GC
MOTHER

BOOKS BY SAM HEPBURN

Gone Before
Her Perfect Life

A GOOD MOTHER

SAM HEPBURN

Bookouture

Published by Bookouture in 2021

An imprint of Storyfire Ltd.
Carmelite House
50 Victoria Embankment
London EC4Y 0DZ

www.bookouture.com

Copyright © Sam Hepburn, 2021

Sam Hepburn has asserted her right to be identified
as the author of this work.

ISBN: 978-1-80019-416-8
eBook ISBN: 978-1-80019-415-1

This book is a work of fiction. Names, characters, businesses,
organizations, places and events other than those clearly in the
public domain, are either the product of the author's imagination
or are used fictitiously. Any resemblance to actual persons, living or
dead, events or locales is entirely coincidental.

In Memory of Susana Quiros Jacomini

PROLOGUE

Thin rain pattered onto the leaves above me. I cowered beneath the branches, gazing at the creeper-covered brickwork of the vicarage. A curtain twitched at the downstairs window. I shrank back. Seconds later, a slit of light split the darkness and widened as a woman opened the front door. White hair haloed in the glow, she looked down at the holdall on the step and glanced up and around before bending down to open it. I heard Finn whimper. Her voice cut through the night, sharp and shocked. 'Gerald! Oh, my goodness! It's a baby! The poor mite must be frozen.'

She lifted him out, one of his tiny fists escaping from the blanket as she clasped him to her shoulder and dipped down to pick up the bag. The door clicked shut behind her.

The sound ripped my heart. I leant back against the tree. She'd be calling the police, alerting Social Services. I couldn't bear it. I heard his cries from inside the house, a mounting distress that I yearned with every fibre of my body to comfort. Voices battled in my head.

Leave him, he deserves better than you.

No! At best, he'll grow up thinking he was unloved and unlovable; at worst, he'll end up in the system, processed, managed and passed around, just like you were, until it's time to spit him out and leave him prey to the worst the world can do.

Before I knew it I was running up the path and slamming my hands against the door, tears streaming down my face. A tall, grey-haired man pulled it open. A man who opened his arms to me and murmured, 'Oh, my dear, my dear,' as he took me into warmth and light and pressed me into an armchair. There was a fire in the grate and hot sweet tea and kind, soothing words.

'Don't worry. We can help you. You've done the right thing. Your baby needs you. Don't cry, my dear. You're not on your own.'

I reached up to take Finn from his wife's arms and glimpsed a tremor of movement through the gap in the curtains behind her. My heart beat hard. I told myself it was the wind catching the creeper, a flicker of reflection, or my wound-up nerves playing tricks.

I turned away and, as I looked down at Finn's crumpled face, he curled his fingers around my thumb and gripped it tightly. In that moment I knew that I would rather kill than ever give him up him again.

CHAPTER 1

'Mum! You're not listening.'

I glance up from the recipe on my laptop. 'Sorry, sweetheart, say that again—?'

Finn pokes the blueberries dotted on his porridge and says solemnly, 'What do you call a bear with no teeth?'

'I don't know.' I switch on the oven. 'What *do* you call a bear with no teeth?'

Straightening up, he flashes me a grin. 'A gummy bear!' He whoops with delight, flecks of porridge spraying from his mouth.

I laugh and pull a face, and he laughs some more, almost falling off his chair. 'All right, sweetheart, finish your breakfast and get your shoes on. Tilly and Henry will be here any minute.'

I add a teaspoon of cinnamon to the mixture in the food processor and press the pulse button. Sharing the school run with another mum has changed my life. When it's Tilly's turn to do the mornings it gives me an extra half an hour to sort out the washing or run the hoover over the stairs before I leave for work, but today I've ditched the hoovering so I can knock up a batch of muffins.

'Come on, Finnsy. Hurry up, you can't be late for school.'

Smile gone, Finn shuffles past me into the hallway to put on his shoes. I grab his bag from the counter, check that he's got his snack, water bottle and reading book, and I'm by the door buttoning up his coat when I hear Tilly pulling up outside. I kiss the top of his head and wave as he trudges out to the car.

Halfway down the drive he turns, as if he's about to run back inside.

'Go on, sweetheart. Have a lovely day.'

I keep waving until the car is out of sight and then I stand for a moment looking out across Juniper Close – manicured hedges, glistening porch lights, here and there the flicker of breakfast television between half-closed plantation shutters, and that all-enveloping quiet. I've been here for three months but after the non-stop soundtrack of shouts, music, slamming doors and whining mopeds that accompanied my life on the Beechwood estate, I still can't get used to it. The noisiest it ever gets round here is when one of the neighbours murmurs a clipped hello, or the organic veg van is forced to back up to make way for a wine delivery.

I hurry back into the house. It's a beautifully refurbished Victorian semi that screams money, good taste and happy families – the kind of house I dreamed of living in when I was a lost, lonely kid traipsing from one foster placement to the next. I still have trouble believing it's my home. I try not to let it bother me that Ian bought it when he got engaged to his ex. After all, I'm the one he married. Though if I'd been him, I think I'd have sold it after they broke up, and started over. But he'd spent so much money and effort ripping out everything he didn't like and redoing the whole place exactly how he wanted it, it's like he couldn't bear to part with it.

I dollop the muffin mixture into the paper cases and slide the trays into the oven. I check the time, take a last gulp from my mug of tea and reach across the worktop to turn off my laptop. My fingers hover for a heartbeat. I glance at the window and drop them onto the keyboard. I type two words into the search bar; sixteen letters; one space; two capitals – I always put in the caps. *Sallowfield Court.* I take a breath and hit return. Google asks, as it always does, if I mean Swallowfield. I don't. It's Sallow, like the old word for willow, not swallow like the bird. There are hundreds of entries. None of them new. Just to be sure, I erase the search and type in another. This time for Ryan Hurley. Nothing new there, either. I clear my history and snap down the lid of the laptop. I used to check every day. After a few months it was once a week. Now, it's only when I can't stop myself.

I look down at my engagement ring sitting above the slim hoop of my wedding band and rock my fingers in the beam of the overhead spotlight, every glint of my beautiful diamond a reminder that I am safe; more than that, that I'm no longer on the outside, hanging on to life by my fingertips – and I have a husband I love. The funny thing is he seems to love me too. Handsome, successful Ian Dexter. He's a partner at Parkview Dental, brilliant at what he does and adored by his patients, particularly the female ones who were pretty astonished, not to say miffed, when Parkview's most eligible bachelor married his dull little nobody of a receptionist. But no more astonished than I was the night he turned up at my flat and proposed. It was so unexpected I thought he must be joking. Of course, I'd fantasised about it from the moment I'd set eyes on him, but the way he'd insisted on keeping our relationship quiet from everyone at work had made me think that I was just a rebound fling, a moment of madness to get over the break-up with his hotshot lawyer ex. When I looked up into his face and saw that he was deadly serious I didn't give myself a chance to think about the practicalities of adjusting to his world or of bringing my lies into his life. I wanted him so badly I just whispered, 'Yes.'

My hands shook as I opened the little box he pushed into my hand. I looked down at the ring glinting in its bed of black velvet and like an idiot I said, 'Oh my God, it must have cost you a fortune!' and he just smiled and said, 'I wanted to show you how much you mean to me.' Then he slipped it onto my finger and said, 'I love you,' and I made an even bigger fool of myself by bursting into tears, because the only other person who had ever said that to me was Finn. He steered me over to my saggy little sofa and as he tugged off his jacket I took in the shift of muscle beneath his carefully laundered shirt, the buffed gleam of his shoes and the glint of his signet ring – and felt the doubts creep back.

'Why me, Ian?'

He wound a finger through my hair. 'What do you mean?'

'You could have your pick of women.'

'You're everything I want.'

I laughed. I couldn't help it. 'A single mother, eight years your junior with a weakness for pot noodles, who's never ironed a sock in her life? I don't think so. What are your family and all your posh mates from uni going to say?'

'Who cares what they think? You'll learn to fit in in no time and I'll be here, right by your side, every step of the way.'

We looked at each other for a moment, then he grasped my head and pulled me close. Gentle at first and then harder and faster, he drove away my fears and I told myself that I could do this. That everything would be all right. Afterwards, as we lay there listening to the estate gearing up for the night – dogs barking, the moped boys revving their engines, a shriek of what might be laughter, I looped names across my mind – *Nicola Dexter, Mrs Ian Dexter, Mrs I Dexter*, like a lovestruck teenager doodling in the back of her diary.

After he'd left, I stayed awake until the small hours staring at the fist-shaped blotch on my ceiling, thinking about dresses, flowers, country house hotels, and sharing my perfect day with the people who had got me through the early days with Finn: Joyce, my old boss, in a new frock and a big floppy hat; my friend, Susy, looking stunning in something outlandish; her daughter, Gaby, hand in hand with Finn, skipping down the aisle behind me in colour co-ordinated outfits; a day of music, fun and laughter.

'I don't want a big wedding,' Ian said the next day, as we drove out to a pub for lunch. 'All that hype and expense. What's the point?' His hand found my knee and gave it a squeeze. 'All we need to make it perfect is you, me and Finn.' He glanced in the rear-view mirror. 'Isn't that right, fella?'

Finn nodded, happy to please. I turned away to the window, any disappointment about flowers and floppy hats swept away by Ian's inclusion of Finn in his idea of perfection. 'What about witnesses?' I said.

'We'll grab a couple of passers-by off the street.'

'Won't your family be upset?'

'They'll understand.'

'But—?' I bit my lip as Ian pulled out and overtook the car in front.

'They know it wouldn't be fair to fill a venue with all my relations when you haven't got any.'

I looked over at him, touched that he was willing to give all that up for me. 'I don't deserve you,' I said. 'I really don't.'

For most people that's something you say: a figure of speech. For me it was – still is – a cold, unforgiving truth.

It's been sixteen months since I got the receptionist's job at Parkview Dental; eleven since Ian dropped a couple of patient files onto my desk and touched my heart by inviting me and Finn out for Sunday lunch at a pub he knew that had a playground in the garden; four since he proposed; and three since our wedding. And he's been as good as his word, doing everything he can to help me adjust to his world: teaching me how to drive, introducing me to all sorts of fancy foods and showing me how to cook them, buying me new clothes. He even bought me a platinum pass for his gym so I can keep in shape. All to boost my confidence – a kiss every time I mess up, a smile when I get things right.

Lyn Burton, last in my long line of foster mothers, used to say it would take a bloody miracle to make anything of me: '*What do you think you're doing, Nicola Cahill? You'd better watch yourself, missy, or you'll end up just like your mother.*' And now, after years on my own, I've found a man who is ready to work that miracle. Someone who wants to teach me about love and who, just as importantly, is ready to teach me about life. All the things you miss out on when you grow up as a name and a number on a file.

CHAPTER 2

'Thank you, Mrs Walmsley, we'll see you again next Wednesday.'
I tear off the receipt and hand her back her bank card. As soon as
she's gone, I scoot my chair closer to Amy, the other receptionist,
dying for an update on her latest foray into the world of online
dating. She has gorgeous, thick fair hair that falls in curls around
her shoulders, huge brown eyes, a degree in drama and wealthy
farm-owning parents, but she's been single for a while and we'd
had high hopes for Tim, 31, *marketing consultant by day, craft beer
aficionado by night.* 'So come on, how was it?'

She pulls a face. 'Awful. He looked nothing like his photo and
all he could talk about was his mother and his bloody beer.'

'Oh, I'm sorry.'

'Oh, well.' Amy sighs and turns back to her screen. 'If you ever
get tired of Ian you know where to send him.'

It's our running joke, one she's been making ever since the day
he shocked the practice by announcing our engagement. Right on
cue I laugh and say, 'In your dreams,' but, as ever, I find myself
wondering why my husband chose someone like me when he
could have been with someone like her.

'Nicola!' Maggie the practice manager walks in from her office.
'Could you tidy the waiting room, please? There's a paper cup on
the floor and the magazines are all over the place.'

'No problem, Maggie.' I get up from my desk, catch Amy's
eye and suppress a smile. I've tried talking to Ian about Maggie's
lousy people skills but they've got this mutual-admiration thing

going. He thinks she's some kind of management genius, and I wouldn't be surprised if she kept a stalkery shrine of photos of him in her attic. She backed off briefly when we got engaged – retired to lick her wounds – but then he took her out to lunch, told her she was such a gem the whole practice would collapse without her and assured her that he would never let his 'personal relationships' undermine her authority. It was like letting an injured Rottweiler off the leash.

Ian refuses to admit it, but if Maggie had had her way she'd have binned my application the minute it hit her desk – she made that crystal clear the minute I walked into the interview, barely waiting for me to sit down before she waded in to point out my lack of qualifications and experience. And she was right: apart from a few GCSEs I didn't have any qualifications at all. As for experience, I'd only ever had one other job – nursery assistant at a children's day care centre and I was only leaving it because Joyce, the owner, was retiring and selling up.

'You're a single mother,' Maggie said, tapping the word *single* on her copy of my application, as if somehow, in the glitzy whirl of my existence I might not have noticed.

'That's right.'

I could feel her getting ready to ask difficult questions about timekeeping and what would happen if Finn got sick when Ian threw me an encouraging smile – a smile that made my throat dry up and my hands tremble – and asked why I wanted to be a receptionist. It was hardly the time to admit that I'd only applied because an employment agency I didn't even remember signing up to had been bombarding me with 'hand-picked for you' alerts flagging up the post of receptionist/office coordinator at Parkview Dental. I was sure that a practice based in one of the massive Georgian houses near the cathedral – all glossy paintwork, manicured window boxes and polished brass on the outside, and three storeys of clean lines, sparkling glass and brushed steel once you stepped through the door was never going to give someone with zero office experience and the wrong kind of accent a second glance, but I'd had so many reminders to apply I thought, why not? What was one more rejection among so many? So I smiled back at him and gave him my pre-prepared line about being ready for new challenges and enjoying working in a team. Maggie sniffed but he soldiered on, took another glance at my ridiculously sketchy CV and said, 'Could you tell us a bit more about this charity you volunteer with?'

'Yes,' I replied, glad to be on firmer ground. 'Next Steps supports care leavers and I'm one of their mentors. Just a few hours a week. I really enjoy it.'

'Why care leavers?'

I looked him square in the eye. 'I was taken into care after my mother died so I feel I know what these kids need.'

That's when Maggie started shuffling papers and looking at her watch. It must have really stuck in her gullet when she had to phone me the next day to tell me I'd got the job. I don't know which one of us was more astonished. 'You were up against some highly experienced receptionists, most of them with medical experience,' she said, bemused and indignant. 'Mr Dexter had an extremely hard time convincing the other partners to hire you.'

I wasn't sure how to respond to that, or if I was even meant to. 'Thank you for letting me know,' I said finally. 'I'm... glad he managed to persuade them.'

'Well, he's a very persuasive man who usually gets what he wants,' she said tartly. 'For some reason, it appears that what he wanted was you.'

I don't know what she was making such a fuss about. The job isn't exactly difficult, at least not once Ian gave up a few of his lunch hours to get me up to speed on the computer system. Aside from dealing with Maggie I enjoy it, and it's important to me that I'm still earning and not totally dependent on my husband. But 'dental receptionist'? It was never the dream; just a way to survive until I found a way to train to be a social worker.

The minute Jenny, the other half of my job share walks through the door, I grab my coat, and hurry out to my car. Cutting down my hours was Ian's idea – he thought it would help me to fit work around the school run. He's booked me in for a Pilates session – I have a tendency to slouch – and a spin class but when I get to the crossroads, instead of taking a right towards the gym I turn left and head out towards the canal.

You can still see the spire of the cathedral as clearly as anything from this end of town but once you cross the bridge it's as if the cobbles, craft boutiques and cafés of the old town belong to a different world.

I cruise past street corners and chip shops and check down alleyways, doing what I've been doing every afternoon this week: looking for Leon. Of all the kids I've mentored he's the one who worries me the most. Three months ago he was out with some kids who decided to rob a corner shop. He swears he didn't know what they were planning but he comes up for sentencing next week. He promised me he'd stay out of trouble but in the last few weeks I've watched his bright-eyed good nature turn into surly resentment and I've got a nasty feeling I know why. I slow into a queue of brake lights and then, with a sinking heart, I turn left and head out towards the industrial estate. I drive around for a while and then I see them – a bunch of teenage boys straddling push bikes. They're all lean and wary and they're keeping their heads down but even from here, parked fifty yards away beneath the shadow of the overpass, I can see Leon right there at the back. I lean across to get a shot of the slab-faced man doing the talking: Dylan Greaves – Sean Logan's number two. From time to time he looks up, surveys the passing cars and glances at the lorries rumbling overhead. Eyes everywhere. Then he takes a drag of his cigarette, thumbs his phone and goes back to doling out instructions. After a few minutes the boys vault onto their saddles, standing high as they swing into the road and pedal away.

I flick through the photos and check the time. I'll have to be quick if I'm going to collect Ian's suit from the dry cleaners and get to the farmers' market before the end of school. I squeeze the soft flesh at the top of my thigh. Shame about the gym. I'll have to make up for it at the weekend.

I turn the key in the ignition and glance up. A black BMW is pulling up beside Greaves. He leans in to speak to the driver. Moments later, the driver makes a U-turn and accelerates towards me. At the last moment he slams on the brakes, and stops when we're eye to eye.

Heart stumbling, I shove my phone between my knees.

The driver looks at me thoughtfully through my open window. 'I know you,' he says.

'I… I don't think so.'

Head cocked, he waggles a finger to silence me. 'Nah… I'm good with faces.' A drag on his cigarette then, still pointing at me, he snaps his fingers. Data retrieved. 'You're the receptionist at that flash dentists opposite the park. I brought my daughter in the other week. Tanya. She broke her tooth falling off her bike. You got her an emergency appointment.'

'I don't remember,' I say. It's a lie. I'd seen enough photos of him to know exactly who he was, though in the flesh it was his drabness that had struck me. Paunchy and red-faced with fair eyebrows, pale eyes and receding hair, the man ushering a weepy ten-year-old to the reception desk could have been any harmless, doting dad. Only he's not harmless. He's Sean Logan, local scrap merchant and owner of dodgy clubs. At least, those are his sidelines – his core business is dealing drugs and getting other people's kids to deliver them, picking on the weak and vulnerable, luring them in with offers of easy cash and threatening them with violence when they try to break free.

'Why are you watching my lads?'

I open my mouth to deny it.

'No need for lies,' he says, his voice an unnerving mixture of reason and menace. 'This is the third time this week we've clocked your car.'

'I… I was looking for Leon.'

He grins. It's nasty. 'Bit young for you, isn't he?' His eyes slide to the back of my car. *What's he looking at? There's nothing there. Just Finn's booster seat and my gym bag.* The eyes flick back to me. 'So what's a nice dental receptionist like you want with a scrote like Leon Travis?'

I drop my eyes and ride the wave of anger. 'I'm his mentor.'

'His what?'

I breathe deeply, my voice strong. 'I volunteer with a charity that supports care leavers.'

He takes a moment to assess this then he laughs, a deep gravelly sound that shakes with genuine amusement. 'Oh, right. A do-gooder. I should have guessed. And what does this *mentoring* consist of exactly?'

'We help kids cope once they leave the system. Shopping, cooking, paying bills, finding a job.' *Trying to protect them from people like you.*

'Spying on them.'

'I was worried about him. If he gets caught with drugs before his sentencing hearing he'll go to prison.'

A muscle clenches and unclenches in his jaw. 'Who said anything about drugs?'

'He's just a kid, Mr Logan.'

'So you *do* know me.'

'You mentioned bringing your daughter into the surgery. It jolted my memory.'

Logan flicks his cigarette onto the road and spreads his fat, nicotine-stained fingers across the steering wheel. 'I like you.' I flinch. 'You helped my daughter. Which is why I'd feel bad if anything happened to you' – he lifts his chin and points his gaze at Finn's booster seat – 'or your kid. So I'm going to tell you this just once. Stick to the cooking lessons and keep your nose out of my business.'

He floors the accelerator and roars away. A chill runs through me as I pull away from the kerb, returning in sickening waves as I dash to the dry cleaners and hurry around the farmers' market.

I make it to the school just as the first flood of children erupts through the doors. Boys, girls, dark, fair, skipping and jumping, pairs forming and laughing, groups merging and whispering as they head towards their waiting parents – grown men and women who are just as guilty of cliques, hierarchies and casual blankings as their kids: the popular, the awkward, the loud and the shy, the solitary and the over-eager. I smile and nod my way through the buggies and shopping bags, a spasm of tenderness as the flood of children dries to a trickle and Finn comes dawdling out on his own, clutching his latest artwork and leaving a trail of paint-smeared macaroni.

'Where's Henry, sweetheart?'

He pivots around and points forlornly to a group of boys clambering over the newly installed adventure playground: a pirate ship hung with ladders, chutes and rope nets, paid for by the blood, sweat and bake sales of the PTA. In my role as the newly elected secretary – Ian put me up for it, he thought it would boost my confidence – I had to say a few words at the grand opening, and he and I cheered when the first children swarmed up the rigging and hurtled down the slide. But when I saw Finn stuck halfway up one of the ladders, frozen with fear, I started to wish we'd spent the money on computers or a new bike shed instead.

'Come on, Henry,' I call.

I want to get away quickly tonight. Once we drop Henry off there's something Finn and I need to do on the other side of town.

CHAPTER 3

'Go on, Finnsy, you can do it.' His gloved fingers tighten around the sides of the ladder, his six-year-old frame stiff with determination. 'Think how proud Daddy's going to be when we tell him you went down a big slide!'

He darts a look at me, small and scared, his face pinched with cold. I force a smile, wishing we were at home, in the warm. He turns back to his task, carefully lifts his right foot onto the next step and drags his left one up to join it.

'That's it. Keep going.' I make sure my voice stays gentle. No hint of impatience, no betrayal of the sour taste left by my encounter with Logan. He takes another tentative step. And then another, moving painfully up the rungs. I cross my arms against the bitter wind and glance around the recreation ground. It's a good twenty-minute drive from the school but it would be just our luck if one of the other parents came jogging past with a cheery wave and a knowing smile. Thankfully it's almost deserted: just a couple of women pushing muffled-up tots in strollers, a dog walker throwing sticks for an ancient bull terrier, and two girls hunched on a bench. Shivering in their red and black school blazers, they share a cigarette and watch the litter tumble across the battered grass.

I turn back to Finn. The sight of my brave boy up there in his Spider-Man beanie hat battling his fears so he can make his stepdad proud prompts a clash of emotions – joy for who he is and fear for what life might do to him. He tries so hard but he's never going to be the confident, athletic kid that Ian wants him to be. Finn is Finn: clumsy, uncoordinated, funny and loveable. Ian does love him, of course he does; it's just that when you've always been an achiever, it's difficult to understand how much it hurts to hear a groan of frustration from someone you look up to.

I tried telling Finn that he didn't have to prove himself to anyone and it didn't matter if he got teased for being too scared to tackle the slide on the pirate ship. He gave me such a look.

Which is why we're out here in the freezing cold practising in secret. I kick my heel against a buckle in the tarmac. Ian's right, these things *do* matter, and I'm grateful that he cares about Finn and wants him to succeed. There aren't many stepdads who are as hands-on and invested as he is. He's even started giving up his Sunday mornings to help coach the Bellvue Booters football sessions which, according to their website, are specially designed to help children build confidence and make friends. All to help Finn.

He is still climbing. I hold my breath and silently will him on. *Come on, sweetheart, just two more steps.* My heart swells. For the first time ever he makes it to the top, his scarf catching the wind as he looks down at the chute dropping away beneath him: fifteen feet of steeply angled steel rubbed shiny by years of excited whoops.

The weighted safety gate clangs behind me. My antennae twitch. I spin around. The girls I saw earlier are sauntering across the play area. The leader – a scrawny, tight-faced blonde, who can't be more than thirteen, approaches the slide, a straggly ponytail that could do with a wash, swinging as she walks. She stops, throws a look at her friend and shouts up at Finn: 'Get a move on!' Her laughter is shrill and hollow.

'The baby slide's over there,' the other girl says, but her heart's not in it, I can tell. She's just a hanger on, doling out a crushing comment here, a vicious elbow jab there. Doing what she has to to survive.

Finn wavers. For one heady moment I think he might just go for it and soar down the slide. But he's wilting, tilting backwards, his right foot searching for the rung below. He finds it and begins his shaky descent. Ponytail grins. A buzz of victory, a tiny triumph to ease the emptiness inside.

She thumbs her phone and locks her eyes on mine, challenging me to react. I want to scoop Finn off the steps and tell her how much happier she'd feel if she tried to be kind, but I know better than to destroy what's left of my boy's frail dignity and right now I don't have the energy to get sucked into this girl's games. There's nothing she'd like more than a playground spat with an angry, protective mum to post online. *I didn't do anything. Why are you having a go at me?* The shriek of innocence, the jutting jaw, the rocking head. Step by step, Finn backs his way to the bottom of the ladder and ducks between the girls. Shoulders slumped and flapping his hands, the way he does when he's tense or upset, he shuffles towards me.

'Well done!' I whisper. 'You got to the top!'

'Are you going to tell Daddy I bottled it?' The expression, one of Ian's, makes me flinch.

'Of course not. I told you, this is our secret.'

'A zippy secret?'

I nod, pinch my thumb and forefinger together and zip my lips tight shut. 'We're going to practise and practise and then we're going to give him a big surprise. Do you want to go on the swings?'

He shakes his head. 'Can we go home now?'

'Course.' I pull his scarf a little tighter. 'What do you want for your tea?'

He gazes at the ground.

'How about… macaroni cheese?' I suggest. Comfort in a bowl.

He lifts his shoulders in a listless shrug.

'And guess what I made this morning—? Banana muffins.' Consolation or celebration – I'd known he'd need a treat when we got home. His sigh is heavy but he nods.

'Come on, then.' I slip my arm around him, needing to feel the solidity of his little body. To anchor him to me. After a few

moments he moves away, out of my grasp and scampers ahead
to the car park.

I'm rummaging in my bag for my keys when his cry of 'Mum!'
startles me into a run. I cut across the grass. He's standing beside
the car, transfixed by something on the bonnet. I hurry over to
see what it is and stand rooted to the ground, my chest rising
and falling. It's a bird. Black. Broken. Dead. Its beak open, its
pecked-out eyes staring at the sky, the tip of one fanned-out
wing wedged beneath the windscreen wipers. Revulsion rushes
through me, icy black waves that dash the air from my throat as
I'm assaulted by a memory.

Cracked ceiling, torn green curtains, stained woodchip, the
smell of damp. I'm cornered, invaded, breathless. I fling the covers
over my head and gasp and choke for someone to come but the
bird goes on thrashing at the glass: beak, claws, wings, thudding,
scraping, whirring. The door creaks open. 'Open the window!
Please, open the window!' A hand rips the cover from my face. I
look up into cold, green eyes.

'Mum! Mum!'

Finn's faraway voice is pulling me back but the panic keeps
hold, trapping me in that room with the flapping bundle of fear.
The breathing, Nicci. Do the breathing. I try to suck air. My throat
clamps tight. I cross my arms, tap my elbows, find the rhythm.
Tap, tap, tap. Tap, tap, tap. The blood begins to subside. Tap, tap,
tap. My throat loosens, oxygen fills my lungs. As if I'm adjusting
the zoom on a lens, the image of the room begins to shrink.
Smaller and smaller. A grubby moon, a copper coin, a speck of
dirt floating on a sea of black.

'Mum!'

I blink at him. 'Don't look, sweetheart. It's just… just a bird.'
My lips are numb. Glad of a reason to keep my head down I
scrabble in the bushes bordering the car park and pick up a stick.
Eyes averted, I grasp it tightly and poke at the limp corpse. It won't

budge. I have to get closer. I have to lift the windscreen wiper with the tip of my finger and jab and push until the dead thing slides off the bonnet and falls to the ground.

I close my eyes. *It's all right. It's gone.* When I open them again there's still a telltale smear of gore on the bonnet.

'How did it die, Mummy?' Finn is calm, not evenly mildly disgusted, just curious.

'I don't know.'

It's getting dark. I scan the shadowy screen of trees and the crouched outline of the bushes. 'Quick, get in the car.' With jittery fingers I yank open the door, almost push him into his booster seat, and snap the seat belt tight. I switch on the radio, heavy thumping bass to blast away the panic. A dead bird on the bonnet of my car. Not any bird.

A blackbird.

I look at Finn in the rear-view mirror. He's watching the world go by, nodding to the beat on the car stereo. Who put the bird there? Who wedged its shattered wing beneath the wiper blade so I'd be forced to dislodge it? Had they been watching me from the trees? Was it a warning from Logan? I mull that over. It would have been easy enough to get one of his thugs to follow my car, but wouldn't they have keyed the paintwork or smashed the windscreen? A dead bird feels too subtle for an oaf like Greaves, and why a blackbird? A headache stirs, unwanted thoughts grating on my skull. More deep breaths. *In. Two. Three. Four. Out. Two, Three. Four…* until we reach Juniper Close. A twitch of movement as Vera across the road watches my arrival, then a final exhale as I swing the car into our driveway.

The house is warm and smells of polish, fresh washing and the faint scent of baking. I switch on the lights. The hallway fills with soft pools of amber. Finn shakes off his puffa and waits, one hand pressing the top of my head while I kneel down to take off his shoes. He's perfectly capable of doing it himself: Ian spent hours teaching him how to tie and untie proper laces as soon as he started school – Velcro's for babies – but it still takes him ages. And anyway, Ian's not here and Finn is tired. Though not too tired to remember to put his shoes on the wooden rack next to his wellingtons: heels to the wall, the way Daddy likes them.

I watch Finn skid down the gleaming, woodblock floor in his socks and swerve around the corner into the kitchen. I follow behind, pour him a glass of milk and make myself a cup of tea. In a pot. Real leaves. No tea bags or instant coffee in this house. No brown sauce, sliced white bread or pot noodles, either.

Finn gets out his crayons and I cradle my mug and do the walk of the house. The steady tick of Ian's father's carriage clock fills the sitting room as I straighten the portrait of him that hangs above the fireplace. He died when Ian was still at school and I don't think he ever got over it. The pain of losing a parent is the one aspect of his life I understand. Something we have in common. Perhaps that's what he sees in me. A chance for us both to heal.

I've always liked this picture of Bill Dexter. Although it's one of those formal oil paintings they put in boardrooms, if you look past the tweed jacket and stiff shoulders the artist has captured something a little lost and appealing in his face, which makes me sorry that I never got a chance to meet him. If he'd still been around it might even have taken some of the edge off Ian's mother. There's nothing remotely lost or appealing about Gwen Dexter. The only time I've ever seen that woman lost for words was the day she met me, though once she'd recovered from the initial shock the words flooded back pretty quickly. Mostly in the form of probing questions about my 'people' and fond little anecdotes about Ian's ex. I tried not show that I was upset, and in the car going home Ian did his best to cheer me up. 'Don't worry, she'll come round once she gets to know you. She's just having a hard time at the moment, what with Hugh walking out on her and everything.'

She'd seemed pretty chirpy about her divorce to me. She'd even joked about the fun she'd had setting fire to everything that reminded her of husband number two. But I'd just smiled and said, 'Of course, it must be very upsetting for her.'

I check that the cushions are plumped and the water in the flower vases is still fresh. I straighten a couple of chess pieces and wipe my sleeve across the framed photo of our wedding day: a snatched selfie of Ian, tanned and smiling in his black suit and crisp white shirt, me gripping his arm in the blue flowery shift he'd presented me with the day before, a sprig of orange blossom tucked into my carefully pinned hair. It was so thoughtful of him to buy me a dress I hadn't had the heart to tell him I'd already bought one – a silly, strappy, cream-coloured, ankle-kicking number from Monsoon. They'd taken it back, though. No questions asked, seeing as it was unworn and still had its tag on. I move on upstairs and make sure the bedding is smooth and the towels are straight. It only takes a few minutes but, as Ian says, it's the little things.

CHAPTER 4

The radio murmurs, the hob hisses and the pasta bubbles in the pan. I glimpse myself in the dark mirror of the kitchen window: flyaway brown hair, dark eyes in a pale face, a too-wide mouth. Outside it's starting to rain. Tiny spits of water slake the glass but we are on the inside, warm and dry.

I retreat from the window and unpack my haul from the farmers' market: two wild salmon steaks from the fish stall – plump, pink and four times the price of the ones in the supermarket; half a dozen spears of tender stem broccoli; and, just for Ian, some tiny new potatoes dusted with earth. I don't do carbs. Not anymore. Tyres crunch on the drive as I rinse my fingers. Finn looks up. I hear Ian's key in the front door. I glance at my watch. He's early. I run my hands through my hair and pull at my shirt.

'Daddy!' Finn runs towards him, grinning with delight as Ian swings him up into his arms.

'Hey there, fella.'

I look at the two of them framed in the doorway, backlit by the light from the hall. My tall, handsome husband, with his thick dark hair and deep-blue eyes. My darling son with his gawky limbs and winning smile. My beautiful home with its tasteful décor and designer fittings. Ian sets Finn down and comes over and kisses me on the cheek. I'm turning back to the sink when he slips his arm around my waist and nuzzles my neck. 'Where were you?'

I suck in my tummy and twist around. 'What do you mean?'

'Finn's extra football training? We'd arranged it for tonight. You were going to bring him to Bellvue.'

I glance at the little square allotted to today on the kitchen calendar. There it is, pencilled in Ian's small, even writing, beside the discreet little cross marking it as one of my fertile days. According to Ian's ovulation app there are six of them a month. Who knew?

'I must have got confused. I was sure it was tomorrow.' How did I get that wrong?

'I had to change it. I told you. It's a shame, he could really do with the practice.'

'I'm sorry,' I say, quickly. 'I completely forgot.'

'Never mind, we can do it next week.'

'Silly Mummy.' Ian rolls his eyes at Finn – who makes a squiffy attempt to roll his back – and turns away to grab a beer from the fridge. But I know how much he hates it when I forget things. So do I. I have to get more organised.

'I'm doing salmon for supper,' I say, brightly. 'With dill and capers. And I got some of that tender stem broccoli you like from the farmers' market.'

'Great.'

'We saw a dead bird,' Finn says, kicking his heels against the rung of his chair. 'Mummy didn't like it.'

'Feet, Finn.' Ian waits until the kicking stops before he snaps the cap off his beer. 'Your mummy doesn't like birds. Especially not dead ones. Where was it?'

'On the car. It was stuck and she had to poke it off.' He pulls his face into a grimace, jumps off his chair and jabs the air manically with an imaginary stick. Is that how I'd looked? A crazy woman, jousting with a lump of roadkill?

Ian gazes my way. There's amusement in his expression, and something else I can't quite make out. 'What was a dead bird doing on your car?'

For a moment it feels as if I am on a rudderless boat drifting towards deep and dangerous waters. Somehow I manage a shrug. 'Kids messing about, I expect. I'll clean it tomorrow.'

He presses the bottle to his mouth, takes a sip and gives me a playful pinch on the thigh. 'How was the gym?'

'Oh… a bit rushed.' I squeeze past him and get out milk and cheese for the sauce. 'I'll do a bit extra at the weekend.'

He leans over and picks up my phone from the worktop. 'Look at the state of your screen. I don't know why you won't let me buy you a new phone.'

'Honestly, Ian, I don't know why it bothers you so much. I like my phone. But, I promise, the minute it dies I'll get myself an upgrade.'

'Up to you, but we'd get a much better deal if we had a joint contract.' He turns away. 'Hey, Finn, how about a chess lesson?'

Grinning with happiness, Finn runs to the toy drawer and fetches out the junior chess set Ian bought him for Christmas. I said he was far too young to even think about learning and I worried that chess would be another thing he'd struggle with. But Ian's working him through a programme he found on the internet for the very young. It teaches them one piece at a time, and uses quizzes to chart their progress, and somehow all those moves and strategies seem to speak to Finn in a way that letters and numbers just don't.

I watch the two of them as I stir milk into the cheese sauce: Finn, who's usually so restless and fidgety, bent forward over the board, his hand wavering over his pieces; Ian's voice, firm and measured, talking tactics.

I've been trying to get Finn to teach me the moves so we can play together. He's a bossy teacher, '*Nooo, Mum, not like that!*' but I'm sort of getting the hang of it and I've picked up quite a few tips from watching Ian replay the grand master games he knows by heart. He insists that playing the same moves over and over again helps him to unwind, but to me there's something horribly depressing about knowing that the loser is always going to fall into the same old traps.

They finish their lesson, Finn eats his tea and the rest of the night unfolds like any other. Bath, book and bed for Finn. A meal, a couple of episodes of a Scandi thriller, bed and sex – I'm a bit tired but we can't waste a fertile day – for Ian and me. His stare is hard as I emerge from the bathroom. He pulls my T-shirt from my shoulder and pushes me onto the bed with a force that makes me feel wanted and needed. I throw back my head and grasp his muscled shoulders as the smell and taste of him overwhelms me. I dig my fingers deep into his flesh and breathe deeper and faster, matching the pulse of my body to the rhythm of his until he shudders and groans into stillness.

In the crimson glow of the digital alarm I meet his eyes as he looks down at me, and then he smiles and rolls away onto his side of the bed. I wait in silence for his breathing to steady. It doesn't take long.

I ease my feet onto the floor and tiptoe into Finn's room. It's awash with ghostly stars: white on blue sweeping the walls in gauzy arcs. One hand presses Robbie the robot to his cheek, the other is flung above his head like a highland dancer. I kiss him on the forehead, inhaling his sweet, drowsy smell.

I turn away and reach up on tiptoe to take my old rag doll Maisie from the row of rejected baby toys lined up along the top of his bookcase. I must have been on my third or fourth temporary foster placement when I found her dropped on the floor of a bus and somehow, amidst all the chaos, I managed to hang on to her. She's nothing special: a home-made rag doll – woolly braids, chain-stitched mouth, coat-button eyes – but when I saw her gazing up at me from among the empty cans and crisp packets I remember feeling really sad for the kid who'd dropped her. But deep down I knew that whoever they were, they couldn't have needed Maisie as much as I did. I still treasure the moment when, years later, I placed her into Finn's pudgy grasp – the grin on his face as he'd snuggled down beside her, the happiness I'd felt that Maisie would always be there to comfort him the way she'd comforted me.

'Big boys don't play with dolls,' Ian said, the first night we stayed at Juniper Close, the night he presented him with Robbie. After we got married, Ian wanted to chuck Maisie in the skip with the rest of the junk from my flat. *You don't want that old thing. It's falling apart.* But I did want Maisie. So I fixed her up a little, re-stitched her seams, made her a completely new outfit, tied fresh ribbons to her braids and persuaded him to keep her. *Just in case we have a daughter*, I said. Ian's really keen for us to have kids. He's even picked out names. Gwen, after his mother, if we have a girl. William, after his father, if it's a boy.

I unbutton Maisie's striped pinny, lift up her petticoats, unsnap the popper hidden in the seam down her back and dig deep into her raggedy insides for the little brown tub of Valium. I shake my nightly dose into my palm: one little white pill to slow the ever-playing loop in my head, and a second to freeze the juddery frames before the moment that would otherwise fling me thrashing and gasping from my sleep. I drop a third pill into my palm: one extra tonight to blot out the blackbird.

I chase them down with a gulp of water from the beaker by Finn's bed, tidy Maisie's skirts and put her back on the shelf. At the door I look back. Her head has flopped to one side and her black, coat-button eyes stare straight past me into the darkness of the landing.

I slip back into bed and huddle into the silky cool of the pillow. Usually I make lists in my head as I wait for the pills to kick in: tasks to do, people to call, things to buy. Tonight, the show starts up as soon as I close my eyes: a figure, thin and pale, dancing on her own in a whirr of blue light, her skinny body gyrating to a silent song. Her face bruised, her hair mussed, her eyes bleary, her mouth cracked in a hollow smile. Blood on her lips. Blood on her teeth, blood spattered across her thin white top. I try to run to her. My leaden legs won't let me. I let out a cry. Her face begins to melt and as I watch her, the girl becomes my mother, teetering on the edge of darkness just out of my reach.

I jolt upright in the gloom, shivering to the frenzied flap of wings.

CHAPTER 5

THEN

My mother's name was Shelley. I thought it was lovely, like a film star. She was pretty too, especially when she smiled. But when she was sad she used to cry all the time, which made her face go red and puffy. The crying got worse after Nana died. Sometimes Mum would tell me I was the only chink of light in her gloom, the anchor that kept her from drifting into darkness. It made me feel loved and important. Even on her worst days I thought that just by existing I was helping to make her feel better.

The day she died started like any other: better, in some ways. It had been raining all week and when I woke up the sky was a clear, shiny blue. Mum had been happy for a while, the kind of happy where she giggled and danced and sang silly songs and swung me around the kitchen and I went along with the fun, hoping that this time it would last for ever: my all laughing, singing, dancing mum who forgot to sleep and burnt the toast. It was a Friday. The day my school awarded stars to the 'achievers of the week' and I had high hopes for my story about a stray dog with secret powers.

It was a terrible blow when Zoe Evans got the writing star for her stupid poem about a rabbit. It didn't even rhyme. I was doodling a picture of Superdog on my pencil case when my teacher, Mrs Lane, called out my name, only she said it in this really strange way, like she couldn't find the breath.

'Nicola.'

I looked up. She was standing with Mrs Miller, the school secretary, and the two of them were looking at me as if I was the only person in the room. I said, 'Yes, miss?' and she said, still in that thin, wobbly voice, 'Can you come up here, dear.' The word sounded funny coming from her. She never called anyone *dear*. 'Mrs Sugden wants you to pop along to her office. Mrs Miller will take you.'

Mrs Lane never said things like *pop* either. But who cared? The only reason the headmistress sent for people on star day was to give them the triple prize for attendance, achievement and being kind, which was the award that everyone wanted because it came with a special certificate. Bursting with excitement, I jumped up from my desk and followed Mrs Miller down the corridor.

There was no triple prize for me, no certificate signed in the headmistress's curly handwriting to take home and stick on the fridge, next to my swimming certificate, to make Mum glow with pride whenever she fetched milk to make a cup of tea. Instead, there was a policeman in a black uniform and a woman who said her name was Hannah and she was from Social Services. She knelt down so we were eye to eye and said, 'I'm so sorry to have to tell you, Nicola, there was an incident in town this morning and your mummy died.'

I wasn't too sure what 'Social Services' were or what 'incident' meant but I knew about being dead. That's what had happened to Nana.

Hannah said that the other children in my class might say silly, untrue things so she was going to tell me exactly what had happened.

She said that after Mum walked me to school she got the bus into town, only instead of getting off at the precinct and going to her job at the supermarket she stayed on for another six stops. She sat on a bench outside the library and took some pills and then she walked onto the bridge and jumped into the river. Hannah said it wasn't anybody's fault and that when you're sad like Mum was, it's an illness.

But I was Mum's anchor, her chink of light, and I knew that if I'd been stronger, nicer, prettier or cleverer she'd have had a reason to hang on.

Hannah said she was taking me to stay with some people called Gina and Ross and they would look after me until she could find me a long-term foster placement. More words I didn't understand.

When we got to their house Gina stripped off my clothes and scrubbed me down in a boiling hot bath until my skin smarted, because she didn't want me 'bringing anything' into her nice clean house. Then she took me downstairs and gave me a plate of horrible fatty sausages and watery tinned tomatoes, which she 'put by for tomorrow' when I ran to the toilet to throw up. Later, she put me to bed in a big, cold room and turned off the light.

I lay in the dark on a strange lumpy mattress and all I could think about was the twenty-five meters swimming certificate with my name on it stuck on the fridge at home. The certificate was a lie. I'd done the test in the shallow end with six other girls from my class and I'd had one foot bumping along the bottom all the way, and if I hadn't cheated at the test and I really had learned how to swim I could have leapt into the river the minute Mum jumped in and I could have saved her.

Next day a boy in my class called Kieran showed me a picture of Mum in the paper. Underneath it they'd written about what had happened. It said that a man saw her jump and he was the one who rang the police. The man said that as she fell, her white mac came open and lifted out 'like wings in the wind'. Those were his actual words. He said that just for a moment in the sunshine, she'd looked like an angel.

Kieran said I had to give the newspaper back because it was his dad's, but he let me tear out the picture of Mum.

CHAPTER 6

Tilly looks up from buckling Finn into the back of her SUV. 'Are you going to be all right getting into work?'

'Yes, why?'

'Your back tyre's flat.'

'What?' I stick my feet into my slippers and shuffle outside to take a look. She's right, the back tyre is so deflated the hub is resting on the ground. I let out a groan as my plans for the afternoon evaporate.

'I'd come back and give you a lift but I've got to take Mimi in for her vaccinations.'

'It's OK. I'll get a cab in to work and I'll call the AA as soon as I get back.'

'That could take forever.'

'I can always call another cab to pick up the kids.'

'That's crazy. I'll call Matt. He's working from home today.'

'You can't do that.'

'Why not? He won't mind. It'll only take him five minutes to change it.' She's already on her phone, talking to her husband as she gets back into the driving seat.

'Thanks, Tilly, you're a star,' I call as she drops her phone in her lap and pulls away.

I walk around the car kicking the other tyres, my heart plummeting when I notice a scratch on one of the hubcaps. Before I met Ian I'd always cycled everywhere with Finn bumping along on the back – even getting the bus had been a treat, a chance for

Finn to sit up front and pretend to be the driver, and I'm still not used to the stress that comes with owning a car, especially a flashy one like this.

I walk back to the house wishing – not for the first time – that I'd managed to buy the battered old Micra that one of the mums from Finn's school had been selling. It was the perfect run-around for a nervous new driver, and after years of dancing the shaky line between payday loans and small-time loan sharks just to own a working fridge and cooker, I'd looked forward to buying my own car with money I'd earned and saved. I'd just about scraped together the cash when Ian shoved a key into my hand, dragged me outside and presented me with this one – a brand-new Honda Civic, with a big pink bow tied to the bumper. An early wedding present, he'd said. I knew he expected me to be ecstatic but all I could muster was a whimper of thanks. It wasn't just the fear of driving something that big or even of denting the shiny new paintwork that sucked the thanks from my throat, it was the dread realisation that here was something else I'd have to have to wash, wax and worry about.

I run upstairs two at a time, calling Amy on the way to tell her I'm going to be late and to beg her to placate Maggie. I've barely had time to get dressed before Matt arrives at the door. Tanned, tousled and wearing a worn tracksuit, he looks like a beach bum when in fact he's some kind of tech genius who runs his own company.

'Thank you so much,' I say, handing him the keys. 'Do you want a coffee?'

'Sure.'

'Do you need tools or anything?'

'There should be some in your car but I brought mine anyway, just in case.'

By the time I bring Matt his coffee he's got the car jacked up and he's digging a screwdriver into the side of the deflated tyre.

'Here's your culprit,' he says, working a thick, L-shaped shard of glass out of the tread. 'Looks like a piece of a bottle. Bubble bath or perfume or something. Went right through the inner tube.'

I put the mug on the ground and hold out my hand. He lays the chunk of glass in my palm. I turn it over with my fingers. In the light it has a pinkish tinge. 'That's so weird. I'm sure that tyre was fine when I drove home.'

'You probably ran over it when you were parking. Tilly's always complaining about the bin men spilling trash.'

'Maybe.' I look up and down the pristine sweep of Juniper Close. Not a scrap of litter in sight. Is this Logan's doing? Another warning to back off? Is it anything?

'Go on, it's freezing out here, you get back inside,' Matt says. 'I'll drop the keys in when I'm done.'

'Honestly, you saved my life.' I run back up the steps and close the door. I shiver as I drop the piece of glass in the bin, even though the heating is on full.

Upstairs I drag a brush through my hair, twist it into a bun and pin every stray strand into place. On mornings like this putting it up is a faff I could do without but Ian's right – the receptionist is the front line of the business: the first person anyone sees when they walk into the surgery; the last one they see when they leave.

Thanks to Matt turning up so quickly I pull into the surgery car park barely fifteen minutes late, but even so I dash up the steps, braced for a lecture from Maggie. With a grateful eye-roll at Amy I shrug off my coat and reach for the flashing phone. 'Parkview Dental. This is Nicola. How may I help you?'

A beat of silence then the line goes dead. I drop the handset back in its cradle and wait for Amy to finish her call. 'Where is she?' I whisper, gesturing to the window of Maggie's office.

'You're in luck. She's up in the meeting room talking to that drug rep.'

'The one she fancies?'

'Yep. They've been in there ever since she got in. Get us a coffee, would you?'

I rush off to the staff kitchen and I'm filling our mugs from the coffee machine when Ian walks past the door. He stops as if he's surprised to see me.

'What's wrong?' I say.

He falters for a second, looking me up and down as if he's searching for an answer. 'Why are you still wearing your scarf?'

'Oh.' I loosen the knot and unwrap it from my neck. 'I only just got here. Flat tyre.'

'Oh, no. Did you have to get a cab?'

'No need – Tilly got Matt to change it for me.'

'*Matt?* What was he doing at home?'

'No idea. I'll have to get him a bottle of something to say thank you. Maggie hasn't noticed I was late, though, so *please* don't say anything.'

'Course not.' He leans in and kisses me, his hand lingering for a moment in the small of my back before he walks back to his surgery.

CHAPTER 7

Friday is my day, every second of it precious. I double-check the kitchen calendar. It's fine. No pencilled additions to the day's doings. No chance of another mix-up. Once I've waved Finn off I text Joyce, my old boss. She's not been well and I feel terrible that I haven't been to see her since she moved to Margate last year. She's dying to meet Ian and she invited us down for the day, just after we got engaged. But a few days before we were due to go Ian seemed upset, and I finally got it out of him that that weekend was the anniversary of his father's death. He hadn't wanted to say anything, but he always spent it at his family's weekend cottage in Norfolk because that had been one of his dad's favourite places. I was touched when he said that he'd wanted to share those special memories with me and Finn. Of course, when I explained the situation to Joyce she insisted that we go to Norfolk instead, and somehow with everything that's been happening, we still haven't managed to get to Margate.

I send her a couple of pictures of Finn and lots of hugs from me and whizz around the house making the beds, running the hoover over the floors and giving the kitchen and both bathrooms a swift clean before I run downstairs and load up the car. With a quick, sharp sense of being watched I slam the boot shut and glance up to give nosy Vera across the road a wave, just so she knows I've seen her. For once her curtains are closed, and her little red Mini isn't in her drive. I swing around the other way. Save for a mangy fox the close is empty. I glance at the smear of blood still streaking the bonnet of my car and turn to look back at the house. The tall wooden side gate is open a little, creaking in the wind. We always keep it locked. In fact, Ian has just put in a new combination lock that clicks in as soon as you close it, and I'm pretty sure – almost certain in fact – that I shut it last night after I put the bins out. I move on down the path, treading quietly and kick the gate wide open. There's no one there. I hurry down the side of the house and out into the garden. Nothing. I walk back to the gate and inspect the lock. It doesn't look like it's been tampered with, and I haven't given anybody the code; Ian definitely wouldn't have, and it's not as if it's a number a stranger would be likely to guess. It's the year Finn was born.

Rolling my shoulders I pull the gate shut, rattle it to make sure the lock has engaged and keep rolling them as I hurry back to the car and ram the key in the ignition. Caught in a flow of uneasy thoughts I swing out onto the main road and almost cut in front of a van. The driver blasts his horn, gives me the finger and veers away. Shaken, I mouth 'Sorry!' and sit up stiffer and straighter, hands gripped tightly to the wheel.

I swing past the surgery and the entrance to Bellvue Park and stop at the traffic lights by the iron gates of Dunelm. It's a private school – all gothic turrets and sweeping lawns. Ian wants to send Finn there for secondary. But the entrance exam is notoriously tough and even with the extra tuition he's been talking about, I worry that we'd just be setting Finn up to fail. If, by some miracle, he did manage to get in I'm not sure he'd be happy in such a pressurised environment, and the thought of those pushy parents and all that formality and discipline terrifies me.

I cross the canal, drive on to the railway arches and with a hurried glance in the rear-view mirror I turn into Riz's car wash.

It's a basic-looking operation: a few hoses and buckets and a bank of dirt-caked hoovers, but the staff do a brilliant job and, best of all, no one from the surgery would be seen dead entrusting their car to a place like this. If Ian ever asks if I spend my Friday mornings cleaning and polishing my new car, I'll tell him the truth. Until then, well, as my nana used to say, why rock the boat?

Riz is a decent guy and over the last few months I've managed to persuade him to offer a few shifts to some of the kids from Next Steps, the latest of them being Leon. When it works, they get money in their pocket, experience of the workplace and something to put on their CVs. When it doesn't, he grumbles for a while then chalks it up to experience.

As I pull up on the forecourt I can see Riz watching me through the grimy panes of his office window. From the look on his face I get the feeling that Leon's placement is one of the ones that isn't working out. No surprises there. Riz beckons me inside. I hand my car keys to one of the men hosing down a transit van, pick my way around the puddles in the concrete and push open the door.

Riz plonks himself behind the metal desk and gestures to the easy chair reserved for clients. I perch gingerly on the ripped vinyl seat while he leans back and clasps his hands over his swollen belly. 'I fired him,' he says.

'Oh, Riz! I thought he was doing OK.'

'He's a hard enough worker and polite with clients, but last week he missed three shifts in a row. What am I supposed to do?'

'If I talk to him, is there any way you could give him another chance?'

He throws his hands in the air. 'If my staff don't turn up I lose business. How can I feed my family if I lose business?'

'Please, Riz, as a favour to me.'

He eyes me over the top of his glasses. 'Why do you care so much about this boy?'

I take a Tupperware from my bag and snap off the lid. 'I don't know. Maybe because he's reached that point where his life could go either way. Or maybe it's because he's got no one else.'

He stares at me for a moment then he switches his gaze to the box of neatly packed muffins I'm sliding across the desk. 'What flavour?' he asks.

'Banana.'

He selects one and inspects it carefully, his mouth turning down at the corners and his head dipping from side to side, before he tears off the paper case and takes a delicate bite. He chews for a while then grunts and says grudgingly. 'It's good. Maybe better than last time.'

He works his way through the muffin and helps himself to another while we chat about skyrocketing business rates, the impossibility of getting your children to respect you and his forthcoming knee replacement.

'So, will you give Leon another chance?' I say.

He swallows the last morsel of muffin and smacks the crumbs from his palms. 'One chance. That's it.'

'Thanks, Riz,' I say, relieved. 'I really appreciate it. Oh, I nearly forgot. Can you ask your guys to pay special attention to my bonnet? Some kids thought it would be funny to drop a dead bird on it and it's left a mark.' I wince a little. 'And is there anything you can do about a scratch on one of the hubcaps?'

'No worries. Once my boys are finished it will look like new.' He gives me wink. 'Your husband won't notice a thing.'

We shake hands. I hitch my bags onto my shoulder and set off to confront Leon. Walking fast and blinking into the wind I avoid the main road, cutting through the criss-cross of shabby metal warehouses and bulky industrial units and make my way to the Rosemead estate. The Beechwood estate where I used to live was pretty bad, but Rosemead is legendary for its vandalism and youth crime. You just have to look at it to see why. It's one of those shoddy 1970s housing experiments that time and the council forgot: ugly concrete blocks, stained walkways and broken lifts. Glancing behind me, I hurry past a stack of old mattresses piled up by the dustbins and step over clusters of tiny silver gas canisters left by kids in search of a quick high, gathered in the corners of the stairwell like the eggs of some alien reptile. I walk up to the third floor, make my way along the concrete walkway to Leon's flat and ring the bell. I wait for a while and ring it again.

I'm about to give up when he opens the door in a pair of jogging pants and a T-shirt and walks back into the living room without a word. I step inside, closing the door behind me and squeeze past the gleaming mountain bike propped against the wall in the hallway. The whole place stinks: dope, cigarettes, takeaways, and there's a roll of cash and a pair of flashy trainers, still in their box, on the coffee table. He flops onto the futon we salvaged from the street and looks at me, wide-eyed. 'What?'

'Where'd you get the bike?'

'Borrowed it.'

'How about the trainers?'

'Saved up.'

'And the cash?'

'Looking after it for a friend.'

Tread gently, I tell myself.

It's three years since I answered the call for volunteers pinned up in the local library: '*Have you got what it takes to mentor a vulnerable young adult? A few hours of your time could change a life.*' I thought I'd ace it. All I had to do was remember the way I'd been treated and do the opposite. Turns out it's a lot harder than you'd think.

I fling open the window and head into the tiny kitchen. Leon had been thrilled when he'd first moved in. His own flat. A place to call home. He'd taken a real pride in keeping it clean but now, after six months, it's disgusting. Dirty cups, empty pizza boxes, overflowing ashtrays. I dump my carrier bags on the table, switch on the kettle and start crushing beer cans and scraping cold chips into the bin.

'How's work?' I call through the half-open door.

'All right.'

'Really? I just talked to Riz. He says he fired you for missing three shifts in a row.'

'It was a shit job.'

'Call him and apologise,' I say, firmly. 'He promised me he'd give you another chance. Go on. Do it now.'

I wait, straining to hear what he says to Riz. Instead of the low murmur of his voice I hear the click and slam of the front door. Annoyed that he's run out on me I dart into the sitting room. Two boys are standing over him. The taller one turns deadened eyes on me. Not much older than Leon, this boy is pure threat: arched brows, smooth skin, unblemished save for a jagged scar on his left cheek: a blade wound left untended and unstitched, worn as a badge of honour. 'Who are you?' he says.

'It's OK, Flex,' Leon murmurs. 'She's from the council. Checkin' out the flat.'

Still holding eye contact with me the boy dips down, picks up the roll of notes from the coffee table, stuffs it into his back pocket and ticks his head at his companion. Without a word they walk out, the menace still lingering as the front door bangs shut.

'What was that about?' I say.

'Nothing.'

'It didn't look like nothing. How did they get in? I didn't hear the doorbell.' And then, when he didn't reply, 'Leon?'

'Flex has got a key.'

'Why?'

His gaze stays locked on the coffee table. He spots some dried debris on the glass and picks it off with his nail. 'He's a mate. He stays here sometimes.'

I take a breath and look away to the window to compose myself. My face turns to meet me, clouds scudding behind me in the glass. 'You mean he uses your flat to stash Sean Logan's drugs.'

'What are you on about?'

'I know you're working for Logan. I saw you with Dylan Greaves.'

He shoots up from the futon and glares at me, breathing hard. 'Butt out, all right!'

I want to shake him. Instead, I stare him down and say, 'Come and help me unpack the shopping.'

'What shopping?'

'I'm going to show you how to make chilli so you can stop eating rubbish.'

I stomp back to the kitchen. After a while he comes in after me. I point to the bags on the table. He takes out a packet of mince, a jar of flaked chillis, a couple of tins of tomatoes and a net of red onions. He scrumples up the empty carrier bag and opens the second one. His hand slows and his lip lifts as he takes out a white shirt in cellophane packaging. 'What's this?'

'What's it look like?'

'I ain't wearing no—'

'It's for court. Going in there looking smart, with your head up, won't do you any harm with the judge. Try it on. If it doesn't fit. I'll change it.'

He hesitates, then grabs the back of his T-shirt and pulls it over his head. I feel a jolt of helplessness when I see that his torso is newly taut and defined. I look away. I've seen this before, kids awaiting sentencing bulking up in case they get sent to prison. 'There's a good chance they'll go easy on you this time,' I say, softly, 'but if you're caught with Logan's drugs while you're out on bail, there'll be nothing anyone can do.'

He blinks his long dark lashes and throws me a look: part fear, part defiance. 'You just don't get it, do you? You don't say no to Logan. Not if you live on Rosemead.'

'I do get it, Leon,' I say, reaching for the bag. 'And I'm going to try and get you moved.'

'Yeah, sure,' he says. He shrugs on the shirt and does up the middle button, stretching and twisting his arms to see if the cuffs reach his wrists.

'Looks good,' I say. 'Try it with this.' I pull out the tie I've bought him.

He stands for a moment, shoulders drooped, frowning at the neatly rolled tie in my hands.

'Don't you like it? I thought maroon would look smart without being flashy.'

He shrugs awkwardly. I feel my face reddening. I should have realised. He doesn't know how to tie it because no one has ever bothered to teach him. I say quickly to save his face, 'My husband does this fancy Windsor knot. If I do one for you, and you're careful you can slip it off without undoing it.'

He shrugs again but lifts his chin. I slip the tie through his collar and with brisk fingers loop and tuck until there's a smooth fat knot sitting at his throat. He meets my gaze for a moment, then twitches his head away. 'Thanks.'

I step back. 'All right so now slide it off and hang up the shirt so it doesn't get creased.'

He snatches up his T-shirt and slopes off to the bedroom. When he gets back I dump the net of onions in front of him. 'Go on, get chopping.' I find a pan in one of the cupboards and rinse off the dust while he rescues a knife from the brown, grease-scummed water in the sink. As he peels and chops I clear the draining board and wash up. He likes cooking – he pretends he doesn't, but he once let it slip that it was something he used to do with his aunty, way back before her death catapulted him into care.

'They're enrolling for NVQ catering courses at the local college,' I say. 'I brought you the forms. Do you want me to help you fill them in?' He stays quiet. 'It would be something good to tell the court. Show them you're getting your life back on track.'

He drops the knife and pushes his arm to his eyes. 'What's the point? Logan's not going to let me do a course.'

I look down into the sink. The cheap crockery blurs in front of me. I know exactly what he's feeling, what it's like to be frightened and alone. No sofas to surf, no family to call up when you're struggling, nowhere to hide. Before I can stop myself I'm breaking all the rules and putting my arm around him.

He flinches and tries to shake me off, but not that hard and I wrap the other arm around him. For an instant it's like holding Finn, wanting to stop the world from hurting him. Knowing that I can't.

'It's the onions.' He pulls away, darting his eyes to the window, as if Logan might be out there watching.

'Here.' I hand him the frying pan and while he fries the onions I text Susy and tell her I need to shunt our lunch date back an hour.

By the time I leave Leon's flat all the rooms are tidied and swept, there's a pan of chilli bubbling on the stove and he's completed the college enrolment forms. It's not enough, though. He's eighteen and on his own. How's a kid like that supposed to survive in a world full of men like Sean Logan and Dylan Greaves?

CHAPTER 8

Famous for bacon rolls and sweaty slabs of bread pudding, Mildred's Café is way beneath the radar of the soya latte and flat-white-drinking brigade, which is part of its appeal. Susy is already there when I walk into the steamy din. She's ten years older than I am, though you'd never know it. Tall, willowy and crazy-haired, she sits among the weary pot plants and yellow-jacketed workmen looking about twenty-five as she glances up from her phone and waves. She's a criminal defence lawyer but somewhere between doing her day job and bringing up her daughter, Gaby, she found time to think about why she spent so much of her time defending care leavers for petty crimes and decided to try to catch them before they fell. So now she splits her days between heading up the youth court team at her firm and running Next Steps. She's terrible at admin, amazing with the kids and funds the whole project by targeting CEOs and celebrities with a lethal combination of flirtation and threat.

'You look tired,' she says.

I squeeze in next to her and take a gulp of the mahogany brown tea she's got waiting for me. 'I haven't been sleeping too well.'

'What's wrong?'

I drop my voice. 'I had a run-in with Sean Logan.'

'What?' She sits forward, horrified.

'Leon's been missing our meetings and ignoring my calls so I took a few drives around town to see if I could find out what was going on. Twice this week I saw him hanging out with Logan's boys. Then, yesterday, I saw him with a group of bikers taking orders from Greaves.'

Susy groans.

I look up as the door opens and more customers stream in. 'Five minutes later, Logan turned up and came over in person to warn me off. The scary thing was he recognised me from the surgery.'

'Jesus, Nic. You've got to be careful.'

'I'll be all right but what are we going to do about Leon? It's not just the deliveries. I think they're using his flat as a trap house.'

'Oh God,' she says. 'He's only got a fifty-fifty chance of avoiding custody as it is.'

'Are you serious? It was a first offence. Wrong place at the wrong time.'

'It'll all come down to how he comes over at the hearing. But if I were you I'd start packing him a bag.'

'I wish you were defending him.'

'The woman who is knows her stuff, but I'll call her and see if she'll let me see the pre-sentence report.'

I pick up my mug, grasping the chunky china with both hands, and take another sip of tea. 'If he does get off we've got to get him out of Rosemead. There's no escaping Logan while he's in that flat.'

'It won't be easy. He's got no chance of getting a private landlord to take him on and now the council have finally housed him, he'll be way down the list for any kind of move.'

'There must be something we can do. Even if it's just a temporary solution.'

'I'll make some calls.'

'Why don't the cops do something about Logan? Some of the kids he's got working for him can't be more than eleven or twelve. Look at this.' I show her the photos on my phone.

She flips through the pictures and glances round the café before leaning in and dropping her voice. 'It's deliberate.'

'What do you mean?'

'One of our partners has a contact in the vice squad. Apparently they're staying hands off and keeping Logan under surveillance, hoping he'll lead them to his wholesaler. It's part of some nation-wide operation to crush a network of county lines gangs, and the top brass doesn't want anyone rocking the boat by arresting what they see as a minor player.'

'Meanwhile kids like Leon end up in prison.'

'Yep.' She lets out an angry breath. Then she tips her head to one side and gives me a long, hard look. 'Leon's not the only thing that's worrying you, is it?'

'I just need a good night's sleep.' I look away. When I'd had trouble finding the money for childcare so I could see my mentees, Susy had insisted that I leave Finn with her au pair anytime I wanted. I'd be doing her a favour, she'd said, he'd be company for Gaby. She'd busied herself digging a lipstick out of her bag, acting as if the offer was nothing, but somehow I think she knew that those snatched hours I spent trying to help a kid from Next Steps were my way of dealing with my own past. Maybe she'd even sensed they were an attempt at atonement. And right now, Susy being insightful is the last thing I need.

'Bacon roll!' The raw, throaty voice of Mildred's only waiter is a welcome interruption. Susy half stands and reaches for the plate being handed over the ducked heads of the other customers. Eyes lift, glancing our way. I feel some of them lingering, but then Susy is quite something to look at. I watch her take off the top of the roll and daub a zigzag of brown sauce across the strips of bacon.

'Want some?' she says.

'I don't do carbs, remember?'

'Don't be ridiculous, you're turning into skin and bone. Here.' She saws the roll in half and pushes the plate towards me. The smell creeps into my nostrils, rich and delicious and, before I know it, my fingers are lifting my half to my mouth. My teeth sink through crisp layers of crust, doughy butter-soaked softness and hit the fruity tang of sauce and the greasy crunch of bacon. I close my eyes and giggle at the bliss of it.

'Good, huh?'

I nod enthusiastically, my mouth too full to speak. My phone beeps as I chew. I read the message and automatically check the time.

'Everything all right?' Susy asks.

'Finn's teacher wants me to get there ten minutes early so she can have a quick word. Probably some PTA thing. Sometimes I wish I'd never joined that committee.'

For a few blissful seconds I pretend that my time is my own. I take bites of bacon roll, wash them down with gulps of tea, and listen to Susy telling me about her latest court battle.

'Ooh, I meant to tell you,' she says, picking up a frizzled shred of bacon and popping it into her mouth. 'I went to one of those Women in Law dinners a couple of nights ago – boring as hell, but you'll never guess who I met there.'

'No idea.'

'Annabel Oakshott.'

A fragment of bread catches in my throat. 'Ian's ex?'

'Yep.'

'How did that come up?'

'I mentioned where I lived and she went a bit weird and said she'd nearly moved here a couple of years ago but she'd split up with her fiancé just before their wedding. I kind of remembered you saying Ian's ex was a lawyer so I did a bit of probing and out it came.'

'Was she pretty?' I ask, as if I'd never trawled the internet to see for myself, or sat staring at her smooth pale skin, glossy auburn hair and shiny smile.

'Not a patch on you.'

I grab another napkin from the dispenser and push it to my lips. 'Did you ask her why they split up?'

'She was clearly still upset about it so I had to tread carefully but a couple of glasses in she just opened up. She said that Ian had never got on with his stepfather but about six months after they got engaged, his hatred started getting obsessive. She put it down to the stepdad being so tough on him when he was a kid and she thought that once they were married and started a family of their own he'd find a way to put it behind him and move on.'

I push away the remains of the roll, feeling slightly sick and more than a little confused. 'He hardly ever talks about his stepfather to me. He just goes on about his father all the time.'

'Well, she said that Hugh, the stepdad, and Ian's father, started a finance company together after they left university but it was Ian's dad who built it up and ran it day to day and made them both a shedload of money. Then, after his dad died, Hugh moved in on Ian's mum — what's her name, Gwynneth?'

'Gwen.'

'That's right. Anyway, he offered Gwen a shoulder to cry on and an arm to lean on, organised the funeral, sorted out the probate and generally made himself indispensable. Then suddenly they're married and he's taking over the house and her finances and making her and Ian's lives hell. Mr Nice Guy in public and a complete bastard behind closed doors.'

Across the room the waiter yells out an order of pie and chips, his voice cutting through the chatter and the clatter of plates. I lean in closer. 'What did he do?'

'According to Annabel he turned into a total control freak, putting Ian's mum down the whole time and acting like nothing Ian did was ever good enough. Apparently he taunted him when he failed to get into med school and sneered about him becoming a dentist. I think he might even have got physical with Gwen behind closed doors, but she put a brave face on it because this guy had done some crafty accounting thing which put him in control of Ian's father's share of the company and if she'd left him she'd have lost the lot.'

'Did Annabel say why Ian left her?' I say, hurt that my husband had shared all this with her but never mentioned a word of it to me.

Susy narrows her eyes and looks at me hard. 'He didn't. She left him.'

'What?' I scan her face.

'She said he was getting more and more obsessed about his stepdad and started taking out his frustration on her, so she told him if he didn't get counselling and deal with it she'd leave him. He refused, so she walked out.'

'That doesn't sound right. I know his stepfather's still on the board of the company, but he's totally out of Ian's mum's life and, as far as I can see, she got a pretty cushy divorce settlement: kept the family home, drives a big car and spends a fortune on clothes, hair and holidays. And actually, the company – DRB – has just paid off Ian's mortgage. Some tax-efficiency deal Ian said, but his stepfather must have okayed it.'

Susy raises an eyebrow.

'What?'

'Nothing. I'm just telling you what Annabel said.'

I take another sip of tea, and glance up sharply. All I see are heads hunched over mounds of today's shepherd's pie special. 'Did she ever meet his stepdad?'

'A couple of times. She said he was all old-school charm when she was around, but it was obvious he was pretty overbearing.'

'Did she know about me?'

'She'd heard that Ian had got married. I didn't tell her that I knew you.'

I close my eyes, then open them. I don't want to think about Annabel. She'd obviously spun Susy this crazy tale to make herself feel better about the break-up.

Susy licks the last smear of grease from her fingertips. 'So how *is* the demon dentist? All set for my birthday lunch?'

'Stop it,' I say, trying not to giggle. 'You'll like him once you get to know him.'

'Chance would be a fine thing.'

'I know, I'm sorry. He's always so busy.'

'You'd better turn up this time. What's the point of lumbering myself with a huge mortgage I can't afford if I can't show the place off to my friends?'

'Of course we'll be there, and I promise to be impressed.'

'I'll hold you to that!'

I fold up my napkin, first one way, then the other, and score my thumb along the crease. 'There is one thing, though. I've told Ian I've cut down on the hours I do for Next Steps and that I work mainly from home now, doing online support.'

'Why did you tell him that?' Her voice is casual, but she's looking at me closely.

'He worries that I've got too much on my plate and he doesn't like me doing house visits. He thinks it might be dangerous. So maybe don't tell him I'm still working with Leon—?'

A brief, uncertain pause before she nods. 'I'll get us some more tea.'

I watch her as she edges her way around the crowded tables, envying the easy way she tosses back her hair and laughs with the man behind the counter as she gives him her order.

My head twitches away to catch the door swinging shut behind a figure bending low into the wind. A quiver of suspicion hangs in the drift of damp air, a lingering feeling that while I'd been watching Susy, the person who's just left had been watching me.

CHAPTER 9

It doesn't matter how prepared or distracted I am: whenever I push through the swing doors of Finn's school, The caustic smell of disinfectant spins me straight back to my own days at primary school; or, rather, to the cruelly vivid memory of one particular day, skipping down the corridor past handprints blobbed across squares of sugar paper, big-eyed self-portraits and swirly-stemmed versions of Van Gogh's sunflowers to Mrs Sugden's office, each step bringing me closer to the end of childhood and the beginning of life as a name on a tattered brown file.

A woman I half recognise – Liam's mother? Sian? Shan? – clacks towards me in high-heeled boots, her hands stuffed deep in the pockets of her coat. Finn's always going on about Liam and I'm about to stop her and suggest we get the boys together after school one night when she throws me a scorching look and hurries on without a word.

I'm waiting in reception inspecting a banner-length painting of a brick wall, topped with thirty grinning Humpty Dumpties, all of them oblivious to the disaster ahead, when Finn's teacher comes hurrying out to meet me. I like Liz Cooper – she's fortyish, caring and dedicated, and Finn thinks she's great.

'Thanks so much for coming in. Let's go in here.' She ushers me into a small, square room. I can tell from the way she closes the door and points me to one of the grey plastic bucket seats that this isn't about the PTA. A dull ache stirs in my stomach.

'Has something happened to Finn? Is he all right?'

'Don't worry, he's absolutely fine.' She rubs the thumb of one hand over the knuckles of the other. 'But for the last couple of days he hasn't wanted to go out to play at break or lunchtime. He wouldn't tell me why, but I could see he was upset about something so I let him stay inside and help me clear out the art cupboard. He wanted to stay in again today but I hoped that whatever had been worrying him had blown over and I sent him outside. Unfortunately, there was an incident in the playground.'

That word shoots fear through my heart. 'What sort of *incident*?'

'I'm afraid he got pushed over – nothing serious, just a grazed knee, but I think the boy who did it also trod on his glasses and cracked one of the lenses. We know who it was and we've taken appropriate action to make sure it won't happen again, but Finn was very upset and he may need a little extra support and cheering up.'

I swallow hard. 'Was it Liam?'

'I've spoken to the boy concerned and I've made it very clear to his mother that there will be serious sanctions if it happens again,' she says, with a diplomatic smile. 'She understands. She's going to speak to her son and she's offered to pay to replace Finn's glasses.'

'I don't want her money,' I say, fuming. 'Tell her to shove it… in the school fund.'

'Please don't worry, Mrs Dexter. These things flare up and blow over again just as quickly. We are all very fond of Finn – he's a lovely boy, but some children just take longer to form a friendship group than others.'

'So what can we do?'

'Well, we can both monitor the situation, and I've taken a couple of practical steps to boost Finn's morale. I've appointed him full-time art cupboard monitor and I've asked him to act as official buddy to Jamal, who's going to be joining us next week. Perhaps you could look out for Jamal's mother, Lisa—? I'm sure she'd appreciate a friendly smile at the school gates.'

*

As we set off home, I watch Finn in the rear-view mirror. He's staring at the passing cars and although he's not speaking, his hands are restless and his lips are moving.

'Mrs Cooper says you didn't want to go out to play today,' I say.

His eyes stay fixed on the window. 'Henry wouldn't play with me.'

'Why not?'

'He was playing with Liam. They've got a club. It's secret.'

'Oh, right.'

'I tried to join in but Liam pushed me.'

This is the worst part of being a mother: seeing your child in pain and knowing there's nothing you can do to make it better. 'I tell you what,' I say, quickly. 'Why don't I ask Tilly if she'll bring Henry to the park after school one night next week? You can bring your scooters and we'll have tea in the café?'

He lifts his shoulders in a miserable shrug.

Finn is upstairs playing with his train set when Ian gets back.

'Sorry I'm a bit late,' he says.

'Did you get held up at the surgery?'

'No.' He unbuttons his collar and loosens his tie. 'I dropped a bottle round to Matt's to thank him for mending your tyre, and ended up staying for a beer.'

'Oh, thanks for that. I was going to pick one up for him today. In the end I didn't have a spare minute.'

He reaches for a wine glass and eases the cork out of a half-full bottle of red. 'Really? Julie Gibbs says she saw you this morning, going into some greasy little caff in West Street.'

I bet she did. Ian's fan base of female patients don't come any more hardcore than Julie Gibbs, who always arrives fresh from the hairdresser's, ready for a giggle and a gossip as soon as her taut little backside hits Ian's chair – and what better way to get the conversation rolling than by a nasty little swipe at his wife's downmarket taste in coffee shops. 'I popped in there for a quick cup of tea,' I say.

'I thought you were going to the gym. Catching up on lost time.' He glugs wine into a glass. 'West Street's nowhere near the gym.'

I get up slowly and move over to the worktop where I've left two chicken breasts marinating in garlic and herbs. I think fast as I peel the cling film off the bowl. 'I had to go to Marks to get Finn some new pyjamas.'

I look up as he holds the glass to the light and swirls it around. 'This isn't the first time you've lied to me, is it?'

'What?' I break out in a sweat.

'About going to the gym.'

I let out a little gasp of relief. 'I know. I need to get organised.'

Finn's feet thump on the stairs and he comes running in. 'Can we do chess, Daddy?'

'Play,' Ian says, absently, his eyes fixing on Finn's face. 'What happened to your glasses?'

'It's fine,' I say. 'He's going to wear his sports ones until we get them mended.'

'How did it happen?'

Finn bites down on his bottom lip. 'Liam pushed me.'

'Did you push him back?'

'Ian,' I say, quietly.

Finn shakes his head.

'If he does it again you've got to fight back,' Ian says. 'I've told you before, you've got to give as good as you get.'

'Ian,' I say, only louder this time, 'that's not—'

'No, Nic, he's got to learn. If you don't stand up for yourself, nobody else is going to do it for you.'

Finn looks at me, pale and unsure, hands flapping. I slip my arm around him. 'It's getting late, sweetheart. You can do chess another night. Say goodnight to Daddy. I'll be up in two minutes to read you a story.'

'Don't let the bugs bite,' Ian says, lifting him up.

'Night, Daddy,' Finn says, and scoots upstairs as soon as Ian deposits him back on the floor.

'Honestly, Nic, it doesn't help that you baby him all the time. The sooner he gets a sibling the better. It will make him feel grown up and responsible.' I can hear the annoyance in his voice.

'Can you take a look at the side gate?' I say, quickly.

'What's wrong with it?'

'It was open this morning.'

'Is the lock broken?'

'I don't think so.'

'Any sign of anyone snooping around?'

'I had a good look. It all seemed fine. Weird, though.'

He flicks on the outside light and goes out through the bifold doors while I hurry upstairs to Finn. I lie next to him and stroke his hair as I read *The Gruffalo*, one of our favourites from when he was little. His eyes grow heavy and I kiss the top of his head and swing my legs off the bed.

'Is Daddy cross with me?' he says, as I reach the door.

'Of course not,' I whisper. 'Daddy was cross with Liam for being mean.'

Ian's searing the chicken breasts when I come back downstairs. 'The lock's fine. You must have forgotten to shut the gate.'

'I'm pretty sure I shut it last night.'

'Oh, come on. We both know how scatty you can be. And I thought you said you checked to see if anyone had got in.'

'I did. I walked right around house.'

He sighs and says quietly, 'So how come you missed those?' He points to two pieces of glass lying on the table.

'Where were they?'

'By the gate. You must have stepped right over them.'

'They definitely weren't there this morning.'

'So how did they get there?'

Bewildered, I pick up one of the pieces of glass. It gleams pink as I turn it in my palm – it's exactly like the chunk Matt took out of my tyre. I look up at Ian. His expression oozes concern. A sharp pain shoots across my hand. I look down.

Blood trickles from a V-shaped cut at the base of my thumb. I watch the thread of red roll down a crease in my palm and pool around the puckered edges of a crescent-shaped scar.

CHAPTER 10
Then

I was hunched in a corner of my bedroom at Ma Burton's, sucking at the cut on my palm and knocking my head against my knees when this new girl walked in. It was the day after my thirteenth birthday, which I'd celebrated with a card from my current social work team – *Best wishes from Loretta, John and Debbie* – a slapping on the way back from school from some kids in the year above, and a stony silence from the Burtons.

The head knocking was a tic, a source of comfort, something I'd done since the day Mum died. It got me laughed at, teased, punched, but I still did it. Though I stopped and looked up when I realised I wasn't alone. The girl had dark hair and green eyes and gave off a buzz of energy like a force field. She dumped her bag on the floor and looked around the room, her eyes flitting from the stain on the wallpaper to the peeling Take That posters left by some long-gone kid I'd never met, then across to the window and finally to me. 'What's up with you?' she said.

I shrugged and slid my hands between my knees, too slow to stop her seeing the blood. She pounced, prised my fingers open and plucked the glass figurine from my grasp. It was a ballerina, hands clasped to her chest, standing on one pointed toe, the curve of her long, rippled skirt missing a chunk along the edge. She frowned at me. Slowly I opened the other fist and showed her the broken fragment lying in my bloody palm. 'I took it,' I said. 'From the cabinet in the front room.'

'Why? It's horrible.'

I felt a flush creep up my neck. 'I was pretending.'

'Pretending what?'

'That I'd got a present.' Tears dribbled down my cheeks. 'I didn't mean to break it. I was going to put it back. Burton's going to kill me.'

'S'all right. Soon as she got shot of my social worker she went out.'

'Then she'll kill me when she gets back.'

She put the pieces on the floor, slid down the wall and squeezed in next to me. 'You know what I say?' She looked at me. 'I say, screw 'em. Screw the lot of them.' She started to laugh. I tried to laugh too. I really tried. Only it came out as a sob. Then she did something so unexpected I gasped. She wrapped her skinny arms around me and rocked me. No one had done that since my nan died. With Mum, it had always been me hugging her, creeping into her bed late at night and curling up small with my hand resting lightly on her hip, not daring to breathe in case I woke her up. And now here was a stranger comforting me, making me feel wanted. It felt so good. I whimpered a little and pushed my head into the soft warmth of her neck. I never wanted to move. Not ever. But after a moment she freed up one arm and waved a finger between the two single beds. 'Which one's yours?'

I pointed to the one under the window.

'Can I have it? I can't sleep if I can't see the door. I like to see who's coming.'

I liked to see who was coming too. But I let her have my bed. She jumped onto it, flung open the window and lit a cigarette.

'You can't,' I said, aghast and impressed.

She took a long drag and blew the smoke out of the window. 'Don't worry. I can handle Burton.'

'You don't know her. One minute she's all smiles, the next she's freaking out.'

'All you've got to do is find her weak spot and play it for all it's worth.'

I licked the blood off my cut and climbed up next to her. 'Supposing she hasn't got one?'

'Trust me. *Everybody's* got a weak spot.' She passed the cigarette to me, butt first. 'I'm Donna by the way. Who are you?'

I took a quick puff and blew it out of the window. 'Nicola. But everyone calls me Nicci.'

'So, tell me, Nicci, what are Burton's rules?'

'Stay in. Shut up. Keep out of the front room and stay out of her way.'

'What time does she and her old man go to bed?'

'About eleven, but you can't get out. She locks the front door and takes the key to bed with her.'

Benjy toddled in at that moment, sucking his thumb. His nappy sagged full and low from his scrawny little hips, his nose was running, his left leg dragged when he walked and he had an assortment of scars and dirty-looking bruises dotted down his bone-white arms and belly. Donna turned from her post by the window and her face crinkled with disgust. I couldn't blame her. Even without the snot, the limp and the scars, bald, bug-eyed Benjy was no one's idea of cute. I stepped off the bed and lowered my hand very gently to touch his cheek. Move any quicker and he'd flinch. He was an emergency placement, removed from the care of a crack-head mum and a dad who liked to use him as an ashtray. He'd been here a week. A 'place of safety' they called it. I suppose even Ma Burton's was marginally better than crawling around in your own filth with nothing to eat for days on end. I had never heard him laugh, I'm not sure he knew how. Come to think of it I'd never heard him cry either but in the last couple of days he'd taken to coming into my room and curling up in the corner. I was glad of the company. I liked to think he was, too.

'You stay with Donna,' I said, as I went in search of a fresh nappy and a packet of wipes. When I got back, she was still hanging out of the window and he was still standing in the middle of the room, exactly where I'd left him. After I'd changed him and wiped his nose, I sat on what was now my bed and lifted him onto my lap. He didn't object or respond; he just stiffened slightly and stared straight ahead. Twenty months old and already a master of survival.

Donna had unpacked her things, had a good look through all of mine and was on her third cigarette when we heard the front door slam. Ten minutes later Burton came stomping up the stairs. I could tell from the sound that she was on the warpath. Donna scraped the lit end of her cigarette against the pebble-dashed wall outside and laid the butt carefully on the window ledge. Calm and unhurried, she picked up the pieces of the figurine and sat down on the edge of the bed. I shrank down beside her.

Burton threw open the door. Lips quivering, she stormed in and loomed over me. 'What have you done with my ornament?'

I put my head in my hands and rocked forward, my tongue thick and dry.

'Come on. What have you done with it, you little thief?' she hissed, bending down to my level. I was trying to find the words to own up when I heard Donna's voice, calm as you like: 'Don't have a go at her. It was me.'

Burton stepped back and Donna pushed herself up. Blinking wide-eyed into Burton's surprise she held out the broken figurine. I was looking up at her, holding my breath when she tipped her head to one side like a dog on a Christmas card. 'It was an accident,' she said, running a bitten finger over the folds of the skirt. 'It's so beautiful I just wanted to touch it and then I… I dropped it.' Burton stared at her, suspicious that this was a wind up, but Donna stood firm, that gloopy look frozen on her face. 'I know it looks bad for carers who ask for kids be reassigned, specially so early on in a placement, so I'll tell my social worker it's me that wants to be moved. I'll think of something that won't make you look like… you know, like you can't cope with damaged kids.'

I stared at Donna in wonder. Burton glared at her, her piggy little eyes cold and narrow. 'Don't push it, missy. I've got my eye on you.' She switched her attention to me. 'As for you, you should have told her no one goes in my front room.' She pivoted around on her stumpy heel and stalked out.

Donna was nearly ten months older than I was but we were going to be in the same year at school, and I was looking forward to showing her who to avoid, which teachers were OK, and the best places to hide. Only Donna didn't need to hide. From the minute she walked through the front gates all the girls, even the mean ones, were wary of her. The boys were fascinated by her and a bit scared of her, too. Nobody sneered at Donna; nobody pushed her head down the toilet or kicked her ankle when she passed them in the corridor. Miraculously, when I was with her, they didn't do it to me either. Overnight, I went from being the grubby, picked-on weirdo to being Donna's sidekick. Instead of the lunchtime agony of eating alone I walked into the dining hall at Donna's side and held my head high as we loaded our trays and found ourselves a table. When the bell rang for the end of school I didn't have to creep away, head down in the hope that I wouldn't get picked on on my way home. That day I walked out of the school gates with my arm linked through Donna's, swinging my bag and laughing a bit too loudly at her impersonation of my most vicious tormentor.

'Let's go shopping,' she said.

'I haven't got any money.'

She grinned. 'Neither have I.'

I tripped along beside her, adrenaline pumping, mouth dry like I was teetering on the edge of a cliff.

'Get yourself a basket, stay about ten feet behind me and keep a lookout,' she said, when we got to the supermarket.

She walked casually through the doors and threw the security guard a little smile. Picking up a basket she wandered towards the shelves of bread and cakes on the far wall, glancing down each aisle as she went and stopping now and then to inspect the tubs of special offers. Heart pumping like it was going burst, I grabbed a basket and went after her. She swerved back on herself, walked past the tinned goods aisle and turned into the meat section, where a smartly dressed woman was checking out the steaks while her toddler wriggled and whined in the designer buggy she was trailing behind her. Donna edged past her, plucked the teddy out of the kid's sticky hand and kept walking. The kid drew in a mouthful of air and blasted it out in an ear-splitting screech. The mother spun around and crouched down to see what was wrong. Donna gave the kid a chance to turn crimson then doubled back, holding the teddy high. 'Is this what he's after?' she said. 'I found it back there by the washing powder.'

'Oh, thank you,' the woman said, with a grateful groan. 'We'd have been up all night if he'd lost his Ted-Ted.'

Donna squatted down. Pulling silly faces at the kid she pressed the teddy back into his hand, and briefly, so very briefly, brushed against the woman's open shoulder bag as she pulled herself upright and walked on. Without missing a beat, she tossed a multipack of crisps and a couple of cans of coke into her basket and made her way to the self-checkout. With the innocence of an angel she beeped her shopping through the scanner, even pressing '1' when the automated voice asked her how many five-pence bags she wanted to pay for. Delving into her coat pocket she burrowed deep and scrabbled for a moment before she brought out a handful of notes. She flicked through them, selected a tenner and fed it into the machine, only glancing round as she scooped her change out of the little black trough.

I trotted after her into the car park, a horrified pounding in my belly. 'That was mean,' I hissed.

'She can afford it. Didn't you see her coat and shoes?'

'What are you going to do with her wallet?'

'Not me. You.' She pressed it into my hand. 'Give it to the security guard.'

'What?'

'She'll be so relieved to get her bank cards and IDs back, she won't go whining to the manager demanding to see the CCTV footage.'

I did as she said. Unable to look the guard in the eye I shoved the wallet at him, mumbling about finding it outside by the trolleys, and bolted out of there. Even so, by the time I got out of the car park, Donna was heading down the high street and I had to run to catch up.

'Where are you going now?'

'Boots. This time you stay close and keep a lookout.'

I trotted after her and watched trembling as a handful of eye shadows and a couple of mascaras disappeared into the depths of her pocket while she tried out the lipsticks. Picking one out she took it to the counter and paid.

On the way home she stopped off at a charity shop. This time I hung around by the door praying she wouldn't steal anything. I needn't have worried. She trotted up to the counter with a china shepherdess and forked out seventy pence for it.

'What did you get that for?' I said.

'You'll see.'

When we got home, she whispered, 'Watch this.'

All downcast eyes and shy smile she presented it to Ma Burton. 'It's from both of us. It's not much but we wanted to make up for the ballerina.'

Burton went red in the face and told her she didn't have to do that, and Donna said she did because she knew she'd messed up and she didn't want them to get off on the wrong foot. Cue more drippy head cocking. Burton didn't fall for it, but it unnerved her enough to keep her off our backs for the rest of the week.

That night, Donna took the broken piece of the ballerina's skirt and cut a nick in her finger, then she caught hold of my hand, squeezed the wound in my palm until it started to bleed again and mingled her blood with mine. 'Blood sisters,' she whispered. 'Forever.'

I looked down at the dark stain in my throbbing hand and whispered, 'Blood sisters, forever.'

The next day I rolled my skirt up like Donna's and loaded my lashes with one of the mascaras she'd nicked from Boots; only the skirt went all bunchy around my waist, and the mascara got smeared down my face when I rubbed my eyes in Physics.

CHAPTER 11

'Susy's going to love this colour,' I say, wrapping tissue paper around the turquoise bowl I bought from the pottery stall at the farmers' market. I bite off a piece of Sellotape and press it across the join. 'Let's see your card.'

Finn holds up his drawing. It's a stick figure of a woman with scribble hair and red high heels, standing beside a bright green cake topped with purple candles.

'That's fantastic.'

Ian walks in, rubbing his hands. 'OK, Finn, I've had an idea. Why don't we take Mummy out for a nice pub lunch and then' – he pauses as if for a silent drum roll – 'how about we drive to IKEA and get you a set of bunk beds like Henry's?'

'Yes!' Finn leaps off his chair and runs around the kitchen, his fist thrust out Superman style.

'Ian, that's a lovely thought but it's Susy's birthday lunch.' I glance at the calendar. There it is – *Susy's Birthday*, with two exclamation marks.

He sighs without looking at the calendar. 'It doesn't say anything about lunch. I assumed that was a reminder for you to send her a card.'

'But I told you she was having a party. The invitation's on the noticeboard.' I swing around to point out the invitation made by Gaby in all its glittery glory. It's not there. I was sure I'd pinned it next to my calorie guide.

He drops a piece of toast into the toaster and snaps down the lever, clearly irritated. 'Nicci, honestly, this scattiness isn't endearing and it's not good for Finn. I've just promised him we can go and get bunk beds and now you're telling him we can't.'

Finn's eyes flick from him to me.

'We can order them online,' I said. 'Susy will be so upset if we don't go. It's going to go on into the evening and she's invited Finn to stay over with Gaby.'

'He's got football in the morning.'

'He's taking his football kit with him, and I'm going to pick him up first thing.'

He sighs, his voice almost kind. 'You of all people should know that children need consistency, but if you'd rather undermine me and go to a party, we'll go.' He rolls his eyes at Finn. 'Silly Mummy, what are we going to do with her?'

Finn climbs back onto his chair and mutters, 'Silly Mummy,' as if he's trying out the words for size.

Ian pours himself a coffee and takes it up to his study. I hear the door close and the faint sounds of classical music drifting down the stairs. I finish wrapping Susy's present and close my eyes for a moment, not liking the way I'm feeling. I fetch Finn's reading book from his school bag and listen while he strains and frowns over the words. I write *Excellent effort!!!* in his reading diary and by the time I'm heading upstairs to get dressed, I'm inching back into party mode. If I'm honest I *was* a bit hesitant when I told Ian about Susy's party because he's so down on the whole Next Steps thing, so it's no wonder he got confused. But this party isn't about Next Steps: it's about celebrating a friend's birthday.

I search through the clothes in my wardrobe and pick out a black cheesecloth gypsy blouse that I haven't worn for months. I put on a pair of jeans and slip on the blouse, enjoying the looseness of the neckline, the softness of the fabric and the feel of the long, floaty sleeves. I tuck my jeans into the old, black cowboy boots with the silver studs I picked up in a charity shop years ago. They've been mended more times than I can remember but the narrow toes and stacked heels always used to give me a boost when I was feeling low. I shake my hair out of its scrunchy, comb it through with my fingers, add red dangly earrings and a slash of bright lipstick and run downstairs.

'You look pretty,' Finn says.

'Thank you, sweetheart. Can you fetch your overnight bag? I left it on your bed.'

He disappears upstairs and I'm writing our names in the card he made, shaking the sparkly pen between kisses, when Ian comes in. He stops when he sees me. 'What are you wearing?'

I pluck at my blouse. 'You've seen this before. I've had it for ages.'

'Black doesn't suit you.'

'I thought you liked this blouse.'

'I don't know what gave you that idea. Anyway, it's freezing outside.'

'I'll take a coat.'

His tone grows tighter. 'I'd like you to change. And to do something about your hair.'

'Why?'

'You know why.'

'No,' I say, confused. 'I don't.'

'If you want me to spell it out, I will. You look… cheap. And scruffy.'

Hurt, I seek his eyes but his glance drops to my feet and the sight of my boots seems to incense him. 'For Heaven's sake, I thought you'd thrown those things away!'

'Why would I? I love these boots!'

The muscles in his jaw are flexing as if he's having trouble keeping control. 'Look, you spring this event on me and if you expect me to drop everything and go with you, the least you can do is wear something that won't embarrass me. It's not as if you haven't got any decent clothes.'

Cold with humiliation, I walk to the door with as much dignity as I can muster. It's true. I do have a wardrobe full of smart new clothes, half of them bought the day Ian presented me with the Honda. We'd been planning on going into town to get Finn new trainers and Ian said it would be a good chance for me to test-drive the car. By the time he'd corrected my jerky gear changes, guided me in and out of the lanes on the roundabout and talked me through a tricky reverse in the multi-storey I was a wreck. When we got to the shopping centre he bought Finn designer trainers, a couple of smart jumpers and a goose down puffa coat that came with a price tag that made me flinch. Then he headed off to one of those designer outlets that's full of snotty staff, elegantly draped mannequins and floating shelves dotted with tiny handbags, intent on getting something for me.

I really didn't want to go in but he was already chatting to an assistant and between them they picked out skirts, shirts, jackets and trousers in what she called an autumn palette – basically brown, beige and rust – and packed me off to the changing room to try them on. They fitted beautifully and the material felt amazing but when I glanced in the mirror it was like I'd caught a glimpse of Ian's mother. Though he seemed to think they were perfect.

Seeing as he'd just bought me a car and spent so much money on Finn I couldn't let him pay for my things as well so I ended up spending a big chunk of the money I'd saved for the Micra on a whole lot of clothes I'm not sure I even like, and none of them are suitable for a party – especially one thrown by Susy.

I take off the blouse and numbly put on a beige blouse and scrape my hair into a ponytail. I hesitate for a moment and then I ease off the cowboy boots and change into flat, zip-sided ankle boots. Avoiding my face in the mirror I swap the red earrings for studs and take out a tissue and blot away the lipstick.

'She's your friend, so you can drink if you want to and I'll drive,' he says, as we leave the house.

'Thank you.' I reach for his hand, but he's hurrying ahead, unlocking his car.

Ian doesn't say much on the way to the party but Finn's excited chatter about sleeping over with Gaby eases the silence.

'That one,' I say, pointing to a rambling red-brick house covered in ivy and clearly in need of work. Ian winces a little at the loudness of the music blaring from the garden. He winces a lot more when he sees that the front door is wide open, and he trails behind me as I walk into the kitchen. Two aproned cooks are busy stirring great vats of food.

'Ooh, that smells good,' I say, knowing that he'll be hungry. I add our gift to a pile on the table by the door and we step outside into the garden, where a huge fabric structure, halfway between a yurt and a marquee, has been erected on the grass. I duck through the doorway into a domed space looped with balloons and fairy lights, the floor covered with overlapping rugs. It's packed with people – forty or so of Susy's friends and colleagues, some of them clustered around the heaters, chatting; others lolling on cushions. Susy is in a slinky red dress, laughing with the crop-haired female DJ, while a few brave souls are dancing to the music pounding from the speakers. In one corner an entertainer in an orange top hat and baggy, acid-green tuxedo is conjuring cards out of the air to the delight of the children gathered at his feet.

'Hey, Nicci!' Susy shouts, squeezing her way through the throng of people. She hugs me and kisses Ian on the cheek.

'Happy birthday,' he says.

'Thanks.' She bends down to Finn. 'Why don't you go and find Gaby? She's over there by the entertainer.'

Somebody is waving at me. I crane through the crowd and see Ginny and Alex from Next Steps and wave back.

'You go and mingle,' Susy says. 'I'll look after Ian. It's time we got to know each other.' He recoils a little as she slips her arm through his but doesn't protest out loud when she drags him away.

'I'll get you something to eat,' I call, as I pick up a glass of wine from the drinks table.

It's all my fault. I should never have left him for so long, but by the time I've stopped to say hello to all the people I know from the Next Steps team and stood in line at the buffet, I must have been gone for at least half an hour. I come back holding two plates heaped with food and feel terrible when I seem him standing on his own, glass of sparkling water in hand, watching the DJ.

'Sorry, you must be starving. Shall we find somewhere to sit down?'

We perch on a couple of floor cushions while he pokes his fork around his plate. All around us people mingle and laugh, and the entertainer tries to teach the children and some of the drunker grown-ups how to juggle.

'This chicken is delicious,' I say, taking another bite. 'Did you have a nice chat with Susy?'

I'm not sure if he's heard me, and he's barely tasted the food, but the music is pretty loud and the chicken might be a bit too spicy for him. I take both our plates, put them on the floor and leap up and grab him by both hands. 'Come on, on your feet. Do you realise we've been married for nearly four months and we've never danced together?'

He frees his hands and pushes himself to his feet. I sway a little to the music, eager for the press of his fingers down my back, the brush of his cheek against mine. He leans in close. 'For God's sake. How much have you had to drink?'

There's nothing but scorn in his voice. My face burns. He shifts his back to me and stares grimly at the dancers as I drop back onto the floor, tucking my feet beneath the cushion and trying to make myself as small as I can. The atmosphere between us grows colder and colder and after about five minutes I get up and go in search of Finn. He's sitting next to Gaby, enraptured by the entertainer's terrible jokes.

I squat down to tell him that Ian and I are leaving and I'll be back in the morning to pick him up. I'm dodging my way back to Ian, trying to avoid Susy, when she catches me by the sleeve. She's slightly tipsy, rocking on her heels. 'Are you having a good time? Let me get you another drink and give you a tour of the house.'

'It's a lovely party and your new house looks amazing, but I've got a bit of a headache.'

'I'll get you an aspirin.'

'No,' I say, quickly. 'I just need to go home and lie down. I'll be back in the morning to pick Finn up.'

She fixes me with a keen, but slightly unfocused, eye and before she can rally her thoughts and kick up a fuss I kiss her cheek and slip away.

Ian doesn't say one word to me on the way home. I follow him into the house and cross my arms and squeeze my elbows to hide the tremor in my hands as I wait for him to speak, but he still doesn't say anything: just gazes at me as if I'm a stranger.

'Ian, I'm sorry I…' I scrabble for words of apology.

'Why do you do this, Nicci?' His voice is low and weary.

'Do what?'

'Go out of your way to hurt me.'

'I would never—'

He pulls the cork from a bottle of red and glugs some into a glass. 'Have you got any idea how hard I've tried to turn your life around? How much money, time and effort I put into giving you and Finn the things you never had?'

'Ian—'

'Please. Let me finish.' I nod, muted. 'I do it because I love you and loving you means helping you to move on from your past. But that woman just wants to drag you back into that whole sordid world.'

I stand in the middle of the kitchen, shaking my head and squeezing back tears.

'What upsets me most is that you're so weak you let her do it. Do you miss the squalor and deprivation? Is that what this obsession with Next Steps is? Huh? An excuse to go back to your hand-to-mouth existence and hang out with scroungers?'

'Ian, that's not fair,' I whisper.

'I'll tell you what's not fair,' he says, in that flat, reasonable monotone. 'That woman. Feeding you bullshit about the *unique contribution* you can make because of the hard time you had as a kid. The truth is, she can't bear to see someone like you making something of themselves.'

'It's not bullshit!' The words burst from my mouth.

He swigs a mouthful of wine. 'There's no need to raise your voice.'

'I'm sorry, but I *do* know what these kids need and please don't talk about Susy like that. She's my friend.'

'She's no friend of yours, Nicci. She just wants to drag you back to the mire because that's where she thinks people like you belong.'

'Working for Next Steps makes me feel useful. Like my life means something.'

He studies me, working his chin. 'So Finn and I are meaningless? Our marriage, this house, the future I'm working so hard to build for us?'

'That's *not* what I meant.'

'If you're so hell-bent on volunteering, there are plenty of other charities looking for fundraisers.'

'I don't want to stand around shaking a tin. I want to do something practical that will make a difference.'

'Then volunteer at the library or the hospital, but for God's sake let this Next Steps thing go and stop letting that woman fill your head with lies.' He takes another long swig from his glass. 'I think it would be best all round if you stopped seeing her.'

'It's not up to you who I see.' The words are out before I can stop them.

He blinks hard as if I've slapped him. 'So you *do* want to hurt me.'

'Of course I don't. I… I love you.'

'Then give me your word that you'll have nothing more to do with her or those deadbeats she claims to be helping. After all I've done for you, is it really too much to ask?'

My lips move. No words come out.

'Well?'

'Ian.' I lay my hands on his arm. Without warning he flings them off and hurls his wine glass at the wall, showering the floor in a cascade of broken glass. Fear kicks in. I keep very still. He picks up his car keys and strides past me and down the hall.

The front door slams shut behind him. My insides feel molten. Tears dribble into my mouth and track down my neck. I slither down the wall and press my head against my knees, struggling between anger and confusion. I don't understand what I've done wrong. I try so hard to make him happy.

When the numbness lifts I reach for my phone, hoping he's texted to say he's sorry. No text, just shots of the party popping up in my feeds: grinning faces, sweaty dancers, twinkling lights, Finn rolling on the floor with a heap of children, helpless with laughter. For one unhinged moment I'm tempted to call a cab and go back to join the fun.

I don't. Of course I don't. I sweep up the glass, sponge the spatters of wine from the wall and catch up on the ironing, pressing and folding to the echoing ring of smashing glass and the sting of Ian's words. *Why do you do this, Nicci? Why do you go out of your way to hurt me?*

*

It's gone midnight when I feel him slip into bed beside me. I want to ask him where he's been and who he was with. Most of all I want to talk about Susy and make him understand why I need her and Next Steps; explain that it's not just about making a difference to someone else's life, it's about finding a way to deal with the guilt of what happened at Sallowfield Court. Only I can't tell him or anyone else the truth about that night. Not now, not ever. So I tuck myself against the curve of his back and whisper that I'm sorry. Too late. He's already asleep.

I get up early and fill my morning with frantic activity. How can I live with myself if I give up Next Steps? And I can't just abandon Leon, especially not now, with Logan breathing down his neck and the threat of prison hanging over him. That's what people have been doing to him his whole life – picking him up and then dropping him when things get tough. I could lie, tell Ian I've stopped seeing him. But in a town this small, there's a risk he'd find out.

By the time he comes down I've put on a load of washing, emptied the dishwasher, stuffed the chicken and prepared the vegetables for lunch.

'I'll pick Finn up after the match,' he says, as he loops his whistle over his head. 'He's going to be too tired to play.'

I open my mouth to say that I'll do it, then I close it again. At least this way I'll avoid getting interrogated by Susy. She's already texted me twice to see how I am.

Lunch is a disaster. I'm not hungry, Finn is too hyped up to eat much and Ian scrapes most of his chicken into the bin, insisting that it's undercooked though mine seems fine. As I stack the dishwasher he catches me off guard by suggesting we drive out onto the downs for a walk. I nod, grateful, and tell Finn to fetch his coat.

Now and then, as Ian navigates the narrow lanes, he looks across at me, an expression I don't recognise on his face. I try a smile. He doesn't smile back. Finn's excited chatter about the sleepover and how funny Mr Smartypants the entertainer was, only notches up the tension.

We step out of the car into the kind of blustery autumn day that I've always loved: crisp air, blue sky busy with clouds, and the sun rushing in and out, sweeping swathes of shadow across the hills. Ian strides ahead and I walk with Finn, a lump growing in my throat as we stoop to pick up a stone with a hole in it or a particularly shiny conker to add to his collection. Tears threaten as we approach a stile. Ian turns and waits for Finn to scramble over it. I climb onto the step, expecting Ian to walk on but he stays where he is and holds out his hand. I take it and jump. As my feet hit the ground he lifts my chin with two fingers and plants a kiss on my mouth. A sign that I am forgiven. I'm pulling back and looking up into his face when those same two fingers find the spot between my shoulder blades and press gently against my spine. A reminder that I am still a work in progress.

I drop my shoulders and straighten up.

'What do you sing at a snowman's birthday party?' Finn says, skipping around us with a huge grin on his face.

'I don't know, Finn,' Ian says. 'What *do* you sing at a snowman's birthday party?'

'Freeze a jolly good fellow!' He kicks through a pile of leaves, hooting with laughter. Ian catches my glance and we laugh too, and I tell myself that I must find a way to be a better person. A better mother. Most of all, a better wife.

When we get home Ian makes us his special fluffy omelettes and reads Finn a bedtime story. Later that night he makes love to me. He's gentle, taking his time, stroking my skin and whispering over and over that all he wants in this world is me.

CHAPTER 12

My cheeks ache with the effort of smiling as I speak – they say it makes your voice sound upbeat, however upset you're feeling inside. I put down the phone and gaze at the raindrops bursting against the wide, sash windows of the waiting room. Hard, dismal rain.

I can't do it. I can't just turn my back on Leon.

I look up as a pretty, dark-haired woman comes in with a newborn strapped to her chest and a little boy clinging to her hand. 'Hello,' she says. 'I'd like to register as a new patient.'

I gather up all the scattered pieces of myself and switch to automatic. 'Of course. If you could just fill in one of our registration forms.'

I snap a form to a clipboard and hand it to her, with a pen. She wanders over to a seat. I watch her as she pats the baby's back with one hand and fills out her details with the other, while still managing to chat to her son. I do that sometimes: focus on other women carrying out ordinary, everyday tasks, and imagine how it would feel to be them.

I close my eyes. If I can just get Leon through this bad patch then maybe I can find a way to make Ian see that it's not about him not being enough. Until then, I'll just have to try harder to keep him happy and make sure I'm extra careful about covering my tracks. The minute my shift is over I grab my coat and slip away.

I walk into the shopping centre with my eyes on my phone, thumbing to the blog post I found last night – an 'insider's' guide to what you can and can't take with you to prison. The official rules say you're allowed T-shirts, track pants, flip-flops. Nothing black, nothing branded, nothing with a hood or pockets. The unofficial rules – according to the blogger – veto anything that makes you stand out or look like a prat. I clatter down the concrete steps and wander through stores already prinking up for Christmas – tinsel and baubles, starbursts and elves – though we're barely out of October. I buy a sturdy holdall and dart around a sports shop throwing T-shirts and jogger bottoms into a basket. In the end, though, it's not about getting the perfect stuff – half of a prisoner's possessions get stolen or bartered the minute they arrive, apparently; it's about letting Leon know that however bad things get, he's not on his own.

I heave my basket onto the checkout and wonder, if it ever came to it, if anyone would be there for me.

I stuff everything into the holdall, hitch it onto my shoulder and set off for Rosemead, taking a back route, head down into the rain, ready to duck out of sight if I see anyone I know. I don't, which is unnerving, because all the way there my neck prickles, as if I'm being noticed. I suppose that's what happens when you're a receptionist: people know you even if you don't recognise them. The trouble is, most of them know Ian, too.

I hammer on the door of Leon's flat, call through the letter box and hang around in the wet for half an hour but he doesn't show up. I worry as I hurry back down the litter-blown staircase. Worry that Leon is couriering drugs for Logan, worry that he'll miss his sentencing hearing, worry that he's going to disappear through the cracks and be lost forever. Worry that it's going to get back to Ian that I was at his flat.

I step out onto rain-swept tarmac and weave my way through the parked cars. An urban fox, scarred and scrawny, lifts its sharp snout and watches me coming. It waits until I'm close then skitters along a parapet, across the row of overflowing dumpsters and slithers nimbly out of sight.

CHAPTER 13

Then

It didn't take Donna long to work out an escape route from our bedroom window: down the pipe onto the garage, across the roof to Terry Burton's shed, a leap onto the fence and a quick jump into the alley. Two or three nights a week she'd disappear around midnight and come back around three, skinny legs first, and drop onto the bed. Eventually I plucked up the courage to ask her where she'd been going.

'My secret hideout. I go there to think.'

I knew better than to ask her to take me with her, though from then on I spent every waking moment longing for an invitation to her 'secret hideout'. Sometimes I'd catch her looking at me with this thoughtful look on her face and I'd hold my breath willing her to tell me that tonight was the night, and swallowing my disappointment when she looked away. I wondered sometimes if she liked keeping me dangling.

I'd almost given up hope when three weeks after her arrival, she shook me awake and said, 'You coming or what?'

Dizzy with excitement I pulled on some clothes and followed her out through the window, almost missing my footing as I lowered myself down the pipe and slithered onto the roof of the shed. The sky was spangled with stars and the air tasted of magic. Casting up and down the alley, Donna set off through the back streets. We walked for nearly mile until she halted, crouched down

and disappeared through a hole in the chain-link fence that ran
along the side of the railway line. I wriggled through after her and
we stumbled along the bank, tripping over discarded trolleys and
plastic bags, feeling the rumble of an oncoming train vibrating
through our heels, jumping back from the thundering whoosh of
the brightly lit carriages, nettles whipping our ankles as we slashed
through waist-high weeds. Suddenly she stopped and pointed to
the dark outline of a building up ahead. 'There you go.'

'What is it?' I whispered.

'The old tyre factory. Been empty for years.'

As we neared it, I made out high metal doors and boarded-up
windows and wondered how we'd get in. I needn't have worried.
Donna had a way with locks and had found her own special way
in: up the rusty fire escape and down through an access door on
the flat roof. At the top I stopped to catch my breath, and looked
down at the lights of the town below us, gleaming like sucked
sweets spilled across a grubby carpet.

As we clunked down a rusty inner staircase, Donna switched
on the torch she kept inside the door and ran the light around
the cavernous interior. Fallen beams, broken gantries, lifeless
machinery. A zigzag of jutting platforms interlaced with metal
chutes and narrow ladders. She beckoned me along a platform lined
with storerooms, creaking open one of the doors and shining the
torch across a stack of wooden pallets. 'Give us a hand.' Between
us we heaved one of the pallets onto the railing that ran along the
edge of the platform. The metal groaned and shifted in its casings
as we pushed the pallet over the top. It fell with a satisfying crash.
She flashed the torch into the darkness. Sick with giddiness, I
peered down thirty or so feet to the broken pieces scattered on
the concrete below.

'Come on.'

I followed her down three more rickety flights, the haunting
clang of our feet reverberating through the rusting ribs of ironwork.

We gathered up the pieces of the pallet and carried them into a partitioned-off area full of old desks and chairs and broken filing cabinets. Donna piled the wood onto a heap of cold ash in the middle of the concrete floor, added scrumpled newspaper, and kindled a fire, flames flickering red in her face as the splintered wood caught light.

We lounged on a couple of stinky old mattresses, drank cheap, sweet cider from a bottle she produced from one of the filing cabinets, and threaded the marshmallows she'd nicked from the corner shop onto bits of stick and toasted them over the fire. I'd never had toasted marshmallows before and I burnt my tongue as I bit off a charred bubble of sweetness. I didn't care. My heart was full. Happiness of a kind I hadn't realised was possible.

'So, what's my weak spot?' I said.

'What?'

'You said everyone's got one. What's mine?'

'You want to be loved,' she said, twirling her marshmallow as she sucked it.

I turned that over in my mind. Didn't everyone need people to love them – friends, family? 'What about you?' I said.

'Me?' She laughed and tossed another bit of wood onto the fire. 'I don't need anyone.'

'No, I meant what's your weak spot?'

'I'm not stupid enough to tell you,' she said, breaking the spell, 'and don't you go blabbing about this place.'

'Course not.'

'You promise?'

I crossed my heart and hoped to die.

'I ran away once and stayed here a whole week,' she said, lolling back on the mattress and looking up at the shadowy vault of the ceiling. Her words seeded a fantasy of the two of us escaping from reality and camping here forever, safe from the horrors of the world.

Every night after that I waited for an invitation to go back. Sometimes it came. More often than not she sneaked out alone, leaving me in agonies of jealousy at the thought of her taking someone else to her secret hideout.

A couple of weeks after Donna had turned my life around I bounded into the dining hall ready to join her in the food queue. She had already got her lunch and was sitting with a group of my former tormenters, who were laughing loudly at something she was saying. The table was crowded, no room for me. I ran out to the playground and sat behind the bike sheds knocking my head against my knees and nursing my misery until the bell went. Later she told me she hadn't seen me and that if she had, she'd have budged up and made room. On one level I knew she was lying. On another it hurt too much to admit it. To make up for it she gave me a makeover, plucked my eyebrows, restyled my hair, and told me it was my own fault that people thought I was weird.

That weekend, we went to the mall, and she lent me some of her clothes. She had some really nice things. I didn't ask her where she got them from. Once she'd done her own make-up she did mine. She looked good but I felt like a freak.

When we got to the mall I had to trail around on my own for ages while she snogged some skinny bloke called Tony who worked on the market. I didn't like him. He had funny teeth and a tattoo on his neck, and strutted around like he was number one and no one else came close.

I bought a bag of chips and waited for her on the benches by the fake waterfall. She turned up an hour or so later with her top all ripped and a red mark on her cheek. She wouldn't talk to me when I asked her what had happened and she went up to our room as soon as we got home and didn't come down for tea. I told the Burtons she'd got a headache and once they'd got stuck into *Strictly* I sneaked out to the kitchen and made her a peanut butter sandwich and smuggled it up to our room.

I found her in bed with her face to the wall. She wouldn't answer when I tried to talk to her but I could tell she wasn't asleep so I got under the covers beside her and put my arm round her. She lay there all stiff for a bit and then she squeezed my hand hard and her shoulders started to shake, only she kept so quiet that if I hadn't been holding her close I'd never have known she was crying.

Life with Donna. I glowed when she needed me. I wilted when she laughed at me. I was bereft when she ignored me.

CHAPTER 14

I check my phone as I leave the office. Leon still hasn't got back to me. I send him a text.

Call me.

'Nicci!'

I look around. My heart sinks. It's Susy, all gussied up in one of the silk shirts and tailored suits she wears for court, her long leather coat flapping against her sides. I glance back at the open door of the surgery, scared that Ian will see us.

'Hey,' I say, and keep walking, hoping she'll start moving too. 'What are you doing here?'

She stays right where she is. 'Hoping to catch you.'

I pivot around. 'Why?'

'You won't answer my calls; you don't reply to my texts. What else is a girl supposed to do?'

'I haven't had a minute. Sorry.'

She hurries after me, patent high heels clacking on the pavement. 'All right, let's grab a sandwich.'

'Can't. Sorry.'

'Why not?'

My brain revs and stalls. 'I've got to get to the farmers' market before it closes.' It's a lie. Anything to shake her off before someone from the surgery sees us together.

'I'll come with you,' she says with a tight smile.

'Shouldn't you be in court?'

'It got cancelled. Client jumped bail. Where's your car?'

'Round the back, in the car park.' I walk faster, only slowing down when I reach the narrow alleyway between the surgery and the office block next door.

'Nic.' I feel her hand on my shoulder. 'Tell me to mind my own business if you want to, but I'm worried about you.'

'Me? Why?'

'What's going on?'

'What do you mean?'

'With you and Ian?'

I shrug her hand away and hurry across the courtyard. 'Nothing. We're fine.'

She teeters after me. 'You're not getting rid of me that easily.'

I look up at the back windows of the surgery. *It's all right. If Ian sees us I'll tell him Susy's car broke down in town and she dropped by to get a lift.* Calmer now, I press the key fob. The car squawks.

Susy wrenches the door open and slides her long legs into the passenger seat. I can feel her studying my face. 'It's well documented, you know. If you're brought up by a controlling man, there's every chance it's going to affect the way you treat your partner.'

'What are you talking about?'

'Ian.' She snaps on her seat belt. 'He might have hated the way his stepfather treated him and his mother, but if being controlling is what you know—'

'Susy, Ian's *not* controlling.' I shove the gear stick into reverse. 'And I told you, Hugh means nothing to him. He barely even mentions him.'

'How is he with Finn?'

'Wonderful.' I back the car up and swing it around.

She flips down the sun visor and inspects her face in the mirror. 'He didn't seem very wonderful with him on Saturday.'

'Well, he is. He's kind, patient and thoughtful. He takes him to football and he's even teaching him to play chess.'

She spits on her finger and scrubs at a smudge under her eye. 'So, what *is* his problem?'

'He doesn't have a problem.'

'He was sulking from the minute you walked into my party to the minute he dragged you out of there.'

'He didn't drag me out. I wasn't feeling well.'

She pushes the visor back up. 'I'm not blind, Nic, and I'm not stupid. No one's saying he has to like your friends, but it wouldn't do him any harm to be civil. And what's all that crap about you only doing online stuff for Next Steps?'

'I told you, he worries about me doing home visits.'

'That's why we have safe spaces at the office. Don't tell me he'd object to you seeing Leon there.'

My hands shake a little as I flick the indicator and turn off the high street. 'He... he associates Next Steps with my past and he doesn't feel comfortable with that.'

'What do you mean *doesn't feel comfortable with it*? It's part of you, part of what makes you so good at what you do. You can't marry someone then pick and choose which bits of them you want and which ones you don't.'

'It's not like that.'

'What is it like?'

She lifts an eyebrow and watches me while she waits for an answer. I stare at the road ahead. Silence engulfs the car but not for long.

'Well?'

'He just wants to help me to be the person I might have been if I'd had different chances. Different choices.'

'Did that mean you signing up to not having any friends or any life apart from him?'

'Don't be ridiculous.'

An ambulance comes balling through the traffic, siren blaring, followed by a police car. I pull over into the kerb, and start speaking before Susy has a chance to say another word about Ian. 'Finn won't stop going on about that entertainer you hired. Can I have his number?'

'Why? He was terrible and after you left he got drunk and tried to get off with the DJ.'

I turn into the car park and park badly in a spot by the fence. 'Well, Finn loved him.' I shut the door on her and hurry off towards the market stalls. I wasn't planning on coming here, I haven't even brought a shopping bag with me, but I elbow my way to the cheese van as if my life depends on nabbing the last of their cave-aged cheddar before they pack up for the day.

Susy catches me up as I reach for my package of cheese.

'Does Ian monitor your phone?'

'Of course he doesn't.'

I swerve away towards the meat section. On the way she stops at a stall selling essential oils in tiny, stoppered bottles. She lifts one of the testers and holds the dropper to her nose, breathing in the smell. 'How about your money? Does he control what you spend?'

'No. He's unbelievably generous. He even cut down my hours so I'd have more time to myself.'

'So why aren't you doing that degree?'

I stare up at the scalloped edge of the striped awning. 'I will do.'

'When?'

'When the time is right.'

'What's wrong with now?'

'We… we're trying for a baby. Ian wants to have as short a gap as possible between Finn and a new sibling.'

She turns to face me, her eyes drilling into mine. 'Is that what you want?'

'Of course it is.' My tongue feels thick and dry. 'I love being a mother. It's the best thing that ever happened to me.'

CHAPTER 15

I dollop honey onto Finn's porridge and pour Ian a coffee. He's leaving early for a meeting with an investor. They're hoping to expand the practice, buy the building next door and hire a team of specialists to take on orthodontics, minor surgeries and more cosmetic work. It's going to cost a fortune but he's done the numbers and he's convinced it's the right way to go. He walks into the kitchen adjusting his cuffs. He looks good, freshly shaven in his newly dry-cleaned suit and a crisp pink shirt.

'Can you book a babysitter for Wednesday night?' he says, coming up behind me and planting a kiss in the curve of my neck. Instinctively, I drop my shoulders. 'If it all goes well today, Mac wants to get the head of the consortium round for dinner to meet the other partners.'

'Sure,' I say, lightly. It's the kind of event I dread – trying to make small talk while I work out which knife to use – but after the horrible time he had at Susy's I can hardly complain. 'I'll give Katy a call.' I wriggle free and drop his toast onto a plate. He butters it quickly and spreads it with dark marmalade, darting hurried glances at his watch.

'Eat up,' I say to Finn.

Ian goes over to the window and peers at the sky as he chews. 'Damn, I lent my umbrella to Maggie and it looks like rain. I can't turn up for this meeting looking like a drowned rat.'

'Borrow mine. It's in my car.'

'Thanks.' He drains his coffee and ruffles Finn's newly combed hair. 'OK, I'm off. Wish me luck.'

'Good luck, Daddy,' Finn says, through a mouthful of porridge.

'Drink your milk, sweetheart,' I say, as the front door closes. Finn jabs his spoon into his porridge and looks up at me. 'What's brown and sticky?'

'Finn!' I pull a face, mock horror as I wait for the inevitably poo-ey punchline.

'A stick!'

I burst out laughing, almost dropping the plates I'm holding and we're standing there giggling at the joyful absurdity of it when the front door slams. My eyes sweep the room in search of whatever it is that Ian has forgotten before I remember that Ian isn't prone to forgetting much at all.

'What the hell is this?' He storms in and tosses a red and white fast-food container onto the table. It's greasy and crusted with lumps of red and brown.

'I've got no idea.'

'No wonder that boy's all over the place. What have I told you about feeding him junk?'

'I don't feed him junk. That box has absolutely nothing to do with me.'

'So what was it doing in your car?'

'I… I don't know.'

I pick up the carton, holding it gingerly between my thumb and forefinger and walk over to the bin, blocking my nose against the smell of stale fat. I press my toe onto the pedal and drop the box onto the rubbish. It flips to one side as it falls. My insides turn molten. I let the lid snap shut and look up. Ian is glaring at me, blue eyes burning. 'We'll talk about this tonight. Thanks for making me late.' His footsteps ring down the hallway and the house shudders as the front door bangs shut behind him.

Finn tugs at my leg. 'Mum, where's my reading book?'

'In your bag, sweetheart.'

Moving like a zombie I dampen a piece of kitchen roll and wipe away his milky moustache. 'Quick, get your shoes on. Tilly will be here any minute.'

He scampers away. I stare at the bin, a dark bubble of terror in my chest.

A horn toots outside. I snatch up Finn's school bag and run into the hall. He's waiting by the door, shoes on, laces tied tight. I smile but say nothing, afraid that if I open my mouth a scream might erupt. I shuffle him into his anorak, kiss his forehead hard and open the door.

'Bye, Mum!'

'Bye, Finnsy.'

I press my fingers to my mouth and waft more kisses down the drive, turning the trembling movement of my hand into a wave as Tilly straps him into the back of her SUV. I watch, still waving, as she drives away. I walk back into the kitchen, one foot, then the other, hook the box out of the bin with the end of a wooden spoon and place it gingerly on the draining board.

There's no address on the packaging, just the familiar red and pink bubble-font logo. *Mojo's.* Someone else must be using the name. Maybe by now there's a whole chain of Mojo's fast-food franchises all around the country. I type Mojo's diner into the search bar on my phone. A picture of a high street takeaway appears. It's much the same as I remember: a perky cartoon chicken winking from a plastic banner slung across the double frontage, rows of cheap plastic chairs visible through the plate glass windows. I scan the website. There are no other franchises. The one and only Mojo's is exactly where it always was: over twenty miles away, just around the corner from Lyn Burton's run-down semi. So how did that box get all the way over here? More to the point, how did it get into my car?

I glance at the keys hanging on the rack by the fridge. The spare is there, where it always is, dangling from the second hook on the right. I step back from the carton as if it's a bomb that might explode.

CHAPTER 16

Then

Donna flounced away from the counter swinging her hips as she wove her way between the packed tables. Bending low to make sure her hitched-up school skirt rode up even higher, she dumped the tray on the table in front of me. 'There you go. Two portions of spicy chicken, two extra large fries, two giant cokes.'

'How much did that lot cost?' I said.

'It's a freebie. Mo thinks we need feeding up.'

I looked around me – bright lights, ketchup-smeared formica – and caught Mo, the proprietor, tipping me a wave with his finger while Jo, his blonde, smiling wife looked on. I opened the box of chicken and inhaled the smell.

'What's in it for him?' I said.

'He knows we're skint. If we want, he'll give us a chance to earn a bit of money.'

I lifted a drumstick, tore off a strip of chicken and folded it into my mouth. 'Doing what?'

'Handing out flyers, wiping tables, helping him with anything that comes up.' She put the straw of her giant cola to her lips and sucked on it until it gurgled at the bottom of the cup. 'If you don't fancy it I can easily find someone who will.' She glanced around the crowded diner and waved at Connie and Sophie from our class. Before I could stop her she was on her way over to talk to them. My stomach twisted, the way it always did when she threatened to desert me.

Donna was the centre of my world; over the last year, Mojo's had become the centre of hers. It was where she came to laugh, flirt and stuff her face. She had this easy way with her, always mucking around with Mo and having a laugh with the other customers. She seemed to know half of them by name. I tagged along, never quite comfortable with any of it, never quite sure if she'd rather I stayed home.

I felt a hand on my shoulder. I looked up. It was Mo. He smiled and glanced around as if he wanted to grab a word before Donna came back. 'Nicci. Look, I was wondering if you could do me a big favour. I had someone lined up to deliver a parcel for me and they've called in sick. There and back on the train will only take a couple of hours, but it needs to be someone sensible. Someone I can trust.' I glowed and looked over at Donna, hoping she'd turn around and see me chatting to Mo. 'I'll pay you of course,' he said. 'Fifty quid.'

'Sure,' I said. 'I can do it on Saturday.'

'It has to be tomorrow.'

'I've got school.'

He shrugged and turned away. 'No good then.'

'It's nothing I can't miss,' I said, hurriedly.

'Good girl.' His smile was wide and grateful. 'Drop by around eight tomorrow morning and I'll have it ready for you. If it works out this time, maybe we can make it a regular gig.'

Next morning I turned up at the diner bang on time. Shivering in my thin mac, I peered inside. It didn't open till eleven but Mo and Jo were in there, wiping down tables and mopping the floor. I stood outside in the cold, hesitating for a minute before I tapped on the glass door. Mo unlocked it and looked me up and down with a frown of concern. 'Haven't you got a proper coat?'

I shook my head. He pulled me inside and called over to his wife: 'Jo, you got a decent coat she can wear? Weather like this, she's going freeze to death.'

Jo propped her mop against the counter and went out back. While she was gone Mo sat me down at a table by the heater and brought me a hot chocolate, a Danish pastry wrapped in cellophane and a smart-looking clipboard with a dangly pen attached. 'Anyone asks why you're not at school you tell them you're doing a project.'

'What on?'

'You're a bright girl, you'll think of something.'

I pulled the lid off my hot chocolate, took a long delicious sip and bit into the Danish. The sugar rush made me giggle. Ma Burton's idea of breakfast was a slice of toast with a slither of marge and a cup of lukewarm tea. He pulled out a chair next to me and sat down, legs slung out to either side. 'Donna says you're a brainbox, top of the class.'

'Not really, but I'm not too bad at English and maths and I really like sociology.'

'Blimey, I was too thick to do any "ologies" when I was at school.' I smiled at him. He didn't smile back, just looked at me thoughtfully. 'Why haven't you got a proper coat?'

'Burton's too stingy to get me one. The social give her loads of money but she never spends it on us.'

'I know what that's like, seeing other kids spoilt rigid when you've got nothing, always feeling like you're on the outside looking in.' His face creased with concern. 'Honestly, if that woman gives you any trouble or you ever need anything, you tell me or Jo and we'll see what we can do.'

Something loosened inside me. A band of fear and uncertainty. I sat at that little plastic table in a fog of contentment, cramming bites of sugary pastry into my mouth, sipping hot frothy chocolate and listening to Mo slagging off Ma Burton and telling me it shouldn't be allowed. 'So, what happens when you leave care?' he said.

'They put you in a hostel. Then maybe, if you're lucky, they find you a flat.'

'On your own?'

'Me and Donna are hoping we'll get somewhere together.'

He nodded and looked over my shoulder. 'Looks like Jo's found something to keep you warm.'

I looked around. Jo was walking across the diner clutching a grey sheepskin coat and a black woolly scarf and gloves. I shrugged off my mac and slipped my arms into the coat while she tugged and patted and did up the buttons. The coat had a fur-trimmed collar and cuffs, flared slightly from the hips, and wearing it felt like being wrapped in a hug.

'Snug as bug,' she said. 'Really suits her, doesn't it, Mo?'

'Yeah,' he said, admiringly.

'I'll drop it back to you on my way home.'

'Don't worry about it,' Jo said. 'It's getting a bit tight for me so you might as well keep it.' Dazed and delighted I did a twirl, revelling in their attention. It was years since an adult had smiled at me the way they were smiling.

Turning to catch my reflection in the floor-length windows I plunged my hands into the pockets. There was something bulky wrapped in plastic in each one. Mo leant in and put his arm around me – not like he was trying to cop a feel or anything, just friendly, like an uncle, and put his lips to my ear. 'Don't take them out till you get to the drop-off. And, look, it won't happen, but if anyone asks where you got them, don't mention me or you'll get us both in trouble. Just give them that lovely smile of yours and say you found them on the train and you were on your way to hand them in to lost property.'

'All right,' I said.

'There's a train ticket in the inside pocket and a phone with a number in the contacts. Any problems text that number. Don't call it.' He gave me instructions where to go and some cash to get a snack on the way back.

Buttoned up in my warm coat with a belly full of pastry and hot chocolate, I sat on the train and watched the town give way to countryside. Stations and farm buildings flashed past and soon I was looking at hills and woods and then, in the distance, the sea. The last time I'd been to the seaside was on a coach trip to Clacton with Mum and Nan when I was seven. Mum had been on a high that day and Nan had got cross with her for spending all our money on the fruit machines and feeding our sandwiches to the gulls.

Mo hadn't told me what was in the parcels and I hadn't asked. I just dropped them in a waste bin in an alley behind a pub called the Queen's Head and walked away, exactly like he'd told me to. I knew it was dodgy but I didn't care. Mo was my friend, he cared about me, and Donna was dead pleased that he'd asked me to do him a favour. I'd been worried she'd be jealous. But she wasn't. Not at all. It was good money too. A trip to the sticks, three, four, five times a month would soon mount up, and having a bit of money put by made me feel a bit less scared about leaving care next year. Independent living they called it. That was a joke. Dumped in a hostel and left to rot, more like.

CHAPTER 17

Even now the feel of sheepskin makes me shudder. The smell of it. The fuzzy thickness of the fur. With clumsy fingers I drop the Mojo's box back into the bin. A fifteen-year-old kid in care swanking around in a £300 coat? Why hadn't Burton done her job and demanded to know where I'd got it from? I force myself upstairs, jab a pair of pearl studs into my ears and scrape my hair into a bun. I want to pretend that nothing is happening but I can't escape the truth. The blackbird, the punctured tyre, the open side gate and now the Mojo's box. I don't know if they are threats or warnings. I do know that whoever is doing this, it isn't Sean Logan. Bile comes up in my mouth, burning my throat. I take out my phone. I inhale, exhale and type in Sallowfield Court. For the first time in five months there's a new mention, though it's not the one I feared. It's a listing on a website for rural properties, offering the farmland, stables and barns for sale by auction, the once imposing manor house described only as a 'fire-damaged development opportunity consisting primarily of main walls'.

A local paper and a couple of tabloids have picked up on the sale but they just recycle the same old photos, and sketch out the details of the long-stalled police investigation. There's nothing new. Nothing to knock a celebrity Twitter feud off the front pages. I delete the search from my history and pocket my phone. The sale should feel like a good thing. The closing of a page. But the timing is disturbing. Have the police unearthed something they're keeping out of the papers. A new lead? Something an estate agent or a prospective buyer found buried in the rubble? Something that's sent somebody from the past looking for me?

I pull up in the car park behind the surgery, smooth my hair and stare at my face in the mirror. I mustn't look sloppy or distracted. Not today. Not ever. My reflection gazes back at me, seemingly calm and unruffled but it won't fool Maggie. One quick glance as I pass her office on the way to hang up my coat and she always knows exactly how I'm feeling and precisely how much needling it's going to take to push me to the brink. If I'm riding high she leaves me alone; the slightest whiff of tension, and she strikes. She's on top form today. No sooner do I sit down and log in to the computer than she's at my shoulder asking for 'a word, please, Nicola'.

It's some nonsense about forgetting to order new printer cartridges and pay the invoice for the cleaning company – both at the top of my to-do list for today – oh, yes, and a hissy little warning about timekeeping. She's on my case all morning, needling and moaning but hardly says a word when Amy rolls in twenty minutes late with a lame excuse and a bad hangover.

I feel her eyes on me as I feed the fish in the waiting room. I know they're supposed to be calming but seeing them darting round and round their over-lit, glass-walled world, with nowhere to go and nowhere to hide, has never worked for me, and this morning it's really cranking up my stress levels.

Chatting with the patients, making the new ones feel welcome and the old ones feel cared about, is the part of my job I like best, but today every swing of the door sets me on edge and every time I lift my eyes from the keyboard I dread whose face I might see staring down at me from the other side of the desk. I make it robotically through the next couple of hours, smiling, filing and scheduling appointments, while the image of that empty Mojo's box bumps around my skull.

A voice jolts me out of what feels like a trance. I look up. It's Mr Halliwell, complaining about his new dentures. There's absolutely nothing wrong with them but it's the third time he's been in this week. He's old and lonely and what he really wants is a chat and a chance to sit in the warm and look at the papers. What I usually say is: 'I'm so sorry to hear that, Mr Halliwell, why don't you take a seat and I'll ask one of the dentists to pop out and see you when they have a moment between patients?' Sometimes, if we're really quiet, I sneak him a cup of tea from the machine in the staff kitchen. Only today I snap at him and tell him to make an appointment if he wants to see a dentist and he shuffles out into the cold, rheumy eyed and resentful. I feel so bad I jump up and run after him and tell him I'm sorry and I'm having a bad day and he takes my hand in his dirty claw and pats it gently and I want to weep.

I usher him back inside, a dull ache in my gut, the sense of an imminent blow when I see Ian standing by the reception desk, his face tight with annoyance. I don't speak. I can't. He tosses down a file of patient notes. 'What's going on with you, Nic? These are for yesterday's eleven o'clock. You gave Amanda the wrong ones as well. Can you hurry up and bring us both the right ones?'

A lump swells in my chest, tears burn my eyes. 'Sorry,' I say, quickly.

I dig out and deliver the right files and for the rest of the morning I double-check every appointment I book, every invoice I pay, every payment I take. It's exhausting, and by the time I leave the surgery I barely have any space left in me.

'Sorry about the mix-up this morning,' I say lightly, as soon as Ian gets home.

He cups his hand around my cheek, his blue eyes warm and forgiving. 'And I'm sorry if I snapped at you. I just worry when you get… forgetful.'

'Well, there's no need.'

He kisses the tip of my nose. I turn away and check the oven.

Humming to himself, he fills his wine glass and sips it as he flicks through the post I've left on the worktop. 'Oh, I meant to tell you. Good news on the football front. The partners have agreed to sponsor the Bellvue Booters.'

'That's brilliant! I didn't even know you'd asked them to.'

'I did tell you, Nic.' A hint of a sigh as he picks out a white envelope and rips it open. 'I suggested it to Mac a couple of weeks ago, we discussed it at today's meeting and it got a unanimous yes. It'll be good for the community and great PR for Parkview.'

'What are they offering?'

'New strip all round and support for any kids who can't afford proper boots.'

'Amazing.'

He rips open the envelope and smooths out a letter. 'More good news. Harris is offering us an appointment in December.'

'Harris?'

'Paul Harris. The fertility specialist I told you about.' I stay silent and perfectly still. 'The one Annabel and I went to see,' he adds, as if I need reminding that the two of them had passed all their tests with flying colours. A wonder couple of perfect, prospective breeders, ticking off another little task on their pre-wedding to-do list.

'It's normal for it to take at least a year to get pregnant,' I say, surprised how calm my voice is, how casual my words. 'We haven't even been trying for six months.'

'Maybe, but you have to admit it's a bit concerning seeing how easily you got pregnant with Finn.'

He's been trying to fill in the gaps in my story ever since we started going out, pressing me for details about my relationship with Finn's father. Each time it's come up I've stuck to my tale about a drunken one-night stand with a stranger, and I'm not about to change that now.

He's still talking. 'The problem might be something minor caused by your last pregnancy, which can be easily rectified. If not, the sooner we get it looked at the better.'

'You should have talked to me before you spoke to the clinic.' It's an effort to force out the words.

'What's there to talk about? We both want a baby.'

That, at least, is true.

'Male fertility can fluctuate too,' I say, testily.

'Sure. That's why we're both going.'

'When is it?'

'December third. Harris splits his time between the UK and the States and he's not back until the end of November. Meantime, it wouldn't do you any harm to think about some lifestyle changes.'

I step past him towards the cutlery drawer. 'What kind of changes?'

'Cutting out caffeine, keeping a closer eye on your weight, trying to destress as much as you can, improving your sleep.'

I look up and meet his eyes. Complete silence for a moment.

'You're a twitchy sleeper,' he says. 'A mumbler too. You must know that. I often come in late and catch you talking to yourself.'

'Saying what?'

He grins. 'All sorts of things.'

I say nothing, my breath coming too fast to carry words. I just stand there dazed and trembling. 'Everybody talks in their sleep,' I say at last.

'Do I?'

'Sometimes.'

It's a lie. He sleeps like the dead. Spark out the minute his head hits the pillow. I take a knife and a fork from the drawer.

'Aren't you eating?' he asks.

'I had something with Finn.' Not true, but my appetite has gone. 'Actually, I'm really tired. I think I might have an early night.'

'You do look a bit weary.'

I walk upstairs and turn on the shower. I stand under the pounding water and scrub my skin until it's raw. I thought it would get easier. I thought that once I was married I would be able to find peace and let go.

I was wrong.

Every day my past creeps closer and I don't know how much longer my wall of lies can hold it back.

CHAPTER 18

Then

'Mo says we can forget their stinking hostel,' Donna announced one night, as she climbed in through our bedroom window. 'He's going to let us live in one of his flats.'

I sat up and flicked on the bedside light. She was wriggling out of a pair of tight white jeans that I'd never seen before. 'How would we pay the rent?'

'We won't have to. Not if we keep up the deliveries and do a bit of waitressing.'

'Waitressing? At Mo's?' I laughed.

'Not at the diner, stupid.' She unclipped a silver hoop earring and dropped it on the top of the chest of drawers. 'At events. You know. Parties and stuff.'

'What kind of parties?'

'Private ones. For businessmen.' She peered into the little wall mirror, her eyes holding mine as she unhooked the other earring. 'We'd be working evenings so you could still go to college in the daytime.'

'What would I have to do?'

She turned around and laughed. 'Depends how much money you want to make.'

I wasn't stupid. I knew what she meant.

'Oh, come on,' she said, when she saw my face. 'You just down a few drinks, close your eyes, and think about something else.'

'Is that what you've been doing all those nights you said you were out with your new bloke? *Waitressing* for Mo?'

'You up for it or not?'

I nodded. Anything to please Mo. Anything to be with Donna.

Three months later, we moved in. The flat was a small two-bed that hadn't been decorated in a while. Scuffed woodchip on every wall, cheap curtains and heavy, old-fashioned furniture, but it had everything we needed and, more importantly, there was no foster carer breathing down our necks and writing reports packed with words like 'defiant', 'defensive', 'demanding' or 'belligerent', and no warden telling us what we could and couldn't do. Our first taste of freedom.

Donna was thrilled that we each got our own room. I wasn't so sure about sleeping on my own. Mo's only stipulation was that we kept ourselves to ourselves and didn't cause any trouble with the neighbours. Now and then he used the spaces under the bath and behind the wardrobes for storage; a couple of times a week he gave us money to go out so he that he and his new sidekick, Gary, could use the flat for business meetings. It never bothered us: as far as we were concerned, it was Mo who was doing us a favour; as far as the neighbours were concerned, Donna and I were students renting the basement flat from Donna's uncle – nice, quiet girls who kept their music down and never forgot to put their bins out. As far as Mo was concerned, we were just two more of his 'Bics' – cheap, easy to come by and disposable. Though it took me a while to realise it. At the start I thought of him as family.

Mo made up these little cards with our photos on – fully clothed, nothing crude – and our names and a few details so the punters could pick out who they wanted, and leave a message on his private phone to arrange a time. 'Old school' he called it – nothing online that could get us into trouble if his computer got hacked.

Nothing that could lead the police back to him.

He did his best to prepare us for the work, but I never got used to it. The first time was the worst. He took me to London, drove me there in his car, just me and him. The client lived on the top floor of a mansion block overlooking Battersea Park. His flat was huge and full of antiques. I don't think I actually looked at him because I can't really picture his face. It was the clock I remember. It was on the table beside the bed. Four white marble pillars holding up a plinth with a black lion on it. The lion's mouth was open and it was resting one paw on a golden ball. The rest of the clock was glass and you could see the little brass pendulum swinging from side to side inside. I kept my eyes on that pendulum, tilting my head so I could see it as the unbearable weight pushed down on me and the tick, tick, tick counted down the seconds.

It was easier when we did parties. Mo would send along a bunch of us and there'd be music and plenty to drink. The punters were usually older, always posh and mostly all right. Even when they weren't, it was our job to keep them happy. If it ever got weird, Mo gave us a bit of time off to get over it and paid us a bit extra. Some of them wanted drugs: fat old blokes popping pills like rock stars. Some wanted to stroke your hair afterwards and talk about their problems. Gross. But after that first time in London I took Donna's advice about downing a few drinks first, closing my eyes and trying to think about something – anything – else. Sometimes I imagined me and Donna lying on a beach drinking cocktails out of coconuts with little umbrellas stuck in them, like in the adverts, but it worked best when I pictured the family I was going to have when I got older: the kids, the husband, the house, the caterpillar birthday cakes, Little Mermaid lunch boxes and holidays at Center Parcs.

Sometimes, after college, I'd go for coffee with some of the other girls on my course and they'd invite me out to clubs and parties or back to their houses. I always said no. I told them my mum was sick and I had to stay home to look after her. It's not that I didn't want to do the things they did; it's just that I felt too grubby and ashamed. But it wasn't like we had to work every night and, anyway, it was only until I finished my A-levels. After that I'd be getting a grant, moving away, going to uni, starting over.

To be honest I'd been worried about telling Mo I was doing A-levels. But he'd been fine about it, especially as the clients who liked to talk seemed to get off on the idea of spilling their woes to a girl who was heading for uni. If he needed me in the day to do a delivery or anything, I'd just bunk off and borrow someone else's lecture notes to catch up. They were always nice about it because they thought I'd had to stay home to look after my mum.

Sometimes I got a bit jealous of the other girls Mo looked after. Some of the ones he brought to the parties were good for a laugh, but a couple of them were blank-eyed and scary. Mo said the other girls weren't special. Not like me and Donna.

CHAPTER 19

'Stay where we can see you, boys.' Tilly lifts Mimi out of the buggy and eases herself onto the bench beside me. 'And keep an eye on Jabba!'

Finn and Henry are already speeding away on their scooters, with Henry's new rescue spaniel hurtling after them.

'Jabba?' I say, laughing. 'Isn't that a boy's name?'

Holding her squirming daughter with one arm she laughs and unzips her bag. 'I know. But what can I do? Henry chose it. Her last owner made the poor little thing frightened of her own name by calling her inside to beat her, so the rescue centre told us to give her a new one. Honestly, why get a puppy if you're just going to hurt it?'

Mimi whines and wriggles as Tilly digs around in the bag. 'It's all right, hungry girl,' Tilly coos. 'Mummy find your bottle.' She rolls her eyes at me. 'God, I hope I brought it.'

'Here, give her to me.' I reach out my hands and waggle my fingers invitingly at Mimi.

Tilly throws me a hopeful look as she hands her over, and I wonder if Ian has been sharing his frustrations about my slowness to conceive with Matt.

I take hold of the baby, enjoying the unresisting weight of her and the muscle memories of Finn at that age. She eyes me cautiously and pushes a small, plump finger between my lips, momentarily forgetting her hunger and squealing with delight when I make growly noises and pretend to bite it off, but it's not long before the screams of hunger start up again. Finally, with a gasp of triumph Tilly finds the bottle, snaps off the lid and takes her baby back, sighing with relief as Mimi's tiny pink lips close around the teat.

'How's the building work?' I ask.

Tilly groans. 'Nightmare. The whole thing was supposed to be finished last week but they haven't even started the plastering, the Aga still hasn't arrived and now my mother tells me that the marble worktops I ordered for the kitchen are a complete waste of money because they'll stain the minute you drop anything on them *and* she says I've bought the wrong fridge and dishwasher…'

I don't say anything, just murmur sympathetically. I might have moved on from a stained sink and a free-standing cooker with an oven door that won't shut, but I'm running on empty when it comes to Agas, appliances and interfering mothers.

'Mum!'

I look up. Henry is hobbling towards us, his trousers ripped at the knee, Jabba the spaniel barking at his heels.

Tilly looks up. 'What happened?'

'I fell off.' Still cradling Mimi, Tilly leans down to inspect his knee. She spits on a tissue she pulls from her pocket and rubs at the graze. 'You'll live.' She glances back up the path. 'Where's Finn?'

'By the drinking fountain.'

I stand up. I can see the fountain in the distance and a boy on a scooter. But the boy isn't Finn. It's that little bully, Liam, freewheeling towards the café with his mother. There's no other kid in sight, just a flat expanse of grass leading away to distant trees. I drop to my knees in front of Henry. 'Are you sure?'

He nods unconvincingly and looks up at me from beneath knotted brows. 'What happened, Henry? I won't be cross.'

'Liam raced me to the bandstand.'

'And you left Finn on his own.'

He stares at the ground.

'It's not nice to leave your friend,' Tilly says.

I don't care about the finer points of play-date etiquette. I grip Henry's shoulders. 'Did you see any grown-ups nearby. Did he talk to anyone?'

He shakes his head. A woman cycles towards us with a toddler in a trailer. I spin around, checking the paths leading to the football pitch and the bandstand, searching for the blue and red of a Spider-Man hat. A man jogs past, checking his Fitbit. I shoulder my bag and set off towards the drinking fountain, walking quickly at first then breaking into a run. 'Finn!' I shout. 'Finn!'

A white-haired woman approaches with a terrier at her heels. 'Dog or child?'

'Child. He's six, glasses, small for his age.'

'What's he wearing?'

'A Spider-Man hat… and a… a dark green puffa.'

'He wasn't back that way,' she says. 'I'll look by the tennis courts.'

I swing around. Tilly is snapping Mimi into her buggy with one hand and holding her phone to her ear with the other. 'I'm calling the park-keeper,' she shouts.

As I stumble towards the café, a jogger brushes past me, a blur of black lycra. The café comes nearer. I stretch out my fingers. The door jerks open. I blunder past an elderly couple and bump into a woman juggling takeaway coffees. 'Sorry. I'm sorry.' The interior is heaving. I see Liam and his mother at the counter.

'Liam!' My voice rings out, shrill above the noise. Faces turn. Eyebrows rise. Disapproval and curiosity crackle across the room. I elbow my way to the front of the queue, ignoring the glares and tuts. Liam blinks up at me, suspicious and unsure. His mother drops a protective hand to his shoulder.

'I'm Finn's mother, Liam. Do you know where he went? Did you see him talking to anyone?'

Voices swirl around me, the energy switches. Concern, sympathy, just a hint of blame. What kind of mother lets her kid out of her sight? Liam is shaking his head. I lock my eyes on his mother's and grope for her name. Shan? Yes. It's definitely Shan. 'Liam went off with Henry and left Finn on his own. Now he's gone.' She glares at me, bristling at the criticism of her son, yet aware that she's also being watched and judged by the turned faces.

'I was… on my phone. I didn't see him.'

I pivot around and address the room. 'Has anyone seen a little boy on a purple scooter? He's wearing a Spider-Man hat and a green puffa.' The room quietens. My voice cracks. 'His name is Finn.'

A man in a navy donkey jacket downs his tea and stands up. 'We're strimming by the main gate. If we see him we'll bring him back here.'

The woman serving teas calls from behind the counter. 'Yes, anyone finds him, bring him back here.' She comes out pulling her phone from her apron pocket. 'Give us your number, love.'

I crush my eyes shut and murmur the digits.

'We'll help you look.' Less chippy now, Shan reaches for her son. 'Come on, Liam.'

He pulls away. 'You said I could have a cake.'

Her jaw tightens and she jerks him by the wrist. 'You can have one once we find Finn.' She catches me up as I stumble to the door. 'We'll try the car park. Did you check by the lake?'

The word snatches the air from my lungs. Finn is endlessly drawn to the lake – the ducks, the ripples, the clumps of bulrushes fringing the slippery edges.

I push my way out of the café and run back up the slope. Casting across the playing fields I make for the woods and cut through the shrubbery, beating at the overhanging foliage. 'Finn!' My voice is a wail of terror. I plunge on. A flash of purple. Finn's scooter, lying in the undergrowth. Time stands still. The pulse of guilt throbbing through my veins beats harder, stronger, faster. I grab the handlebars, the rubber grips cold against my palms. *This isn't happening.* Panic swirls and swells. I throw down the scooter. Deafened by my own heartbeat I stumble on, brambles springing across my face as I slash through the undergrowth towards the lake.

The water stretches out before me, dark and viscous, scummed with weed. My hands fly up and bury themselves in my hair. My vision swims in waves of red. I see wide eyes, a pinched mouth, a pale face sinking beneath the murk. A shape humped on the ground, limbs spilling, flesh dripping. Retribution. Vengeance. This is my fault. My punishment. Payback for the things I did and the things I should have done.

'No! No!' I'm screaming now, trying to ward off fate, spinning around in full-blown panic.

A fisherman frowns at me from the opposite bank, annoyed at this madwoman blundering into his quiet.

'Have you seen a little boy in a Spider-Man hat?' I yell, and pat the empty air to show his height.

He leans forward in his deckchair and points. I follow his finger. A flash of blue and red behind the railings.

'Finn!'

He's coming towards me, head down.

'Finn!' I break into a run and scoop him up and hug him to me, inhaling the smell of his skin as the pain inside me eases and the panic retreats. Slowly, as the emptiness fills relief gives way to fury. I stand him back down and grip his shoulders. 'I told you not to go out of my sight! Why didn't you stay by the fountain and wait for Henry and Liam?'

His lip trembles and tears trickle down his cheeks. 'Liam's not my friend.'

'Oh, Finnsy.' I squat down and fold him back into a hug. As I rock him to me something presses into my side. I look down and pull a Mars bar from his pocket. 'Where did you get this?'

'A lady gave it to me.'

'You know you mustn't take things from strangers.'

'She said you wouldn't mind.'

'Did she… hurt you?'

'No. She was nice. She rubbed some dirt off my face, and she said she was playing hide and seek with her little boy and I could join in.'

I stand up and spin around. 'Where is she?'

'I don't know. I ran off and hid by those trees but she didn't come to find me.'

'What did she look like?'

He stares at me blankly, hands flapping.

'What was she wearing?'

He frowns. 'A hat.'

'What kind of hat?'

'A red one. With a bobble. And she had glasses. Big dark ones.'

'Was she young or old?'

He frowns. 'I don't know.'

'Did she tell you her name?'

He shakes his head. 'No, but—' His face brightens, as if he's remembered something that will please me.

'What?'

'She knew you.'

'How do you know?'

'She said, tell your mummy I said hello.'

Vague fears of a nameless stranger solidify into something sharper and far, far more worrying. My phone buzzes. It's Tilly. I press it to my ear. 'It's all right. I've found him.' I start to cry. Great blubbering sobs. Tilly's voice telling me she'll meet me in the café floats through my head, vying with the sound of a woman in a red bobble hat whispering, 'Tell your mummy I said hello.'

I take Finn's hand, gripping it tightly as I drag him away, refusing to let it go as I trample through the foliage to retrieve his scooter.

Back in the café, Shan insists on paying for all the children's meals but refuses to look me in the eye, Tilly makes stilted conversation about the upcoming PTA elections and Finn munches his taco in silence while Liam and Henry exchange sideways looks and nudge each other under the table.

I barely touch my coffee and hardly speak. My fears are spiralling. I look at Tilly and Shan without really seeing their faces or hearing their voices. I don't want to be here. I want to take Finn home and slam the door on the outside world. A tinny Christmas tune floats from a radio behind the counter. *Christmas.* Even when it was just me and Finn, I'd always tried to pull out all the stops – a tree and a turkey, mince pies and a home-made pudding: a proper celebration like the ones I'd never had. As I think about the plans I've been making for this year, a darkness descends.

On the way home I stop at the garage and buy ten Benson & Hedges. I haven't had a cigarette for years, but I need one now. I smoke it in the garden while Finn does his homework at the kitchen table – furtive puffs behind the shed like when I was a kid. *Tell your mummy I said hello.* I run inside and clean my teeth, and rinse and floss and gargle with mouthwash, and spit and rinse again.

Finn is in his pyjamas and we're snuggled up together in front of the television. He's watching *Charlotte's Web* and I'm staring at the screen silently reliving the horror of losing him, when I hear the slam of the front door and the thud of Ian's squash bag as he drops it in the hall. My cue to act the happy housewife. 'Hi, darling, did you win?' I call.

He pokes his head around the door of the sitting room. 'We drew. Three games all. What happened in the park?' I look up at him, a smile of welcome nailed to my lips. 'Tilly called Matt. She said you lost Finn.'

'It was nothing. He wandered off and I overreacted.'

'Where was Henry?'

'He went off with Liam,' Finn says. 'They wouldn't let me play with them.'

'That boy who pushed you? We need to do something about this, Nic.'

'I'm going to speak to his mother. I didn't want to do it in front of everyone. I'll call her tomorrow.'

'That's only going to make things worse. Kids like that need to be taught a lesson. I've told you before, Finn, next time you think he's going to push you, you push him first. Do it hard enough and he'll think twice about hurting you again.' There's real anger in his face and a tremor of something I can't make out.

Finn's eyes travel from Ian's face to mine then back again, scared and confused.

'Ian,' I say, as calmly as I can. 'That's not going to solve anything.'

'It's the only way, Nic. Hurt them before they hurt you.'

Finn's face puckers and he bursts into tears.

'For God's sake.' Ian's voice is harsh and brittle. 'What are you crying about? No wonder you get pushed around.'

Finn slides off the sofa and runs upstairs, hands flapping. Ian looks as if he wants to follow him.

'Let him be,' I say. 'I'll go.'

'You mollycoddle him, Nicci. He needs to toughen up.'

I run upstairs to find Finn curled under his duvet. I lie beside him and stroke his hair. 'I'm going to talk to Shan and sort this out,' I whisper. 'I'll make things better, I promise.' But it's not Liam or Ian or even Shan that I'm thinking about as I pull the dinosaur duvet up to his chin and kiss his forehead. It's someone else I made that promise to a long time ago. A promise I never kept.

CHAPTER 20

Then

One afternoon, after we'd been living in Mo's flat for about six months, he walked in with a girl trailing behind him. He'd been in a right mood for the last few weeks – money problems, Donna said, but that day he seemed almost cheerful. The girl looked grubby: skinny legs, ripped black jeans, sullen mouth, hair a mix of dip-dyed braids and greasy tangles. She smelled, too – the sickly, sour stench of the street.

Donna circled her, looking her over, like she was a runty calf at an auction. 'Who is she?' she asked.

'Jade. From Manchester.' Mo made it sound like he was introducing an act on a low-rent talent show. 'She's going to be staying here for a few days.'

'Where's she going to sleep?' Donna said.

'In here.' He twitched his thumb at the sofa. Jade flopped onto it, trying it out for size and relit a half-smoked cigarette. I noticed her gnawed-down fingernails and a bracelet of DIY tattoos circling her skinny wrist.

'How old is she?' I said.

'Sixteen,' the girl said, glaring at me. 'And I am here, you know.'

'Yeah,' Mo said. 'Sixteen.' He laughed like he'd just made a joke and we should be laughing too.

'When did you leave Manchester?' I asked.

She shrugged. 'Couple of months ago.'

'Did your parents chuck you out?'

She shook her head. 'It's just my dad. He probably hasn't even noticed I've gone.'

'Where have you been living?'

'Around.' She gave the room a quick calculating glance, taking in everything from Donna's phone lying on the coffee table to the new TV.

'Don't even think about it,' Mo said, following her gaze.

Donna glared at Jade. 'Yeah. Any nonsense from you and you're out. You hear me?'

'Maybe you'd like a shower,' I said. 'Bathroom's down the hall.'

'Yeah,' Donna said, wrinkling her nose. 'Do us all a favour.'

Jade picked up the tatty carrier bag she'd dropped on the floor.

'Is that all you brought with you?' I asked.

She didn't answer, just hauled herself to her feet.

'How long's she going to be here?' Donna demanded, before Jade had even got to the door.

'Not long,' Mo said. 'There's a room coming free in one of my other flats.' He tossed a few quid onto the table. 'There you go. Bed and board till she can pay her own way.'

'Pay her own way doing what?' I asked.

'Deliveries, pick-ups, this and that.' His eyes locked on mine. 'Better than living rough.' He eased himself into our only armchair and stretched out his legs. 'Go and make us a coffee, Nic. I want a word with Donna.'

I retreated to the kitchen and flicked on the kettle. It unnerved me when Mo had these private chats with Donna. I was pretty sure she was doing jobs for him that she wasn't telling me about and I felt left out. As I spooned out the granules I strained to make out what he was saying. All I could hear were the pipes knocking as Jade took a shower. I went into my room and looked out some of my old clothes for her. She was so skinny my things were going to swamp her but I found an old belt she could use to hold up the jeans. I dropped the clothes on the floor outside the bathroom and shouted through the door. 'There's some clean things for you out here.'

I took the coffees back to the sitting room and sat with Donna while Mo told us about the parties he'd got lined up for us over the next few weeks. I was surprised when he mentioned that one of the clients was the man we called Roo. They all had nicknames. That was part of the deal. No surnames, no insights into what they did for a living or who they really were, though there were the usual nudges and whispers about them being judges and MPs and lords. Roo had a big swanky place in the country and we used to do a lot of gigs there. But recently Roo and Mo had fallen out. Something to do with Mo owing him money. Still, if they'd settled their differences it was good news for us. Roo was always nice to us and he tipped really well. Mainly because he had a thing for Donna.

Half an hour later, Jade walked back in. All cleaned up, with her make-up scrubbed off, she looked even more pitiful than when she'd been filthy.

'How old are you really?' I asked when Mo had left. 'Thirteen? Fourteen?'

'What's it to you?'

'I want to know.'

'Fourteen,' she said, lighting a roll-up and taking a deep drag. 'But I'm not a kid.'

I dumped a clean ashtray in front of her and went out to the bathroom. She'd thrown her old clothes in a heap in one corner. The jeans were falling apart and stiff with grime, the T-shirt and hoody were stained and ripped, and the worn-through trainers stank like rotting cabbage. I picked the whole lot up and carried the bundle at arm's length into the kitchen.

Jade came in while I was stuffing them into the washing machine. 'Why are you doing that?' she said.

'Someone needs to.' I threw in the trainers. 'If they fall apart I'll lend you a pair of mine.'

She stared as I scooped powder into the drawer and turned the dial to boil wash. 'Thanks,' she said, uncertainly.

'What happened to your mum?'

She shrugged. 'Buggered off when I was six. Don't know where. I can't blame her. My dad's a right bastard.'

That night I made us all beans on toast with sausages. Jade ate fast, eyes flicking left and right, barely stopping between mouthfuls like she thought I was going to snatch her plate away. Afterwards the three of us sat on the sofa and watched a romcom on TV. Donna and I had seen it so many times we were howling with laughter and shouting out the lines, but for the first hour or so Jade never made a sound, just sat there, eyes glazed, shoving popcorn into her mouth. Donna and I cheered when our favourite scene came on – a bunch of friends throwing up in a posh bridal shop. It must have tickled Jade too because out of nowhere she started to giggle, rolling around like a little kid and swinging her bare feet onto my lap. When she stopped laughing she left them there. I didn't mind. In fact, I quite liked it; but Donna reached over and smacked them off. Told her to have some respect.

Jade was sound asleep when I looked in on her the next morning, one skinny white foot sticking out from under the blanket. Cracked toenails, grime still etched into the hardened skin of her heel. She didn't even stir when the drilling started up in the road outside, and I wondered how long it had been since she'd slept indoors. After college I went to Tesco's to buy food, got to the checkout and discovered there was twenty quid missing from my purse. I ran back to the flat, quietly let myself in and crept down the hallway. I could see my room was empty but Donna's door was closed. I flung it open, and there was Jade going through Donna's drawers.

'What are you doing?'

She glanced up, a lipstick in her hand. 'Just looking.'

I ran at her and grabbed her shoulders. 'Empty your pockets. *Now!*' She twisted away. 'Do it. Quick, before Donna gets back.'

'I didn't take anything!'

'Yes, you did. And you stole money out of my purse. Come on, hand it back. All of it.'

'You can't make me.' Her eyes flicked over my shoulder. Her sneer shrivelled. I glanced round. Donna was standing behind me. She pushed past me and walked towards Jade, hand outstretched. Jade understood the silent order. She reached in her pockets, took out a twenty-pound note and a pair of gold hoops that Donna had bought the week before and dropped them into Donna's palm. Donna passed them to me, drew back her hand and slapped Jade so hard across the face she fell back onto the bed.

Jade clamped her hands to her cheek and ran into the lounge, sobbing. 'I hate you! I hate you both!'

Donna pulled out her phone.

'Who are you calling?'

'Mo. I want that little bitch out of here.'

'She's just a kid.'

'She's a thief.'

'Come on. We nicked loads of stuff when we were her age.'

Her finger paused on the keypad. '*I* nicked loads of stuff. You just whinged and got in the way.'

She catches my gaze and we both start laughing.

'Well, I *would* have nicked loads of stuff if I'd had the nerve. Come on, Don, at least if she's here we can keep an eye on her.'

'She's not our problem, Nic.'

'I know but—'

'But what?'

'*Please.*'

Donna gave me an odd look. 'What's it to you what happens to her?'

'She's had a crappy time.'

'And we didn't?'

'We had each other.' I poked her in the ribs. '*Blood sisters forever.*'

She shook her head and pocketed her phone.

Donna went out that night and I got a takeaway for me and Jade. I let her choose. She sat close to me on the sofa, nibbling pizza. Halfway through she slipped her hand into her bra, pulled out a pill, snapped it in two and popped half on the tip of her tongue. 'Here.' She pushed the other half into my mouth and giggled loudly, showing stubby little teeth.

I spat it into my hand. 'What are you doing?'

Her face crumpled. 'It's a present. To say sorry for taking your money.'

'Spit yours out.'

She shook her head and pulled away. I shoved my fingers into her mouth and scraped the pill off her tongue. 'Who gave you this?'

'I did a delivery for Mo.'

'And helped yourself to a freebie. Bad idea, Jade.'

She pushed me away and I stomped into the bathroom, rinsed the gritty remains of the tablet down the sink and wiped my hands on a towel. I came back in ready to let rip at her, but she was all curled up on one end of the sofa. I've never seen anyone look more crushed or more lonely.

'Jade, come on.' I tugged at her shoulders. 'You don't need that stuff. You shouldn't even be here and you certainly shouldn't be doing deliveries for Mo. You're just a kid.'

'Where else am I going to go?'

'I'll find you somewhere. Somewhere safe. I'll make things better, I promise.' I meant it too. Though I had no idea how. After five minutes in any foster home Jade would wreck the place and haul herself back onto the street. But there had to be someone who could help her.

I sat in the half-dark, watching headlights slide across the dingy wallpaper and holding her wiry little body. When she fell asleep I pulled a blanket over her, turned out the light and left her.

Next day I had an early lecture. When I got back to the flat she was gone. I called Mo. 'Where's Jade?'

'Went back to Manchester.'

'To her dad's?'

'Staying with her aunty, she said.'

I knew he was lying. I also knew I should ask him what had really happened to her. I didn't, though. Mo didn't like to be crossed and I was scared of losing my home, my only source of income and my chance of going to uni. When I asked Donna about it she just shrugged and said, 'More trouble than she was worth, that one.'

CHAPTER 21

I lie in bed, steadied by the pills but sleepless as the panic of losing Finn in the park comes back in waves. I watch the numbers on the digital alarm lighting up in sequence, morphing through the seconds, and listen to the rise and fall of Ian's breath. All at once the numbers and the breaths sync up and then his breaths slow down, leaving the numbers to flip on at their own relentless pace, staining the room with their luminous red glow. I can see the shapes of the chair and the chest of drawers, the pale outlines of the windows and the patch of dark where Ian has hung his jacket on the wardrobe door. I get up and see myself reflected in the long mirror, a ghost in a white cotton T-shirt. I pad down the landing to Finn's room, stand at the door and watch for a while as he sleeps. I step back, slither to the floor and sit hunched against the wall. The tick of the carriage clock in the sitting room drifts up the stairs, filling the silence, picking up the countdown where the alarm left off. The bird, the tyre, the box, the woman in the park. I knock my head against my knees. A day, a week, a month, a year. It can only be a matter of time.

The carriage clock chimes five. I lift my head; light is seeping through the landing window, I'm doing the morning school run today – Tilly's taking Mimi to the clinic, so there's no point going back to bed. I tiptoe around, gathering up clothes, and get showered and dressed in Finn's bathroom. By the time Ian comes down to breakfast I'm ready for the day, hair extra smooth, smile screwed on tight, a second cup of coffee in my hand.

*

I watch the boys run into the playground, Henry veering away to join a noisy kick around, Finn dawdling over to the benches on his own. I turn away and glimpse Liam's mother walking back to her car. 'Shan!'

She pivots on her shiny heel and pushes her hands into the pockets of her coat but makes no other move. I walk towards her, throat dry, heart beating hard. I ignore the riot of noises in my head and keep going, running over the words I've planned to say. I plant myself in front of her. 'Look, Finn was really upset about what happened in the park yesterday and, to be honest, so am I. Liam doesn't have to be Finn's friend, or to play with him, but he does have to stop being so unkind to him.'

'I've spoken to Liam,' she says, grey eyes as flat and unyielding as her tone. 'And I'll speak to him again, if that's what you want, but it's a hard old world out there Nicola, and…' her nostrils twitch.

'And what?'

'Well, you know what they say about bullied kids.'

'I didn't use that word.'

'They bring it on themselves by playing the victim. I hate to say this, but Finn needs to toughen up. You won't always be there to fight his battles for him.'

She turns a sudden shoulder, cold and studied as any playground shunning, and calls to a woman I don't know, who waves back. Shan walks towards her, leaving me standing there gaping and stung. How dare she? How *dare* she?

I start work with more coffee, extra strong, and by the time the first patients arrive I'm wound up and jittery with caffeine, but I've finished the invoicing, arranged a locum for Amanda's half-term cover, and made sure that every dentist in the team has the right patient files for their morning appointments. I fill every moment, plugging the gaps, clogging the crevices. No time to think. Shut out the past, hold back the dam. It's going to burst. I'm going to burst.

In my break I sneak out to the car park and call Leon, surprised when he picks up. There's shouting in the background and the heavy throb of music.

'Leon, thank goodness, where are you? Why haven't you been—?'

A voice behind him – hard and angry – barks his name. He hangs up.

I text him. *Call me.*

I'm starting to the think the worst, that Logan is sending him out of town, lending him out to someone further up the chain of supply. If he is, there's nothing I can do. It's not as if the police are going to see a six-foot youth with a sentence hanging over him as a victim in need of rescue, even if it is for a first offence. I just have to pray that Logan lets him come home in time for his hearing. I text my fears to Susy, who replies with an explosion of angry-face emojis and a promise to call me when she gets out of her meeting.

I've just sat down at my computer again when Maggie appears behind me. She drops a couple of envelopes onto my keyboard. 'Sorry. I opened them before I realised they were addressed to you.'

'Don't worry.' I slide a sideways look at Amy and turn back to my screen. That's a new one: Maggie apologising to me. And for something as petty as opening a couple of pharma mailouts. We get sent them all the time. Who knows how these companies get hold of our names but now and then the freebies are worth having – bottles of wine, pamper hampers, vouchers. She was probably after a free spa day. Let's hope she got one. It would do her good to lighten up. I reach for the phone, aware that she is still hovering at my side. I look up, smiling the tight-lipped smile I keep especially for her. 'Was there something else I can do for you, Maggie?'

She flushes a little. 'Just to remind you of our policy on receiving personal mail in the surgery.'

'What policy is that, Maggie?' *The one you've just invented?*

Her lips tighten. 'It's not permitted.'

'Well, thanks for the reminder.'

I sit there expecting her to stomp away. Instead, she opens the glass case on the wall behind me and for no reason at all starts rearranging the display of oral hygiene products. No reason, because I filled it earlier and I know for sure that there isn't a floss pick or a stain eraser out of place. So why is she still here? Unless… my skin prickles. Unless she's hanging around to see my reaction to my post. Well, Maggie, sorry to disappoint. I push the envelopes to one side and dial a number.

'Mr Mason? Hello, this is Nicola from Parkview Dental. I'm just ringing to let you know your new crown has arrived. Can I make an appointment for you to come in and have that fitted? We could do ten am Monday or four pm Thursday. Yes, that's fine, Thursday it is. We'll send you a confirmation. Thank you.' When I hang up and dial again Maggie slinks back to her office, but I feel her watching me through the glass window above her desk. Just to taunt her, I busy myself making calls and working through emails until curiosity and rising unease win out.

I swivel my chair a little so she can't see my face and look down at the envelopes. They are large, glossy, emblazoned with the logos of a big drug company and addressed to Nicola Dexter. I pick them up and push my chair back to retrieve a third envelope that drops into my lap. It's small, white, addressed in blocky blue biro to Nicola Cahill, and jagged down one side where Maggie has slit it open with her thumb. A jangling sound starts up in my head, harsh and out of tune. It gets louder as I slip my fingers inside and pull out a folded sheet of paper. It's a photocopy of a grainy photo, but I'm holding it upside-down. I turn it around.

There are two figures in the shot – two skimpily dressed, long-haired girls teetering on high-heeled shoes, locked in a struggle. The taller one grips the arm of the shorter one, whose head is flung back in pain or fury. Caught on the turn, their outlines are blurred: hands, hair and faces a low-lit smear. My throat shrinks. My vision swims, I yank breath from the air as I smash the paper into a ball and suddenly I'm rushing into the waiting room, my clenched fist scraping the wall, the other hand flailing for the door of the toilets. I jolt it open, stumble inside and I'm drowning, plummeting, falling, folding into that night at Sallowfield Court.

CHAPTER 22

Then

Music. Laughter. Bodies bumping and grinding, the flicker of candlelight reflected in massive gold mirrors. I brush past the man they call Tommo – late fifties, grey-streaked hair, red in the face. He scares me. I've been with him just once. He was into weird stuff, whips and masks, and he hurt me. Badly. When I showed Mo the welts and bruises he handed me a bundle of fivers and told me to keep quiet.

Tommo is pawing a skinny girl in a white crop top and a blue satin mini skirt. I can only see her from behind and I don't recognise her. No reason why I should. Mo's sidekick, Gary, turned up with a carful of girls I've never seen before. This one squirms and wriggles, her bleached-blonde hair swinging low as she beats on his back with her fists but it's feeble and half-hearted and I hear her laughing, like it's a game. I should warn her about Tommo. Someone grabs me from behind. He spins me around. Sweat drips onto my face, hands slip on my skin. I pull away. Mo is watching me, frowning. So I stay where I am and go on dancing, hoping this guy is too stoned to want more than a sympathetic ear. Turns out he isn't. But at least he's quick.

I leave him in the downstairs bathroom doing up his trousers and hurry up the wide oak staircase to look for Donna. Muffled grunts and giggles as I pull open doors to the swanky bedrooms. I reach the end of the landing. The master suite. I turn the handle and peek inside. Roo, the owner of the house, is lying on a huge four poster bed half-naked, arms tied to the bedposts. Donna is leaning over him, wrapped in a skimpy towel, doing this stupid dance – wiggling her hips and laughing. She turns around and tells me to get out. I close the door and hear Tony, one of Mo's regulars, calling my name, telling me to get him a line of coke and a whisky. I fetch him what he wants and stumble out onto the terrace.

It's cooler out here. Pale marble tiles stretch away into darkness, and a light breeze ruffles the potted palms. I see a movement. The girl in the white crop top is dancing all on her own in the aquarium-light from the pool, swaying on high heels. She's got her back to me and she's gyrating to the music, arms curling up through the air then snaking down to clasp her body. She turns. I flinch. Beneath the blotched make-up and mussed-up hair, it's Jade. What's she doing here? I step closer. She's bruised and bloody, her skirt ripped, her roots dark. She's bleary-eyed and off her face.

'Who did this to you?' I say. 'Was it Tommo?'

She frowns as if she's trying to remember something that happened a long time ago, then her mouth cracks into a smile. Blood on her lips. Blood on her teeth. Blood on her skimpy white top. 'S'all right. He gave me some molly to stop it hurting.' She opens her palm and shows me a bag of coloured pills stamped with jazz hands and smiley faces – the kind Mo has been supplying to any of Roo's guests who fancied a change from their usual coke. The bag is half-empty.

'Don't be stupid. Don't take any more of that stuff.'

Her voice slurs, her lip curls back in a snarl. 'You're just jealous cos Tommo picked me.'

'Give me the tabs.'

Her fist snaps shut.

I grab her wrist. 'I said, give them to me.'

'Get off! You can't tell me what to do.' She breaks free and pulls away. I lunge at her and clamp two hands on her clasped fist. We tussle on the edge of the pool. There's a wiry desperation in those bony wrists and she's getting the better of me, the fingers of the other hand digging deep into the flesh of my arm. I summon all my strength and fling up my elbow, breaking her grip. Her heel catches and snaps. She wobbles for an instant, her hands fly high and she tips backwards. I feel her slipping through my fingers. Her body cuts the water, a juddery blur slicing the blue. I stumble back, panting, looking down at the shimmering patch of dark, waiting for her to splutter to the surface screaming obscenities. She lies there on the blue-tiled bottom, humped and still, playing some stupid game, trying to freak me out. Seconds tick by, swelling and growing. She's still not moving. The night sky folds in. My muscles shut down. Water fills my vision, time blurs and bends. I'm faking my swimming test, gagging and gasping, one foot on the bottom, reaching the side. If I hadn't cheated I could dive in now and save Jade, like I could have dived in and saved my mother. But I am a liar. A liar and a cheat. I couldn't swim then, and I can't swim now.

I see myself from above, a lone figure, helpless, useless, frozen on the poolside. I have to get help. My legs are leaden, weighing me down as if I'm moving through jelly. Heart pumping faster with each slow-motion step, I stumble into the house and push through the dancers to the writhing bodies sprawled across the gilded sofas, looking for someone sober. I open my mouth. A sob thrusts its way through my lips. I can't find a scream. I try again and manage a strangled cry: 'Help me!'

Eyes turn to look at me, then swivel away. One face looks up, dazed and dreamy. He sees my panic. I grab him by the wrists and pull him upright onto unsteady feet. He sways back and forth, tie awry, lipstick on his cheek. I drag him through the crowd and out onto the terrace. I point at the blob at the bottom of the pool. He staggers and squints and topples into the water. I watch him sink through the blue, down and down. Blurred arms grapple to get hold of Jade. Hours seem to pass before he kicks himself up from the bottom. Red and spluttering, he bobs to the surface, one arm circling her neck, the other churning the water as he gasps for air and thrashes for the side of the pool. I slither onto my front and reach out. My fingers find cold, wet flesh. He lifts Jade higher. I catch her under her arms and pull hard, scraping the soft dip of her stomach against the edge of the pool. Light floods the terrace. The music stops. A shout cuts the silence. People trickle through the French windows to see what is happening; a ripple of shock when they see Jade. A hefty man in a blue polo shirt pushes to the front and drops onto his knees beside her. He pumps her chest, blowing air into her bloodied mouth, his huge pink hands crushing her chest. He pumps and pumps. I watch, willing her body to spasm into life, water to erupt from her mouth, her eyes to spring open.

Gary runs out onto the terrace and shakes me hard. 'What happened?'

'I… I can't swim.' I start to sob, trembling and hysterical.

He slaps my cheek hard. I stumble back. He leans into my face, cold and angry. 'What happened to Jade?'

'That bastard, Tommo. He beat her up. She was all bloody and bruised.' My head wobbles and drops.

He grabs my chin and jerks it up. 'How did she drown?'

'He gave her a bag of molly. She was already off her head so I tried to take it off her and she… she fought me.' My words slur. My teeth clatter. I'm fighting for breath. 'We struggled and she fell in the water. I thought she'd swim to the side but she sank and I… I can't swim, and no one came when I yelled.'

The man in the blue shirt is still pumping Jade's chest, harder now, jerking her limp, skinny arms. Tears well in his eyes. Mo comes running out, waving his phone.

'It's no good, mate.' He grabs the man's arm. 'You've got to get out of here. Come on, I'll sort this.' He turns to the rest of the guests, who have gathered in a ragged circle, his voice hard and controlled. 'Get out. Everybody. Now! You were never here, all right? None of you. Don't talk to anyone. One slip up, that's all it'll take.'

Dazed and dumb, they look from him to Jade's body, a slow ripple of realisation spreading through the crowd. Lying there in a puddle of water, she looks exactly what she is: a drugged-up, underage runaway who's been used, abused and discarded.

They start to back off, tottering and swaying. I lunge forward, cutting off Tommo's retreat. 'You bastard! She was fourteen!' He tries to dodge past me. 'Just because she was a runaway you thought you could slap her around, pump her full of crap and toss her away. Well, she was… she was… *somebody*.' I slam my fists against his chest, venting my own guilt and grief.

He grips my wrists. 'Get off me, you little bitch.'

Fury makes me strong. We rock and tilt, his small, bloodshot eyes glaring down into mine.

'Cut it out, Nicci!' Mo grabs me by the shoulders and flings me aside.

I crumple onto a wooden lounger and watch Tommo stride away. Cars start up outside, rubber crunching the gravel, engines revving as the party guests screech back to their posh, privileged lives, their snotty wives and their spoiled kids. What's it to them if some scabby little tart is dead? All they care about is saving themselves.

Donna appears in the doorway, eyes unfocused, mouth unlatched. I start forward and reach out to embrace her. 'I couldn't swim! I couldn't save her.'

Her eyes stare through me and swerve, not to Jade's body, but to Mo. She calls his name. One syllable, edgy and cracked. He swings around. She lifts her hand. Beckons him to her. My ears strain to sift their words: *tabs… not breathing… doctor*. Somewhere in the folds of my brain I know it's not Jade they're talking about. I fall back as the two of them go running upstairs. Panicked feet pound on the polished oak. Ten minutes later, Mo comes back, angry, white-faced, barking orders. He lines us up: five girls shivering with shock in flimsy partywear.

'You weren't here. All right? None of us were. You even think about naming names, pointing fingers, blabbing to anyone, you'll regret it. I mean that. Not one word about tonight to anyone.'

We shuffle and nod, too scared and upset to speak. He motions to Gary. 'Donna'll stay here and help me sort this. You take the others home.'

I hear myself sob. 'I want to stay with Donna.'

'Shut up.' Mo's voice slams me back. 'You've done enough damage.'

All the way back in the car the other girls are silent, Gary is silent and I am silent, panic seizing my throat every time I think about the grotesque, lifeless shell that was Jade. If I'd grabbed her as she fell, if I'd been able to swim, if I'd got help sooner, she'd still be alive. Thoughts spin tighter and tighter as the car speeds through the darkness.

Gary pulls up outside the flat. I open the car door. As I swing my legs onto the pavement he turns to glare at me. 'You pushed her in and you let her drown. So keep your mouth shut. If the cops start sniffing around, Mo will make damn sure it's you who takes the rap.'

I run into the flat, eyes clenched shut, heart pounding, sobs jerking deep in my body.

CHAPTER 23

'Nicola. It's all right. Can you hear me? Nicola!'

I'm looking at a light. A recessed bulb staring down at me. An unblinking eye. Cold tile beneath my cheek. Gary's words fizzing in my ear: *If the cops start sniffing around, Mo will make damn sure it's you who takes the rap.*

'Can you sit up?' A hand presses into my back, helping me to sit up. 'Here, drink this.' A silver pendant swings back and forth as the dark-haired woman kneeling over me holds a plastic cup to my lips. Someone else is standing behind her, looking on. The far figure ripples into focus. It's Maggie.

I pull my wavery gaze back to the stranger. 'What happened?' The words stagger off my tongue.

'I was sitting in the waiting room when you went stumbling in here, looking like death, so I came in to see if you were OK and found you laid out on the floor. Looks like you hit your head on the sink. I don't think you're concussed but you're going to have a hell of bump on your forehead. I'm Gail, by the way.'

Glad of her capable fingers and steady voice, I whisper, 'Are you a doctor?'

'Midwife. Best we could do at short notice, I'm afraid.'

I taste blood. I bring my hand to my mouth and realise I'm clutching something. The scrunched-up printout. I squeeze my hand tight as if to keep the image frozen in my fist, but it seeps through the cracks between my fingers and crawls into my skull.

I throw back my head and stare at the tiled ceiling. Breathe, Nicci. Breathe. *In. Two. Three. Four. Out. Two. Three. Four.*

'Shall I fetch Ian?' Maggie asks.

'No. I'll be fine.' I grasp the cup of water.

'I'll cover reception until you're back on your feet,' she says, and lets herself out.

'Who's Ian?' Gail asks.

'My husband. He's one of the dentists here.'

'He should take you home.'

'Honestly, I'll be fine. He's doing a root canal this morning.'

She sits back on her knees. 'I think you had a panic attack.'

I press my knuckle to the cut on my forehead.

She looks at me closely. 'You've had them before.'

I nod. 'I think I must have tripped, though. I don't usually faint.'

'Have you talked to a doctor about getting help?'

'He gives me something to help me sleep and I've got some… coping strategies.'

'You should talk to him about therapy. They say CBT can work wonders.'

I don't tell her that my GP has been pushing me to get therapy for months, telling me I need to find my hidden demons so I can lay them to rest. The trouble is, my demons aren't hiding: they're right here, bubbling up from beneath whatever lid I try to jam them down with.

I grasp the edge of the sink and with Gail's help pull myself up to standing. 'Thanks so much for looking after me. I'll be fine now.'

'If you're sure.'

'Absolutely.' I squeeze her hand and retreat to the nearest cubicle, rip the balled printout into tiny pieces and sprinkle them into the toilet, making sure to flush between handfuls so I don't clog the system and rouse Maggie's wrath. When I'm done I stare into the empty bowl. The jangle starts up in my head again, low and accusatory: *You could have saved Jade from Mo, but it suited you to buy into his lies about her going back to Manchester. You could have saved her from Tommo. You could have grabbed her as she fell, but you thought a dunking in the pool would do her good, sober her up. So you stood there and watched her die. You're worthless and pathetic. No wonder your mother couldn't be bothered to stick around.*

By the time Ian has finished his root canal, I've splashed my face with cold water, drunk the mug of sugary tea Amy made me and I'm back at my desk, booking appointments and making small-talk with patients.

He drops a pile of files in front of me. 'Hey, what's all this about you fainting?'

'It was nothing, honestly. I forgot to eat breakfast and I stood up too fast.'

'Maggie says you got something in the post. She thought it upset you.'

I throw her a look through the internal window. She drops her head and starts tapping at her keyboard. What a cow. First she opens my mail, then she has the gall to snitch to Ian.

'It was just a couple of pharma mailouts. I didn't even bother to open them.'

He looks at me for a moment, a frown creasing his forehead. 'Can I see them?'

I feel a throb of annoyance.

'Nicci?'

What's the matter with you? He's worried about you. He's your husband. I roll my chair back, lift up the bin and rummage among the bits of paper. 'Here you go.' I hand him the two glossy envelopes.

A muscle twitches under his eye. He hands them back. 'Are you going to be all right to drive home?'

'Course I am.'

'Promise?'

'Promise.'

'Well, make sure you eat something before you leave.'

'I will.'

He squeezes my shoulder. 'See you later, darling. I'll try to get back early.'

Amy watches him stride back to his room, tall and purposeful in his crisp white coat, and makes a swoony face. 'If you ever get tired of him, don't forget to send him my way.'

It's my usual cue to laugh and say, 'In your dreams.' Today I pretend not to hear her. I slide the pile of files to one side and greet a hovering patient, professional smile in place. I'm good at that. It's what I do.

I check the bonnet as I hurry out to the car, and scan the faces of passers-by all the way to the supermarket. Far from making me feel safer, the brightly lit aisles and cavernous interior make me feel vulnerable and exposed.

When I get home, I unpack the shopping and stand alone in the middle of the kitchen. I look at the windows and imagine eyes out there, in the gloom, looking in. I jump up and close the blinds and do the tapping. Arms, face, hands. *Tap, tap, tap. Tap, tap, tap.*

I didn't save Jade. There's nothing I can do to save my own future, but I might just be able to save Leon's. I text him. *Where are you? I'll come and get you. I'll find somewhere safe for you to go.*

I switch on the radio, turn up the volume, and hoover and tidy, fold and dust, filling every moment until it's school pick-up time.

I get to the school gates and stand on tiptoe to wave as Finn comes down the steps, shirt hanging out, jumper trailing from his bag. He's not on his own. I crane to get a better look. He's talking to a thin, dark-haired scrap of a boy. And now they're stopping to laugh and share a joke. Tears prick the back of my eyes.

'Nicola Cahill?'

A claw grips my heart. *No, please. Not now. Not yet.* I swing around sharply and see a stranger. She's about my height, thirtyish and dressed in a black jacket, her thick brown hair pulled back from her face in a ponytail. Her face is pale and thin. 'Lisa Henderson.'

She smiles quizzically as if I should know who she is. 'Jamal's mother? Mrs Cooper said I should look out for you.'

'Oh!' The claw lets go. I let out a jagged breath. 'Yes. How's he settling in?'

'Really well. Finn's been doing a great job of looking after him.'

'Oh, good.' I switch to autopilot. 'I'm on the PTA committee, so if you ever fancy getting involved, just let me know.'

'Yes. Maybe.'

'Have you just moved to the area?'

'Yep.'

'What brought you here?'

'I just got divorced and what I got for my half of the house meant moving out of London or living in a shoebox.'

'Well, my husband helps to run a kids' football club on Sunday mornings at Bellvue Park. It's a community thing, all ages and abilities welcome. You might like to bring Jamal along.'

'I might take you up on that. He's not played much football but Sundays can be tough when it's just the two of you.'

'Don't I know it.' I smile again, only more warmly this time. Is it just because she was nice about Finn, or is it because there's no hearty, football-loving partner to get sucked into the gossipy post-match chatter with Ian, that makes me suddenly long to be her friend?

We swap numbers and she asks tentatively if Finn would like to go to Jamal's for tea next week.

'He'd love that,' I say. I should be the one doing the inviting, making her feel welcome. I need to get organised. I need to get a grip. But my head is full of Sallowfield, and who, out of all the people who were there that night, is coming for me now.

CHAPTER 24

Then

Snotty tears tracking down my face, I stumbled into the kitchen and banged open the cupboard doors looking for the drink that Mo kept in the flat for his business meetings. Gulping from a half empty bottle of Bourbon, I dragged myself to my room and sank onto the bed, swallowing swig after swig until the bottle dropped from my hand and rolled across the floor.

I lay there drunk, but not drunk enough, drifting in and out of consciousness, my brain glitching and rebooting on the moment when I knew Jade was dead. A whirr filled my head. She was so limp, so pale, so empty. A shudder of revulsion. Is that how Mum had looked when they pulled her from the river? I didn't save Jade. I didn't save Mum. The whirr grew louder. A ragged shadow skimming, swooping, circling, churning the air. Jade falling from my grasp, her body slicing the water. I should have reached out. I should have caught her. I should have looked for her when she disappeared from the flat. It's all my fault. I saw her sinking, gasping, drowning, dying as the shadow swooped closer, brushing my face.

My eyes sprang open. Pale dawn light outlined a gaping orange beak and black wings thrashing at the glass. Jade flailing as she fell, that terrible moment spooling and unspooling on endless repeat. A frenzied scrape of claws. Fear and horror as water fills her lungs.

A scream rose from my belly. It stuck in my throat. I couldn't breathe. Why? Why couldn't I breathe? It felt like I was having a heart attack. Death was coming for me, too. Of course it was. I was a killer. Death was what I deserved.

Pain tightened around my head, my eyes lost focus, blurring everything to grey. I tried to call out. A weight pushed down on my lungs, crushing the sound, the bird kept flapping – growing ever more frantic in its suicidal panic to be free, just as Jade must have gasped and struggled as death closed in.

Cornered and breathless, I flung the covers over my head and gasped for someone to save me. I heard the door swing back on its hinges. A scream burst from my mouth. 'Open the window! *Please*, open the window!'

A hand ripped the cover from my face. I looked up into Donna's cold, angry eyes. 'Shut up. You'll wake the neighbours.'

'Get rid of it, please, *please*, Donna! Get it out of here.'

She threw open the window and walked out. I cowered beneath the covers and lay in a trembling sweat until the whirring and flapping had stopped and the bird had escaped. Slowly the panic subsided. But I was left with the horror of what I had done to Jade.

Still struggling to breathe, I ran to the bathroom and threw up in the toilet bowl. I pulled myself to my feet and, using the wall for support, I made my way to the kitchen.

Donna was in there, staring out of the window, smoking. She didn't turn around, just said: 'What the hell's wrong with you, screaming and carrying on about a bloody bird?'

I sank down shakily onto one of the kitchen chairs. 'What will happen to her body?'

'I told you to keep your voice down,' she hissed. 'It's all your fault. You shouldn't have interfered.'

'Mo said she'd gone back to Manchester.'

'He lied.'

'What did he do with her?'

'She wasn't some little innocent. She knew how to look after herself.'

'She was fourteen, Donna! What was he doing taking her to Sallowfield?'

She took a drag of her cigarette. 'She was there by special request.'

'Whose request?'

'Tommo's. He likes them young.' She turned around and glared at me. 'Don't look at me like that. She was totally up for it. Money for her, money for Mo. But, thanks to you, she's dead and now Mo wants us out of his flat.'

'When?'

'By tonight.'

'Why?'

'Because you're a fucking liability, that's why.'

'Where are we supposed to go?'

She pulled out a bundle of cash and threw it on the table. 'He said to find a cheap hotel while we look for jobs and another place to live.'

She saw my horror. 'Yeah. Get it now? You've screwed us both.'

'What do we say if the police come?'

'For God's sake! Don't you understand? We're not going to be talking to the police. No one is. If everyone keeps their heads down and their mouths shut, they'll never know who was there.'

'What about fingerprints and DNA?'

She looks away. 'It's sorted, all right?'

'What do you mean, *sorted*?'

She got up and walked to the door. 'You weren't there. None of us were. If anyone asks, you've never even been to Sallowfield Court.'

'Why did you come rushing down to get Mo? It must have been something bad. Jade was lying there dead and you didn't even look at her.'

She kept walking down the hall.

'Donna? What happened upstairs?'

Her bedroom door slammed shut.

Four hours later, a story hit the breakfast news.

> *The badly burned body of wealthy entrepreneur Ryan Hurley and that of an unidentified teenage girl were found in the early hours of this morning when fire fighters arrived to put out a fire at his Essex home, Sallowfield Court. Tests indicate that both victims had consumed large quantities of narcotics before their deaths.*

I wanted it not to be Roo, but the photo of Ryan Hurley lolling on the deck of a luxury yacht told me it was. I flashed back to that glimpse of him passed out on his bed, hands tied to the bed posts, and Donna dancing around him in a towel.

I ran down the hall and kicked open her door. The curtains were closed and Donna was lying slumped on the unmade bed in the half-light, her face to the wall. There was a fire at the house. Roo's dead.' She rolled over and looked at me, her face bloated from crying. 'You did it. You and Mo. You killed him.'

Donna sat up, wearily. 'It was an accident, I swear.' She pushed her hand to her mouth. 'Roo was using all night – anything he could lay his hands on – and washing it down with vodka. He wouldn't listen.' Tears ran down her face. 'I thought he'd just passed out but then I touched him and… he wasn't breathing.'

'But it was Mo who set fire to the house.'

'Two people were dead. It was the only way to destroy the evidence of who'd been there when it happened.'

'Two dead bodies full of drugs that *Mo* had supplied. All *he* was worried about was himself.'

She wiped her sleeve across her face. 'It was your fault Jade died. She'd still be alive if you'd left her alone.'

'It's Mo who got her into this. Mo who sold her to Tommo. Mo's drugs that got her so stoned she could hardly stand up.'

She pushed her hair off her face and glared at me, distress souring to a snarl. 'Yeah, but it was you who pushed her into the water and you who stood there while she drowned. Mo saw you. From the upstairs window. So just remember – if this gets out you're the one who'll take the rap.'

I could see then that the Donna I'd idolised and adored was slipping away, but I hung on, hoping she would come back. She was all I had. And deep down it scared me that she knew the terrible thing I had done.

CHAPTER 25

I'd give anything not to go to the dinner at Mac's tonight but there's no getting out of it. Some of the partners' other halves aren't too bad, but Mac's wife, Orla – botoxed queen of the not-so-subtle put-down – has never forgiven me for snaffling Ian when she had him all lined up for some newly divorced PR guru from her book club. I heard her discussing it with Maggie at a grim practice drinks-do soon after we got engaged. I didn't catch everything they said, but 'rebound', 'tragic waste' and 'come to his senses' gave me the gist.

Orla has narrow hips, suspiciously pert breasts and filler-plumped lips which she smothers in crimson lipstick even when she's putting out the bins. She and Mac have got an older son, Oscar, who's just dropped out of uni, and a pair of late arrival twins, Maddy and Wilf, who are in year seven at Finn's school. Oscar won't get a mention, that's for sure, but what's the betting that Orla will spend the evening describing her absolute *astonishment* that *both* twins have won scholarships to Dunelm. I mean, she knew they were *bright* but the competition is so *unbelievably* intense – even though I, and everybody else within ten feet of her, heard all about it in coma-inducing detail at the last PTA fundraiser. To make things even worse, Adam Downing, the head of the consortium investing in the expansion will be there, and I mustn't put a foot wrong because the whole dinner is about saying the right things and keeping him sweet before the final sign-off.

I arranged for Katy, the babysitter, to come at six to give myself time to get ready. I shower and wash my hair, and take heart from the sound of Finn's laughter drifting up the stairs. He likes Katy and she always comes armed with some new jokes to add to his collection.

I lean in to the bathroom mirror in my bra and knickers and study my face. Ian's made it very clear that he doesn't approve of 'war paint' – at least not on me – but this evening I need a mask to hide behind: concealer and foundation for the blemishes and dark circles, and a few subtle strokes of eye shadow and lip gloss to disguise the tension lines around my eyes and mouth. According to the YouTube tutorial paused on my phone, getting 'that dewy, fresh, natural look' is all about careful layering, then blending it all in with a damp sponge. When I'm done I step back and inspect the result, tilting my head from side to side. It's not bad. Even under the harsh bathroom spotlights it's impossible to see the join between the real me and the patched up, airbrushed version. I reach out my hand. 'Hello, I'm Ian's wife, Nicola. Lovely to meet you.' Now smile, and smile, and smile.

I drop the tubes and bottles into my bag so I can slip to the loo and touch up the cracks between courses. I pin up my hair, smooth down the flyaway bits at the side and lock in the look with a heavy squirt of extra-hold hairspray.

Ian is going for a drink with George, one of the other partners, straight from work, and meeting me at Mac and Orla's at eight. He chose what he wants me to wear before he left this morning. I'm glad. I couldn't face getting it wrong again, especially not for an occasion like this. I step into the clothes he's laid out on the bed. The grey trousers were a size too small when he bought them but they zip up easily now. I slip on the aubergine silk shirt, the mid-heel pumps and the pearl earrings and take another look in the mirror.

Eat your heart out, Gwen Dexter.

I squirt perfume behind my ears, grab my coat and run downstairs to say goodbye to Finn. He's playing snap with Katy, barely looking up as he submits to my kiss.

For once, I time it just right, and I'm in the hall, handing my coat to the Quinns' au pair just as Ian arrives with George. I smile at him, looking for approval. He runs his eyes from the top of my carefully tamped-down hair to the tip of my shiny pumps – and frowns a little. I pull back my shoulders. He gives me a tiny nod. We move into the sitting room and accept drinks from Mac, who is tall, bald and clearly on edge. The men join Orla and Amanda, the only female partner in the practice, and George's wife, Lennie, who are waging a full-throttle charm offensive on a man who must be Adam Downing. I'd imagined he'd be a hard-bitten, slick-suited City-type but this man is tall, thoughtful-looking and casually dressed. I nail on a smile and move away to where Amanda's husband, Luke, who's a big-wig consultant at the local hospital, is talking to an unbearably chic woman who must be Downing's wife: fair hair swept into a chignon, slanting cheekbones, ice blue eyes, a grey silk dress with what looks like a cashmere cardigan draped over it, and almost no make-up. I stand there feeling frumpy and awkward as Luke introduces us. 'This is Lydia Downing, she's a writer and this' – the tiniest of panicked pauses before a blink of relief – 'is Nicola Dexter. She's married to Ian, over there, and she helps out at the surgery.' His phone bleeps. He digs it out of his pocket and glances at the screen. 'Sorry, got to take this. I'm on call.'

'What do you write?' I ask, as he hurries away.

'Historical fiction.'

'I used to read a lot when I was younger, but I don't seem to get the time any more.'

'That's a shame,' she says. 'What sort of books do you like?'

'Oh, you know – thrillers, a bit of romance. Sometimes when I was a kid I'd run off to the library and stay there all day.' I smile, remembering my favourite corner of the fiction section, the narrow spot between the bookcases where, just for a few hours, I'd felt safe. 'I liked the smell, and the quiet, and after one of the librarians introduced me to Agatha Christie and Georgette Heyer, I think I must have devoured the lot.'

She smiles politely. I take a nervous sip of my fizzy water and it's a relief when Orla pokes her head around the door and calls us in to eat. Annoyed that Luke's hurried return to the hospital has messed up her seating plan, she whisks away a place setting, which leaves me sitting between Lydia and George. I groan inside. They don't seem particularly thrilled about it, either.

I unfold my napkin, slide a glance at the people around the table, a sheen of privilege and wealth on their candlelit faces, and look down at the gleaming array of silver cutlery laid out in front of me. *Outside in*, I tell myself. *Outside in.*

CHAPTER 26

Then

There was £500 in the roll of notes Donna threw on the table that morning, though looking back on it I'm sure Mo had given her more and she'd kept the rest for herself. The money covered a couple of nights in a Travelodge and a deposit on our new home – a dank little flat with a bedroom split into two by a flimsy partition that cut the window in half, a narrow kitchenette, an electricity meter that devoured an endless supply of coins, and rent we'd have to do pretty much anything that came our way to pay, which put an end to college and my dreams of getting into uni. When I got upset about it, Donna snapped at me to shut up because it was my fault we'd lost our cushy ride.

For the next few weeks I couldn't stop reading the updates on the investigation into the deaths at Sallowfield Court. Most of the coverage focused on Ryan Hurley – his playboy lifestyle, his grieving father, stuff like that. When they mentioned Jade they didn't know her name so they just called her 'the girl'. There was one piece I kept reading over and over.

> *The girl, who is believed to have been in her early teens, is described as being 5ft 3inches tall and of slim build. The police are asking any members of the public who may know her identity, or who may be concerned about the well-being of someone they know, to get in touch.*

After what Jade had told me about her family, I knew there was no one who had ever been concerned about her well-being, and no one who would be coming forward to identify her. Donna said that was a good thing. The less the police had to go on the better it would be for us.

For the next few months I got drunk every night to try to forget. Only I never could. Every time I closed my eyes I saw Jade's bruised, bloodied face. Sometimes she was dancing. More often she was dead.

Donna seemed to deal with it much better than I did. She'd got a new bloke, Marcus. Narrow head, dark spiky hair, cocky smile. He worked on the oil rigs and she met him at a club while he was down south on onshore leave with his mates. I only saw him once – he was a loser, everyone could see that. Everyone except Donna. They had this long-distance thing going: phone calls late into the night, texts pinging back and forth. She'd only known him for five minutes but all she could talk about was going up to Scotland and moving in with him. Meanwhile brown envelopes were piling up on the mat. Council tax, water rates… who cared? We couldn't pay any of them. If we'd had anyone to turn to we might have got help. As it was, we just muddled along, hoping that if we ignored them it would be all right. Two lost, vulnerable eighteen-year-olds who thought they knew it all and who, when it came to it, didn't have a clue about anything.

It was the same with the pregnancy. Who knew it was even possible to fall pregnant, still have your periods and not get morning sickness, weird food cravings or any more of a bump than you get from a hangover bloat, or to wake up one morning and go from zero to full-blown, gut-wrenching labour without you or your best friend suspecting a thing? Not Donna, that's for sure. Certainly not me.

CHAPTER 27

Orla serves Persian lamb sprinkled with pomegranate seeds and some kind of spinach and herb frittata, which arrives in neat little squares. The compliments on how amazing she is and how wonderful it all looks are barely out of the way before she starts in on Maddy and Wilf's academic success.

'What about Finn, Nicci?' Orla says, her tone swerving sharply from triumph to sympathy. 'How's he doing, now?' It's the *now,* pitched oh-so-perfectly to imply some long-simmering problem, that puts her up there with the best.

'He's fine, thank you, Orla.'

But she's not done with me yet. 'Remind me to give you the number of the private tutor that helped our neighbour's son. He works with *all* sorts of children, and I've heard he does *wonders* with dyslexia.'

'Finn doesn't have dyslexia,' I say quietly. 'He's very mildly dyspraxic.' I hate that I'm having to explain my gentle, sensitive boy to her in front of strangers – so what if he can be a bit clumsy and uncoordinated?

She waves a dismissive hand. 'Well, whatever it is, I'm so glad you've finally got a diagnosis. It must have been such a worry not knowing what was wrong.'

Wrong? I glance at Ian. He's watching me levelly. I look away, flustered and annoyed. Has he been discussing Finn with Orla?

'Are you still working with that Next Steps charity, Nicci? I've heard they do wonderful work.' It's Amanda, throwing me a lifeline, but why did she have to pick this one?

I'm struggling to come up with an answer when Ian cuts in: 'It was so draining and thankless she decided to give it up,' he says. 'You need proper training to deal with kids like that. Well-meaning amateurs usually end up doing more harm than good.'

'Oh, I don't know,' Orla says. 'I would have thought Nicci's first-hand experience of the care system would trump professional expertise any day.'

It's a low blow even for Orla, and I find myself blushing hot and red. I reach for my glass of sparkling water and sip it slowly, wishing I had the guts to chuck it in her face. Thankfully the flow of chatter moves on to the pressing topic of second helpings of lamb, and my thoughts turn inwards, staggering queasily from the blackbird, to a woman in a red hat whispering *Tell your mummy I said hello,* to the photo of me and Jade on the edge of Ryan Hurley's pool.

Lydia is speaking to me. I turn to look at her. 'Sorry, I was miles away.'

'I was asking how old your son is?' she says, her voice warm.

'Six.'

She studies my face. 'You must have been very young when he was born.'

'I… I was.'

'I take it he's not Ian's.'

'No. But he's a great stepdad.'

'And so looking forward to being a *real* dad.' It's Orla, butting in. That woman has the hearing of a bat.

'Any news on that front and you'll be the first to know, Orla,' Ian says, levelly.

Lydia spears a shred of lamb with her fork, concentrating hard on her food. She waits until Orla has switched her attention back to Adam – some raucous story about a woman at her gym – and then she says quietly: 'It must have been hard for you having a baby that young.' There's real sympathy in her eyes, no judgement or pity, just concern. I sit for a moment, not saying anything. 'Sorry, I didn't mean to pry.'

'It's all right. I don't mind. It *was* hard and the worst thing was, back then I didn't have a clue about taking care of myself, let alone a baby.' The silence between us grows intimate and strange, as if somehow we are connected.

'And you were brought up in care?' she says at last.

I nod.

'Well, I admire you even more. It must have been doubly difficult without family to support you. Did you have anyone to help out?'

I feel my pulse jumping. 'There was a neighbour who helped with the birth.'

'No midwife?'

'No time. Finn decided he was ready and just popped out.'

I look away, remembering the otherworldly moments after Finn was born, holding him in my arms, looking down at his crumpled face and feeling a gush of love like a physical burn that ran down my spine and sent a shudder through every muscle in my body. He was so tiny, so vulnerable. So perfect.

'You must have missed out on university,' Lydia is saying, her voice so low I can barely hear her.

'I always hoped I'd find a way to do it later,' I say. 'You know, distance learning or something. I wanted to be a social worker. Catch the lost, angry kids before disillusion set in. Do all the things the system failed to do for me. But Ian... well, he's not keen.'

'Why not?'

'He thinks I've already got my work cut out, what with the job and the house and Finn.'

Mac tips a bottle of wine in my direction and raises a bristly eyebrow. I hold my hand over my glass and shake my head, a smile fixed on my face.

Lydia nods a yes and keeps her eyes on her glass until Mac has refilled it and moved on. 'Did you ever think of giving your baby up?' she says, barely moving her lips.

The question is so shocking, so intrusive, I'm stunned. Her hand trembles as she raises the glass to her mouth and all at once she seems close to tears. 'I'm sorry,' she says. 'That was unforgivable. It's none of my business.'

I stare at my plate not knowing what to say. Cutlery clinks on china, laughter ripples, my heart hammers.

'I got pregnant in my last year of school,' she says, her voice dropping so low it's as if she's talking to someone I can't see. I lean in closer, feel the brush of her arm, smell the spicy sharpness of her perfume. 'I wanted to defer my place at Oxford, have the baby and find a way to go back to my studies. Instead, my mother organised an adoption. I saw my daughter for a few minutes before they took her away. I think about her every day.'

My indignation thins and melts. 'Have you tried to trace her?'

'Yes, as soon as she turned eighteen. I found her, too.' She presses two fingers to her mouth and swallows hard. 'She didn't want to see me. It's ironic. All through the pregnancy my mother kept saying, why destroy your life when you can have all the children you want once you've got a career and you're married and settled? But Adam and I tried for years and it never happened.' Her expression is glacial but beneath the table, her slim fingers worry the hem of her dress. I reach down and squeeze her hand. 'We even bought a great big house with a garden, all ready for the kids we never had.'

'I came close,' I say.

She turns to look at me. 'To what?'

'To giving Finn up. Just once. When he was about two weeks old.' In an instant I'm back in that moment: rain on my skin, the shimmer of wet leaves, the smell of damp earth, the sound of Finn's cries, the slice of light in the darkness as the door of the vicarage swings open. The flood of certainty when he was returned to my arms.

Lydia is speaking. I blink hard. 'Sorry?'

'I asked if that charity you worked for is still looking for volunteers?'

'Um... probably.'

'I'd love to get involved, especially if there was a teenage mum who was struggling. It would be good to help.'

'Sure,' I say. I shift around a little and drop my voice. 'Give me your number before we leave. I'll pass it on to the director.'

'Well, Nicci,' Orla says, loudly enough to pierce the chatter around the table. 'Now you've given up working for that charity, the membership secretary at the tennis club would love some help. Seeing as Mac says you do such a good job with the practice admin, it would be a shame to waste your talents.'

I glance at Ian. He gives me that look. The one that keeps me in line.

'I'm glad Mac's happy with my work,' I say. 'Unfortunately I've got more than enough on my plate at the moment.'

'Adam's wife seemed a bit of a cold fish,' Ian says, as I nose the car out of the Quinns' driveway.

'She was hard work,' I say, keen to divert suspicion from our shared confessions, 'but I did my best.'

'What were you talking about? It looked pretty intense.'

'Oh, you know...'

'I don't know. That's why I'm asking.'

'She was telling me about her books.'

'What books?'

'She writes historical novels. Tudor intrigues, scandals at court.'

'Why did you swap numbers?'

How did he even see? I thought we'd been so subtle out there in the hallway as we'd slipped on our coats.

'She thought I might like to go along to a talk she's giving at the community centre. I won't, though. Not my kind of thing.' I accelerate into the silent street.

'You should go,' he says. 'Keep her onside.'

'Why? Are you worried Adam's not going to approve the financing?'

'Oh, no.' A satisfied smile as he crosses his arms and settles back against the headrest. 'After tonight, the practice expansion is pretty much a done deal. But if it goes well, I've got a couple of other projects I'd like him to back.'

He closes his eyes and I blink into the darkness ahead, my heart heavy with Lydia's loss. To be forced to give up her child. I don't know how she survived the pain.

CHAPTER 28

'Smile!'

Finn hugs his football and beams up at me, a big gappy grin on his face, so proud in his brand-new blue and black team strip. I snap a couple of close-ups to send to Joyce. 'Now, one foot on the ball and hands on your hips.' I widen the shot to get the Parkview Dental logo in the frame for the team album and click. 'Look at you, Finnsy.'

Finn giggles. I pull an 'Oops' face and glance back to the house to make sure that Ian hasn't heard me use that silly baby name. 'OK, now go and stand by the goal.'

I take a couple more shots and slip my phone into the back pocket of my jeans. 'All right. Pancakes coming up! Ready in five minutes.'

I leave him kicking the ball at the wall and go inside. There's already a rich herby smell coming from the slow roast lamb I put in the oven as soon as I got up. I pop in two scrubbed baking potatoes so lunch will be ready as soon as we get back, and turn my attention to the pancakes. I've made the wholemeal batter exactly as the recipe said and set out the sliced bananas and blueberries in little bowls.

Ian, bronzed and handsome in his navy tracksuit, a whistle dangling around his neck, sips coffee as he looks at his phone.

'Mum just texted. She wants to come over on Tuesday evening.'

My heart sinks. 'Oh. Right. Any particular reason?'

'She's decided she wants to go on a winter cruise. Apparently, she needs my help to choose where.'

I flash back to what Annabel told Susy about Gwen's second marriage: the years of torment that Ian has never mentioned to me. 'Is she looking for love?'

'What?'

'Well, you know what they say about cruises.'

'No, I don't.' He laughs. Quick and spiky. 'And I don't think I want to.'

'I just mean she must get lonely now she's divorced.'

'I doubt it.' He stops laughing and goes quiet for a moment. 'Hugh was a mistake. Now he's out of her life, she's happier than she's been for years.'

'What about you?' I say, as casually as I can. 'How did you feel about him?'

'He was loathsome.' His mouth twitches. His eyes deaden and grow distant.

I wait for him to say more. Nothing. That's it. All I get. But it looks like maybe Annabel was right.

He goes over to mark Gwen's visit on the calendar and I drop two spoonfuls of batter onto the griddle. I'm waiting, spatula in hand, for the bubbles to form when the doorbell rings. I look up as Ian puts down his coffee and goes to open it. Voices. The front door shuts. Voices again, coming down the hall. Ian's and a woman's. She's laughing. I know that laugh.

'Hey, Nicci!'

I falter forward, a tiny step and grip the edge of the counter.

Donna. Unmistakeable yet utterly changed.

Beneath a heavy layer of make-up her skin is bloodless and her thin jumper is slightly felted and worn at the cuffs. She flings her arms around me and hugs me tight. I close my eyes, rocked by the smell of cheap perfume, cigarettes and something earthy that spins me back to another time, another life, another me; a lonely kid craving comfort – and then the fear surges back and I hold the spatula and the batter bowl high, glad of an excuse to keep my hands to myself.

'My God, you look amazing! And this house! Just wow! It's been ages,' she says.

I look imploringly at Ian, hoping he'll tell her we're about to go out. He sees my unease. His eyes dart back to her, almost as if he's enjoying seeing me squirm. 'So, Donna, how do you know Nicci?'

'We were in care together. Survivors of Ma Burton's school of hard knocks.'

'Actually, Donna,' I say, 'this isn't a good time. We're about to go out.'

I glare at Ian, willing him to back me up and throw this living, breathing flotsam from my past out of his house; to slam the door on her and extract a promise that I'd gladly make: to never speak to this woman again.

Instead, he goes on gazing at her, strangely fascinated. 'How long were you at the Burtons?'

'A couple of years, give or take. Nic had already been there for ages when I arrived. I was like a big sister to her, always there to pick up the pieces when she messed up. Which was pretty much all the time.'

To my horror Ian laughs. 'No change there, then.'

Donna relaxes, enjoying herself. '"Cack-handed Cahill" Burton used to call her.'

Ian lifts the cafetière. 'Coffee?'

'I wouldn't want to disturb you.'

'It's not a problem.'

'Then, yes. I'd love one.'

She's pitching her voice, raising the tone, making it posher and sexier. She always was a chameleon. Always skilled at reading her audience. Finding people's weak spots, telling them what they want to hear. And it looks like what Ian wants to hear right now is details about my teenage years.

The years I've always been so careful to gloss over.

'Black, please.'

'So what was Nicci like as a kid?'

'To be honest, she let people walk all over her and she got bullied left, right, and centre. I asked her once what she wanted to be when she grew up. You know what she said? She said, "I want to be like you, Donna, tough." I told her to fake it. But it wasn't in her nature.'

She smiles and so does Ian, but she's not looking at him; her eyes have pulled away and she's gazing at the garden through the bifold doors to where Finn is crossing the lawn. He walks up the steps, sits down and pulls off his new football boots.

'Like I said, Donna, now's not a good time. Give me your number and we'll meet for a proper catch-up in the week.'

'There's no rush,' Ian says. 'You don't need to be there for the warm-up, and the match doesn't start till eleven.'

The door slides back and Finn comes in. He looks from me to Donna, surprised to see a stranger in the kitchen.

'Hello, Finn,' she says.

His mouth falls opens in wonder. 'How do you know my name?'

'Oh, I know all about you. Your mummy and I are old friends.' She steps a little closer to him and drops into a stagey whisper. 'In fact, I was holding her hand when you were born.'

'Do you want to see me shoot a goal?' Finn says, making for the door.

I feel sick, unable to speak, glad when Ian intervenes. 'Not today, fella.' He turns his eyes on Donna and hands her a mug of coffee. 'You can show Mummy's friend your football skills next time she comes.' He glances at me as if he's waiting to see my reaction.

The fire alarm shrieks. I spin around. Smoke is rising from the griddle. I grab the iron handle and scorch my hand. I let out a gasp. Tears of pain sting my eyes as I reach across the counter for the oven gloves. Donna gets there first and slips them on. With swift, easy movements she lifts the griddle to the bin and scrapes the burnt pancakes into the rubbish. An oily hiss as she dumps the hot pan in the sink and runs the tap. I dash over to the alarm and poke the handle of the spatula at the override button, standing on tiptoe and spattering batter onto the floor with each jab. The shriek stops but the scream in my head goes on and on.

I fling open the back door to let the smoke escape. I shove my throbbing hand under the tap. Fresh pain shoots up my arm. The water's hot. I ram the mixer tap the other way and test the flow with my left hand as I wait for the water to run cold.

'Oh, Nicci, clumsy as ever,' Donna says, rolling her eyes in a play of affectionate despair but it's Ian she's looking at.

He frowns and shakes his head. 'Darling, how many times have I told you to use the gloves? Is your hand all right?'

'It's fine,' I say. 'Can you pass me a frying pan?'

'Don't worry about the pancakes.' He snaps a couple of bananas from the bunch in the bowl and takes a handful of protein bars from the cupboard. 'These will keep us going. I don't want to be late. Bye, Donna. See you again, maybe.'

'I hope so,' she says, with a sideways look at me.

I ignore her and hurry into the hall. One-handed, I help Finn into his puffa, my burnt fingers cupped into a useless claw. 'Have fun, sweetheart.' I drop a kiss onto the top of his head.

'Don't forget the oranges,' Ian calls over his shoulder, as they head to his car.

I shut the front door and lean into it, trying to steady my breath before I force myself back down the hall to the kitchen.

Donna is looking at the photos on the fridge, her coffee mug cradled between her fingers.

'What do you want?' I ask.

She turns and looks at me, cold green eyes in that too-familiar face. 'My son.'

CHAPTER 29

Then

Bathed in sweat, Donna let out a deep groan and dropped to her knees, one hand gripping the side of the bath, the other clamped around mine as she threw back her head. I thought she was dying.

'It's all right.' The words skidded on my tongue. 'I'll call an ambulance.'

'No!' A hiss of pain. 'Get Anja.'

'What for?'

Donna rocked forward, a shudder catching her bent body. 'Just get her. She'll know what to do.'

'Anja!' I yelled for our Polish neighbour, glad for once that the walls in our dingy little block were paper-thin. 'Come quickly. Please! It's Donna!'

Within seconds Anja was banging on the door. I ran to let her in and dragged her to the bathroom.

Donna, who was bucking and writhing, let out a long slow moan.

'I'm calling an ambulance,' I said.

'No time.' Anja lurched forward. She pulled down Donna's track pants, snatched a towel off the bathroom door and thrust it between her legs. The next few minutes unfolded in slow motion as I realised what was happening. Pale sunlight through the frosted window, tendons tightening in Donna's neck, a rush of watery blood and mucus, a bellow of pain, a baby slithering onto the towel, a gasp bubbling to my lips.

'It's a boy, Donna. You've had a baby boy.' Anja moved quickly, scooping him up and lifting him up by his ankles. His arms sprang wide as if to embrace the world. A moment of silence and then his tiny ribcage shuddered out a cry.

'Here, go to Mamma,' Anja crooned, swinging him upright and folding the corners of the towel across his body.

Donna let out a low animal grunt, pushed herself up to standing and shook her head. 'You take him, Nic.'

Her voice was flat. Her eyes lifeless. I put it down to shock and pain. I sat on the edge of the bath and held him as Anja reached for a pair of nail scissors and cut the cord. Then she dampened the corner of a towel and wiped him clean. I watched her face. I watched her mouth.

'What's wrong?'

She tutted quietly. 'He is very small. When babies come early like this, sometimes they get problems with their breathing.'

I stroked one of his tiny hands. 'I'll call an ambulance.'

'No!' Donna said, suddenly animated. 'No doctors. I'm not having the authorities poking their noses in.'

The baby let out another cry. High and sharp. She didn't look at him, she just kept looking at me, watching me as if she was scared I might go ahead and call an ambulance anyway.

'See,' she said. 'He's fine. Lungs like an ox.'

I clasped him to me and rocked him. 'Did you have any idea you were pregnant?'

She shook her head, her face suddenly contorting in agony.

'Take baby outside, Nicci,' Anja said. 'Placenta is coming.'

I carried him into my room and sat with him by the window, gazing out across the rooftops while he slept. The sky was pink, the world was stirring, a little life had just begun.

*

Donna refused to feed him herself – she said it would make her boobs droop – so I went rushing out to buy bottles and formula. I even managed to grab a few baby things from the Oxfam shop. When I got back, Anja had gone and Donna was lying in bed staring at the wall, the baby bedded down in an old suitcase on the floor beside her, still wrapped in a towel. I held up the things I'd bought – little cardigans, tiny babygrows and a wrap-around carrier thing for newborns. 'Look at this,' I said. 'Half of it's brand new, still got its labels on.'

She swivelled around and rolled her eyes. 'Any chance of a cup of tea?'

I made us both one and fixed a bottle for the baby, testing the temperature by squirting it on the inside of my wrist like I used to when I fed the toddlers at Ma Burton's. I brought the bottle and the mugs into her room and hovered by her bed. 'Do you know who his father is?'

She accepted the mug I was holding out. 'Does it matter?'

'Of course it does.'

'That's a shame.' She lifted her chin and tugged a hand through her damp hair.

'You've really got no idea?'

She shook her head. I looked down at the sleeping baby, sadness stirring inside me, cresting beneath my ribs. No father for this little one. No aunts, uncles, cousins or grandparents, either.

'I've been thinking about names,' I said, perching on the side of her bed and making an effort to sound upbeat. She gazed at me, her eyes blank. 'What do you think about Aiden or Jamie, or maybe Finn?'

'Give it a rest, Nic, can't you see I'm knackered?'

'He needs a name.'

'All right… Finn. If that's what you want.'

The snap of the letter box caused the baby to stir and half open his eyes.

'Can you take him?' she said. 'I need to sleep.'

I lifted him onto my shoulder, gently rubbing his back as I walked to the door and tugged the letters free. I tore them open using one hand and my teeth. One was a summons for non-payment of rates. The other was an eviction notice from the landlord, giving us two weeks to quit.

Donna went through the motions of giving Finn his bottles and changing his nappy to keep him quiet; other than that, she was numb to his needs. It was me who cuddled and cosseted him, took him to sleep in my bed and rocked him when he fussed. I was so worried about the way she was with him I went online and read up about postnatal depression. Was that what she had? She seemed happy enough when she wasn't with him and she'd perked up no end when, two days after the birth, she'd jammed herself into her tightest jeans, slapped on some make-up and gone out.

I begged her to forget about Scotland; I said I'd find somewhere for the two of us to live and we could look after Finn together, Donna and Nicci against the world, the way it used to be. But she was adamant she was still going. I'd hear her on the phone to Marcus, chatting and laughing, making plans. No mention of the baby. Sure, he wasn't the father, but you'd think he'd have shown some kind of interest. All the while I wandered around in a daze, exhausted by the broken nights and too upset at the thought of losing them both to think about where I was going to live.

Donna was a ruthless packer. The night before the bailiffs were due I stood in the doorway of her room, holding Finn, begging her not to go, while she divided everything into two piles: stuff to take, stuff to leave behind.

I was firmly in the leave-behind category.

'Give him here,' she said, when she was done. She held out her hands.

I clutched him tighter. 'Donna, please don't do this. We can look after him together. You and me. Please.'

She came towards me. 'Come on. We've been through this. I've got a train to catch.'

She slipped one hand around him. I pulled back, thinking she was going to grab him and tear him away. Instead, she dropped her other hand onto my shoulder, pulled me close and dropped her forehead against mine. For a moment we stood there entwined, the three of us, so close I could smell the smoke on her breath. Softly she said: 'I'm sorry, Nic. I have to do this. Can't you see? This is my one chance to have a proper life instead of living on the edge and struggling to make do. Marcus is a good guy. He's got a nice flat, he earns decent money, and he loves me.'

Tears trickled down my face. 'You'll let me come and visit?'

'Sure. Once I'm settled you can come up on the train.'

She slid both hands around Finn's tiny body. I let him go and watched as she buckled him into the baby carrier and picked up her bags. 'See you, Nic.'

I heard him cry out as the door slammed behind her – a startled mewl of distress. Hearing his cries fade with her footsteps was a physical pain, a piece of my heart being stretched and stretched, as terrible as the grief I'd felt the day my mother decided I wasn't worth living for. I ran to the window, tripping over a bag of babygrows and a packet of nappies, and watched, bewildered, as Donna moved in and out of the dirty yellow glow of the street lamps, clutching a holdall with one hand and dragging her suitcase with the other. Why hadn't she bothered with any of the baby stuff I'd bought her? Surely she couldn't afford to buy it all new once she got to Scotland? Struck by a terrible thought, I grabbed my coat and ran out after her, darting into driveways and ducking behind hedges so she wouldn't see me. Just before the station she turned off. Finn's yells grew louder. She didn't seem to notice. She was more interested in checking her phone. She passed a church and stopped at the end of drive that led to a big old house. The sign on the gate said 'St John's Vicarage', picked out in faded gold paint. I crouched behind a tree and watched as she walked up the drive. She lifted Finn out of the carrier, laid him in the holdall and set it down on the doorstep.

She stood for a moment looking down at him, then she rang the bell and darted back to the road.

CHAPTER 30

'You gave up your rights to him the day you dumped him. I'm the one who rescued him, loved him, and gave him the chance of a decent future.'

'I'm still his mother,' Donna says. 'It's only natural I should want him back.'

'Natural? *You?* It's been six years, Donna. Don't kid me this is some sudden burst of maternal feeling.'

'I would have come before if I could.'

'What stopped you?'

'I had… some trouble.'

I look at her dropped head, the greyish pallor of her skin, the hard line of her mouth, the DIY tattoos on her hands.

'You were in prison.' She doesn't answer. 'You've just got out, haven't you? What were you in for? Theft, drug trafficking, fraud, *arson?*'

She's lifted her head and she's moving now, circling me, taking control. 'I'm not here to answer your questions. I'm here to take back my boy.'

I turn with her. 'How did you know I had him?'

'I went back to the vicarage that night and looked through the window. Just to check they'd taken him in.' She runs a bitten nail along the smooth edge of the granite worktop, picks up a peach, takes a bite and drops it onto the worktop. 'And there you were, doing the whole desperate teen-mum act. Tears and everything, as I recall.'

I feel a flicker of hope. If Reverend Michaels is still alive, then he and his wife can help me prove that Finn had been abandoned. When I tell them I lied about being his mother to save him from a life in care, they'd be on my side. 'No judge is going to give you custody when they find out you left him on a doorstep in the freezing cold and then ran off to your boyfriend.'

'You're right. If you got your day in court you'd most likely get to keep him, even though lying to the registrar when you register a birth is a crime. The thing is, this won't get to court.'

'Oh yes, it will. My friend's a lawyer, a good one. She won't let you—'

'I don't care how many lawyer friends you've got. You're going to hand Finn over without a peep. What's more, you're going to tell the authorities that I had... oh, I don't know, postnatal depression and I left him with you so I could get the treatment I needed to straighten my life out, and that we've been in contact all this time. You're going to say I sent you money when I had it and of course there have been all those calls and photos that kept me going when things didn't work out and I ended up in prison.'

'You're insane. Why would I lie? I won't do it.'

'You don't have a choice.'

'Try me.'

'You got the photo of you and Jade.'

'You can't prove that's me.'

'That's just a screen grab. Hurley had cameras everywhere, and there's plenty of footage that shows your face, clear as day. It doesn't look good, Nic. Not good at all.'

'It was an accident.'

'That's what you tell yourself. It's not what it will look like to a jury. At best they'll see manslaughter; at worst, well, who knows?'

Her words plunge me into a whole new world of horror. I need to get my bearings but the roaring in my head won't die down.

I close my eyes, barely able to speak. 'You know that's not what happened. I was trying to help her.'

She opens her bag, takes out a thumb drive and holds it up. 'See for yourself.' Moving over to the worktop she deletes the pancake recipe from my laptop and shoves the drive into the USB port. 'Go on. Take a look.'

So many tiny noises from all around the house: the tick of the carriage clock, the whirr of the fan oven, the sigh of the boiler.

I click, stroke the mouse pad, click again. The file opens. The air around me presses in. Four grainy views of Ryan Hurley's lamp-lit terrace flicker into life. There's Jade, pale and slight, haunting the frame on spindly heels, one arm hugging her body, the other snaking above her head. And there I am. Taller than she is, sturdier too, and clearly angry and aggressive as she turns towards me. Watching myself on this silent loop of film, I see what the world would see: a skinny kid dancing on her own, minding her own business, and me rushing at her, grabbing her, fighting with her, pushing her into the water and standing there watching while she drowns.

My mouth opens. Words come out. 'Where did you get this?'

'Mo got me to empty the recorders before he set fire to the house. He wanted to make sure all the discs were destroyed, but I… kept a few. I had some half-baked plan to give it a few years, then auction off edited highlights to the interested parties. Stupid idea – far too dangerous. I realised that as soon as I worked out who some of those guests actually were. So I hid the discs away and forgot about them. Who would have thought it was the footage of you that would come in useful? Just goes to show you never can tell.'

'If you send this to the police I'll tell them the truth and take you down with me.' For a few feverish moments I think I've won. Even Donna isn't crazy enough to risk mutual destruction.

She takes a sip from her mug. 'What truth would that be, Nic?'

'How about that Mo was a pimp and a drug dealer who rented Jade out to that creep Tommo who raped her, beat her up and pumped her full of drugs because he got a kick out of hurting underage girls? That it was *you* who fed Hurley the drugs that killed him, and you and Mo who set fire to Hurley's house to destroy the evidence.'

Donna shrugs. 'Good luck with proving any of that. I destroyed every frame of footage that put me and Mo in that house.' She pours herself more coffee and wanders around, mug in hand, touching glasses and crockery, moving jars, inspecting labels, deliberately leaving everything askew.

'Everyone at the party knows you were there.'

'How are you planning on finding them? You don't even know their names.' She comes so close I can see the make-up clogging her pores. 'And believe me, if you did track any one of those people down, they'd find a way to keep you quiet. Money, fear and influence. It's a powerful combination.'

It crashes in on me all at once, that there's no way out of this. I resort to pleading. 'Please, Donna. Finn needs me.'

'What's so special about you?'

I want to say I'm his mother, only I know that would rile her. I take a breath and say, 'I love him. I understand him. I know what makes him happy. There's more to bringing up a kid than feeding it and clothing it. It's a full-time job.'

'I'll manage.'

'It's hard on your own.'

She picks up a framed photo of Ian with me and Finn on a Norfolk beach, a laughing, windblown selfie. 'Who says I'm on my own?'

'Are you still with that Marcus guy?'

'I moved on. Turned out we weren't compatible.'

'What does your new bloke think about being a stepdad? It's not easy taking on someone else's kid.'

She tips back her chin and laughs. 'Oh, he just can't wait.'

'You could have a kid together. You and him.'

'But we want Finn. And we're going to have him.'

I look at the grime etched beneath her nails, the scabby jumper, the chunks missing from the heel of her boot.

'How are you going to live?'

'Don't you worry about that,' she says, a note of triumph in her voice.

'Why not? Have either of you even got a job?'

'No need,' she says. 'I'm… going to be coming into some money.'

I stare at her, incredulous. 'Where from?'

'You're not the only one who deserves a bit of luck, you know.'

'It's some scam, isn't it?'

'No. That's the beauty of it. It's all perfectly legit. In fact I'll be seeing the lawyer in a couple of weeks and once we've got things rolling I'll be back for Finn.'

'Ian won't stand by and let him go to a stranger.'

'If your husband makes any trouble, that footage is going straight to the police. So you'd better talk him round. Oh, wait. Does he even know that Finn's not yours?'

I shake my head. 'I didn't want him asking questions about you. I wanted a clean break from the past.' I look up at her, barely able to hide my contempt. '*Our* past. It felt safer that way.'

'Oh dear, then he won't be best pleased when he finds out what a liar he married. Still, I suppose it's better than seeing his wife go down for manslaughter.'

It's what she always used to do: stick the knife in, then give it a little twist just to show me who was in charge.

She plants herself in front of the calendar, lifting the pages. 'Well, look at you, missy, with your PTA meetings, gym sessions and half-term play dates.' She tosses her head and stalks off into the sitting room, still holding the photo, bumping her fingers along the bookshelves, picking up the chess pieces set out mid-battle and putting them down in the wrong places.

'Why are you doing this, Donna? You don't even like kids.'

She looks up, her eyes hard and cold. 'Because he's mine and because you owe me.'

'I don't owe you anything.'

'I had a future working for Mo. Prospects. Because of you I lost it all. But you, you got to play happy families in a nice house with a cute husband and *my* son! Well, not anymore.' She lets go of the photo. It falls face down on the polished floor. Overcome by a suffocating sense of helplessness, I watch her lift her foot, press it into the back of the frame and swivel it until the glass cracks.

She plonks herself down on the sofa, leans back and stretches up her arms. 'You know what? Right now I'd kill for a long, hot bath.'

'You're not having one here.'

'That's not very hospitable.'

'There isn't time. I have to get to Finn's match.'

'No problem. I'll have a bath while you're out, then I'll take him with me when you get back.'

'Oh, for God's sake.'

She stands up leisurely. I walk her up to the family bathroom and throw open the door. She looks down at the basket of plastic toys and the blue whale bath mat. 'Come on, Nic, you can do better than this.' She flounces away down the landing, peering around doors until she finds the master bedroom. She does a twirl, taking in the fitted wardrobes, silk curtains and king-size bed. She fingers the smooth cotton of the duvet. 'Nice,' she murmurs, and strolls into the en suite.

I stand frozen in the doorway, watching her in the glare of the vanity lights as she turns on the taps and glugs half a bottle of scented oil into the tub.

'Why bother taunting me with the dead bird and the Mojo's box? Not to mention picking the lock on my back gate and putting broken glass in my tyre. Why not just confront me?'

'Broken glass?' She picks a fresh towel from the unit in the corner. 'Nah, that wasn't me, but yeah to the rest of it.'

If the glass wasn't her then who was it? Is she lying? My mind whirrs as she speaks, uneasy thoughts stirring deep in the back of my brain.

'I was watching you in your shiny little bubble and I thought hey, missy, you need reminding that people like you don't get to walk away from who you are and what you did.'

'How long have you been watching me?'

'Long enough.'

'To do what?'

'To make sure that the kid you were palming off as yours was Finn. I mean, what would be the point if you'd dumped him and popped out one of your own?'

'Make sure? How?'

'That time in the park. I got him to spit on a tissue so I could clean his face. Then I had his saliva tested. It's easy these days. Though one look at him was enough.'

'He doesn't look anything like you,' I snap.

'Maybe not.' She throws me a look that seems to darken the already bad energy in that room 'But he's the image of his dad. Same hair, same eyes, same nose.'

'You told me you didn't know who his dad was.'

'I lied.'

That hurts, even now. I'd thought back then that we'd shared the important stuff. The way sisters do.

'Why?'

'It was none of your business.'

'Is his father the bloke you're with now? Is it him who wants Finn back?'

'No. His real dad's... out of the picture.' A flash of something, pain or maybe regret, flickers across her face. 'Permanently.' All at once the hardness is back. 'Are you done with the interrogation?'

She peels off her jumper, dangles it for a moment and drops it languidly to the floor. Her body is pale, and there are thin white scars on her wrists and faded track marks down her arms. Turning to face me, she undoes the fly of her jeans, button by button. With the last one unfastened she hooks her thumbs through the belt loops and wriggles the jeans over her hips, revealing the pale flesh of her belly. I look away.

'Do you remember the night he was born?' she says, her voice low and taunting. 'Plopped out of me like a scrawny little pig, and you stood there and cried.'

'Can you hurry up? I've got to do the oranges for the match.'

'Don't let me stop you. While you're there, make me a sandwich, will you? Bacon, lettuce and tomato. White bread.'

'I don't have white bread. Or bacon.'

'Brown then, and cheese, ham – whatever you've got.'

I hesitate, loath to leave her up here on her own, but what more harm can she do than threaten to take my boy? She drops her shabby bra and knickers onto the tiles and tests the foaming water with her toe. The black varnish on her nails is chipped and her feet are grimy, as if she's been crashing in a place where hot water isn't on tap.

'Go on then.' She dismisses me with a flick of her hand. 'I'm starving.'

I walk out and lean back against the bedroom door. I've never felt fear like this before. I've felt scared, sad, miserable and angry, but this is a whole new level of terror. And there's no one I can turn to. No one who can help me. No one I can trust with the truth.

Downstairs I move around the sitting room, my legs buckling, my hands unsteady as I rearrange the cushions, straighten the vases and put the chess pieces back where they should be, four moves back from the shocking finale of Ian's favourite game. I fetch the dustpan and brush and kneel down to pick up the smashed glass. With a tremor in my hand I turn over the photo frame. Finn's face stares out at me – wide set eyes, thick fair hair, that dimple in his chin. From upstairs comes the faint sound of Donna singing in my bath, careless and off-key.

I hurry into the kitchen, empty the dustpan into the bin and put the photo back onto the shelf. If Ian notices the glass is missing before I can get it replaced I'll say it was me who dropped it. It might even amuse him. Cack-Handed Cahill, at it again.

I take an orange from the wooden crate on the counter and a knife from the rack. I touch the blade – hardened Japanese steel – against my thumb, and stab the tip into the peel. A spurt of juice burns my scorched palm. I jam the handle against my wound and slice down, again and again, cutting into the soft flesh of the orange, working the blade, letting anger and hatred numb the pain.

By the time Donna comes downstairs I've slapped bread and cheese into a couple of slices of bread, cleared up the kitchen and filled a large Tupperware with quartered oranges. She's been through my drawers and helped herself to some of my favourite clothes: skinny jeans, and a white T-shirt under a pink cotton jumper. Her damp hair is fragrant with my shampoo, her newly cleansed face shiny with my moisturiser.

She scrapes out a stool and sits down at the counter.

I drop the plate in front of her and draw in a deep breath. 'How long have I got?'

She sinks her teeth into the sandwich and chews, taking her time. 'Like I said I should be seeing the lawyer in the next couple of weeks when he's back in the country then I'll be renting a place to live as soon as he advances me some money. Finn can stay with you till then. It will give you a bit of time to come clean with Ian and get Finn used to the idea that you're not his mother. I don't want him kicking up a fuss when he moves in with me.' She pulls out her phone. 'Give me your number.'

I murmur it to her. She chews as she punches it into her contacts and then, with a sideways look my way, calls it to make sure I've given her the right one. She throws down the remains of her sandwich and picks up her coat. On the way to the door she passes my handbag. She stops, unzips it and takes out my purse. She snaps it open and pulls out the notes. 'Is this all the cash you've got?'

'Yes.'

She stuffs the money into her pocket. 'Get me another couple of hundred, will you? I'll drop by for it on Wednesday. It'll give me another chance to see my son.'

I follow her down the hall. She turns in the doorway. 'Just so we're clear. You try any tricks to stop me getting him back, that footage goes straight to the police, along with a note explaining exactly who you are and where to find you. You never know, they might even pin the fire on you, too.'

She yanks the door open and slams it shut behind her.

I press my hand to my mouth and run upstairs. She's trashed the bedroom, strewn clothes across the floor and ransacked my drawers. I run around, shoving everything into the bottom of the wardrobe, hoping I'll get a chance to sort it out properly before Ian notices the mess. The en suite is disgusting: dirty water splashed all over the floor, Donna's old clothes dumped in a sopping heap, and hairs and grime floating in the bath. I pull out the plug and waste precious minutes with a cloth and a bottle of spray cleaner trying to erase every trace of Donna.

Only, I can't.

The girl who for so long has been a memory, a name from my past, a scar on my heart, is now back in my life threatening to take my child.

CHAPTER 31

I drop Donna's clothes in the bin and drive to the park. The route is snarled up by roadworks and it would have been quicker to walk. Pale sunlight, cathedral bells chiming, a small-town Sunday throbbing with threat. I sit in the traffic running over and over everything Donna said. There's no way wanting Finn back has got anything to do with her having any feelings for him. She wants him for a reason. The only way to stop her from taking him is to work out what it is. I shunt forward a few yards and stop, halted by the temporary traffic lights. I watch a stream of pedestrians flow across the crossing: smartly dressed couples heading to church, a blue-jeaned backpacker, a bent-double old man shunting a tartan shopping trolley who turns to glare at me as he approaches the kerb. Donna was clearly desperate for cash and I don't buy the idea that someone has left her any. The only family she ever mentioned was an uncle in prison and a distant cousin who never replied to her letters and refused to visit her in care.

The match is in full flow when I finally pull into the car park. I pick out Finn among the children on the pitch, arms flapping helplessly as a tall red-headed girl from the other team tears past him.

'Come on, Ginny!' a woman yells.

The red-head thunders across the pitch. Hair swinging, she hammers the ball into the net. A gaggle of kids in orange shirts erupt in cheers and Ginny wheels away, skinny arms raised in triumph. I look away and head over to where Tilly and some of the other parents are gathered on the touchline: mums and dads whose lives and hearts are intact; people for whom this is just another, infinitely forgettable, Sunday morning; whose children are theirs to keep; whose lives aren't built on lies; who never stood helpless at the side of a pool and watched a young girl drown.

What if I take my chances and tell the police everything? Even if they believed me, Mo would find a way to silence me before it ever got to trial, and Donna's right, the only evidence of what happened that night is the footage of me and Jade. My thoughts spin. It all comes back to why. Why does she want Finn? And why now? Is this some scam she hatched in prison, sparked by something she heard from one of the other inmates, or saw on the news? Whatever it is, I'm certain she needs a kid in tow to make it work.

'You OK?' Tilly is looking at me oddly.

'Sorry. I was miles away.'

'Coffee?' It's Janine, mother of a fierce little girl in Finn's class.

'Yes, please.' She pours from a giant thermos and leans in closer as she hands me a steaming paper cup. 'Did you hear about Danny Morgan's dad running off with their au pair?'

I feign interest in her tale of adultery committed by a man I hardly know, wondering what the touchline gossips will make of the news that I'm being prosecuted for manslaughter and arson, maybe even murder, or that Finn was never mine and Ian has left me because I'm a liar.

I hear him shouting Finn's name. I turn to see Finn approaching a lithe, curly-haired boy who has got the ball. Clattering forward, Finn lunges at full speed but the boy sidesteps him and Finn goes sprawling in the mud. Ian's groan carries across the pitch. Finn raises his head, lip trembling, and pushes his glasses up his nose.

'Come on, Finn!' Ian yells. 'Focus!'

Finn struggles to his feet and stands perfectly still as the other players sprint past him. He watches Henry tap the ball forward, swerve deftly and pass it to Liam. He looks so small and lost I can hardly bear to watch.

What if we ran away? Tonight. Me and Finn. A new life. New names. Where would we go? How would we live? I think of Ian panicking, calling the police; of Donna releasing the footage of me and Jade; a nationwide hunt to track us down. I turn away, felled by the bleak impossibility of escape.

The whistle screeches behind me.

'Hey, Nic, what kept you? Where are the oranges?' Ian is striding across the pitch followed by a straggle of muddy children. I dash back to where I've left the Tupperware.

Somehow I make it through the second half. Our team wins, four–two. Finn hangs back, downcast and a little bemused as the other kids share high fives, revelling in the thrill of victory, while Ian walks around showering the star players with praise.

'I bet they're all rubbish at chess,' I whisper, as I lead Finn back to my car. I keep up the chatter as we drive home. He doesn't say much in reply and it hurts to see him looking so defeated.

As soon as we get in I strip him off, stand him under the shower and rinse the mud off his scraped knees and bloodied hands. I wrap him in a towel, lift him onto my lap and sit on the edge of the bath rocking him to me. I remember the first time I held him, I remember the musky newborn scent of his hair, I remember the shape of his bones and that feeling of falling in love. I close my eyes. I won't let Donna have him. I don't care what it takes, I won't give him up. As if sensing something is wrong he curls into me. For a moment as we sit there, anchored and inseparable, I think back to the night Donna dumped him, the night I claimed him for my own.

The front door slams. I hear Ian hurry up to our bathroom to take a shower. *Act normal*, I tell myself. *Don't let him see there's anything wrong.*

I ease Finn off my lap and send him off to get dressed while I gather up his muddy football kit and hurry downstairs, relieved I don't have to do more than cook a pan of green beans to go with the slow roast lamb and the baked potatoes I put in the oven before my world imploded.

Ian comes down freshly showered, full of plans for the team. I barely listen – just nod and smile and serve up the lunch. As if I'm saving them to memory, I study Finn's features while I spoon beans onto his plate. Is he really the image of his father? I think back to the deadbeats who'd drifted in and out of our lives in the months before he was born. He was small – just over five pounds when I'd weighed him on Anja's kitchen scales – but seeing as Donna had never shown any signs of pregnancy, it was impossible to know exactly how premature he was, and impossible to even guess who she'd been seeing when she got pregnant. Something brushes the edges of my mind.

'That's enough beans.'

I gaze blankly at Finn, trying to catch the trailing end of the thought, but it's gone, whisked away as quickly as it came.

'What happened to *thank you*?' Ian says.

'Enough beans, thank you, Mummy,' Finn says, dutifully.

Hearing that word in his mouth makes my eyes smart. I hold back the swell of tears and switch to automatic. Here I am, Nicola Dexter, loving mum, happy wife, eating Sunday lunch with my husband and son. I force down a few mouthfuls and feel Ian watching me. 'Are you all right, Nic?'

'Fine,' I say, quickly. 'How's the lamb?'

'Bit heavy on the salt.'

I bite down hard on the inside of my cheeks. A trick I learned in care. *Don't let them see you cry.* 'Any thoughts on what I should cook for Gwen?'

'Something simple that can't go wrong. How about aubergine parmigiana?'

It's not simple if you're not sure what it is or even how to spell it.

'And something for pudding. With that sweet tooth of hers, I've got no idea how she keeps so trim.'

Me neither, but a metabolism like a nuclear meltdown, three spin classes a week and the daily attentions of a personal trainer probably help.

'I'll do that apple tart you like,' I say. 'I've pretty much perfected it.'

Finn lays down his knife and fork. 'Finished. Please can I get down, Daddy?'

'Are you sure? You haven't eaten very much.'

Finn drops his head and nods.

'All right then, off you go. But no snacking before teatime.'

I wait until I hear Finn moving about in his bedroom before I gather up the plates. I set them down on the draining board and brace myself. 'I know we thought signing him up for football would help his confidence, but I'm worried it's having the opposite effect. He was miserable after the match today.'

Ian brings over the glasses. 'That's exactly why he needs to persevere. If we pull him out now, he's always going to feel like a failure.' He plants a kiss on my forehead and opens the dishwasher.

I glance at my laptop sitting on the worktop. 'What are your plans for this afternoon?'

'Actually, I want to take another look at the costings for the expansion.'

'That's fine, you go ahead. I'll finish clearing up,' I say, knowing I'll get it done in a quarter of the time.

'No, don't worry,' he says.

I count the seconds, jittery with frustration, while he rinses each piece of crockery and fills the racks with mathematical precision. Finally, he turns on the dishwasher and goes upstairs to his study.

I settle Finn with a jigsaw and curl up in the big armchair in the sitting room with my laptop on my knees. I would be far more comfortable on the sofa but over here, in the corner, I get a clear

view of the door and there's no chance of Ian walking in unexpect-
edly and catching sight of my screen. I type in *Donna Stephens
arrest* and search for coverage of her trial. My finger trembles on
the mousepad as I click on an article in the *Daily Record*. A listing
of minor members of a Glasgow-based gang involved in fraud,
racketeering and weapons sales. She got four years. Mugshots of
the men involved fill the screen, their stares made more sinister
by the details of the accusations against them. Two of them got
off on a technicality. A moment passes. Then another. What if
one of these stubble-jawed, cold-eyed thugs is the man Donna is
setting up home with? The man who 'can't wait' to play stepfather
to Finn? If one of them really is her latest partner, then maybe this
money she's coming into is her share of the stolen cash. But then
why would she need to see a lawyer about it, and why would she
need an advance before she can rent somewhere to live? Surely
they'd give it to her all in one go? A bag stuffed full of used notes,
kept safe for her while she was inside. And why on earth would
she need Finn back in order to get her hands on it?

   Whatever scam she's pulling, she had to have started planning
it when she was in jail. Can prisoners get access to the internet?
If they can, was she like me? Did guilt and fear drag her back to
Sallowfield every time her fingers touched a keyboard?

   I tap in *Sallowfield Court*. This time I scroll back to the date
of her sentencing and work forwards. There's a short interview
with Ryan Hurley's father, Gordon, on one of the morning
programmes, when he was lobbying – unsuccessfully – for the
attorney general to order a second inquest into his son's death.
Perched uncomfortably on a curved red sofa, he looks gaunt and
ill, worn down by the pain of not knowing the truth about the
death of his only son. I caught it live when it first went out and
switched over after the first few minutes, unable to deal with the
depth of the old man's grief. This time I force myself to sit through
it to the end. It's almost unbearable to watch but there's nothing

there for me. Just a grief-stricken father looking for answers. Six months later he was dead. A heart attack. Another victim of the fallout from that night. Some of the papers carried obituaries of him. I scan them quickly.

Gordon Hurley has died aged 68 at his home in Essex. A successful businessman, he is best remembered for his tireless campaign to find the truth behind the death of his only son, Ryan, who was found dead at his fire-ravaged home along with the body of an unknown teenage girl…

Between announcements of Hurley's death and the recent For Sale notice for the Sallowfield property, there's an interview with Hurley's lawyer explaining the legal minefield left when someone fails to update their will after the death of their sole beneficiary. I skip through photos of Gordon's middle-aged nephews and cousins once, twice and three times removed, screaming at each other on the steps of the courthouse, and pause on a photo, taken just before he died, of handsome, suntanned Ryan.

CHAPTER 32

'How come you never mentioned Donna before?' Ian says later that night. He's leaning back on the sofa, one eye on the television news, the other on the chess board, but his attention fully focused on me.

'Why would I? We weren't nearly as close as she made out. What game are you playing?'

'Anderssen versus Kieseritzky.' He makes a move, wincing a little as he sacrifices the white queen. 'She seemed to know you pretty well.'

'We just happened to be at the Burtons at the same time. If she turns up again I'd rather you didn't invite her into the house.'

'Sorry. I thought you wanted me to make an effort with your friends.'

'I told you. She's not my friend. If she wants to see me she can meet me in town.'

His glance lifts from the chess board. 'I don't understand. If you two weren't close, how come she was holding your hand when Finn was born?'

Cold fingers squeeze my insides. 'He was premature. You know that. No time to make it to a hospital, and she just happened to be there. I can't even remember why.' As soon as I've said it I regret it. It would have been safer to admit we'd lived in the same flat for a while, stuck as close to the truth as I dared.

'So, why did she look you up?'

My heart beats so hard I'm scared he'll hear it. 'To tell me about someone we used to know.' A lie blossoms on my tongue. 'A girl who was in care with us for a while. Her husband's just died and left her on her own with a couple of kids. She thought I might want to get in touch with her.'

His eyes drift to my handbag. I always leave it lying around and there's a chance that he might, just might, know how much money there'd been in it. 'Donna's going to see her so I gave her a bit of cash for the children.' I ease myself to my feet. 'You know what? I'm going to have an early night.' He catches my hand as I move past him. His fingers are cool. Mine, I know, are hot and sweaty. He gives them a squeeze. 'I'll be up in minute.'

I light a scented candle and download a recording of whale song on my phone while I run a bath. I have no intention of relaxing and I can't stand whale song, but it will give me an excuse to be on my own while I think. I sink my body into the bath and sit in the steamy half-dark, chin on my knees. The room smells faintly of bleach – my attempt to purge Donna from my life. But she's not going anywhere. I close my eyes, slump back and let the water close over my face. Tears seep beneath my lids. Ian suspects something, I know he does. He wasn't convinced by my story about Donna just happening to be there when Finn was born. But the part about there being no time to call an ambulance was true. One minute Donna was lolling on her bed smoking, the next her cigarette was burning a hole in the carpet and she was dragging herself to the bathroom doubled over in pain. In a way it's a mercy Finn was so small. Any bigger and his sudden arrival might not have been so straightforward. As it was, he was skinny and small but he had none of the problems some preemies are born with. I smile at the memory of the hefty cry he'd let out when Anja had swung him upside down and the way he'd guzzled the bottle as soon as I put it to his lips. I gaze at the candlelight shimmering on the surface of the water above me. Slowly I lift my hands, grip the sides of the bath and ease myself up. I scrape my wet hair off my face and blink into the flame. What if he wasn't premature? What if he was underweight because Donna smoked and drank all through the pregnancy? That would widen the possible time of his conception right back to when we were working for Mo.

I step out of the bath. Dripping wet, I fumble among my dropped clothes for my phone. Finn's face fills the screen, the photo I look at maybe twenty times a day. The eyes, the hair, the dimpled chin.

I reach for a towel and dry myself, my brain stumbling between the questions I've been asking myself all day and the sparse scattering of facts I've gleaned from my encounter with Donna. Finn's father was 'out of the picture', that glimmer of pain when she'd added *permanently*. The way she'd laughed when she said her boyfriend couldn't wait to become Finn's stepdad. The lawyer, the wait for the money, the dates.

It all fits.

I call Donna's number. The phone rings out. I call again. Another six rings. She picks up.

'What do you want?'

'Can we meet?'

'Why?'

'We need to talk.'

'What about?'

'I know why you want Finn back.' A male voice rumbles in the background. 'In private,' I say. 'As soon as possible.'

'I'll text you,' she says, and hangs up.

CHAPTER 33

I'm in the car on the way to work when I get a call from Susy. I flick on the hands-free. 'Hi.'

'Got to be quick – I'm on my way into court.' She's breathless, the sound of her high heels clacking on polished wood as she runs. 'I've managed to get an appointment this afternoon with the housing officer about Leon and a couple of other kids I'm worried about. I pushed hard to get them to squeeze me in and now I can't go. You'll have to do it.'

'Me?'

'I'll forward you the details. Don't worry about the other two. I'll rebook a time to talk about them. Concentrate on Leon. He's the emergency.'

'What do I tell them?'

'The truth. Seeing how deeply Logan's got his hooks into him, the only answer is to get him moved to another town. Say he's willing to downsize and take anything that comes up. It will push him up the waiting list.'

'Won't they want him there too?'

'Ideally, but if you can't get hold of him go on your own and get the ball rolling. Oh, and Gaby wants you and Finn to come to this art workshop we're doing at half-term. Shall I book you in?'

'Yeah, maybe, but Susy—'

'Sorry, they're calling my case. I'll text you about the workshop. Let me know how it goes with the housing officer.'

She's gone before I can tell her I can't do it, that I don't have the headspace for anybody's problems but my own. Her forwarded email from the council beeps onto my phone. A name. A time. A place.

I pull off the road and sit on the kerbside, thumbs poised to text back and tell her she'll have to reschedule for a time when she can do it herself. But as I sit there with the engine idling, doors open in my mind onto a rosy daydream I've had so many times before, in which someone cared enough to step in and help me and Jade to escape Mo's grasp before that night at Sallowfield. A dream where I make it to university and live a happy, humdrum, guilt-free life, and Jade gets to grow up and find out how it feels to be safe and happy.

I type *Leave it with me* and call Leon. His phone goes to voice-mail. Of course it does. I forward the email and without much hope I tell him to meet me at the council offices at one forty-five so we can decide what we're going to say.

All morning I keep my phone in my lap, desperate to hear back from Donna. I have to be careful. Maggie doesn't approve of staff phones on display during work hours and I have to keep things normal. Avert suspicion. Play my role. Nicola Cahill – blameless wife, doting mother, unflappable receptionist.

As soon as my shift is over I head for the council offices. No sign of Leon when I pull up outside the drab, concrete building – and still no text from Donna.

After years of living at the mercy of the click of a keyboard or the tick of a pen, dealing with the authorities usually crushes me into tongue-tied submission. Today I'm too distracted to be nervous. I step into the lift. The doors slide shut. I see my face in the scratched steel walls, hazy and half-there. No trepidation as I walk to the reception desk. No notes or preparation as I'm ushered into the meeting room and introduced to Olive White.

She's plump and weary, limp, grey-streaked hair pulled back from her face and rammed into place with a claw-tooth clip.

'Ah, Mrs Dexter. I understand you're here about an emergency placement for–' – she frowns at her computer screen – 'Leon Travis.'

'That's right. He—'

'Susana Quiros from Next Steps sent me his file.'

I start to speak. She cuts me off again. 'I really can't see why you think this is an emergency. He's not homeless. Far from it. There are hundreds of people without any kind of roof over their heads who would give their right arm for a newly renovated one-bed flat like his.'

'It's not the quality of the accommodation that's the problem.'

'Then what is?'

'The drug gang on the Rosemead estate—'

She sighs and turns her pen in her plump pink hands. 'We have this all the time. Care leavers making risky lifestyle choices and expecting other people to step in and bail them out when things go wrong. I'm afraid it's not our job—'

I lift my eyes to the window. Anger seeps up from my gut, runs through my lungs and clots in my throat. I squeeze out the words. 'That's just it, Mrs White. Kids like Leon… vulnerable teenagers with nothing and nobody in their lives, make bad decisions because they don't *have* choices! They live day to day, doing what they have to to survive, preyed on by the wrong people because there's no one else who gives a damn. Worrying about consequences is a luxury they can't afford and by the time they realise what's happening, they're in too deep to get out in one piece and their whole lives are ruined.'

Ten minutes later I'm stumbling out of there, past the lift and along the corridor to the stairs. I grip the rail, miss the first step and almost fall. I squeeze my eyes shut. If it wasn't for the two

women coming up from the floor below I would scream. I reach
the bottom and burst out into the cold.

My phone buzzes in my hand. I look down at the screen.
Finally. A text from Donna.

Builders Arms Canal Street 8pm
Bring the £200

Ian is more than happy to babysit when I tell him I want to go
to a body sculpt session at the gym. He even offers to put Finn
to bed so I can get there in time to do a warm-up first. Shame I
nearly blow it by walking out of the house without my gym bag.
At least he manages to catch me before I drive off.

I stop at a cash point to get the £200 Donna had demanded,
park down the street from the pub and wait. My phone buzzes.
Panicking that it might be her blowing me out I flick to the text.
It's from Lydia, saying how much she enjoyed meeting me and how
keen she is to get involved with Next Steps. I quickly text her back
and I'm deleting the thread when a figure in a raincoat emerges
– head down, hood up – from a side road. I edge forward and
adjust the wing mirror. It's Donna. I'd know that walk anywhere.
It looks like she's on her own but I'm not taking any chances.
The last person I want to be faced with tonight is her boyfriend.
She enters the pub. I give it a moment. When I'm sure no one's
following her I get out of the car and follow her inside, hanging
back, head angled towards the giant TV as if I'm distracted by
the football. She orders what looks to be a vodka and drinks it
quickly at the bar. She's pale and nervous but she's not making
eye contact with anyone, not even looking around. She orders
another, a double, and takes it out to the courtyard at the back.

It's pretty deserted, just a couple of old men huddled on a
bench sucking on roll-ups, and two middle-aged women in coats

and scarves leaning against the wall, deep in shivery conversation, the smoke from their cigarettes threading through the gloom. She picks a table in a corner, beneath one of the overhead heaters and as far from the other smokers as possible. Good choice. I buy an orange juice and shift a little so I can see her through the open door. She takes out a cigarette and half turns her body to shelter her lighter. She shakes it and thumbs it again.

I carry my drink across the courtyard, kick back the seat opposite her and sit down.

She glances up. 'You got the two hundred?' she says.

I push it across the table. Ten crisp, new, twenty-pound notes.

I watch her fold the money into the pocket of her coat, wondering if she's slit the seam for easy shoplifting like when we were kids.

'So, what do you want?'

A dog barks down the street. Small blobs of colour dot the sagging rope lights. The commentary from the football game rises over the chatter in the bar behind me.

'Finn wasn't premature, was he?' I say. 'At least not by more than a couple of weeks.'

She lifts her shoulders in a wide-eyed shrug. I lean forward so we're eye to eye. 'He was underweight because you went on drinking and smoking even after you found out you were pregnant. You didn't give a toss about him then and you don't give a toss about him now.' She bends down and tries the lighter again. 'You want to use him to get your hands on Gordon Hurley's money.' She tries not to react, but the flame from the lighter jumps. 'He's Ryan Hurley's kid, isn't he?'

She takes a drag of her cigarette and looks away. In the neon light from the street I see a flush spread up her neck, dark against the pallor of her skin.

'I cared about Ryan. In his way he cared about me, too. If he'd been alive he'd have seen me and the baby right.' She drops her head. For a second, sitting there in the half-dark, I glimpse the girl I used to know. Curled up on that narrow little bed at Ma Burton's, hurt, frightened, weeping at the wall. She blinks and back comes the brittle stranger. 'Why shouldn't I have some luck for a change? The old man had a massive house, a couple of cars, half a dozen holiday cottages, a fifty per cent stake in an insurance business and everything he inherited from Ryan.' She takes a long drag of her cigarette. 'Feels weird, doesn't it? A son's money going to his father. Most men Ryan's age would have had a wife or a live-in girlfriend to leave it to. Luckily for me, he wasn't cut out for commitment.'

'How are you going to prove Finn's his?'

'They've got his DNA on file.' Her voice drops. 'The papers said that's how they identified his body.'

I lean over and take a cigarette from her pack. I put it to my lips and reach for her lighter. 'What happens when someone works out you were seeing Ryan around the time he died and starts asking if you were with him that night?'

She stares into her glass, then knocks back what's left. 'That's why I kept quiet until now. But with the old man dead, no one's going to be pushing to reopen the investigation. If they do, I'll say we had a one-night stand the week before. No one can prove I ever went to the house.'

I take a sip of my orange juice, wishing I'd got the barman to put a shot of vodka in it. 'Doesn't it worry you that they've put it on the market? All the land, and what's left of the house?'

She shrugs. 'Why would it? It's the first thing I was going to do, anyway.'

'If they're selling things off, it means they've already decided who's getting what.

'That will all change when the laywers find out that the old man had a grandchild. As soon as they do, it'll all go to Finn.'

'Exactly. *To Finn.* That money won't be yours. With an inheritance that big there'll be trustees, lawyers and accountants watching every penny they pay out and keeping an eye on everything you do until he grows up. One false move and they'll cut you off.'

She smiles long and slow. 'Then I'll just have to put up with living in Hurley's big old house, driving his fancy cars and spending whatever allowance they give me to keep my son in comfort.'

'They'll find out you've done time. You know that, don't you?'

'I'll tell them I've reformed. Seen the error of my ways.'

'You'll have to convince them.'

'That's where you come in. Backing me up, pleading my cause. Respectable, married, pillar-of-the-PTA Nicola Dexter.' She shifts slightly and flicks ash onto the ground. 'Anyway, they can't take your kid away just because you made a few mistakes.'

'The first hint of drugs, drink, dodgy associates or neglect and there'll be trouble. They'll vet that boyfriend of yours, too. How long do you think he's going to stick around when he knows his every move is being monitored?'

'Thanks for your concern but I'll take my chances.' She takes the smouldering end of her cigarette from her lips and mashes it to pulp in the ashtray, head moving slowly from side to side. 'Is that it?'

For all her bravado I can see I've got to her. *She hasn't thought this through at all. Good. Now's my chance.* 'If it's cash you want I can get you some.'

She raises her head and gazes at me, her choppy hair lit by a single orange light bulb dangling from the wooden beam above us.

'I'll give you whatever I can get hold of upfront, then I'll extend my hours at the surgery and pay you monthly. It wouldn't be a fortune but it would be yours. Money in your pocket. No risks, no strings, no hassle. No one breathing down your neck. No one poking their nose into your past and, most importantly, no possibility of anyone connecting you to Hurley's death.'

She slides two fingers down the shaft of her lighter and turns it upside down. 'How much?'

I've gone over and over this in my head. My salary wasn't much even before Ian arranged for the surgery to pay a chunk of it into the fund for Finn's school fees. I do have a credit card I can use for emergencies and big household items, but it's in Ian's name and has a monthly limit of £1,000 so it will all come down to how much I can borrow.

'Ten thousand upfront, then once I go full-time at the surgery again I'll pay you something every month.'

'Ten grand? Are you joking?' She laughs, genuinely amused. 'Think what I'd be giving up.' She shoves back her chair and stands up.

'Fifteen then, twenty if I can get it.' I'm desperate now, snatching numbers out of the air. 'And a few hundred a month for as long as you want after that.' Anything to get her to agree.

'Tell you what. I'll think about it.'

I close my eyes. 'Thank you.'

'Don't get excited.' She picks up her cigarettes and her lighter. 'I'll call you,' she says, and walks away.

She has to say yes. She has to.

CHAPTER 34

A visit from Ian's mother is the last thing I need but I can't put her off; Ian would start asking questions and I can't have him getting suspicious that anything is wrong. I'm jittery all morning, barely able to concentrate on anything except my phone concealed beneath a carefully positioned file on my desk. I leave work as early as I can, determined to have everything looking perfect when Gwen arrives.

I pull into the drive and I'm checking my phone again, just in case Donna texted me while I was on the way home, when Vera comes trotting out of her house, immaculate in full make-up and a pink velour tracksuit, twirling an umbrella like an ageing Mary Poppins. It took me a while to realise that Ian's female fan base reaches far beyond his adoring patients, but Vera is yet another fully paid-up member, second only to Maggie in her slavish devotion to him and her surly suspicion of me.

I lower the window and gaze into her heavily mascara-ed eyes. 'Hello, Vera. You all right?'

'I took in a parcel for Ian this morning.'

'Thanks for that. I'm in a bit of a rush right now, but I'll come over later and get it.'

'Well, it's rather heavy. Probably best if he comes for it himself.' She leans in closer, lipstick on her teeth. 'Actually, while he's there I was rather hoping he might take a look at the light bulb on my landing. It's gone again and I'm worried about tripping over in the dark.'

She is in excellent nick and can't be a day over sixty. You'd think that at some point over the last five decades she'd have worked out how to change a light bulb. But that would mean missing out on her cosy little chats with my husband.

'Of course,' I say, with a smile. 'I'll text him and get him to pop in on his way home.'

By the time Tilly drops Finn off, the aubergine parmigiana is in the oven, the apple tart is cooling on the worktop, the house is heady with the scents of Pledge and fresh flowers, and I've filled in three online loan applications and been rejected by all of them because, guess what? I have no credit history. It doesn't matter that I practically lived off loans when Finn was little and paid back every penny in full and on time: the people I was forced to borrow from aren't the kind who report back to the credit bureau. I can't apply to our bank because Ian's a joint signatory on my account and any loan application would get referred straight back to him.

I feed Finn early and put him in his best pyjamas with the bribe of an hour on my laptop tomorrow night if he goes straight to bed as soon as he's said hello to 'Granny Gwen'. Ian came up with that one. It makes me wince almost as much as it does her. Maybe he thought it would give us something to bond over.

'What's in your parcel? Something exciting?' I say, when Ian comes in lugging a large cardboard box and a carrier bag with a couple of bottles of wine poking out of the top.

'A home security system.' He puts down the carrier bag, deposits the box on the worktop and slashes it open with the bread knife. 'After that business with the side gate and the glass in your tyre, I don't want to leave anything to chance.'

'We don't need CCTV,' I say, lightly, 'we've got Vera.' My attempt at a joke falls flat.

'That's not kind. She's old and lonely. I wish you'd be a bit nicer to her.'

'She's not that old and she's not nearly as doddery as she makes out. I've seen her nip up the road like lightning when it suits her.'

I watch as he lifts away a chunk of polystyrene and shakes out the instruction leaflet. I glance at the window. 'Does it set off an alarm if there's someone outside?'

'Yes. The floodlights come on and the system sends an alert to our phones. But we can log in and check the live stream or the recording any time we want, and all the cameras have got microphones, so if a delivery turns up when we're out we can speak to the driver.'

'Can he speak back?'

'Of course. It says here that each camera records distortion-free audio for up to sixty meters.'

My voice falters. 'How many are there?'

'Six. But I was thinking of getting a couple of extras.'

'Where are you going to put them?'

'Front door, back door, French windows, side gate, one over the garage and one up there.' He points to a spot above the bifold doors. 'The lenses are wide-angle so we'll get a full view if anyone tries to break in through the kitchen windows.'

I look down at the cameras. Six little round eyeballs stare back at me from their polystyrene nests, waiting to record every sound I utter and every move I make. When I'm in and when I'm out. What I do and who I call. I'll even have to own up about not spending my Friday mornings cleaning my car.

Ian is looking at me as if he's expecting a reaction. I swallow very hard and go over to the sink and fill the kettle. 'Are you going to install them yourself?'

'Bit beyond me. I'll have to get Derek to do it.'

'Derek?'

'The guy who set up the system in the surgery. He's pretty busy but I'm sure he'll fit us in.'

I blink down at the stream of water spurting into kettle. No one told me there was surveillance at the surgery.

'Mmm, the parmigiana smells good,' he says, coming up behind me and putting an arm around my shoulders. I straighten up and ask him to whip the cream for the apple tart.

'Don't worry. I picked up a tub of stracciatella and some of those little almond biscuits from the Italian deli when I got the wine. You know how picky Mum is about pastry.'

I don't say anything. I'd like to think it's because I'm bigger than that. Truth is, I don't have the energy. All I can think about is hearing back from Donna.

He stashes the ice cream in the freezer, arranges the biscuits on one of the bright ceramic dishes he picked up on a mini break in Rome with Annabel, and goes upstairs to shower.

Gwen arrives right on time, pulling up outside the house in a brand-new Mercedes convertible.

'Nicola,' she says, as I let her in, as if she can't quite get over the surprise of seeing me in my own home. 'And Finn.' Her plucked eyebrows shoot high as if in amazement that he is still living here as well. 'Well, isn't this lovely?'

We don't kiss. Never have. Never will. It's a relief to us both. Finn disappears upstairs and her face lights up as Ian comes down the hallway. This is the first time I've seen her since Susy's revelations about Ian's stepfather and as she strides past me in a haze of scarves, expensive tailoring and Estée Lauder Youth Dew, clutching an armful of glossy brochures, it's hard to imagine her getting pushed around by anyone. But then who knows what goes on in other people's marriages? She follows him into the sitting room and I retreat to the kitchen to make the salad, pour myself a large glass of wine and check my phone.

I'm grinding pepper into the salad dressing when Donna finally calls. I glance around to make sure I'm alone, back quickly into the utility room and click the door shut.

'I've thought about what you said,' she says, spinning it out, taking a long noisy drag of her cigarette. 'You know, about old man Hurley's lawyers breathing down my neck and making me live like a nun.'

'And?' I whisper.

Another pause. I stand frozen to the spot not daring to move.

'Well, maybe it *would* be easier to take your money.' The room spins, I topple back against the wall and let go of the breath I didn't even know I'd been holding. 'You get me fifty thousand in cash by next week and I'll walk away and leave you to your cosy little life.'

'Fifty thousand? Donna, you know I can't get that much.' A male voice rumbles in the background, gruff and aggressive. She must have me on speaker.

'Deal's off, then,' she says.

'No! Don't hang up. I can get you… twenty thousand upfront, and the rest in instalments once I increase my hours at work.'

The man's voice growls again. He's pushing her into this. Jerking her strings. Maybe the whole bid for Hurley's money was his idea.

'Forty,' she says. 'By next Monday.'

'That's less than a week.'

'Tuesday then,' she says, grudgingly.

'But—'

'If you're serious about keeping Finn, you'll find a way.'

'All right! Forty.'

'You'd better not jerk me around.'

'I'm not, Donna. I swear I'm good for the money.'

She hangs up.

Forty thousand pounds. The atoms in my head spin apart struggling to grasp the enormity of the sum. I walk back into the kitchen, down what's left of my wine in one gulp and reach for the bottle. I stare at my trembling fingers curled around the stem of the glass. My engagement ring and my car are the only possessions I own of any value and what I get for them isn't even going to touch the sides of forty grand. I pour myself a refill and take another glug of wine. Enough. I push the glass aside. I have to keep a clear head. I have to act like nothing is wrong. I toss the salad and put the bowl on the table, then I smooth my hair, pop my head around the door and call, 'It's ready!'

Ian fills Gwen's glass and I slice a spatula through the aubergine parmigiana, which is now golden, bubbling and sprigged with torn basil. I cut again and carefully remove a perfectly melded stack of aubergine, tomato sauce and melting cheese. Gwen unfolds her newly ironed linen napkin and inspects the portion I'm holding up. 'Did you breadcrumb the aubergine before you fried it?'

'The recipe I used didn't mention breadcrumbs.'

'*Do* try it next time. It will absorb all that excess moisture and keep the layers from falling apart.'

I slide the portion of parmigiana onto her plate, the air crackling between us as I offer her the salad and the basket of warm olive bread.

'Have you decided where you're going on your cruise?' I say, tempted to suggest the Bermuda Triangle.

'Not quite,' she says, already tiring of me and turning away to Ian. 'What's happening with the practice expansion?'

He holds out his plate for parmigiana, a slight shake of his head as I offer him an extra spoonful of the crispy bits of mozzarella clinging to the edges of the dish. 'The architect's plans have all been approved and the investors are signing off the first instalment of the money as we speak.'

Lips tight and pink, Gwen spears a piece of woefully unbread-crumbed aubergine. 'I just don't understand why you went to that Downing man instead of approaching DRB. The new chair was more than happy to invest in all that new equipment you bought last year. Even Hugh agreed to it. A good business deal is a good business deal when all's said and done.'

Ian's jaw stiffens and I'm conscious of him taking care to control his expression. 'I wanted to do this one on my own,' he says. 'Prove I could do it without DRB backing.'

'Prove it to whom?' she says, clearly mystified.

He puts down his fork and says crisply: 'Myself.'

The intricacies of Ian's stake in his father's company and his relationship with the DRB board have always been a mystery to me, and this tense little exchange isn't making it any clearer. My eyes wander to the wall calendar. Next week is half-term. I should be thinking about excursions and activities but I just keep counting the days until Tuesday. I can't have Finn with me when I hand over the money. I'll have to ask Tilly if he can go to hers.

What if I can't raise it? The enormity of losing my son hits me hard, a blast of such intensity I gasp out loud.

Two pairs of blue eyes dart towards me across the table.

'More wine, Gwen?' I wave the bottle in her direction. She holds out her glass while I pour and I wonder, for one wild moment, what the DRB board would say to a request for £40,000 to enable me to keep my child.

CHAPTER 35

I hardly sleep and get up at five, terrified thoughts crashing down on me as I sit at the kitchen table filling out applications to ever-more dodgy-looking loan companies. But even the dodgiest of them only offer maximum loans of £25,000 and come with repayment terms and interest rates that make me gasp.

'I've been thinking,' I say, two hours later, as Ian pours himself a coffee and I drop his perfectly timed toast onto the plate in front of him. 'If I sign Finn up for the after-school club, I could go full-time at the surgery again.'

A beat of silence before he lifts his head. 'Why would you want to do that?'

'I've been looking at the price of school fees. By the time he gets to secondary, they're going to be huge.'

'Darling, you can hardly cope with the hours you've got already.' Ian swallows a gulp of coffee and runs a hand down my thigh. 'You're always complaining that you're too pushed to get to the gym.' He glances over at Finn, standing bleary-eyed in the doorway. 'We don't want Mummy getting pudgy again, do we, Finn?'

Eager to please, Finn shakes his head.

The 'again' leaves a sting but I say lightly, 'I'd manage.' I'd have to. Just like I'd have to find a way to stop the extra money getting siphoned off into the school fees fund before I could get my hands on it.

Ian drains his mug and checks his watch.

'Shall I mention it to Maggie, then?'

'Let me think about it. Can you pass me my jacket? I want to get in early and have a word with Mac.'

On his way out he leans in and gives me kiss, brushing my ear with his lips as he whispers, 'Who knows, once we've seen Dr Harris you might have a reason to give up work altogether.'

I stand rooted to the floor, a tremor spreading up my arms and through my body as I gaze at the calendar. Three weeks until our appointment at the fertility clinic; three weeks until Harris examines me and finds out that I have never given birth and, given the way things are going with our all-out attempts to conceive, possibly discovers that I never will.

I sit at the reception desk and stare out of the window at the passing traffic, my brain splintering in every direction trying think of anyone who might lend me even a few thousand pounds. Joyce would help me if she could but she's living on her pension. Susy? She's broke after buying her house and anyway it would take her about two minutes to work out that I was being blackmailed and she'd want to go to the police. My mind trips on an unthinkable thought: Ian's credit cards. I know his pin numbers. I found them by accident months ago when I was cleaning his study. I close my eyes. No! I can't do it. I can't steal from my husband.

'Fiona Clarke, ten thirty with Mr Quinn.'

I snap back from the dark abyss of my thoughts to focus on the ruddy, square-jawed face staring down at me. I tap the keypad, run my eye down the screen and offer up my most diplomatic smile. 'I'm so sorry, Mrs Clarke, your check-up is booked for the thirteenth.'

'No, I definitely booked it for today. It was you I spoke to. I recognise your voice.'

I ignore the hint of disdain and wrack my brain to remember. 'Did you get a confirmation text?'

'I did indeed. Two in fact. One last week after you gave me the appointment and one yesterday to confirm it.' She thrusts her phone at me. 'Look for yourself. It says here quite clearly ten thirty on the third. I've taken time off work and rearranged meetings. It's just not good enough. Can't you fit me in? Cancel somebody else?'

I read the texts and scroll hurriedly through the diary. 'We do have a cancellation at twelve, but I'm afraid it's not with Mr Quinn.'

Her face flushes from rose to a nasty shade of fuchsia. 'I always see Mr Quinn and, anyway, I can't sit around here for an hour and a half because of your incompetence.'

Heads are turning in the waiting room: Mrs Clarke in meltdown offering a welcome alternative to a tank full of go-nowhere fish or a muted rerun of *Location, Location, Location* on the overhead TV. Two more patients are now queuing up behind her, and Amy is still on her break.

'I'm so sorry,' I say again, but she's turning around, raising her voice even higher and demanding to see my boss, and now Maggie is coming out of her office shooting daggers at me and placatory smiles at Mrs Clarke.

'Is there a problem, Mrs Clarke?'

'I'll say there is. Your receptionist has completely messed up my morning by giving my appointment to someone else.'

Staring at them both, I'm felled by the sensation of one nightmare colliding with another: Donna's voice demanding £40,000, and the job I need to hang on to to raise the money, falling apart.

I shake my head. 'That's not what's happened, Mrs Clarke.'

'Don't contradict me. You gave me an appointment and when I get here it's not available. What other explanation is there?'

'It must be a problem with the system.'

Now Maggie's annoyed. 'We've never had a problem with it before,' she snaps.

'What's happened?' Mac says, appearing as if from nowhere.

In a prickle of sweat I scrub my hand over my face. 'There's been a mix-up. Your ten thirty has been double booked.'

'That's all right,' he says. 'Come this way, Mrs Clarke. I finished with my last patient a little more quickly than I'd expected, so I'm sure I can shunt things around and squeeze you in.'

Their departure leaves me alone with Maggie. I stare at the screen. 'I just don't understand it. Someone must have mixed her up with another patient and moved her appointment.'

'Are you trying to blame this on one of the other receptionists? Or perhaps one of the dentists?' Her little mouth quivers in an ecstasy of reproach.

'No, but somebody must have—'

'I don't know what's got into you, Nicola. You need to pull yourself together.' With a little shake of her head she hisses, 'As a favour to Ian I cut you a lot of slack, but there are limits even to my patience.' She spins on her heel and goes back to her office, leaving me to the humiliating stares of the waiting patients.

I keep my head down and stare at the computer screen. Disquiet moves in on me like dirty grey mist. Has Ian spoken to her about giving me extra hours? Is she sabotaging my work to give herself a reason to say no? I wouldn't put it past her.

CHAPTER 36

I leave the surgery at 1.30 p.m. sharp, my heart pounding at the thought of Ian's fury when he hears about the mess up. Then I remember he's playing squash with Matt after work so at least he'll have a chance to cool off before he gets home.

I drive twenty miles to Guildford: a town where no one knows me, where none of Ian's patients are going to spot me on the street and let it slip at their next check-up. I park the car and cut down the high street looking for the brash yellow signage of the 'We Buy Gold' shop I found on the internet. In the window, stacked tiers of second-hand rings peep from padded boxes: tiny diamonds in heavy, old-fashioned settings; chippy little sapphires; eternity rings that clearly failed to live up to their name; wedding rings pulled from the fingers of the dead, the desperate and the divorced; all on sale for knock-down prices. I wiggle the fat solitaire from my ring finger and jiggle it in my palm. Going by the rings I've compared it to online, it's got to be worth at least £800. If I'm lucky I should get at least £500 for it. Ian's going to be so upset when I tell him I've lost it but it can't be helped. I press the entry button. The woman behind the counter – short, plump and businesslike – looks me up and down before she buzzes me in.

I lean in to the glass security screen and slide the ring through the slit at the bottom. 'How much can you give me for this, please?'

The woman puts an eyeglass to her eye and holds the ring up to the light, turning first the stone and then the band to face the lens. She puts down the ring and removes the eyeglass. 'I can do you eighty quid.'

I laugh and shake my head. 'For a diamond?'

'It's fake, love. Cubic zirconia.'

I glare at her. *She's lying, trying to con me.*

'Whatever he told you, I promise you, it's fake.'

I hear Ian's voice in my ear, the rough warmth of his cheek as he slipped the ring onto my finger. 'I want you to know how much you mean to me.' It must be him who got conned when he bought it, though it's hard to imagine any jeweller, however persuasive, managing to palm off a fake diamond on my careful, detail-driven husband.

'Do you want the eighty?' the woman is asking.

I gaze at her blankly and shake my head.

'If it's any consolation, you wouldn't be the first,' she says, and pushes the ring back beneath the screen.

Face burning, I shove it back onto my finger and walk out into the street. A few hundred pounds wouldn't have been much out of forty thousand but that first fistful of notes would have given me hope.

Six days. That's all I've got, and the minutes are slipping away.

I'm heading back towards the car, poised to cross the road, when my eye catches a pavement blackboard offering gourmet food to take away. A chalked arrow at the top points to the kind of high-end emporium I'd have barely noticed when my food shopping consisted of snapping up yellow-tagged bargains teetering on the brink of their sell-by dates.

The bell dings as I push open the door and step inside. There's a smell of freshly ground coffee, the tiled walls are hung with vintage signs, and whole hams and rows of knobbly salamis dangle from the ceiling. Grey marble counters groan with cheeses and baskets of artisan bread. I inspect the display of 'cheat eats'. They come in a choice of overpriced earthenware dishes or plain waxed cartons – no telltale branding to betray the time-stretched cook who needs to lie.

The shop assistant leans over the counter. 'What would you like? I can recommend the coq au vin.'

I hesitate, half tempted to shake my head and leave. Ian doesn't approve of ready meals, only authentic, top quality, home-cooked food for my picky husband.

It's fake, love. Cubic zirconia… You wouldn't be the first. I blink away the look of pity on the jeweller's face, think of all the extra time I'd buy myself if I didn't have to shop or cook every day, and hear myself say, 'Can you freeze this stuff?'

'Of course.'

'Great. I'll take two portions of the chicken, and two each of the lamb tagine, the Spanish bean stew, the boeuf bourguignon, the smoked haddock and bacon gratin, the mushroom stroganoff, and the meatballs.' I point and smile.

I pay her in cash so Ian won't see a Guildford-based transaction on my bank statement and walk out of there swinging two brown paper bags packed with a week's worth of cooking-free days, and a punnet of olives and a sourdough loaf to act as cover in case anyone saw me go in. I stash the bags in the boot and drive on through town.

I park on the forecourt of Austin's Car Mart and sit with my hands on the wheel, imagining Ian's reaction when he finds out I've sold my car and the lies I'll have to tell to explain why I did it. But it is mine after all – an 'early wedding present'. I'll tell him the money was for the girl I was in care with who's lost her husband. I'll say she helped me once when I was in a bad way and I owe her. If he wants to know why I didn't go to him for help I'll say it was to pay off a bad gambling debt and I knew he wouldn't approve. Anyway, once it's done, it doesn't matter how incensed he is, there'll be no going back. I open the door and swing my legs onto the tarmac. If it comes down to losing Finn or facing Ian's wrath, there's no contest.

I'm wandering along the rows of cars trying to pluck up the courage to go into the office when a voice calls from over my shoulder. 'Can I help you, there?'

I spin around. The salesman is tall, blond and scrubbed. He's around my age, maybe slightly older, wears a white shirt and a grey suit with narrow lapels and has a fresh, uncomplicated face. The old Nicci might even have swiped right on his photo in the hope of a drink and a laugh and a hurried hour or two of hushed, single-mum sex to stave off the loneliness.

'Yes, I'm… looking to sell my car,' I say. 'It's the blue Honda over there.'

He seems impressed. 'Any accidents?'

'No, and I've had it from new.'

He saunters over, pulls open the door and sits in the driver's seat, one long leg sticking out onto the tarmac as he looks around the interior.

'It's a nice motor.'

'How much can you give me?'

'Are you interested in a part exchange?'

'I need cash.'

My abruptness sends a frown flickering across his brow. 'I see. Well, I'd have to check out its history and get our workshop to give it the once over.'

'I can bring it back tomorrow, but could you give me a rough idea of price now?'

I follow him back to the showroom. He points to a chair at one of the workstations. 'Take a seat, Mrs—?'

'Dexter.'

His fingers peck at the keyboard. 'OK, so six months old, excellent condition and if, as you say, there's no crash history and the workshop gives it the all clear we'd be looking at… ballpark… thirteen thousand.'

'I'd been hoping for fifteen.'

'We could do you a better deal on part exchange.'

'No.' I've got no idea if he's ripping me off or offering me the going rate. Either way, I don't have time to shop around. 'That's fine.'

'Can you drop the logbook into the office tomorrow when you bring the car into the workshop?'

'All right.'

I drive home, running the numbers in my head. Thirteen thousand pounds out of forty thousand. That leaves twenty-seven to find. I walk into the house, stash the cheat eats at the very bottom of the freezer behind a bag of ice cubes and stand staring at the calendar, as if seeing the days laid out on a grid will somehow increase the six days I've got left. It doesn't. The peppering of pencilled reminders and appointments actually makes them shrink. But if Finn goes to the family art workshop on Monday with Susy and without me, that will buy me a last, desperate day before the deadline.

I'm not forbidden from entering Ian's study, in fact I go in there once a week to hoover and dust, and on Saturdays, when he does his paperwork, I often pop up there to bring him his post or a cup of coffee. But today, even though I'm armed with a duster and a can of Pledge, there's a feeling of trespass as I open the door, a shiver of guilt as I hurry to the window and pull down the blind before I switch on the desk lamp. The room is perfectly neat and orderly. Not a paperclip out of place. The big mahogany desk, the filing cabinet and bookshelves, the team photo of his university rowing team – Ian in a line-up of sweaty red-faced young men. I lift up the framed snapshot of him as a child with his father. A handsome, red-cheeked little boy holding the hand of a tall gentle-looking man in shirtsleeves. I turn it over, prise open the metal tabs at the back and lift away the rectangle of cardboard. I run my finger down the list of initials and numbers taped inside: the PINs for Ian's three personal credit cards and the one for the practice account. I gaze at them for a moment, then quickly drop the backing in place and close the metal tabs.

I pull open the drawers of the filing cabinet. It's all there, neatly filed: guarantees, instruction booklets, bills, receipts, accountants' letters. He deals with all of it. When I first moved in I'd offered to do my share and he'd laughed and asked if I didn't get my fill of boring admin in the office. He had a point. I flick through the plastic envelopes and pull out the registration document for my Honda. It's in his name. I don't understand. And then I do. A peculiar emptiness descends on me. Legally, the car that my husband gave me as a wedding present is still his. It was my only asset and without his permission – which I know he'll never give me – I can't sell it. I turn to the insurance. That's in his name, too. I'm not even named on the policy. I'm just 'any driver' allowed to drive it with his permission, a concession he can renege on any time he chooses. In a burst of frustration I pull open the next drawer, flip through the files to the household insurance policy and scan the named 'items of value' – his watch, his father's carriage clock, our laptops, the new television. That's all there is. No listing for a diamond engagement ring. I search through the folder of carefully dated receipts. No ring there, either. My mind hurtles from one explanation to the next and lands on one inescapable conclusion.

It's not Ian who was conned. It was me.

I drop into his leather swivel chair and hold up my hand, turning it so the fake diamond winks in the lamplight. It looks so real. If I hadn't tried to sell it I would never have known it was worthless. But why say all that stuff about wanting to show me how much I meant to him? Why pretend? A thought worms its way into my misery. Had he given Annabel a real diamond? After all, he'd been all set to give her a big posh wedding. But what did

I expect? For a girl like Nicola Cahill, a registry office and a cubic zirconia would do just fine. How can I blame him for that? I am soiled goods, an outsider, a liar and a nobody pretending to be something I'm not. It was always just a matter of time before my past caught up with me and brought my new life crashing down. And now it has.

But even as I sit there with my eyes stinging and my heart pounding, I'm ready to lose everything and to beg, borrow, lie and steal if that's what it takes to keep Finn. Brim full of pain I pick up the photo of Ian with his father again and lift away the backing. Another glance at my ring and the hurt bubbles up, helping to mask the shame and guilt as I get out my phone and take a photo of the PIN numbers.

A car pulls up outside as I'm reassembling the frame. I jump out of the chair. A woman's voice drifts up from the driveway. It's all right. It's Tilly dropping off Finn. I turn off the desk lamp, reopen the blind and hurry downstairs.

I wave and smile as Tilly drives away. When I bend down to kiss Finn the touch of his skin sparks another overwhelming urge to scoop him up, throw him into the car that isn't mine and run away. Instead I hurry him inside.

'What's for tea, Mum?' he asks, untying his shoes.

'Daddy's out tonight so I thought we'd have scrambled eggs with ham.'

'Can I help you make it?'

I hesitate. He never asks to cook when Ian's around – Ian doesn't like the mess, so when we're on our own I usually indulge him. But I'm tense and on edge and I want to get supper over quickly so I can think.

'*Please.*'

I gaze into his pleading eyes, struck by the sudden fear that if I can't raise the money this could be the last chance we'll ever have to cook together. The horror of it hits me hard, a slam so intense

I have to grip the edge of the table to stay upright. I shut my eyes and nod. 'All right, sweetheart. Go and wash your hands.'

He trots off to the sink then kneels up on a stool beside me and watches carefully as I crack eggs into a bowl. I hold the bowl down with one hand and grip the top of the whisk with the other while he cranks the handle, but somehow the whisk skids and rocks in his fingers, slopping egg onto the worktop.

'Stop!' I say. I mop up the puddle and he tries again, his face scrunched with concentration. When the eggs are frothy, I tip salt into my palm and show him how to take a pinch but it takes a couple of tries before he manages such a delicate operation. I transfer a splash of milk into a cup – there was a disaster last time I let him loose with the whole carton – and when he's poured it into the bowl I send him off to the fridge to get the butter and ham. I let him drop the slices of bread into the toaster while I chop the ham and drop it into the egg mixture but rather than dealing with a saucepan and a hot hob we cook the eggs in the microwave and I show him how to take them out, stir them with a fork and pop them back in to get just the right consistency. By the time he's finished the toast is cold and the eggs are rubbery but he's so pleased with his efforts he can't stop grinning and my heart is on the edge of breaking. As soon as we've eaten I shoo him into the sitting room and to his astonishment I hand him the remote and plant him in front of the television.

'Aren't you going to watch with me, Mum?'

'Not just now, sweetheart. I've got some things I need to do.'

I return to the kitchen to fret and pace, my heart thumping to the beat of my calculations and Finn's excited, sing along to the *SpongeBob* theme tune. I flirt fleetingly with the idea of using Ian's cards to buy valuable things like computers and jewellery and selling them on, but where would I buy that kind of stuff, where could I store it, and how could I find enough cash buyers in time? No. Withdrawing cash has to be the safer option. I'm guessing that each card will have a £500 daily withdrawal limit. If I'm lucky and Ian doesn't get wind of the withdrawals before I'm done, that could get me ten, maybe even twelve thousand pounds. But I would still be thirty thousand short. I look up at the wall calendar again. If I open my mouth a howl like a wounded animal will come out, a howl that will tear me apart and go on and on ripping through the house.

CHAPTER 37

When Ian gets back from his dinner with Downing I pretend to be asleep, though I can tell by the upbeat way he cleans his teeth that the discussions have gone well. It sounds like he's tipsy too – good. It means he'll fall asleep quickly. I lie very still, listening to the wind rippling the trees outside the window as he gets in beside me and cups a hand around my breast. I wait until his breathing steadies before I unclasp his fingers and edge out of his grasp. I give it ten more minutes before I wriggle out of bed. Keeping my eyes on his sleeping form I move backwards, step by tentative step, towards his suit jacket hooked over the back of the chair. I slip my hand into the inside pocket and feel for the soft leather of his wallet. Holding it behind my back I retreat to the door. A floorboard creaks beneath my foot. Ian stirs. My muscles lock. I screw up my eyes, he grunts, stretches and goes quiet. I hurry downstairs, pull my gym bag out of the hall closet and dress quickly in the black joggers and black hoody I stuffed in there earlier, scraping my hair into an old black baseball cap. I wrap a black scarf around my throat, pull it up and over my mouth, drop the hood over the cap and tweak the peak low over my brow. I slip my umbrella into my backpack, check that I've got the list of PIN numbers and let my myself out of the back door. I close it quietly and wheel my bike out of the shed and down the side of the house.

Damp wind gusts wisps of cloud across a moon that's as pale and thin as a nail clipping. With a quick glance at our bedroom window I swing myself onto the saddle and pedal down the drive to the road, letting my stiff muscles warm up as I sweep around the silent close. The gabled roofs of the houses stand serrated against the dark of the sky, a square of light in an upstairs room, a distorted silhouette playing on a half-closed blind. I turn onto the main road, a sudden feeling of hope and freedom as I pick up speed, wind on my face, the squelch of rubber on wet asphalt as I move up the gears, A police car slows a little and draws parallel. I stare straight ahead and keep peddling. The car glides away. I ride on. The tree-lined streets give way to pubs, high-rises and semi-lit office blocks. Street lamps glint on the bonnets of parked cars, a blare of rap bursts from a passing van, a sharp rattle of wind.

By the time I get to the Megamart there's a thin drizzle swirling around the car park, streaking the unnervingly strong light from the sulfur lamps. Spotlights burn from the ceiling of the covered walkway housing the ATMs. Only the furthest edges of the tarmac and the recycling area are in darkness. I can't see any cameras but I know they're there. I want to turn back but desperation stops me. *You'll be all right. Just keep your head down.* A car pulls up. A woman jumps out in a blue nurse's uniform and hurries towards the ATMs. Keeping to the outer fringes of shadow I leave my bike behind the recycling bins and watch as she withdraws her money and walks quickly back to her car. I pull my scarf up over my nose, slip on a pair of tinted glasses that someone left in the surgery and flick the umbrella catch so it springs open. Cowering beneath it I dart towards the walkway. Halfway there, a low whirring sound stops me dead. The sound grows louder. *Don't look up and don't look round.* A lone skateboarder swings close. I see his feet as he circles around me, jeans and dirty trainers, legs leaning effortlessly into his turns. I keep moving. His arcs widen. The whirring fades as he slaloms away. Breathing hard I make it to the ATMs. Even beneath my umbrella I feel so exposed in the lurid wash of the lights I can hardly get the first card into the first machine. I squeeze my eyes shut. *I'm stealing from my husband. It's an emergency. He won't find out it's me, he'll think he's been hacked or cloned or whatever it is fraudsters do when they steal credit card data. And he's insured. It will be all right.* I think of Finn, open my eyes and punch the keys. My stomach clenches. The mechanism clunks and grinds. I punch again. The slot opens and spews out £500. I stuff the money into the zip-up pocket of my backpack. I tilt the umbrella a little and check the ground around me for approaching feet. It's OK. I'm still alone. I try again, working through all the cards until I've exhausted Ian's credit for the day and collected £2,000. Giddy with triumph, I shoulder my backpack and step out into spattering rain.

There's movement at the far side of the car park, a chink of bottles, the rumble of a trolley. I hurry back to the recycling area and peer into the darkness. My bike's not there. I run along the row of bins, tripping over a mess of ripped bin bags, rain-soaked catalogues and broken glass. No bike. I look around for the skateboarder. He's gone, too. A fierce gust of wind tugs my umbrella and whips it inside out. I snatch at the flapping canopy and wrench it down, snapping one of the struts. I hurl it into a dumpster and start to trudge home through the rain, feeling bereft at the loss of my trusty old bike and worryingly conspicuous, even though I keep to the shadows.

A man lurches out of a doorway. He leans in close, yellow teeth, a grizzled jaw, a stench of piss. Fear swells inside me, a rising tide that floods my senses.

'Got any change, love?'

I plunge my hand into my pocket, pull out a handful of coins and tip them into his cupped hands. He grunts and ambles away.

My clothes are wet through and my teeth chatter with fear and cold as I open the back door. I'm exhausted, and tomorrow night I'll have to do this all over again, only walking both ways. I yearn for a hot shower, but I daren't turn on the water in case I wake Ian. I peel off my sodden clothes and once I've stashed

them in the washing machine I pull on a T-shirt and tiptoe up to
Finn's room. He stirs as I take Maisie from the shelf and murmurs
a little as I unsnap her seam and shove the money into the cavity
in her back. My fingers close around the tub of Valium. I gaze up
at the sweep of stars wheeling across Finn's walls and push the tub
back down. I daren't take any. I have to be up in four hours' time.

I creep along the landing to our bedroom, slip Ian's cards back
into his wallet and crawl into bed beside him.

I've been a liar for a long time. Now, I'm a thief.

CHAPTER 38

At breakfast, Ian doesn't mention yesterday's disaster with Mrs Clarke. He obviously left the surgery before Maggie had a chance to vent about my incompetence. What does it matter? She'll definitely be popping by to have one of her 'little words' with him today.

All morning I feel her eyes on me, hungry for another slip-up. Woozy with tiredness I double-check everything: files, appointments, invoices. There's too much at stake to let her edge me out of this job. At eleven Ian drops by the reception desk. I look up at him and feel my heart rate rise.

'I'll be back a bit late tonight,' he says, 'I want to have a drink with a guy from the planning department – good to keep these people onside. Is that all right?'

'Of course,' I say, and drop my eyes to my keyboard as I exhale.

'Any chance you could get home by two this afternoon? Derek says he can install our cameras. He's got a last-minute cancellation.'

Pain and frustration roil inside me. Once the cameras are installed it will put an end to my midnight trips to the ATMs, desperate calls to lenders, and lies about being at home.

'Nicci?'

I can feel him looking down at me, waiting for a reply.

'I… um… actually, next week would work better for me.'

'No problem. I'll tell him to drop into the surgery and pick up my keys.'

Crushed and helpless I murmur, 'No, it's… it's all right. I can be home by two.'

'Thanks, darling.' He gives me a smile and heads back to his room.

I stare at my computer screen, pressure tightening around my skull, a band of steel pushing at my temples. The morning drags on in a haze of phone calls, filing, dealing with awkward patients and trying to mend the broken photocopier. I try everything, including kicking it, and give up in despair.

Amy hands me a coffee. 'Don't worry, I'll call the engineer. It's ridiculous, the damn thing's brand new.'

I gaze at her for a moment, and feel a sudden easing of the tension around my skull.

As soon as my shift is over I hurry out of the surgery, keen to get home as quickly as I can. Despite yesterday's downpour the sky is clear, there are even little patches of sunlight breaking through the clouds and catching the brass tips of the railings.

I stand in the dim light of the garage running my eyes along the carefully arranged shelves. Finally I see it, the red metal toolbox that belonged to Ian's father, rammed between the electric sander and a pot of the Elephant's Breath emulsion he chose for our bedroom. I raise my phone, take a photo of its exact position and carefully lift it onto the workbench.

It's heavy. The paint is chipped and rubbed, but the snap locks and hinges are well oiled and the cantilevered trays pull out smoothly. I take another photo of the layout of the tools and screws and bolts and select a couple of screwdrivers and a pair of pliers. I carry them back to the kitchen and remove the slim black recorder from the box of security cameras. Resisting the urge to hurl it against the wall, I carefully unscrew the bottom. A fat black cable bulges out from the innards. Pulse throbbing in my fingertips I grip it with the pliers. A satisfying snap as they slice through the plastic casing and expose the bright copper wires inside. I lay down the pliers and use a flathead screwdriver to work some of the metal pimples loose from the circuit board. Calmer now, I screw the bottom back on, slip the recorder back into its plastic wrapper and bed it down into its polystyrene cradle. I take the tools back to the garage, use the photos I took to put them back in the toolbox exactly as I found them, and heave the box back onto the shelf.

I put the ironing board up in the kitchen and I've just fetched the basket of clean washing when the doorbell rings.

Smile at the ready I pull open the door. A dumpy man with a mat of close-cut brown hair stands on the step. 'Derek,' he says, looking over my shoulder into the house.

'Oh, great come in,' I say, as if his arrival is the high point of my day. 'Can I get you a cup of tea?'

'You're all right.' He swings his canvas tool bag onto his shoulder, picks up his aluminium ladder and walks past me into my kitchen.

'It's all in the box on the kitchen table,' I say, following him down the hall. 'Shall I show you where to put the cameras?'

He shakes his head. 'Your husband's told me where he wants them.'

It rankles that he's treating me as if I'm the help whose opinions don't count but maybe he's used to his clients' partners kicking up a fuss when he comes to install spy cams in their home. I force another smile and move back to the ironing board. I roll my head, first left then right, a crunch of tension as I spread a pink, Hawaiian cotton shirt across the ironing board. When I look up he's unpacking the cameras, carefully inspecting each one before he deposits it on the table. I dab a spit – moistened finger against the flat of the iron and nose the tip across the collar of the shirt as he opens up his ladder. Three screechy bursts of his drill, three short sharp whizzes of his electric screwdriver and there it is: the first camera installed above the bifold doors. It fixes me with its intrusive stare as he adjusts the little antenna and heads outside to put up the others. By the time he comes back, I've swept up the sprinkling of plaster dust he left on the floor and there are three, newly ironed, precision folded pastel shirts on the chair beside me.

He picks up the recorder. 'Where's the utility room?' he says, still without looking at me.

The tensions I've been holding at bay for the last two days surge to the surface and suddenly I want to yell at him that this is *my* house and he should be asking me where he should put the damn recorder, which is stupid seeing as I don't want him to put it anywhere. 'Through there,' I say, with a helpful tip of my head.

I shunt the ironing board very slightly so I can watch him. He's plugging it in. I lay another shirt across the ironing board. Flick. He's switching on the socket. Flick. Flick. He grunts, comes out and looks around for another socket. Without a word he plugs the recorder into the one next to the cooker and tries again.

'Problem?' I say.

'Yep.' He takes the recorder over to the table, whips a screwdriver from his top pocket and with a few delicate twists of his calloused fingers he unscrews the back. He pokes around for a couple of seconds, pulls out the severed cable and shakes his head, as if the damage is a personal affront.

'Can you mend it?' I say.

'No point.' He peers at the rest of the components. 'Circuit board's buggered as well.'

'I'm sorry you've had a wasted journey.'

'Tell your husband to give me a call when he gets a replacement.' He packs up his tools. The iron hisses as I tilt it back onto the board, ready to see him to the door.

'I'll let myself out,' he says.

'You do that, Derek.'

The door shuts behind him. I lean back against the worktop, a weight lifted, a hurdle scaled. But it's only a temporary reprieve.

Ian catches sight of the recorder sitting in the box as soon as he walks in. 'What happened?' he says, as he kisses me.

I turn away and pull on the oven gloves. 'There's something wrong with the recorder. Derek wants you to call him when you've got a replacement.'

I brace myself as he reaches for a bottle of wine and twists off the cap. 'That's annoying,' he says. 'If I repack it tonight, can you drop it into the post office?'

'Sure,' I say, bending down to open the oven.

'That looks good. What is it?'

'Lamb tagine.'

'New recipe?'

'I… thought I'd give it a try.' I set the dish on the table and say quickly, 'that friend Donna told me about, the one whose husband died. She's desperate to get her hands on some money and she needs it quickly. I said I'd ask you if you knew anywhere that might give someone like her a loan.'

'How much does she need?'

'A few thousand, I think. More if she can get it.'

I turn back to the sink and drain the couscous, taking my time so the steam will account for my burning cheeks.

'Has she got a job?'

'Part-time. In a shop, I think, so she could pay it back over time if the interest rate was reasonable. But she's getting a no from all the banks and building societies.' I toss oil into the couscous and spoon a single portion into a small earthenware serving dish – no carbs for me. 'Are there any other options?'

'For people like her? With nothing to offer as security and no credit rating? Not really. I suppose she could try joining a credit union but that's not a quick fix. They still check your credit score and expect you to save with them for a while before they'll give you a loan.'

I bring the dish to the table, squeezing it hard to hide the tremor in my hands. The tagine goes down well with Ian, though I can barely taste it. After we've eaten we clear up together and I feign a headache and leave him watching the rugby while I crawl up to bed. I set the alarm on my phone to vibrate at midnight and push it beneath my pillow. I needn't have bothered. I'm exhausted but far too wound up to sleep.

At ten to twelve I leave him sleeping. I hear the rough rasp of his breathing as I descend the stairs in my bare feet. I pull on my gym gear in the dark and gently open the back door. A shaft of moonlight falls across the package sitting on the worktop: the damaged recorder, all labelled up ready for me to drop off at the post office tomorrow morning.

I slip outside, close the door gently behind me and jog to the ATM at the garage on the bypass. I come back a couple of hours later with another £2,000 in crisp new notes stuffed in my bra. No rain tonight and no cameras to record my departure or my return. But there's no cause for elation. Even if I manage to keep this up until Tuesday, I'll still be £30,000 short of the sum I need to keep my son.

CHAPTER 39

Four days left. What am I going to do? I glance at my watch. It's parents' assembly this morning. I have to be there. On the way, I rip the labels off Ian's package and drop the recorder into the gaping mouth of a roadside litter bin, the sky flat and grey as I get back into my car and drive on to the school.

I arrive at the gates just as Tilly is making her way up the school steps.

She and Matt are wealthy. That massive extension they're building on their house is costing a fortune, and last Christmas they took their kids to Thailand. They're generous too, always first in line to donate to school fundraisers. I run to catch up with her. The words tumble out: 'Tilly, can you lend me some money?'

The request quivers in the air. I step back, embarrassed.

'Sure.' She takes out her purse and pulls out a couple of ten-pound notes. 'Sorry, that's all I've got on me. I never carry much cash.'

I look from her to the money. Small change to someone like Tilly, it's the kind of life-saving amount the mums on the block would scrape together when one of us was desperate. Women whose so-called boyfriends had done a flit with their housekeeping, the television and anything else they could shift while their partners were out at work. We'd have a whip round. Five or six women, all without safety nets, chipping in a few quid each to feed a kid, pay a bill, buy a pair of school shoes or keep a debt collector at bay. Money the lenders could barely afford to do without and the borrower would raise heaven and earth to pay back the minute she could. But I'm not living on the block anymore. In the world I inhabit now, people don't bail each other out of financial trouble, not even the ones who can afford it. And even if I did manage to convince Tilly to lend me some serious money, she'd never agree to keeping it a secret from Matt. Why would she?

'Oh, no.' I laugh awkwardly. 'A fiver will do. I wanted to buy some raffle tickets and I left my purse at home.'

'Don't worry. I'll treat you. I need to get some anyway.'

She waves to Jake Turner's dad, who's sitting beneath an arch of balloons by the front desk, clutching a ticket book.

I accept the little wad of tickets she hands me and trail after her into the hall. We pick our way to seats at the front and Tilly launches into a tirade about her builders, but the fear of losing my son is jangling my nerves so loudly I struggle to make out the words.

'Nicci?'

I look up. The room is shivering, blurry lines play around a smiling face. 'Oh, Lisa. Hi. Sorry, I was miles away. Do you, erm… do you know Tilly, Henry's mum?'

The two women lean across me and nod and smile. The doors open and a line of children shuffle to the front of the hall, some staring at the floor, some grinning at their parents – Finn giggling with Jamal. They seem thick as thieves and he looks happier than I've seen him since he started school. I wave at him. When he lifts his hand and waves back it's as much as I can do not to burst into tears.

Lisa glances at me and we share a smile. 'It would be great to get the boys together over half-term,' she says. 'Jamal's going to his dad's for the first few days but would Finn like to come over on Thursday?'

Thursday. My vision bends and the walls tilt in. Will Finn still be mine by Thursday?

'Nicci? Are you all right?'

I try to reply. Words and sobs wedge in my throat. I sniff up my panic and press the back of my hand to my nose. 'Thank you. He'd love that.'

'Great! Text me your address and I'll come and pick him up.'

It strikes me again that at any other time I would be offering to have Jamal over to our house and doing everything I could to encourage Finn's new-found friendship. Not today. Today all I can think about is money.

Who do I know who might lend me some? Who can I trust not to tell?

CHAPTER 40

The Downings' house is a white-pillared villa set back from the road by a sweep of pale pea-gravel. There's a small blue hatchback parked in front of the garage. I walk slowly up the front steps and stand for a long while before I work up the nerve to rap the knocker. It feels like I stand there for ages staring at my feet and I'm almost at the point of running back to my car when the door jerks open and I'm eye to eye with Lydia, effortlessly elegant in jeans and a taupe-coloured top. Her feet are bare, her hair is loose and she's wearing enormous tortoiseshell glasses which she pushes onto her head. 'Nicci,' she says.

'I hope I'm not disturbing you.'

'Actually, I'm on a deadline.' Her eyes scan my face. Whatever it is she sees there causes her to step back and motion me inside. 'But come in. I was just about to break for a coffee.'

I follow her down an airy hallway and catch my reflection in a long, gilded mirror. I'm looking peaky, eyes over-bright, fists clenching and unclenching. I look away into a wide sitting room: pale sofas, a polished floor, a marble fireplace over which hangs a portrait of Lydia in shades of cream and ochre that leaves half her face in shadow. I hurry on into a huge yet welcoming kitchen: hand-painted units, a Belfast sink and a big range cooker flank a long pine table dimpled with wear – the kind of elegant shabbiness only serious money can buy. An elderly dog lifts its head as I walk in, then loses interest and nestles back onto a tartan rug.

'Grab a seat. Tea or coffee?'

'Coffee, please.'

Lydia pushes back her sleeves and busies herself at the worktop scooping coffee beans into an electric grinder. 'Is everything all right?' she says.

'Not really.' Glad of her half-turned back, I take a breath and launch into my carefully prepared lie, a new riff on the one I told Ian. 'This is a bit awkward and I wouldn't be doing it if it wasn't an emergency, but one of the young mums we mentor is in trouble.' The words are coming out too fast. I push back my hair and slow down. 'She'd been struggling to hold things together and when she got desperate she borrowed money from a loan shark. It was a stupid thing to do and now he's threatening her.'

'She should go to the police,' Lydia says.

'That's not an option for someone like her. If this guy got arrested his people would make it their business to make an example of her.' My face burns. I look down at the tiled floor, feeling like a street beggar trying her luck for the first time. 'This is completely unofficial but I'm trying to raise the money to pay off her debt.'

There's a beat of silence and then the blast of the coffee grinder. I stare out of the window at a wide expanse of lawn and a line of trees leading down to a white-painted summer house. I can feel her watching me but I daren't meet her eyes. The grinding stops. 'What'll happen to her if she doesn't pay?' Lydia says.

'They'll probably beat her up.'

'How much does she owe?'

'She borrowed five hundred pounds. But with that kind of loan the interest balloons and now she owes… five thousand.' I'd been tempted to ask Lydia for more but I've thought this through and carefully calibrated the sum.

'That's a lot of money.' She pours water into the lower chamber of one of those bright red Italian coffee pots.

'She's got a job and she can pay it back with normal interest. The only reason she got into trouble was because of the extortionate rate this creep was demanding.' I stop and swallow hard. 'But she needs it by Tuesday.'

She spoons coffee into the funnel of the coffee pot, screws the top and bottom together and sets it on the stove before turning around. 'Would a bank transfer do?'

The offer is made so casually, it takes me a moment to register what she has said. To my horror when it sinks in I find my eyes filling with tears at her sheer, unquestioning generosity, though I wince a little at the answer I'm forced to give her. 'Not really. She… she needs cash.'

'I just haven't really got time to go into the bank today. If she doesn't have a bank account, I could transfer it to you and you could get her the cash.'

'No!' She blinks at my vehemence. 'Sorry, Ian deals with all our finances. If it goes through my account he'll ask questions.'

She eyes me steadily. 'Why don't you tell him the truth?'

I feel myself flushing and look away. 'He… doesn't approve of me working with Next Steps.'

'I kind of gathered that at the dinner. To be honest, I don't see what business it is of his.'

'It's just easier to keep it off his radar. But please don't mention it to your husband. I don't want him getting the wrong idea about Ian.'

'I could get you the cash by Saturday.'

'Thank you. Thank you so much.'

'All right. I'll have it ready for you. And don't worry. Adam's away this weekend.'

'Thank you,' I say, again, croaky with embarrassment.

'This girl,' Lydia says. I look up into her smooth, impassive face. 'Is she being abused by someone? A boyfriend? A partner?'

'Oh, no,' I say, quickly. 'Nothing like that.'

'Abuse doesn't have to be physical.'

'I know.'

'Tell her I don't need the money back.'

'However long it takes, she'll want to pay it back.'

'Well, let's talk about that once she's paid off this loan shark.'

'I can't tell you how grateful she'll be.'

She pours coffee into two blue pottery mugs and offers me a jug of milk. 'Do they run workshops for prospective mentors?'

'Who?'

'Next Steps.'

'Oh, yes. Every couple of months.'

'Do they give you a chance to meet any of the mentees?'

'Definitely.'

'Will you let me know when you have a date for the next one? I'd really like to come.'

'Sure. But I should warn you, some of the kids are pretty hard work.'

'It must be rewarding, though.'

I sip my coffee. 'It can be.'

'Are you working with anyone at the moment?'

I tell her about Leon, how it's impossible to get through to him and how half the time I want to shake him. 'The thing is, however impossible they are, you mustn't give up on them. They're so used to people disappearing out of their lives they're basically just waiting for you to abandon them.'

'I'm not sure how patient I'd be, but I really would like to help.' She runs a finger around the top of her cup.

'Anyway, thanks for the coffee,' I say. 'I mustn't hold you up.' I take my coat from the back of the chair and try to look casual. 'If you do go along to one of the workshops, it's probably best if you don't mention the money to the rest of the team. Financial involvement with any of the kids we look out for is strictly off limits, but I can't bear to see this girl suffering.'

She raises her eyebrows very slightly. 'Of course.'

At the front door she takes my elbows, grasping them firmly in her long, slim fingers. At first I think she's going to kiss me goodbye but she just holds me there so we're standing face to face. 'I've got a little cottage in Oxfordshire,' she says. 'I use it as a writing retreat. If one of your girls… or your boys, ever needs a safe place to stay while they sort themselves out, just let me know.' Her eyes linger on mine almost as if she's trying to see inside my head. 'No one need know. Not even Adam.'

I stammer my thanks and walk back across the pea-gravel to my car.

Turning around in the driveway, I do the sums in my head: £5,000 from Lydia, £4,000 so far from Ian's credit cards, and £1,000 from the one he lets me use. I do the calculations again as if a frantic recount might alter the reality. It doesn't.

As soon as I get home I hit the phone again, calling credit unions and asking about emergency loans. The best I get is the offer of an appointment to see a loans officer in two weeks' time.

I feel like a film director creating a set: from certain angles my life looks just like the real thing, while behind the scenes it's chaos; a flimsy illusion held together by lies and deception.

Our home was a picture of order and calm when Ian got home. Now, when he looks up, he sees his wife and stepson enjoying a perfect evening in their perfect home. All the right sounds and smells are in place – the haddock and bacon gratin bubbling in the oven, the clink of pans as I empty the dishwasher, the rasp of Finn's breath as he pores over the chess problem Ian has just set him. Ian even gets his own lines pitch perfect as he murmurs advice: 'Sometimes it's worth sacrificing a really important piece if it helps you win in the end, especially if your opponent thinks you've haven't got the guts to do it and you can catch them off guard.'

Finn stares up at him, guzzling the words, though I have no idea how much of it he understands. He looks back down at his pieces and pushes his glasses up his nose.

This is how I must keep it. Everything normal, everything smooth.

'There's a couple of new gym classes I wouldn't mind trying out on Saturday,' I say. 'Any chance you could look after Finn for a couple of hours?'

'No problem.' He throws Finn a glance. 'How about we go swimming. I don't know why your mummy never takes you.'

'You know I don't like water,' I say, too quick and too sharp. I soften my voice. 'Anyway, he gets swimming lessons at school.'

'I spoke to Maggie today,' Ian says, getting up to refill his glass. 'We've agreed to advertise your job.'

The set wobbles, a sudden crack in the flimsy veneer exposing the void beneath. Slack-jawed with fury I turn away and place a ceramic bowl just so on the shelf above me.

'It's clearly too much for you at the moment, even part-time.'

I turn back, face composed. 'No, it's not. I told you, I want more hours.'

He sighs and shakes his head. 'She told me about the mistakes you've been making. If Mac hadn't stepped in and calmed Mrs Clarke down, we'd have a lost a very well connected patient.'

Everything blurs. 'I don't want to stop work. I can't.'

'It's not as if we need the money and, look at you, you're all over the place. Stressed out, leaving gates open, fainting at work, overreacting all the time, having trouble sleeping, not to mention the state of this place.' He glances at Finn and then back at me and leans in close, dropping his voice. 'No wonder you're not getting pregnant.'

I look away, torn between anger that he's done this without even consulting me and panic that he's snatched away my only source of income. 'I should be the one who decides when I stop work.'

'It's done now. Believe me, darling, it's for your own good.' His voice is soothing and measured, as if he's talking to a crabby child who's refusing to go to bed. I slam the dishwasher shut with my hip and force my lips into a compliant smile – the ever-ready duct tape that holds my crumbling world together. I'll fight this. I'll talk to the other partners, kick up a fuss. But not now. At this moment it's as much as I can do to stay upright.

Five hours later, I stand panting in front of the ATM, one hand pressed to the wall as I feed in the first of Ian's cards and tap in the maximum withdrawal.

Card declined

The machine grinds and spits it out. I shove the second one in and tap in the PIN.

Card declined

No! Please, no! I tug my hoody down lower and try the third one.

Card declined

I try his card for the practice account and watch in horror as the machine clicks, clacks and swallows it whole.

Please contact your bank

CHAPTER 41

Saturday comes. I leave Ian stuffing Finn's towel and swimming trunks into his backpack and head to Lydia's. She invites me in, but I tell her the girl who needs the money is waiting for me and I'm in a hurry to get to her.

She darts back inside and returns with a fat brown envelope. 'Here.' She pushes it into my hand. 'Like I said yesterday, there's no rush to pay me back.'

I look up at her, struck by a sudden desperate thought. 'Were you serious about lending your cottage to someone in trouble who needed a place to lie low? Just for a few weeks.'

Her eyes lift to mine. 'Of course, if it would help.'

Hope fizzles out before I even get back to the car. As soon as Donna realised I'd disappeared she'd send that footage to the police and they'd hunt us down in no time.

On the way back into town I pass Sean Logan's scrapyard. Logan's BMW noses its way out of the entrance and the heavy iron gates clang shut behind him. I drive on quickly, afraid he'll clock my car.

I park in the multi-storey and walk through the old town, past the branch of Monsoon where I bought the frothy wedding dress I never wore, past the restaurant we went to after the ceremony, just me and Ian and an overbearing waiter who fussed and hovered and made a big deal about bringing me another fork when I dropped mine on the floor. I walk down to a café, buy a coffee and sip it as I cross into the cathedral gardens. The rumble of traffic fades, muffled by the trees. It's cold and damp but I need the quiet and the calm. I feel so distracted, empty and frightened I lose track of where I am and I find myself on the bridge where the canal meets the river. I look down into the swirl of muddy water and think about my mother, how she must have felt the day she decided I wasn't worth living for.

Someone is touching my sleeve. I spin around.

'Are you all right? You've been… standing there a while.'

I look into the face of stranger. Lipstick, headscarf, a dusting of powder on wrinkled cheeks.

'Yes, yes, I'm fine.'

'Are you sure?'

'Yes.' I stare into pale, watery eyes. 'Thank you, though.'

'However bad it feels, there's always a way to work it out,' she says. 'Believe me.'

I want to tell her that my life might be crashing down around me but I would never do to Finn what my mother did to me; and it warms me that this stranger cared enough to stop.

When I get back I find Ian dealing with a flurry of texts about 'unusual activity' on his credit cards. He checks his wallet, discovers that one of them is missing and spends what seems like hours on the phone to the police and various fraud teams who, he tells me, are all setting up investigations.

My hands are steady as I slice avocado and mozzarella for lunch but inside I am squirming, my stomach flopping and writhing like a fish on a hook.

'Thankfully I've got insurance for this kind of theft,' Ian says over his shoulder as he empties the swimming bag, 'and the good thing is they only managed to take a few grand before the cards got stopped.'

I nod silently. A few grand. It's a minor irritation to my husband, but to me it could mean the difference between losing and keeping my son.

*

The next morning, I tell Ian I feel sick, which I do, and he brings me peppermint tea in bed.

'You stay there. I'll sort lunch when we get back from football,' he says.

'Really?'

He cups my cheek. 'Of course. Like I told you yesterday, you need rest.'

I roll onto my side and shut my eyes, counting the minutes until the front door slams shut. Then I sit up and make a call.

'Yeah?' The voice on the other end is chipper yet non-committal. Michael Cronin – a spotty little loan shark who preyed on the women on Beechwood: small loans at extortionate interest rates. All smiles and a helping hand while he doled out a few fivers; threats and a brick through your window the minute you faltered on a payment.

'Mikey? Mikey Cronin?'

'Who's asking?'

'Nicola Cahill.'

'Nicola.' A grunt of surprise. 'I heard you'd gone up in the world.'

I look at the pale stripe of the curtains. I look at the antique Windsor chair in the corner by the window. I look at my face in the gilded mirror above the chest of drawers. 'I need to borrow some money.'

'How much?'

'Thirty thousand pounds.'

Silence, then a snort of laughter. 'You're talking to the wrong bloke, love.'

'Do you know anyone who can help me?'

'Well,' he says, silkily. 'I suppose I could make some calls, ask around.'

'How long would that take?'

'That kind of money? A few days. Maybe a week.'

'I don't have a few days.'

'I don't have thirty grand.'

'How much do you have?'

'I could let you have five. Ten at a pinch. Rates would go up, though.'

You don't say. 'I'll get back to you.'

I'm in cold sweat as I hang up, and totally unprepared for the howl that spurts from the throat of the woman in the mirror. I look at her a little closer and realise that she is sobbing.

Ian is cooking a stir-fry when I come down, tossing strips of chicken with bright chunks of pepper and broccoli in a heavy iron wok.

'How was football, Finn?'

He looks down at the table. 'We lost.'

'Afraid so,' Ian says. 'He missed a couple of really easy passes, but that girl Ginny's a marvel. In a couple of years I think one of the academies might be interested in signing her up.'

I give Finn a smile. 'I bet she's terrible at telling jokes.'

'There was a new boy there from Finn's class – Jamal?' Ian says.

'Oh, good. His mum said she might bring him. Did he have fun?'

'I have no idea. But let's just say he's not one of the world's natural athletes.'

Ian sprinkles cashews into the wok and brings it to the table. What little appetite I have disappears when he asks if Donna has been to see me.

'No. Why do you ask?'

'She was at the game with some bloke in tow. Didn't stay long. They waved to me, chatted to Finn at half-time and then wandered off. I assumed she'd gone to see you.'

'No.'

This bloke has to be Donna's boyfriend, the one who 'couldn't wait' to become Finn's stepdad. Why would she take him to football? To see what he was missing? To keep me on my toes?

'What did they say to you, Finn?'

'He was nice. His name's Steve and he said not to worry about missing passes. I just need to work on my weak foot.'

Ian piles stir-fry onto his plate. 'It's going to take a bit more than that, old son.'

I lay down my fork. 'Sorry, I don't feel at all well. Do you mind if I go back to bed?'

'Go on,' Ian says. 'Up you go. We'll be fine, won't we, fella?' Ian tousles Finn's hair. 'It'll give us a chance to get in some serious practice in the garden. Can't have the coach's kid letting the side down all the time.'

The pills aren't working. Of course they aren't. It's two in the morning and tomorrow is Monday. My last day to raise the cash. After another hour of lying in a tortured, half-dream – Donna's threats colliding with visions of my boy slipping from my grasp – I creep downstairs and make myself a pot of coffee. Dawn creeps through the shutters as I sip it, the thin light bringing with it a glimmer of calm and the makings of a plan. If I borrow the £10,000 from Mikey Cronin and give it to Donna along with the £10,000 I've raised from Lydia and from Ian's credit cards, that will be £20,000. It's a lot of money. More than enough for a deposit on a flat and to keep her and her bloke in style while Mikey gets hold of the rest.

I make Finn a packed lunch to take to the art workshop. All his favourite things: a cheese and Marmite sandwich, a carton of blackcurrant smoothie, a muesli bar, a pot of grapes and a banana, packed neatly into his Spider-Man lunch box.

On the way there, I glance in the mirror and say casually: 'Sweetheart, something's come up and I can't go to the workshop today, but you'll be all right with Gaby and Susy, won't you?'

'But I wanted you to come with me.'

'I know, but you and I are going to do loads of fun things together later in the week. OK?'

He bites his lip but manages a small, 'OK.'

I give it a beat. 'But let's not tell Daddy that you went with Gaby and Susy.'

'Why?'

'Well, he doesn't want me to work for Next Steps anymore and Susy does, which makes him a bit cross. I'm going to sort it out but at the moment it's best if we don't mention that we're seeing them. Poor Daddy works so hard and we don't want to stress him out.'

My heart squirms as he nods and zips his fingers across his lips. So many lies. So many deceptions.

I pull up outside the church hall. Susy and Gaby are waiting for us beside the multicoloured banner announcing a creative fun day for all the family strung across the railings. Mums, dads, kids, grannies and granddads are pouring through the double doors, unwinding scarves, laughing and joking. I yearn to join them and spend the day sploshing glue and paint around, having fun with my son.

I wave at Susy and walk around to open Finn's door.

'Hey!' She comes up behind me and gives me a hug. 'You never told me how it went with the housing officer.'

'Not good. I kind of lost it when she started talking about care leavers making risky lifestyle choices. I'm going to email her and apologise.'

I meet her gaze, unnerved to find myself facing the same narrow-eyed concern I'd seen when I left her party.

'Not like you to go off the deep end,' she says.

'I've been a bit… wound up, lately.'

'Sounds like today is exactly what you need.'

'I'm sorry. I can't.'

'Why not?' Susy looks a little hurt, which makes me feel even worse.

'I've got a work thing.'

'I thought you'd got the week off.'

'Staff training. Got to go.' I plant a kiss on the top of Finn's head, thrust his lunch box into his hands and jump back in the car.

As soon as I get home I call Donna. As always, she takes a while to pick up.

'Donna, it's me.'

Her voice is slurred and heavy. 'What do you want? What time is it?'

'Just gone nine thirty. Look, sorry if I woke you. I'm... I'm still waiting for some of the money I'm borrowing to come through. Nothing to worry about. I can definitely get you twenty thousand in cash by tomorrow and the rest as soon after that as I can.'

The man cuts in, deep and aggressive. 'Is that her?'

Seems like this time I'm not on speaker because I can hear Donna's voice, low and muffled like she's covering her phone. '... twenty now... more time to get the rest.'

'No way.' The man's voice again, so loud I have to hold the phone away from my ear. 'You swore I'd have it by tomorrow.'

'I know but—'

'If she wants the boy she'll find the money.'

'Donna,' I say, talking over him. 'This is your decision, not his.'

'We had a deal.' There's an edge of fear in her voice. 'I told you not to jerk me around.'

'I'm not jerking you around. I said I'll get you the money and I will. The full forty grand. I just need... a few more days.'

'You with your swanky house and your posh car?'

'Donna, it's not how it looks.' I'm sobbing now, gasping out the words. 'None of that stuff is mine, not even the car.'

'My heart bleeds. If you want Finn as much as you say you do, prove it. You've got till one o'clock tomorrow.'

'Donna, please—'

She hangs up.

An abyss opens at my feet and I feel myself toppling into it. If I want to keep Finn I've only got one option left. One that will bring all the misery and darkness I've tried so hard to shut out, roaring back into my life.

CHAPTER 42

Sean Logan's scrapyard is spread over an acre of waste ground enclosed by a wall of graffiti-sprayed corrugated iron, topped with razor wire and taut lines of electric fencing. I've driven past it hundreds of times and watched the entrance from afar. Until now, I've never had a reason to go inside. There's a buzzer by the gate. I hesitate for a moment, then I rub my sweating palms against my jeans and jam my thumb against the button. I tilt back and look into the winking eye of a security camera.

'Yeah?' A voice crackles through the speaker.

'I'd like to see Sean Logan.'

'Who are you?'

'Nicola Dexter.'

'He expecting you?'

'No.'

There's a pause. I listen to the roar of traffic on the overpass and the strange tick-tick of the electric fence. I'm about to press the buzzer again when there's a squeal of metal against metal and the electric gates grind open. I slip through the gap and enter a vast, decomposing landscape: twisted metal, battered oil drums, muddied tarpaulins and the mechanical shriek of an electric saw. A crane swivelling overhead dips down, plucks a clawful of pipes from a pile of scrap and drops them with a ringing crash into the back of a waiting truck. A twitchy-looking man – cropped hair, small eyes, tattooed neck – steps out, crowbar in hand, from behind a mountain of old tyres. Without saying a word to me or taking his eyes off mine he shouts, 'Dyl!'

Dylan Greaves emerges from the back of a rusty container and walks towards me, running his eyes over my legs and what he can see of my top half through my gaping coat. For one sickening moment I think he's going to search me. I glare into his pouchy face. He glares back, taking a moment to enjoy my discomfort before he beckons me to follow him. He leads me past chunks of broken cement, heaped packing cases and a stack of splintered door frames and walks up the steps to a green prefabricated hut. He holds open the door and stands back to let me in – less a show of gallantry, more a ploy to force me to brush against his sagging belly as I step inside. Close up, he stinks of oil and burned rubber.

Sean Logan sits behind a metal desk, talking on the phone and smoking. The windows are tacked up with black mesh, whether to keep out daylight or prying eyes I'm not sure. The mesh spreads a diffuse grey light punctuated by the flicker from two monitors placed on a table opposite the desk. On one a football match plays out in silence; the other shows a grid of feeds from the security cameras dotted all around the yard. No secrets from Logan around here.

He cuts his call and plops his cigarette butt into a paper cup. I hear it fizz. 'If this is about Leon—'

'It's not.'

'So, what do you want?'

I glance behind me. Greaves is leaning against the door, arms folded, enjoying the show. 'It's private,' I say.

Logan sends him out with a grin and a jerk of his head and points to the metal chair on the other side of the desk. I wait for the door to shut then I sit down and come straight out with it. 'I need to borrow thirty thousand pounds.'

In the glow from the monitors, Logan's pale eyes shine cold and unblinking. 'Why come to me?'

'I've maxed out my credit cards.'

'Go to the bank. Get a loan.'

'I… I tried. For that kind of money they need my husband to guarantee it.'

He's opened a drawer in his desk and he's poking around inside it. 'So ask him.'

'I can't. I'll pay you whatever interest you want but I need to keep this between you and me.'

He closes the drawer and says slowly, 'Why don't you want your old man to know?'

'That's private.'

'Not if you want me to fork out thirty thousand quid it isn't.'

I look down at the cracked vinyl flooring. I feel jittery and hot. 'It's… for my son.'

'What kind of father won't cough up for his kid?'

'My son isn't his.'

'Is the boy sick?'

I pause for a beat too long before I nod and say, 'Yes. Yes, he's sick.'

'Don't lie to me. I don't like it.'

I have to gasp to get out the words. 'Someone's… threatening to take him.'

He turns this over. 'And you can't go to the police.' It's a statement, not a question. 'Is it the kid's real father?'

'It's more complicated than that. I'm desperate, Mr Logan.'

'You wouldn't be here if you weren't.' He lights another cigarette, tilts his head back and slowly blows out the smoke. 'How are you proposing to pay me back?'

'Out of my salary. It might take me a while but I'll see you get your money. And my car. It's a Honda Civic, less than a year old. I can't sell it because it's in my husband's name but I could report it stolen and you could strip it down and sell off the parts as a first repayment.'

He blows out a stream of smoke. 'That bad, eh?'

I nod.

'Tell you what. I'll think about it.'

'I need an answer now, Mr Logan. If you can't help me I need to find someone who can.'

A suffocating silence, then: 'You've got balls, lady, I'll give you that.' He scratches his eyebrow with his thumb. 'When would you need this money by?'

'Tomorrow morning.'

He opens his mouth, then seems to reconsider. 'Give me your number. I'll let you know when I've got it.'

I walk away from there, torn between relief at getting the money and despair at having to turn to a man that I loathe and despise.

I pick Finn up from the workshop, glad of the distraction of the garish loo roll marionettes that he and Gaby and Susy are jiggling around: a dachshund, a dragon and a unicorn held together by glitter glue, staples and knotty lengths of string. My oohs and aahs of praise are a handy way to hide the tension in my voice.

'You should have come,' Susy says, eyeing me hard. 'You'd have loved it.'

'Next time,' I say. With an awkward hug I leave her and hurry Finn out to the car.

I'm cooking his tea when my phone rings. I glance at him, busy crayoning at the table, and turn away as Logan's gritty voice comes on the line: 'I'll have your money by eleven tomorrow morning. There's a row of garages round the back of the Rosemead estate. Leave your car by the one at the far end. Lock it and bring me the keys when you pick up the cash.'

'What about the CCTV?'

'Don't you worry about that.' He laughs. A sound that manages to be both smug and threatening. 'There's a problem with the cameras on Rosemead that the council just don't seem to be able to fix.'

CHAPTER 43

Tuesday arrives. I'm calm as I step into the shower. Calm as I towel myself dry and pull clothes from my drawers. Calm as I contemplate the things I'm going to do today to keep my son safe. The doorbell rings and Finn shouts up the stairs. 'Mum, there's a parcel on the step!'

I come running down, shrugging a jumper over my T-shirt. 'Sweetheart, I've told you a hundred times not to open the door unless you're with a grown-up.'

'But it's for me. Look.' He picks up the package and swings around, grinning. 'Can I open it?'

I look down at the package in his hand. I don't like this. Something feels off. 'No,' I say. 'I'll do it.'

'Why can't I? It's for me.'

'Just in case it's... a mistake.'

I take the package from him and hurry into the kitchen. While he hops excitedly from foot to foot I lay it on the worktop, rip open the packaging and pull out a plastic pack. There's a picture of a boy in football kit on the front. He's kicking a ball that's strapped into a plastic harness and attached by a length of elastic to a vinyl belt he's wearing around his waist. *Improve your shooting, passing, and receiving*, it says on the label. *Build ball control without the chase.*

I breathe out. A little hiss of relief. 'It's for football training so you can practise on your own and get really good.'

His face lights up. 'Can I try it now? *Please.*'

'All right, just for ten minutes.'

I send him off to get his trainers and then kneel down and buckle the belt around his middle. Together we strap his football into the harness and he runs out into the garden. I watch through the glass doors as he skitters and skips around, kicking wildly at the ball and missing. After a few minutes he manages to hit it. I see him grin as the ball bounces back towards his foot and he sends it spiralling high.

I dig through the packaging. There's no note, though it has to be from Ian. It's such a thoughtful gift I feel bad that I've been annoyed with him for pushing Finn too hard in front of other children. This is exactly what he needs.

I go upstairs to finish getting dressed and I'm pulling my hair into a scrunchy when the landline rings. A rarity these days. I lean across the bed to pick it up. 'Hello?'

'Nicci.'

'Donna? Why are you ringing this number?' She's in a vehicle of some kind: I can hear the engine running.

'Maybe I was hoping to say hello to your dishy husband. Just kidding. Though you've got to admit you've done well for yourself. He's quite the catch.'

'What do you want?'

'Have you got the money?'

'Don't worry. I'll have it by one.'

'All right. There's an abandoned pub on Turnpike Road. The Fox and Hounds. I'll meet you in the car park.'

'Fine,' I say, pleased she doesn't want to come to the house.

'Nic?' There's a shift in her voice.

'Yes?' I brace myself for another body blow.

'I never thanked you for looking after him.'

I'm too startled to speak. I never expected this. 'What?'

'You've given Finn a good life. It can't have been easy being lumbered with a baby that wasn't yours.'

'I love him. I've loved him from the first moment I held him.'

'You saved him from the scrap heap.'

'No child deserves that.' For one fleeting moment it's as if we're fourteen again. Two naive, frightened kids with no one to turn to but each other.

'So, no uni for Miss Brainbox, then.' Her voice rings with sadness. 'I'm sorry, Nic. I know it was your dream.'

'It was worth it.'

'How on earth did you manage? At the beginning?'

'That vicar and his wife helped me. I stayed with them that first night then they found me a place at a mother and baby hostel. After that, well, I was back in the system, only this time with a kid in tow.'

'I know you think I'm a coward but that's what I couldn't face. Being pushed around and told what to do and how to live. I'd had enough of all that. But you were stronger than me. You always were.'

I sink onto the bed. 'It was really tough for a while.' I take a breath. 'Then I met this lovely woman who gave me a job in her nursery with free childcare thrown in, and about a year later I managed to get allocated a flat of my own.' I press the phone to my ear, the silence warm between us. 'Donna?'

'Yes,' her voice is breathy, on the brink of tears.

'This money I'm getting for you… please. If you could just give me a bit more time I'd be able to borrow it from a credit union. As it is, I'm having to—'

'Donna!' A man calls her name, the same threatening rasp that's been rumbling in her ear every time we've spoken. It must be that bloke she took to football – what was his name? Steve. A door slides shut.

She comes back on the line, hard and cold. 'All of it. Today.' She hangs up.

I replace the handset, glad that this horrible man won't be getting anywhere near Finn again. I run downstairs, grab a cup of tea and pop a couple of slices of bread into the toaster.

I call through the back door. 'Finn! Toast! You need to eat something before we go to Henry's.' I rinse my cup and stash it in the dishwasher. 'Come on, love. Do you want to take your scooter with you?' I step outside. 'Quick, we've got to hurry.'

The garden is empty. I walk around to the side of the house. The side gate bangs in the wind. This time I know for sure that I shut it. I run out onto the drive and look up and down the close.

'Finn!' My voice shatters the quiet. No small boy leaps from behind a hedge. No smiling face grins at me from a doorway. 'Finn!'

I run down the road, pulse rising, adrenaline kicking in. The houses loom up around me, blank-eyed. Has someone leaped out from one of them and pulled him inside? I spin around, breath quickening, fear squeezing my lungs, gates, hedges, driveways wheeling. How long since I saw him? How long was I on the phone? Five minutes? Ten?

Vera appears at her door and calls out, 'Is something wrong?'

I bolt across the road and push open her gate.

'Have you seen Finn?'

She shakes her head.

'Just now. Was there anybody in the street?'

'Just a delivery van. A scruffy-looking white thing with those sliding doors at the side.'

'A van?' I was scared already but now I'm entering full-blown panic. 'Where was it?'

'Parked by the Davidsons' hedge.' I look over at the house she's pointing to, tucked around the curve of the bend, just out of sight of my home. 'It sat there for a while with the engine running, then it backed up towards your drive so I couldn't see if anybody got in or out.' She's scanning my face, thin lips pursed with disdain. 'Why do you ask? Were they friends of yours?'

A spurt of bile rises in my throat. Acid and sour. The call from Donna. Ringing the house phone to lure me away from the windows. The subtle switch from Donna the hard-bitten stranger to Donna the friend I'd clung to as a kid, the gentle questioning, her voice reaching out to me across the years, the conversation I've been aching to have since the night she left. *Find their weak spot and play it for all it's worth.* The change, chilling and abrupt, when she'd switched back from friend to tormentor.

Fear in my mouth, the smell and taste of it everywhere. I run back to the house and grab my phone. With trembling fingers I call Donna's number. I count the rings… five, six, seven.

She picks up. 'Nicci.'

'Where is he?'

A momentary, heart-stopping silence. What if I'm wrong? What if this time it's not her who has taken him?

'Don't worry,' she says, brisk and businesslike. 'It's just a precaution. You'll get him straight back once you hand over the money.'

'That's not what we agreed. Let me come and get him.'

'Not till I get the cash.'

'He'll be hungry. He hasn't had any breakfast.'

'I'll give him a biscuit or something. Jesus.'

'And lunch. He'll be starving by one. Let me speak to him.'

'Like I said, you'll get him back once you hand over the money. Make sure you come on your own.' She hangs up.

I stand for a few seconds staring down at the keypad and then I call Tilly and tell her that Finn is sick. A tummy bug. I run into Finn's room – his unmade bed and scattered toys scream his absence as I retrieve the cash from Maisie's insides and shove it into my bra. Swinging my bag onto my shoulder I run downstairs, grab a plastic bag to put the money in, stuff a handful of muesli bars and a couple of box drinks into my pockets and hurry outside to my car.

CHAPTER 44

Rain clouds gather grey and heavy as I approach the Rosemead estate. I slow right down, crawling past harassed mums pushing buggies and kids kicking a ball around. Faces stare down from the walkways, clocking my car as I circle the blocks and turn down the narrow strip of cracked tarmac that leads to the garages. I park exactly where Logan told me to, outside the last one in the row. I raise the key fob over my shoulder and press it as I walk away. The car squawks a response. A last goodbye from the wedding gift that was never mine.

Aware of the cash stashed in my bra I keep my head down and my thoughts on Finn. I'm doing this for him. To make him safe, to keep him with me. I check the time on my phone, shove it back into my bag and walk faster.

I glance into the stairwell as I cut past Leon's block, a flicker of guilt as I see him slouched against the wall. 'Leon! I'm so glad you're back. I was worried that you were going to miss your hearing.'

He turns to look at me. Bloodshot eyes full of despair.

'You look terrible,' I say.

'Yeah? I wonder why that is?'

'Look,' I say, hurriedly, 'I'm really sorry, I can't stop right now, I wish I could but I want you to know that if things don't go the way we hope tomorrow I'll visit you and I'll be there for you when you get out.'

He raises a half-smoked spliff to his lips and relights it, inhaling slowly.

'That stuff's not going to help,' I snap.

He opens his mouth and lets a curl of thick white smoke escape. 'What would you know?'

'You can't just give up. You've got to stay positive.' I cringe. Is that really the best I can come up with?

'Why don't you just fuck off and leave me alone.'

'Leon!'

'It's all words with you. Yak, yak, yak to make yourself feel better.' He turns and walks away up the stairs.

He's right. I've failed him, I didn't even manage to give him the bang-up bag, and losing my temper with that woman from the council has completely messed up any chance he might have had of getting moved.

I hear voices, laughter and the scrape of feet. I look up. There are six of them, three rangy youths in black and three smaller boys coming towards me, laughing and swaggering, led by Flex, the boy with the scarred cheek who'd turned up last time I was at Leon's.

Panic fills me. Quick sharp spikes. I grip the strap of my bag and hitch it a little higher onto my shoulder. Flex's pace doesn't slacken as he lopes towards me. He stops when we're nearly toe to toe, so close I can smell his breath. The menace coming off him is as clear and unnerving as the drop in pressure before a storm. The rest of them circle me, moving closer, jostling and pushing, hemming me in. Feral stares, curled lips. On any other day I would have shrunk back and dropped my eyes, but today I look straight into that steely gaze. 'I need to get past,' I say.

Eyes still on me, Flex tips his head to one side and spits. A frothy gob of white lands by my foot. 'You ain't from the council.' A diamond winks in his front tooth.

'It's none of your business who I am.'

His body pulses with the tension of an attack dog straining at the leash. I push past him and keep walking. The boys let out a whoop that curdles into laughter as I break into a run.

*

I get the bus to Logan's, sitting upstairs, staring out of the window at the slanting rain. At the scrapyard gates I go through the same rigmarole as before, pressing the buzzer, speaking into the microphone, standing back so the camera can see my face.

I slip through the gates before they're fully open and cross the yard. The buzzing and clanging from the sheds tells me that his workers are around but I see no one. Though I know I am being watched, every step of the way to Logan's office.

I tap on the half-open door and push it wider.

He's sitting at his desk talking to Greaves, who lolls against a battered filing cabinet. They break off their conversation as I walk in. Logan doesn't say anything to me, just slides four bulky rolls of notes across the desk like he's placing a bet at roulette. I pick them up one by one and drop them into my bag. It's more money than I have ever seen in my life, let alone touched. I zip the bag shut. 'Thank you, Mr Logan.' I place the car key on the desk. 'I've left it by the garages, where you said.'

Using his flat-topped little finger he scoops the key up by the ring and hands it to Greaves, who grunts and slopes out.

'How long should I wait before I report it missing?'

'Give it a couple of hours.'

I turn to go.

'Aren't you forgetting something?'

'Sorry?'

He tips back in his chair. 'We haven't discussed your repayment plan.'

'I thought we'd agreed you'd take what you get for the car parts as a first instalment.'

'That'll be a drop in the ocean compared to what you owe me.'

'It's barely six months old.'

'Stripping it down could end up being more trouble than it's worth.' He scratches at the bristle along his chin.

'You'll get your money back, Mr Logan. I promise.'

'Ways and means. That's what we need to discuss.'

'It'll have to wait.' I glance at my watch. 'I've got to hand over the money.' I turn around and walk to the door.

'I'll be in touch, Nicola.'

I feel sick. I open the door and step out into rain, clutching the bag tightly to my side.

The Fox and Hounds is way out of town on a deserted stretch of Turnpike Road. It used to be one of those big chain pubs with massive photo murals of forests and mountains stuck around the walls, and an all-you-can-eat carvery at the back. But it's been empty for a while and the boarded-up windows, missing roof tiles and ripped quiz-night posters flapping in the rain add to the dreary pall of abandonment.

Feeling uneasy and conspicuous, I hurry down the track that leads to the car park and duck into a rickety lean-to attached to the back of the pub to escape the rain. I ease the money from my bra and stuff it into the plastic bag, along with Logan's cash. I use my last match to light one of the Bensons I bought at the garage and perch on an old metal beer barrel, watching the rain fill the ruts in the mud.

I toss the cigarette butt onto the ground, putting it out with a swivel of my foot. Donna's late. She said one o'clock. It's already ten past. It's twenty past when a beaten-up white van splashes through the puddles. It veers past me and pulls up on the far side of the car park, front bumper nudging the fence.

'Finn!' I break into a run, peering through the slanting rain for sight of my boy.

Donna gets out and slams the door. 'Not yet! Wait there.'

The van lights bleep as she locks it. She opens an umbrella and moves towards me. 'Money first.'

'Oh, for God's sake.' I pull out a muesli bar and a box of juice and crane past her, trying to see into the cab of the van. 'He'll be starving. Let me give him something to eat.'

She moves with me, blocking my way. 'Money first.'

'Seriously?' I glare at her. She glares back. She's not looking good. Her hair's greasy and unbrushed, and her clothes are crumpled. With a queasy lurch of my stomach I thrust out the bag of notes.

She snatches it from me. 'Wait by the pub.'

'Why?'

'I want to count it.'

'It's all there, Donna. I'm not like you.'

She laughs. 'That was always your problem. Still, you never know, worms can turn.'

I think about punching that smirk off her face and wrestling the van keys from her hand. She shakes her head. 'Don't even think about it, Nic. We both know I'm stronger than you. Go on, wait over there. I'll count this in the van, then I'll bring him over.'

I turn, and as I walk back to the lean-to I hear the sound of the van backing up. I swing around. The van is lurching forwards, hurtling towards me. The passenger seat is empty. I splash through the ruts. 'Where is he? What have you done with him?'

She halts the van and looks down at me through the half-open window. I make a lunge for the door handle and rattle it hard. It's locked. 'Donna. Please don't do this. *Please.*'

She smiles and shakes her head. 'Come on, Nic, did you really think I'd give up Hurley's millions for few quid cash in hand? Still, don't think I'm not grateful for the money. My other half's got a debt that needs paying today so it'll come in dead handy. And remember, if you're tempted to do anything stupid, I've got the tape.'

She rams the van into gear and pulls away. My feet scrabble for purchase as I yell at her and try to keep up. Swerving violently she screeches down the narrow track and flings me off onto the mud as she careens into the road. I haul myself up and stumble after her, panting and gagging until her lights are a distant red blur in the rain.

I dig in my bag for my phone. It's not there. I ram my hands into empty pockets and run back to the car park, scouring the ground through a blur of tears. It's not in the lean-to. It could be anywhere. At Logan's, on the bus, in the street. No phone to call her with. No car to chase after her. Plunged into helplessness, I drop onto the barrel. Huddled there, I crush my eyes shut and fold forwards, rocking and keening like a mad woman mourning the dead. *Where is he? What have you done with my boy?* Donna's face floats through my grief, drawn and pale, limp coils of greasy hair. Grubby top, dirty nails. No cash, no hot water. Where are you staying, Donna? Where would you go where no one would question the sudden appearance of a distraught child? Come on, Nicci, think. She played you because she knows you, but there was a time when you knew her better than anyone else in the world.

I sit up and open my eyes. The struts of the lean-to wobble around me, spinning and reeling. After a moment they steady. I push myself up and scramble back to the road. *It's all right, Finnsy. I'm coming.*

I stumble through a puddle, slopping water into my trainers and now I'm running, head thrown back, elbows pistoning, feet squelching, bag banging against my hip. My knees buckle. I push myself on. My lungs burn, my vision bends. Cars roar past, throwing arcs of muddy water across my legs. I keep going until I'm back at Logan's scrapyard. I thump my hand against the buzzer. 'Mr Logan, open up, it's Nicola Dexter. Let me in.'

I step back, look up at the camera and beat on the gates. The door buzzes open. I lurch across the yard and burst into the Portakabin. Logan is in there, and so is Greaves.

'I need my car back.'

He lights a cigarette. Slow and deliberate. 'Too late.'

'Please,' I gasp, 'just for a couple of hours.'

'I couldn't give it to you even if I wanted to. It's not here.'

Blood roars in my ears. 'Where is it?'

'Out of town. Being stripped down as we speak.'

'Then lend me yours. It's an emergency.'

Logan's eyes narrow and Greaves lets out a snort of laughter.

'She's taken my son, Mr Logan. I have to get him back.' I stare him down.

Logan looks at me then up at Greaves. 'Lend her the van.'

'What?' Greaves – sneer dying on his lips – stands frozen.

'You heard me,' Logan growls. 'Go on.'

Greaves fumbles in the pocket of his oil-stained trousers and drops a set of keys on the desk.

'Where is it?' I say.

Logan jerks his thumb. 'Round the back. Leave it in the alley when you're done and stick the keys in the key safe by the gate. Code's 1212.'

The van is dusty inside and smells of stale sweat and cheap cologne. I glance in the back, wary of what I might see. Save for a couple of fuel cans and a heap of dirty overalls it's empty. I turn on the ignition. I've never driven anything this big. I don't care. I slam my palm on the horn, holding it down until the back gates slide open. Empty beer cans roll across the passenger footwell as I peer through the pouring rain and turn into the alleyway.

What do I do if I've got this wrong?

CHAPTER 45

The journey to Ma Burton's is a blur, cars and lorries floating up out of the rain, fat gobbets of water bouncing off the windscreen, headlights shimmying through the gloom. I turn the van into Calthorpe Road, gaze dismally at the house I vowed I would never return to and accelerate through the streets of the housing estate where my tormentors used to lie in wait to slap me around on my way back from school.

At the railway line I swing right and drive on, guided by the rattle and flash of the passing trains. In the distance, through the haze of rain, I make out a lifeless slab of grey rising from a sea of fly-tipped dross. The tyre factory is still there, still abandoned. The only difference is the smattering of 'Danger, unsafe building' signs pasted along the graffiti-covered walls. I slow down and circle the perimeter. One of the side doors is open.

Fifty yards on I spot Donna's van, tucked out of sight between the main building and a row of storehouses. I drive around to the other side of the building and nose Logan's van into a space behind a heap of concrete blocks. I open the glovebox; a shudder of relief when my fingers close around a small metal torch. Gripping it firmly, I scuttle across the cracked concrete and haul myself up the fire escape, the wet rungs slick beneath my trainers.

At the top, I scramble across the flat roof and push open the door. The creak of hinges sounds like thunder. I duck and wince, praying the sound won't carry. I move fast down the inner staircase and look down over the metal balustrade on the upper

platform. In the murky light seeping along the edges of the
boarded-up windows, the cavernous shell holds none of the magic
I'd remembered. It's almost the size of a football pitch, ribbed by
jagged staircases and jutting platforms, criss-crossed by yards of
piping and sheet metal ducts. Half the roof has collapsed and the
floor at one end is heaped with fallen beams.

Beneath me, the door of the office where Donna and I built our
fires and dreamed our dreams stands open. I tiptoe down another
flight and drop low so I can see inside. Donna is in there, shoving
clothes into black bin bags. Behind her I can make out a couple
of sleeping bags laid out on some old car seats. No sign of her
boyfriend. But if he's slunk off to pay his debts with the £40,000
I gave to Donna, he could be back at any moment. I peer closer.
There's no sign of Finn, either. Though I have a horrible feeling
I know where he is.

I sneak across the platform and up the caged ladder that leads
through a trapdoor to the mezzanine level, freezing as the hoops
shift in their casings. Holding my breath, I step around the top of
a rusty chute that hangs precariously from the edge of the platform
and slopes steeply away to the floor below. My heart drums. I look
away and move along the row of storerooms, trying each door and
peering inside. The last one is padlocked. I climb onto a stack of
pallets and shine the torch down through the glass at the top of the
door. My heart leaps. Finn is in there, curled on a bare mattress,
his body shaking to the rhythm of his sobs.

I waggle the beam across his face and tap lightly on the glass
with the tip of my nail. He raises his tear-stained face. His mouth
opens. I zip my fingers across my lips. Eyes wide, he nods and
makes the same movement.

Careful not to make any noise, I slither off the pallets and
run the torch beam around the edges of a grill in the bottom of
the door. It's held in by four heavy screws set deep into the metal

frame. I drop onto my stomach, shove my fingers through the grill and pull. The frame won't budge.

Finn peers at me through the mesh. 'I'm thirsty, Mummy,' he whispers.

I reach into my pocket for the box drink, pierce it with the straw and work the other end of the straw through a hole in the grid. He wriggles onto his stomach and fastens his lips around it.

'All right?' I whisper, as he gurgles the last of it. 'This time when I pull the grid, you push it with your feet.'

We try, but it's useless.

'Hold on. I'll be back in a minute.'

I grab the rail and peer over the edge of the platform, inching my fingers over crusts of rust and caked bird droppings. Rain slaps the boarded-up windows. Donna is coming out of the office, carrying a couple of bulging bin liners. I pull back into the shadows and watch while she picks her way across the debris to the door at the far end of the factory. The minute she leaves I dart down to the office.

It's a sad sight: empty water bottles strewn around, a half-eaten packet of biscuits, a camping stove, a kettle, a spoon and knife sitting in a chipped mug beside the makeshift bed and a battered laptop with Donna's initials gouged into the lid. A red bobble hat lies beside the rolled-up coat she's been using as a pillow. I rifle through the pockets and search the bag she's left on the table. *Damn!* No key for the padlock. She must have taken it with her. There's no screwdriver, either. No tools of any kind. I pocket the knife, slip out again and creep back up the stairs to the storeroom.

I dig the knife into one of the screw heads and twist. It gives just a fraction before it sticks. Finn whispers, 'Shall I push again?'

'Not yet.' I get a bit of traction on two more of the screws but the last one won't budge. I jam the knife deep and twist harder. The cheap blade snaps off and bounces onto the metal walkway.

Before I can grab it, it drops through a gap in the steel plates and clatters onto the concrete below.

I freeze for a second, screwing up my eyes. Slowly, I crawl forward and peer down.

Donna is back. I can see her, casting around for the source of the sound. She stops, alert, when she sees the blade. Frowning she bends, picks it up and looks up at the storeroom.

I crawl back to the trapdoor and lower myself down the caged ladder. Halfway down I hear her coming up the main stairway. I take another step. A rung gives way beneath my foot. Grabbing the nearest hoop I take my weight with my arms and lower myself carefully onto the floor and cower back against the wall. I close my eyes and pray. For a moment I think she might just move on up the stairs. My heart plummets as her footsteps stop and turn towards me. She's coming closer. I lift my head. A fearful flash as her eyes meet mine.

She shakes her head and waggles a bunch of keys in my face. 'Are these what you're looking for?'

I stand up slowly. 'Finn's petrified, Donna. At least give him something to eat and then let's sit down and talk.'

'You can talk till you're blue in the face, you're not getting him back. You've screwed up my chances of a decent life once already. I'm not letting you do it again. For God's sake, don't you get it? Hurley was worth millions.'

'I told you, the lawyers won't just give you the money, especially when they find out you're shacked up with some loser. They'll be on your back the whole time, making sure every penny is kept in trust for Finn.'

In the half-light her face looms heavy and vicious. 'You forget. I'm Finn's next of kin.'

'What difference does that make?'

'All the difference in the world. If anything happened to him it would all come to me.'

She's goading me, looking for a reaction. She gets one. I fly at her, propelled by a dark surge of fury. Braced and waiting she hurls herself at me. With a wiry strength she swings me around and shoves me against the railing of the platform. I feel it give. 'Donna, for God's sake!' Summoning all my strength I shove back. Surprised, she twists awkwardly and the keys drop from her hand. I lunge for them.

'Get back!'

I look up. Then I see it. A gun in her hand, pointing straight at me. My throat closes up. 'Where did you get that?'

'I'm looking after it for a friend. But don't worry, he won't mind if I use it.'

'Donna, put it away.' My mouth is dry. I lick my lips. 'What the hell has happened to you? We were friends. Sisters. I idolised you.'

Stony-faced, she curls her lip. 'Yes, and I let you hang around because now and then you came in useful.'

A heavy thud from above, followed by a crashing and scraping. I look up. Finn wobbles out onto the gantry above us. 'Mummy!'

'Finn, get away from the edge. You'll fall.'

He hovers uncertainly, then darts back into the shadow.

'You're not going to shoot me, Donna.'

'It wasn't part of the plan, but the idea is definitely growing on me. It would solve a lot of problems once and for all.'

The platform above us vibrates to the thud of Finn's feet.

'Sweetheart,' I call, desperate to keep the tension out of my voice. 'Don't move. It's dangerous.'

'Your concern for my son is touching, but it just proves that if I don't deal with you now, you're going to go on making trouble I don't need.' She raises the gun.

Adrenaline sharpens my spinning thoughts. 'Don't be stupid! The minute you tell them you're Finn's birth mother, they'll know it was you who killed me.'

Sweaty and pale she draws her palm across her mouth and a slow smile appears on her lips. 'That's the beauty of it. Don't you see? All I've got to do is send the footage to the police with your suicide note, telling them how the guilt about killing Jade had been eating into you for years, and once you'd given Finn back to his real mother you lost your reason to live, and decided to end it. Go on.' She waves the gun at me. 'Back up.'

I glance behind me at the gaping space where the safety railings have sheered off. 'I'm not moving an inch and if you shoot me they'll know it wasn't suicide.'

'That depends on where the bullet goes in.' She places the muzzle of the gun against the soft flesh beneath her chin and, staring straight at me, she whispers: 'Bang.'

'Donna, please.'

She lowers the gun until it's pointing at me again. With a practised click she pulls back the safety catch and takes a step forward. I dodge sideways. She pivots around, following me with the muzzle. My eyes travel from the gun to her face. My insides dissolve. She's serious. She's really going to do this.

Metal clangs and rattles behind her. In an avalanche of dust and debris, Finn bursts off the lip of the chute and runs at her, both hands outstretched. With cold, vicious anger he slams them into the back of her legs. Taken off guard, she jolts forward, losing her footing and shunts into what's left of the rusty railing. The ironwork shifts, judders and lets out a grinding screech as one end of it tears free and swings down into empty air.

'Nicci!' Her scream shreds the air, full throated and desperate. I lurch forwards and make a grab for her flailing arm… the brush of her fingers against mine as she tips into nothingness.

The great space holds its breath, a silent exhale as flesh and bone crumple onto concrete.

I run to Finn, jerk him away from the edge and press his face to my chest. 'Don't look, Finnsy, don't look.' My knees buckle. I sink to the ground, holding him close and rocking him backwards and forwards as I stare at the long, steep chute that brought him hurtling to my rescue. 'My baby. My brave, brave baby.'

I scoop him up and carry him down the stairs. At the bottom I turn him away from Donna's body and hurry him to the side door.

'Quick.' I set him down and take him by the hand. Head down through the driving rain I drag him across the concrete to Logan's van and lift him onto the passenger seat. 'I won't be long, just a few minutes, sweetheart. You mustn't worry. I promise I'll be back.'

'I'm hungry, Mummy.'

I pull out the muesli bars, drop them into his lap and open the glovebox. I dig desperately among the empty cigarette packs and crumpled receipts and let out a jagged breath when I find what I'm looking for – a box of matches. I slide the door shut and heave the fuel cans out of the back.

Finn gazes at me through the window, tear-stained and bewildered as I lock the van and carry the cans back to the factory. Inside I look down at Donna's broken body. She's lying face down, her body curled up, her head turned to one side. But for the pool of red seeping across the concrete she might be sleeping.

Tears burn my eyes and sadness wells up. 'Oh, Donna.' I want to hold her in my arms, but I force myself to think of that moment on the platform when she taunted me about being Finn's next of kin.

I run back to the office and dig around in her handbag, searching for the thumb drive with the footage from the Sallowfield security cameras. It's not there. Panicked that her boyfriend could arrive back at any minute, I tear the place apart, ripping the torn vinyl off the car seats, shaking out her sleeping bag and wrenching open the drawers of the dusty filing cabinets. I rip open a crumpled envelope shoved inside the red bobble hat, a weight of dread lifting as I pull out the thumb drive and shove it into my jeans. I take Donna's laptop and look around quickly for anything else that might incriminate me. I pick up one of the petrol cans.

My fingers tremble as I unscrew the lid, douse everything inside the office and walk over to the tower of tyres in the middle of the floor, dribbling petrol as I go. I move on up the stairs to the storeroom where she'd kept Finn, sloshing gouts of petrol onto the spot on the mattress where he'd peed himself, and more up the walls and floor. For good measure I drag in a couple of old pallets and soak the rotten wood. I run up the steps to the roof, rub the doorknob with my coat to clean off any prints, and throw petrol down the door. I bolt back down the stairs trickling fuel as I go. When I get to the side door I set fire to a twist of newspaper, turn at the entrance and hurl it onto the trail of petrol, barely managing to step back before the fire shoots along the glistening path to the office and streaks off towards the tower of tyres.

Is it enough? Will it burn away every trace of me and Finn before the smoke attracts the fire brigade? Heartened by the bright flame and the acrid smell of smoke I run to the van.

Finn is silent as I rev the engine and drive away. Heading home, I make a detour to the river and park behind a screen of trees. 'Stay here, Finnsy. I won't be a minute.'

I take Donna's laptop, open it and throw it down onto a jut of rock. I glance back at the van. Finn is rubbing his fingers across the window. His small, pale face stares out at me through the smeary gap in the condensation. I turn away and jump on the laptop, stamping and pounding, venting the fear and horror of the last few hours until there's nothing but broken pieces. I gather them up and hurl them into the grey water, flinging lumps of metal and plastic in all directions. I watch them sink, one by one. I do the same with the thumb drive and stand staring out across the rain-pocked surface of the river.

A thought ripples through my brain. Donna's boyfriend. He doesn't know I was at the factory, but he knows what happened at Sallowfield and he knows that Finn's not mine. As soon as he hears that Donna is dead he'll be chewing on ways to use that knowledge to screw more money out of me. But I'm not afraid. Not anymore. Without the footage there's nothing left to blackmail me with and if it comes to it, I'll own up and tell the world the truth about Finn. How Donna dumped him and I rescued him.

Like she said, if I ever got my day in court I would win.

CHAPTER 46

In the van I cup Finn's face with my hands. 'No one must ever know what happened today, Finnsy. If anybody asks where you were, you say you were at home with Mummy all day. No Donna, no horrible factory, no smelly mattress, no locked storeroom, no vans, no laptop.' I zip my finger and thumb across my lips.

He nods solemnly. 'Our zippiest secret ever.'

'That's right, sweetheart.'

'Is Donna going to be all right?'

My heart pumps faster. I dig my nails into my palms, and I lie to my boy. 'She knows what she did was wrong and she's decided to go away.'

'Where to?'

'Somewhere where she can't hurt you or me again. Not ever.'

I jam my foot on the accelerator, swerve the van around and tear away from the river. Out of the corner of my eye, I watch him staring at the passing streets. My sweet-faced, trusting, brave little boy. I look away and see the cold fury on his face as he ran at Donna. A flare of something cold and hard that I've never seen before and never dreamt was in him. Will that moment when he pushed her haunt him for years to come? Will it define the rest of his life, or is he young enough to forget?

As arranged with Logan I leave the van in the alleyway behind the scrapyard and lock the keys in the key safe. The rain has stopped but Finn is wet through and shivering. I slip my jacket around his shoulders, mainly to keep him warm but partly to cover the stain where he's peed himself. I take his hand and run with him, jerking him around the puddles, only slowing down as we reach the street. If anyone sees us we need to look normal. An ordinary mother and son, upright citizens of Juniper Close, caught in the rain.

In the station toilets, I lock us into the baby change cubicle and try to wipe away the worst of the grime.

'Donna isn't your friend anymore, is she, Mummy?' he says, as I scrub at his face with a damp paper towel.

'No, darling she's not.'

'If she comes back are you going to make up?'

A sob sticks in my throat as I shake my head. 'If people who we thought were our friends turn out to be unkind, it's best to move on.'

He thinks about this for a moment. 'Like Liam.'

'Yes, sweetheart, like Liam.'

He nods solemnly. 'Jamal's my best friend now.'

I pump the last dribble of liquid soap out of the dispenser and lather my hands, hoping that the cheap, sweet smell will mask the stink of petrol. There's no mirror but I splash my face with water and do my best to scrape my damp hair back into its scrunchy.

My mind is a mess: relief and horror, guilt and hope swirling and mingling. In the scramble and stress I forgot to report the theft of the car. I hurry Finn to the nearest coffee shop and I buy him a sandwich and get myself a strong black coffee. The barista is young and hip. I tell him my car's been stolen with my phone inside it and ask if I can use his to report the theft. He hesitates. I must look even rougher than I thought. I try to smile, which seems to perturb him even more but when I beg he gives in.

On the bus home we don't sit up front and Finn doesn't pretend to drive. He sits very still and stares out at the rain. The porch light of number seventeen glows like a beacon of safety as we hurry down the close. Desperate to get inside, I run up the front steps, key at the ready. Before I can get it into the lock the door swings open and my *Finn-felt-sick-so-we-stayed-home-all-afternoon* alibi implodes beneath my husband's quizzical gaze.

'Ian,' I say. 'What are you doing home?'

'I came back early to work on the staffing plans for the expansion.'

I squeeze past him. Very, very calmly, in a way that I hope looks casual, I kick off my wet trainers and kneel down to help Finn with his. Ian's eyes flick over my shoulder to the empty drive. 'Where's your car?'

Oh God. This isn't how I planned on telling him. I open my mouth. Air whips into it. I press my hand against the wall as if to hold back the weight of my lies. 'Ian, I'm so sorry. I went to the chemist this morning and when I came out it was gone.'

'What?' He slams the door shut. 'Did you leave it unlocked?'

'No, at least, I… I don't think I so.'

He shakes his head and turns his eyes to the ceiling. 'Scattiness is one thing, but this is beyond a joke.'

'I've reported it to the police. Here, they gave me a crime number for the insurance.' I hand him the grubby scrap of paper I used to scribble down the number. 'Ian, I'm so sorry.' I feel ashen and dazed.

He shoves the paper into his pocket and looks down at Finn. 'Where's his coat?'

'We forgot to take it,' I say, quickly. 'Honestly, I'm such an idiot.' I push my hand into Finn's back and propel him forward, eager to get him out of the way before Ian can question him. 'Go on, love, get those wet things off and I'll come up and give you a bath. I think I might have one too.'

Ian blocks my way, his expression darkening. 'I thought he was spending the day with Henry?'

'He didn't feel well.'

'So, where have you been?'

I gaze at him through wet lashes. How much time do I have to account for? How long has he been at home?

'Finn perked up after lunch so we went to Adventure World on the bus.' The lie drops from my tongue, sloppy and unthought out. 'Honestly, if I'd known the weather was going to be like this I'd never have left the house.'

'I called you. Your phone was off.'

'I… I don't know what's wrong with me, I… I've lost it. I don't know how. One minute I had it, the next it was gone.'

'For God's sake, Nicci, what's *wrong* with you?' A vein bulges in his forehead, red and angry. 'First your car, then your phone, then you take Finn out in the pouring rain without a coat.'

He's got every right to be furious but I don't have space in my head to care. I just need him to stop. I lean down and put my trainers on the rack. 'I know. Maybe there is something wrong with me. Maybe I should see a doctor.'

Ian gapes at me, surprised, then lifts his hands and drops them to his sides. 'Go and have your bath before you catch pneumonia.'

When I get upstairs Finn is sitting on the edge of the tub, wrapped in a towel. Despite the heat of the house he's still shivering. I wonder if it's shock. He doesn't say a word as I turn on the taps, add a squirt of bubble bath and take off my clothes. He climbs in, still silent, as I ease myself down opposite him. My body aches for a scalding hot shower but my need to be with him is greater. 'Are you all right, sweetheart?'

He scoops up a handful of bubbles.

I say softly, 'Can you tell me what happened when you were playing with your football trainer? Did Donna come into the garden?'

He nods. 'That man Steve was with her. The one who came to football. She said he was the one who sent me the trainer and he'd got some other football stuff for me in his van. Then we all went to the van and Donna got in the front and she started talking on her phone. But when I went to look at the football stuff Steve shut the door and I couldn't get out.'

'Oh, sweetheart, that must have been really scary.'

He squeezes the bubbles between his fingers. 'Donna's a big fibber.'

'Shhh.' I raise a finger to my lips and glance at the door, afraid that Ian might be hovering on the landing. 'Not so loud.'

'She told the biggest fib ever,' he says in a hoarse whisper.

I put my face close to his. 'What did she say?'

He clasps his arms across his chest and sticks out his bottom lip. 'She said she was my real mummy.'

My mouth opens and clacks shut. 'That's silly. She… she barely knows you. But I can't blame her. If I didn't have a little boy of my own and I saw one as nice as you, I'd be jealous too.'

His pout relaxes a little as I soap a flannel and work it across his neck and chest. 'Let me do your back.' He swivels around, and I run the flannel across his shoulders and down the pale bumps of his spine, scrubbing away the smell of the factory. 'Stand up now.' I soap the flannel again and clean the already reddening skin where he wet himself, and then I take the nail brush to his fingers and toes and unhook the shower and wash his hair. I do the same with myself, but the horror of the afternoon lingers on, clinging to my flesh, grimed into every nook and follicle. After I've dried us both, I help him into his Spider-Man pyjamas and his dressing gown and slippers, and I pull on a tracksuit and thick furry socks. I hold his hand as we go downstairs. Ian looks up from his iPad as we pass the sitting room. 'Hey, fella, fancy a chess lesson after you've had your tea?'

Finn nods and walks quietly into the kitchen to get out the board.

I stand by the sink, a jarring sensation of the day's horrors grinding through my body as I watch him set out the pieces, his brow furrowed with concentration.

Nausea spikes each time I think about what happened at the factory, fuelled by the throb of a ferocious headache. Moving mechanically, I make him pasta with tomato sauce. I set the bowl down on the table and stand in the doorway of the sitting room and tell Ian that I need to go and lie down.

'You see, this is exactly why I want you to give up work. It's too much for you.'

Maisie's supply of Valium is running low. I shake a couple of pills into my hand and return her to her perch at the top of Finn's bookshelf. I move on down the landing and stumble across our bedroom to the bathroom. A slurp of water from the tap to swallow them down. With trembling hands I close the curtains, shut out what's left of the daylight and totter into bed, in search of oblivion that refuses to come.

CHAPTER 47

I pause the breaking news story on my laptop, unable to drag my eyes from the image of the blackened shell of the tyre factory. *Police are seeking to identify the partially burned body of a woman…*

Oh, Donna, Donna…

Grief flips to anger, and then from anger to fear of discovery. My default setting since that long-ago night at Sallowfield.

I scour the image. There's nothing to link me to that place. The fire will have destroyed any traces of me and Finn. Oh God. What if it didn't? I close my eyes. In an instant I'm back on that rusting platform, the railing, snapping, twisting, swinging free of its moorings, and Donna is falling, falling, falling to her death.

'Play with me.' Finn tugs at my leg, his voice dropping into a whine. He's not usually clingy like this. He needs comfort and distraction, but I need space to think. Whatever happens, it's him I have to protect.

I grimace at the mess in the kitchen. If the house starts looking untidy Ian will get even more suspicious. 'Let's play I-spy while I tidy up,' I say, 'and then we'll go to the park.' I wipe and scrub and put away as we play, glancing constantly at my laptop in case there's an update, and trying all the while to think what I should do.

Should I tell the police that I was at the factory with Donna, visiting our childhood haunts? I could say she must have dropped a cigarette and started the fire after I left, then slipped, somehow, and fallen. No, that's crazy, far better to say nothing. But what if someone saw me in the area? Oh God, if I tell them now it will look weird that I didn't come forward as soon as I heard the news. No, it won't. I'll say I haven't seen the news. Why would I? It's half-term. I'm a busy mum. As the morning drags on my headache comes back, pounding my skull. I throw down the mop and pull a packet of aspirin from my pocket. I drop a couple of pills onto my tongue and I'm gulping down a glass of water when the doorbell chimes. The glass slips through my fingers and smashes onto the slate floor. Fear grips my throat.

It chimes again. I step out into the hallway, bare feet on the polished wood, my vision blurring as the door comes nearer. My hand on the knob, I seize a breath. *In, two, three,* I twist and pull. The door jolts open. A blast of cool air.

A young man. Tall, lean, hair gelled down, white shirt and maroon tie beneath a black puffa jacket, white earbuds nestling in his ears.

'Leon! I... I didn't recognise you.'

He shifts shyly and takes out the earbuds. 'I brought your phone back. Sorry it's dead. It's, like, really old so I didn't have the right charger.'

I look down at the phone he's holding out. 'Where did you—?'

'One of Flex's crew nicked it out of your bag when you were at Rosemead. I'd have brought it round before but I didn't know where you lived.'

I slide a glance at Vera's front windows. 'You'd better come in,' I say.

He steps onto the mat and bends down to take off his trainers. He puts them neatly on the rack next to Finn's wellingtons, heels to the wall. Foster care does that to you – gives you an eye for other people's rules. The trick is knowing when to break them.

'Who gave you my address?'

'Dylan Greaves.'

'What?'

'He followed you home one time, after he saw you in town.' Bile rises in my throat. I choke it back and try to focus on what he's saying. It's something about good news.

'Oh, Leon. Your court hearing! I'm so sorry. I… I've had a lot going on.'

Finn scampers down the hall and stops, startled when he sees a stranger. 'Who are you?' he says.

'Finn,' I say. 'This is Leon.'

'Hey, Finn.' Leon offers him a fist. Finn bumps it shyly and slides an arm around my legs.

'Leon's my friend from Next Steps.' I drop to a squat and hold Finn gently at arm's length so I can look him in the eyes. 'You remember what I told you about Daddy not wanting me to work with them anymore?'

He nods.

'So, we won't tell him Leon was here, OK?'

'Is it another zippy secret?'

'That's right, sweetheart.' I seal my lips with a flick of my thumb and forefinger, an all-too familiar rush of guilt that I'm burdening him with yet more deceit.

I look up at Leon and meet a frown. A flush prickles my cheeks.

Finn wriggles out of my grasp and plants himself in front of Leon. 'Do you know any jokes?'

'I'll… have to get back to you on that,' Leon says, nonplussed.

'Why don't you get out your crayons and draw me a nice picture while Leon and I have a chat?' I say.

Finn groans and stomps back into the kitchen. I follow on with Leon. With a glance at the, as yet, unconnected security camera, I switch on the kettle and plug my phone into the charger on the worktop. 'So, what happened at the hearing?'

He's looking around. His eyes flit from the broken pieces of the tumbler I dropped when he rang the bell, to my laptop and linger on the image of the burnt-out factory on the screen. 'I got ten months community service. My brief said it really helped – you know, the shirt and tie and telling the judge I'd enrolled for college.'

'That's great.' I edge backwards and snap the laptop shut.

He leans against the worktop. 'I was out of order.'

'What do you mean?'

'Yesterday. When I told you to… eff off. It wasn't right. Not after everything you've done for me.'

Yesterday. It feels like a lifetime ago.

I shrug, shaking my head. 'I haven't done much at all, except have a row with the housing officer. But I know someone who's got a cottage you can stay in for a while, until we can sort out something permanent.'

'No need.' A smile I've never seen before lights up his face, and he hands me a letter. 'Whatever you said to them it worked – the council's offering me a flat swap.'

'Where?'

'Bedford. I don't even know where that is, and the new place is just a studio, but I don't care. I just want a chance to start over, away from Logan.'

I look down at the letter. The words blur as my eyes well with relief and envy. *A chance to start over.* A tear gathers and trickles down my cheek. I snatch a piece of kitchen towel and press it to my eyes.

'You all right?' he says.

'I've got… a lot on my mind.'

Finn jumps up from the table. 'Mum, I've finished my picture. Can we go to the park now?'

'Oh, Finn, please, just give me a minute.'

'Hey, Finn, you got a PlayStation?' Leon says.

Finn folds his arms and sticks out his bottom lip. 'Daddy says I'm not allowed. I've only got a train set.'

'Okay.' Slightly fazed, Leon runs a hand over his slicked-down hair. 'Tell you what, you go and set it up and then you can show me how it works.'

Finn wriggles off his chair and scampers upstairs.

Leon glances at me. 'Is that all right?'

I nod and find that I'm sobbing.

His voice drops low. 'You're in trouble.'

'No, I'm just—'

'Trouble so bad you had to borrow money from Logan. Thirty grand. That's deep shit.'

I lift my head. 'Who told you?'

'Greaves was telling everyone. He's got a big mouth. How are you going to pay it back?'

'I don't know.'

He sucks his teeth. 'You should never have borrowed off Logan. He'll own you till you pay it back. With the interest he charges, he'll make sure that's never.'

'I didn't have a choice. I needed it fast.' The room ripples and sways. I press a hand to my head to still the panic.

'Hey, sit down.' Leon pushes me into a chair. I hear the spurt of the tap and feel a glass of water being pressed into my hand.

'Does your husband know?' He scrapes out another chair, sits down at the table and flicks at the sheets of drawing paper scattered across the table.

'No. God, no.' My voice rises breathy and shrill. 'And he mustn't find out.'

He picks up Finn's drawing, tipping his head like he's trying to make out what it is. 'Why did you need the money?'

I shouldn't be talking to him like this. He's just a kid, albeit tough and streetwise, but a kid all the same, with more than enough problems of his own. But my brain is so full of secrets the words are already crowding into my mouth. I tip my head back, stare up at the pendant lights above the island. 'Someone was threatening to take Finn. I had to pay them off.' A band of steel loosens in my chest, releasing a ragged breath.

'Why didn't you go to the police?'

'I couldn't.'

Leon's eyes lift from the drawing and narrow as they meet mine. 'So, what's stopping this person coming back for more?'

A silence filled only by the faint tick of the clock in the sitting room and the gentle hum of Finn's electric train from upstairs.

'They won't.' The harshness in my voice jolts us both.

'Leon! It's ready!' Finn is halfway down the stairs, calling through the banister. 'Come on!'

Leon twists his head and calls, 'Give me two minutes.'

'Go on. I'll be all right,' I say. 'He mustn't see me like this.'

I drop my head onto my knees and listen to Leon's fading footsteps, a flood of questions pouring through my head, filling every fold of my brain with new fears and new dangers. I scrub my hand across my face and see the time on my watch. I need to finish clearing up. I lean across the table, gather up Finn's crayons and reach for his drawing. Leon has turned it face down. I flip it over.

A jagged scribble of angry brown felt-pen circles two stick women standing face to face. One is holding something angular and black and pointing it at the other. Above them floats a stick boy with yellow felt-pen hair. Tears well in my eyes.

A key turns in the front door. Footsteps in the hall. I scrunch up the drawing and I'm stuffing it into my jeans as Ian walks into the kitchen. He's followed by a lanky, fair-haired policeman in uniform and an older woman in plain clothes with over-plucked eyebrows and carefully styled hair.

I try to stand up. My legs won't cooperate.

CHAPTER 48

'Hey. What's going on?' I manage to say.

Ian shucks off his coat and drops it on a chair. 'It's all right. The police just want to ask you a few questions.'

'What about?' My voice is faint, raspy.

He motions the officers to the chairs beside me, asserting control. 'Take a seat. Can I offer you a cup of tea?'

'Thanks,' the woman says. 'Milk and no sugar for both of us.'

I'm looking at her. She's looking at me. A fraction of a beat before she introduces herself. 'I'm DS Webb, Mrs Dexter. This is my colleague, PC Dawson.'

Dawson is examining the room, the granite surfaces, the neatly organised shelves, the half-washed floor and the pieces of that damn tumbler still lying in a splatter of water.

I lift my eyes and look at Ian, trying to make sense of their joint arrival. Did he go to them or did they go to him?

Webb seems to sense my confusion. 'We got your name from your phone number,' she says, 'but your phone's still registered to your old flat. A neighbour there sent us to the Parkview Dental surgery and your husband brought us back here.'

'I see,' I say, quietly fuming. Why didn't he call the house phone to warn me? More to the point, how did the police get my number?

'It's about Donna,' Ian says, flicking on the kettle and taking four mugs from the shelf.

'That's all right, Mr Dexter,' Webb says, crisply. 'We'll take it from here.' She takes out a notebook and clicks her pen. 'Mrs

Dexter, you may have seen a story on the news about a body of a woman found after a fire at the abandoned tyre factory out on the A23.'

I hear a creak. I glance at the door, worried that Finn might be listening from the stairs. 'Yes,' I say, softly. 'I think I did see something about it.'

'I'm afraid the deceased has been identified as Donna Stephens.'

I raise my hand to my mouth, the pain of hearing those words spoken aloud enough to make my horror real.

'I understand from your husband that you knew her.'

I shift in my seat, conscious of Finn's scrunched-up drawing pressing against my thigh. *What has Ian told them?* 'Yes. We were in foster care together. I hadn't seen her for years. Then she turned up here last week.'

'Could you tell me when you last spoke to her?'

I try to look helpful as I run over the pitfalls in my mind. *They must have seen my number on her phone. They'll have checked the call logs.* 'It was yesterday morning. Yes, that's right. I called her around... nine, nine thirty?'

'What did you talk about?'

'She'd been upset when she turned up here so I arranged to meet her in town for a coffee.'

'Upset about what?'

'Men, money, you name it.'

'When did you arrange to meet?'

'Saturday morning. At Mildred's in West Street.'

'Mrs Dexter, could you tell me where you were yesterday between 1 p.m. and, say, 6 p.m.?'

I glance at Ian's back as he busies himself with the kettle and teapot. I've got no option. I have to repeat the hasty lie I told him. I edge my focus back to the policewoman. 'It's half-term. I took my son to Adventure World.'

'I see.'

She glances at her sidekick who consults his notepad and says, 'You were seen entering Sean Logan's scrapyard at 2.15 p.m.'

Ian pauses, teapot in hand, and turns. *Oh God.*

'Yes, that's right,' I say, quickly. 'I dropped in there on the way.'

Dawson taps at the keys on his phone and Webb picks up the questioning. 'Can you tell me why?'

I swallow hard. 'I was fundraising. Mr Logan promised to make a donation to a charity I volunteer for.'

Ian's shoulders stiffen as he pulls open the cutlery drawer.

'Which charity would that be?' Webb asks.

'Next Steps. It's local. It supports care leavers.'

I feel the heat of Ian's annoyance and bite my lip, bracing for an explosion of anger when they've gone.

'Oh, yes. I know about Next Steps,' Webb says. 'Had you visited Mr Logan before?' *They know I have. Of course they do. Susy said the police have him under surveillance.*

'Yes. Last week. To see if he'd sign up to our donor programme. He told me to come back yesterday.'

'Did you exit the premises the same way you went in?'

She knows I didn't. 'No. I went out the back gate.'

'Why was that?'

Me head swims but if I don't get this right, everything Finn and I have been through will be for nothing.

'There was a truck blocking the main gate from the inside. They moved it there while I was in Mr Logan's office.'

'Did you know that Donna Stephens had a criminal record?'

'Yes.' I daren't look at Ian so I glance down at my hands. 'She mentioned she'd... been in trouble.'

'These weren't minor offences, Mrs Dexter. She was part of a gang involved in serious organised crime. She served two years of a four-year sentence for extortion.' She swivels around and accepts the mug Ian is handing her. 'You're not aware of anyone who might have wanted to harm her? Any enemies keen to settle old scores? Anyone she might have been blackmailing?' She's good at this: her voice never wavers, her eyes hardly blink.

'Like I said, we'd been out of touch for years.'

'There was a gun found near her body.'

The gun! I should have made sure I found it and thrown it in the river. 'Why are you telling me this?'

'We're working on a theory. Seeing as you knew the deceased, we'd appreciate your input.'

'All right.'

'We think that one of Miss Stephens' blackmail victims arranged to meet her at the factory, intending to shoot her. We think that Miss Stephens either fell or was pushed from one of the upper platforms and that in their haste to start the fire and get out of there, her assailant dropped the gun.'

I strain my ears for the whirr of Finn's train set, praying that Leon will keep him occupied until this nightmare is over. I can't bear the thought of him seeing me being taken away. 'I suppose it's possible,' I hear myself say, 'but I've got no idea if that's what actually happened.'

'Mrs Dexter, did you know that Sean Logan is a known supplier of narcotics?' Webb's eyes flick to Dawson's phone as he leans in to show her something on the screen. It distracts me, momentarily.

'I... um... no... I didn't know that. I would never have approached him for funding if I had.'

'I'm surprised to hear that, Mrs Dexter. I happen to know that the director of Next Steps – Ms Quiros – has complained to us on several occasions about Logan's attempts to recruit vulnerable teenagers into drug related activity.'

The walls begin to ripple and close in. 'She... never mentioned that to me. But then I don't spend much time in the office.'

Webb purses her lips.

'Is that it then?' Ian says, checking his watch. 'I need to get back to the surgery.'

'Almost, Mr Dexter.' Webb glances at Dawson's phone again and turns back to me. 'My only other query is about Adventure World.'

'Yes?' My voice quakes.

Webb takes her time, turning a page in her notebook and fingering her pen. 'According to the company's website it's been closed all week. A problem with the electrics.' She frowns a little and lifts one side of her mouth in a quizzical smile, as if it's her own words, or the information on the theme park's website, that she's questioning. 'So, I don't understand how you could have been there with your son yesterday afternoon.'

I look up at Ian. He looks back at me, sharp and questioning.

'Well, no, we didn't go in. When we found it was closed we came home.'

'Why didn't you tell us that to begin with?'

That's when I know it's over, that she's toying with me, preparing to strike the lethal blow.

'Because it's a lie.' The sound of Leon's voice draws every eye as he walks into the kitchen.

Ian twists around. 'Who the hell are you?'

'Leon Travis.'

'What are you doing in my house?'

'I came to see Mrs Dexter. She's my mentor.'

'Get out. Now.' Ian's voice is low-key, in shocking contrast to his eyes.

Leon lopes past him, approaching Webb in long, easy strides. 'I've been working for Sean Logan while I was out on bail. Doing deliveries. He threatened me and I was too scared to say no. Mrs Dexter went to see him yesterday to try and get him off my back. Then she came back to mine and helped me prepare for my sentencing hearing this morning. She brought me this shirt and tie to wear, we had a talk about the NVQ she's signed me up for and she cooked me a chilli. Check the location on her phone – you'll see she was on the Rosemead estate all afternoon.'

Webb makes a note then darts her eyes back to me. 'If this is true, Mrs Dexter, why did you lie about it?'

I'm floundering for words when Leon jumps in again. 'First off, she didn't want to drop me in it with you lot for couriering drugs for Logan. And, second, she didn't want *him* knowing she was helping me.' He jerks a thumb at Ian and flashes him a look of total contempt. 'He doesn't like her working with people like me, so she has to do it behind his back.'

Webb turns and looks at Ian. 'Is that true, Mr Dexter?'

Ian's face is flushed and shiny. 'My wife isn't well. She gets stressed and struggles to cope, so of course I don't want her hanging around the Rosemead estate with low lifes and drug dealers.' He glares at Leon. 'These people suck you dry if you let them.'

Leon bears down on him like he's going to punch him. He's taller than Ian, definitely fitter, and he throbs with anger. 'Yeah, well, you got no respect, you hear me? Telling her who she can see and when she can breathe. Strutting around, playing the big man because you ain't got the—'

'Leon, stop it!' Shocked, I push myself up from the chair, ready to pull him away, then I realise what he's doing. He's goading Ian on, whipping up his anger to give credence to the story we've just spun about why I lied about where I was. And it's working. I drop back onto the seat and stay there frozen, watching my husband square up to a teenager, the zigzag vein on his temple pumping thick and red.

Webb steps between them, tough and tiny. 'I'm going to have to ask you both to calm down.'

Ian stands firm for a moment and then backs off, wiping his mouth with the back of his hand, and throwing me a look of fury. He's not used to being challenged or wrong-footed. Dawson turns to me. 'Where was your son when you were at Logan's scrapyard, Mrs Dexter?'

'With m—' Leon starts, before Dawson cuts him off.

'I didn't ask you,' he says, holding up his hand. 'I asked Mrs Dexter.'

Leon rocks on his toes and fires me a look from beneath those long dark lashes.

I drop my head, as if in contrition. 'I left him with Leon,' I say.

'For God's sake, Nicola, are you out of your mind?' Ian's voice is measured, but I can feel his anger overflowing, filling the room.

'I'm sorry,' I whisper.

'I took him to the rec for a kick about,' Leon says, gaily.

I glare at him, warning him not to overdo it. As for Ian, I daren't even look at him.

'If that's all, officers, I'll get back to the surgery.' He picks up his coat and plants himself in front of Leon. 'And you. Get out of my house right now and don't ever set foot in it again.' He nods to the police, passes me without a murmur and strides down the hall to the front door. He shuts it behind him with a click.

Webb steps forward. 'May we take your phone, Mrs Dexter?'

'Of course,' I say. I unplug it from the charger and hand it to her. 'And I'll give you the number for Next Steps so they can confirm that I'm Leon's mentor.'

'And, er, Mr Travis, could you let me have some contact details for you, please?'

I make no eye contact with Leon as she takes down his number and address, and he merely murmurs a quick goodbye as he heads for the door. I'm glad we don't have a chance to speak alone.

What do you say to someone who has just put their freedom on the line to save yours?

'Detective,' I say, when he's gone. 'Leon's a good kid, and he's finally got a chance to get away from Logan and start over. Please, *please*, don't hold what he said against him.'

'I assure you, Mrs Dexter, my only interest here is in finding out the truth behind Donna Stephen's death.'

CHAPTER 49

It's nearly eleven o'clock and I'm emptying the dishwasher when Ian gets back. I don't know where he's been and I don't ask; I just close the kitchen door and lean back against it, waiting for him to speak.

He pours himself a glass of wine, then he sits down at the table and says nothing. It's something he does when he's really angry. The greater my sin, the longer he lets me stew.

Only this time, for the first time ever, it's me who breaks the silence. 'Ian, I…'

He jumps in then, and drowns me out. 'I can't believe you, Nicola. After *every*thing I've done to give you the life I thought you deserved, you just go crawling back to the gutter every chance you get. Did you think for one minute about me, or my reputation, or the reputation of the practice when you brought that thug into my home? Do you imagine that men like Downing are going to want to invest in my projects if they know that my wife spends her time consorting with addicts and drug peddlers? No, you didn't. You just decided to look me in the eye and lie and lie and lie.'

It shocks me how much he despises Leon. It shocks me even more how much he despises me for wanting to help a kid who has no one.

'Ian, he's done bad things but he's not a criminal. He's a victim.'

'Let me speak! I bet it was that bloody woman, Susy, goading you on, telling you to go behind my back, sending you off to face down some local gangster for the sake of a scrounging little low life who thinks the world owes him a living!'

I'm bursting to defend myself and to stand up for Susy and for Leon, but I stay quiet. His tone softens a little when he sees tears slipping down my face. But they're not tears of contrition. They're tears of exhaustion and fear for what's to come.

'Go to bed,' he says.

I shuffle upstairs, take my pills and stare at the girl in the mirror as I clean my teeth. A girl steeped in death. A liar and a thief. I crawl beneath the sheets.

Everything is slipping away: my husband, my home, my hopes for the future. And Logan? How am I going to pay him back if Ian refuses to give me back my job?

He comes up late. I keep my eyes closed and he lies on his side of the bed, a chasm between us as he sleeps. He's up before me and leaves before we have a chance to speak.

Lisa arrives early to pick Finn up for his play date with Jamal I wave him off, torn between a burning desire to keep him close and relief that he won't be here if the police start picking holes in my lies and come back with more questions.

I'm in the sitting room, searching for updates on the investigation, when the soft purr of a car pulling up outside draws me to the window. My breath catches. A black BMW. Sean Logan gets out and beeps the lock, glancing up and down the street as he tugs the cuffs of his worn tweed jacket and turns down my front path.

I shrink back against the wall. *Oh God, oh God.* The door chime pierces my skull. I close my eyes. He presses it again, long and shrill. I swallow hard, push away from the wall and walk to the door, my hand trembling as I open it.

'Nicola.'

'You can't come in. My husband's here,' I whisper.

'No, he's not,' he says, affably. 'How many times have I got to tell you I don't like lies?' He pushes past me and strides down the hall, stopping briefly to take a look around the sitting room before he walks into kitchen. 'Nice place.' His eyes slide around the room, and he stops for a moment as if he's digesting what he sees. Then he homes in on the fridge and takes down a photo of Finn.

'This your boy?'

I don't reply.

'Put the kettle on, will you? I'm parched.'

I take the kettle to the sink and turn on the tap.

'I trust you sorted out your little problem after I lent you my van?' His eyes travel down my body as if he is slicing me open. I feel his gaze reaching deep inside me, probing my secrets.

'Why are you here, Mr Logan?'

He senses my fear and he smiles. 'To discuss your repayment plan.'

'You took my car as the first instalment.'

'The thing is, Nicola, your loan's already clocking up interest. Thirty per cent. Compound rates. So I thought you'd appreciate the chance to go over the options as soon as possible.' He lays the photo of Finn on the island.

'I'm increasing my hours at the surgery.'

'Thirty thousand quid at thirty per cent. That's a lot of extra hours.'

'I'm talking to a credit union about getting a loan. Look, whatever it takes, I'll find a way.'

'Maybe we could work out an alternative method of payment.'

I hadn't seen this coming. Maybe I should have. Maybe a year of living in Ian's world has blunted my antennae. Single mums on minimum wage get offers like this all the time; along with the sneers, the scabby flats on crappy estates, and the benefit sanctions if you dare to do a bit of overtime to buy your kid new shoes. It's the price you've got to pay for your 'reckless lifestyle choices.' Landlords, bailiffs – even a bloody pizza delivery kid tried his luck with me once. I kicked his skinny shin and slammed the door in his face. I might have been hard up but even I had to be worth more than a cut-price margherita and an own-brand cola. Only there's no kicking Sean Logan in the shins, and he and I aren't talking about this week's deep-pan special. We're talking about £30,000.

He leans across the island and runs his thumb down his jaw. 'Don't look at me like that. There's quite a few jobs someone like you could do for me.'

I look him square in the eye. 'What sort of jobs, Mr Logan?' They don't like it when you make them spell it out. It makes them feel cheap.

'Customer liaison, new business development, a bit of marketing and, of course, once you got yourself a new car, you'd be doing your own pick-ups and deliveries.'

A van backs up in the close, its alarm a mournful beep in the silence.

'I thought—'

He circles the island and leans so close I can smell the oily stench of the scrapyard. 'I know what you thought. And, maybe, from time to time, there'll be a few other duties thrown in.' His eyes are dead, filled with the same cold poison I saw in Mo's, and Tommo's, and the eyes of every man I've ever met who thinks that other people can be bought and sold; a deep unyielding emptiness.

'I can't work for you. I can't give up my job at the surgery.'

'I wouldn't want you to. In fact, it's your day job and the school run and your *mentoring* that makes you so perfect for the role I've got in mind. Broad-spectrum appeal, I think they call it. Scrotes to yummy mummies. You'd be surprised how many posh housewives are ready to pay good money for what I sell. They just don't know where to get it.'

I step away and spoon tea into the pot. 'What if I refuse?'

'Well, I suppose I could talk to your husband, man to man, see if he wanted to take on the debt, but that could get messy, what with him wanting to know why you borrowed the money in the first place, and I don't like mess.' His eyes sweep the room. 'I get the impression that he doesn't, either.' He turns the photo of Finn in his hands, snapping back one of the corners with his thumb, cracking the gloss. 'But you've got to see it from my point of view. I can't have people thinking I take being fucked with lightly, so I'd have to do some damage.' He's getting a kick out my fear, feeding off it. 'Like I told you before I'd feel bad about it, but if we can't come to an arrangement, I won't be able to vouch for the safety of you or your boy.'

I grip the steaming kettle, imagining his pain if I threw the boiling water in his face. Instead, I fill the teapot and play for time. 'How long would this arrangement last for, Mr Logan?'

He watches as I stir the pot. 'I keep telling my wife she should make proper tea but will she listen? Will she, hell. Too busy getting her hair done.'

'I asked you a question. How long would this arrangement last? Six months? A year?'

'It doesn't work like that, Nicola. Once you start working for me, you only get to stop when I say you do. If this goes the way I'm hoping it will, you're going to be useful to me for a very long time.' His eyes pin me down. 'Milk and two sugars.'

Is that where I'm headed? A lifetime of servitude to Sean Logan? Trapped forever in a sordid rerun of the life I led as teenager? I take the milk from the fridge, set it down between the mug and the sugar bowl and drop a spoon onto the granite surface. It hits with a tinny clatter. A pathetic little act of rebellion that makes Logan grin.

He tosses down the photo of Finn and heaps sugar into his mug. 'He doesn't look much like you, does he, your boy?' He stirs his tea. 'Takes after his daddy, I presume.'

I look at him, the heavy bags beneath his eyes, the flaky skin on his cheeks, the dandruff in his hair, the small nicotine-stained teeth visible beneath his moving lips, and it feels as if I've been lost for a long time in a dark, impenetrable wood and though the trees aren't exactly thinning, a drizzle of sunlight is penetrating the leaves, shedding a glimmer of light into the gloom. I pick up the photo, put it back on the fridge and hold it in place with a smiley face magnet. I straighten it with both hands, aligning it precisely with the edge of the door, before closing my fingers into fists so tight my knuckles gleam like scraped bone.

'Are you listening to me, Nicola?' Logan is saying.

'Yes,' I say, quickly. I reach for the cookie jar and lift off the airtight lid. It comes away with a satisfying pop. 'Do you want a biscuit with your tea?'

He looks at me oddly, as if he thinks I'm taking the piss. 'No, thanks.'

'What if I manage to get hold of the money and pay it back?'

'In full? With all the accumulated interest? Sure.' He shrugs amiably. 'You do that and we'll call it quits.' His face snaps back to stony, along with his voice. 'Until then, you need to start working off the debt.'

I nod, as if I'm conceding his point, and pour myself a mug of tea. 'But how would it work? I can't be seen going in and out of the scrapyard, and you can't come here.'

'Don't you worry about that.' He takes a noisy swallow of tea, relaxed by my compliance. 'I've got the perfect solution. We'll meet at Leon's.' He smiles at me as if I should find that amusing, a mocking, yellow-toothed grin.

I look up at the picture of Finn on the door of the fridge. My fair haired, blue-eyed boy, who looks so much like his father.

CHAPTER 50

It took nerve I didn't think I had but here I am, sitting in the waiting area of a smart London law practice, straight backed and composed with my handbag on my knees. I've worked out exactly what I'm going to say and exactly how I'm going to say it though deciding what to wear wasn't easy. I tried one of my work suits – too dull, fawn trousers and a cream top – too mousey. In the end I plumped for a wrap-around jersey dress in deep red that I haven't worn since I got married, pulled on my favourite black, stack heeled cowboy boots and swept my hair into a messy bun.

'Mr Rustom-Bennet will see you now, Miss Cahill.' I push myself up, smooth my skirt and follow the receptionist through the heavy oak doors. Wood panels gleam in the light from the leaded windows; tasselled curtains, a wall of leather-bound books, a faded Persian carpet, a carved chess set on a marble-topped table, paused mid-game.

Gordon Hurley's lawyer sits at an antique desk making notes in a file.

'Ah, Ms Cahill,' he says, looking up and pulling off his reading glasses.

A pair of small, red-rimmed eyes look straight into mine. A bolt of recognition ricochets between us. I see Tommo, the man who raped Jade, beat her up and pumped her full of drugs the night she died, and he sees, me, the girl who fought with her and shouted at her and stood frozen at the edge of Ryan Hurley's pool while she drowned. He's as shocked as I am, though he clasps his hands together, those fat, ugly hands, and says, coolly: 'What can I do for you?'

I take longer to recover, staring dumbfounded at the bush of grey hair, the florid face, the red-veined nose. The shadow of that night at Sallowfield hangs between us as I struggle to work out the connection. Slowly the confusion clears. Why wouldn't Ryan Hurley have been friendly with his family's lawyer? Friendly enough to have invited him along to his seedy sex parties.

I sit down in the chair across from Tommo, inches from his hands. The memory of those cruel, clammy fingers pressing into my flesh turns my throat dust-dry and my carefully prepared words come out jagged and raw. 'I've come to make a claim on Gordon Hurley's estate.'

To give him his due he stays cool. 'On what grounds, Ms Cahill?'

'On the grounds that Ryan Hurley is my son Finn's father.' I cling to my script. 'That makes him Gordon Hurley's only descendent. I'm willing for him to have a DNA test to prove it.'

He eyes me steadily, taking this in, weighing it up. Seconds pass. I stare back at him, my heart pounding so hard I'm sure he can hear it.

'And will a DNA test prove that you're the boy's biological mother?'

This winds me, a punch in the gut I hadn't been expecting. He stands up slowly and moves around the desk, tall, authoritative, taking back control. 'I only ask because Donna Stephens called my secretary a couple of weeks ago. She told me that she had a son by Ryan Hurley and she made an appointment to come in to discuss how she should go about claiming Gordon Hurley's money on his behalf.' He sidles up beside me and drops his mouth to my ear. 'Miss Stephens was due to bring the boy in yesterday to have his DNA tested. Sadly, she was unable to keep that appointment because she met with a tragic and untimely accident. But I'm sure you know that.'

A brittle silence, the distorted scream of a siren outside the window. I push myself up from the seat and duck away from the reek of his aftershave and the repellent touch of his skin. Distance gives me strength. I'm not powerless. Far from it. He might know my secrets, but I know his. I know what he is. I know what he did to Jade. I remember – all too clearly – what he did to me.

'I'm the only mother Finn knows,' I say. I pause for a couple of beats while I steady my nerves. 'And seeing as we both have secrets we'd prefer to keep, I'm sure we can find a way to make sure that my son gets what is rightfully his.'

He perches on the edge of his desk and turns his pen slowly in his fingers. 'Does your husband know you're here?'

'No.'

'Does he know that the child isn't yours?'

'That's not relevant.' A blink of what might be surprise crosses his face. 'This is between you and me, Mr Rustom-Bennet. No one else.'

Silence. His eyes on mine as he weighs up just how far I might be willing to go to call his bluff.

'Well, Miss Cahill, as you say, it's only right that the boy should inherit what's rightfully his, and that we resolve this matter as quickly as possible. I suggest you bring him here tomorrow and I will arrange for a nurse to take a supervised swab under conditions that none of the Hurley clan could possibly dispute.' He presses the intercom on his desk.

It's all right. It's going to be all right.

I turn my face to the panelled wall and crush my eyes shut, my whole body trembling. His voice behind me is low and unruffled. 'Alison, could you arrange for an evidential DNA swab to be taken in my office tomorrow?… Yes, please. I'd like to confirm a time with Ms Cahill before she leaves.'

My eyelids flutter open. I see my reflection in the glass of a framed photograph. My face strained and gaunt, two bright spots burning in my sunken cheeks. My focus drifts to the image behind it. A black-and-white team photo: posh boys in striped rugby shirts, a much younger Tommo in the middle, arrogant and entitled even back then; the man at his side just as tall but leaner, more boyish and jarringly familiar. I run my eyes along the names printed at the bottom of the mount. The letters warp and slant. *William Dexter.*

I press my hand against the wall, feel the sharp edges of the panelling pushing into my fingers. 'You knew William Dexter.'

He swivels around in his chair and scrutinises my face. 'You really had no idea, did you?'

'Why would I?'

'Bill was my business partner. After he died, I married his wife, Gwen.'

It's as if all my blood is draining from my body. '*You're* Ian's stepfather?'

'*Former* stepfather.'

'He loathes you.'

'I assure you, the feeling is mutual. Though, thanks to me, he learned to play a decent game of chess. I wanted a worthy adversary, you see – otherwise, where's the fun? So I taught him to see it as a psychological battle.'

I glance away to the chess set on the marble table. It's the twin of the one at home. I should know – I've dusted the fiddly little pieces enough times. The same intricate ivory warriors glaring at each other across their tiny battlefield. I venture closer. The pieces are set out in the closing moves of one of Ian's favourite games, a famous one that I've watched him play over and over again, chewing his lip as he set the white traps, smiling as the red warriors met their inescapable fate.

'You taught him by making him replay the games of the masters.'

'You should get him to teach you how to play.' A sneer pulls at his mouth. 'Studying the tactics of the masters has been known to sharpen even the most mediocre of minds.'

I fix my gaze on the vicious battle of wits being fought out on the board and I think about Ian's clearly justified hatred for this man. If what Annabel told Susy was right, he hated him because he stepped into his father's shoes, took over his business and put him down all through his childhood. But most of all he hated him for the iron grip he'd held over Gwen. A grip that he'd so suddenly released.

Dark thoughts begin to bubble in my brain.

'What did Ian have on you that forced you to divorce Gwen?' I say.

He works his mouth as if savouring the answer. 'Isn't it obvious? What he "had on me" – as you so succinctly put it – was *you*. A living threat of exposure.' He pauses, mockingly. 'Oh, sorry. Did you think he married you for love?'

I grip the back of a chair and sink into the seat. 'How did he find out?'

He moves over to a little side table and lifts a cut-glass decanter in my direction. I shake my head. He pours one for himself, takes a sip and swallows it slowly. 'He'd been looking for dirt on me ever since I married his mother and took control of his father's share of DRB. She'd always indulged the cocky little sod, showered him with praise he didn't deserve and made him think the whole bloody world revolved around him, so he didn't like it when I pointed out his failings. He also suspected certain… peccadilloes on my part, and a tendency to wander from the marital bed. But for Gwen's sake he wanted to force me out quietly, no fuss, no scandal, nothing to set the tongues at the bridge club wagging.'

He sips again. 'Three or four years ago, while I was on business in New York, he broke into my study, went through my private files and came across some of those cards Mo hands out to advertise his girls – so much safer than entrusting anything to the internet. I'm sure you remember them – a photograph, a name, an age, a pithy little description designed to give prospective clients the fullest sense of the merchandise on offer. As it happens, I'd marked some of them with my own notes – points out of ten, additional comments. You know the sort of thing.' His tiny blue eyes sweep my body. 'I seem to remember I marked you as a four. Disappointing.'

My eyes drop to the chess game. My insides burn with revulsion. And then anger. I look up and stare at him, steady-eyed. 'How stupid of you to keep them.'

He raises a single bristly eyebrow. 'Stupid, indeed.' He takes another slow sip from his glass. 'The day I got back he confronted me with what he'd found. God, he could hardly contain his delight. I pointed out that the cards proved nothing. They could have been evidence from an old case or research material acquired by one of my assistants. He's no fool, though. Proven or not, he knew that in the current climate, a public accusation of… impropriety by a living, breathing accuser would destroy me, especially if that accuser were now a respectable married woman and' – his eyes pin me down as if I am a specimen under dissection – 'passably articulate. These days you just have to open a newspaper to see what such an accusation can do to the otherwise untarnished reputation of a prominent man. So, the tenacious little fucker set about tracing the girls in the cards. I'm sure it helped that he had names and faces to go on but knowing Ian I'm sure he paid a professional to do the leg work. I have no idea how many of Mo's girls he found, slept with and tried out for size, or why in the end he chose you. Perhaps you were particularly amenable, gullible, desperate or just… local.' He's lashing out, relishing the chance to turn his confession into a means of inflicting pain but I refuse to react. Glass in hand, he meanders over to the chess board and, with rock-steady fingers, moves the white king diagonally out of reach of the red bishop. 'Even so, it took him a while. The first I knew of it was when, out of the blue, he sent his mother a photo of the two of you at your sad little wedding, and suggested bringing you over to dinner to "meet the family". One foolish blunder on my part, two deadly moves on his, and he had me. Fool's mate, they call it. It's the only impressive thing Ian Dexter's ever done.' He sighs, theatrically. 'Later that day I moved out of the house, signed his father's stake in the business back to Gwen and agreed to a divorce on terms that were very favourable to her. I haven't seen either of them since.'

'I don't understand. He never mentioned any of this to me, never pressed me for details of what you'd done.'

'Why would he? He had me in an impossible position, and you were just the pawn that enabled him to put me there. Of course, it involved a huge sacrifice on his part, but I've got to hand it to him, he held his nerve and went through with it. Anything to win. And there was precedent of sorts. Nothing quite on the scale of the depths that *he* was prepared to stoop to, but he'd seen me marry his dull, narrow-minded mother in order to take control of DRB.'

His eyes drop back to the board and he makes the fatal Kieseritzky move, advancing a red rook. Then he switches to white and starts Andersson's remorseless final attack, moving a white rook forward to put the red king in check.

He knocks back his drink. 'I'm sure there were compensations. Knowing at least *some* of your sordid secrets would have given him an enormous power kick. Much needed after that feisty ex of his... what was her name? *Annabel*, that's right, lovely girl, gave him the boot. She was whip-smart, destined for great things and extremely good looking. A man like Ian doesn't take kindly to being outshone and then dumped by a woman.'

He's switched his attention from the board to me: he's watching me intently, keen to see the effect of his words. I stand there trembling, torn between a desire to walk out of there and an overwhelming need to know all the sick, sordid details of his marriage and mine.

'Does Gwen know why you left her?'

He laughs. 'Oh, no. Ian was keen to spare her the details of my extramarital interests, so my ex-wife is convinced that it was her appeals to my better nature that won the day. Anyway, she was disappointed enough with his choice of bride as it was. Why break her heart twice by telling her what kind of girl you really are?' He drains his drink and pours himself another, his hand less steady this time. 'I'm sure that actually marrying one of Mo's girls wasn't originally part of his plan, but after Annabel damaged that oh-so-fragile ego of his, finding you must have been a godsend. A girl he could control, someone who was too grateful and dull-witted to realise she was being used. And then there was the added bonus of the boy; a chance to fulfil his childhood dream of becoming... who?' He taps three fingers to his forehead. 'Ah, yes. *Me.* The all-powerful stepfather whose every whim must be obeyed, the father figure whose praise can never quite be earned. How banally predictable the human psyche can be.'

He throws me a look of amused disdain and, as if I'm not worthy of any more of his precious attention, he turns back to the board and moves the red king sideways out of check.

The intercom breaks his concentration. It's his secretary saying the nurse can do Finn's swab test at 3 o'clock tomorrow. He glances at me for confirmation.

'We'll be here,' I say.

He switches off the intercom.

'I'd like you to have fifty thousand pounds in cash ready for me when I come back tomorrow.'

Without raising his eyes from the board, he laughs. 'Don't push your luck. The trustees aren't going to advance you a penny until the test results come back.'

Willing my knees not to buckle, I pick up my bag and walk towards the door. Halfway across that soft, expensive carpet I stop and walk back to him. I lean over the board, my face close to his, and make the final three moves of the game: white queen forward to check the red king; followed by the red knight in desperation taking the queen; and then the white bishop slipping like a forgotten ghost to check mate.

I step back a little. 'As you say, Mr Rustom-Bennet, proven or not, an accusation of the rape of a minor would destroy you, especially if those accusations came from a respectably married, passably articulate accuser, who has also suffered at your hands. So, I'm sure you'll find a way to talk the trustees round. If not, I suggest you find the money out of your own pocket. I've got some pressing debts to pay.'

His face has turned crimson, engorged with blood, his eyes stare up at me. I swipe my hand across the board and send the exquisite ivory warriors skittering and bouncing into the air, the red king flying into the fireplace and shattering on the brass fender. I walk back to the door and let myself out, leaving Hugh Rustom-Bennet kneeling over the broken pieces of his priceless chess set.

CHAPTER 51

I carry our possessions out to the hire car. There aren't many. Clothes, toys, toiletries, a few books. Nothing else in this house is mine. No pictures, furniture or knick-knacks. No rugs, plates, cushions, mugs or vases. Everything I owned before I met Ian ended up in the skip he hired when we moved in.

When I'm done, I do my final walk of the house, messing up the cushions, tossing a towel onto the unmade bed, throwing open drawers and wardrobes and taking jars and bowls off the kitchen shelves and dumping them on the worktop. Not out of revenge, just to see how these rooms might look if I'd been allowed to live in them as me. The result feels oddly homely.

'Where's Finn?' Ian says, as he walks in.

'Sleeping over at Jamal's.'

'On a school night?'

'It was a last-minute thing.'

'Why are you encouraging him to be friends with that boy? He's a wimp. They'll both get picked on if they hang out together – you know what kids are like. And we don't know anything about the parents.'

'I do. His mum's lovely.'

'Why's this place in such a mess?'

'I've been having a clear-out.'

He casts around for signs of food preparation. 'What time are we eating?'

I reach into the freezer and take out the carton of cheat-eats boeuf bourguignon – a thump as it hits the worktop. 'Any time you want. Just put this in the microwave for about twenty minutes. If you can't be bothered to do vegetables, have it with bread.'

He picks up the carton. 'What is this? Are you still feeling unwell?'

'I'm fine. Never better.' One by one I take the photos of Finn from the fridge door, putting each magnet back with a little click.

'What are you doing?'

I slip the photos into my bag. 'Nicknames are weird, aren't they?'

'What?'

'Who'd have thought that a name like Hugh Rustom-Bennet would get shortened to Tommo? Why not Hughey or Rusty or Benno?'

He looks at me. His face is pale, almost white. His Adam's apple throbs against his collar.

I gaze at him. My miracle worker. The man I'd loved. My too-good-for-a-nobody-like-Nicola-Cahill husband.

'Hugh's a bastard. My mother's well shot of him.'

I move on to the corkboard and unpin Finn's drawings. 'I know he's a bastard. But that's not why you hate him. You hate him because he's just like you, and he sees you for what you are.'

His jaw quivers. 'I'm nothing like him.'

'You're both control freaks who get their kicks out of putting other people down, making them feel like dirt,' I say, quietly. 'The only difference is that Tommo likes inflicting physical pain on people, especially young girls, while you prefer a more psychological approach. Crushing someone's spirit, squeezing the life out of them, controlling their money, their time, their thoughts, their every move, sapping their self-esteem so they won't ever dare to threaten yours.'

His eyes flare. He raises his hand and I think he might hit me. I stand with my head up, almost daring him to do it. He lowers his hand. 'You're drunk.' His voice is icy with contempt.

'Did it turn you on?'

'What?'

'It did, didn't it? Knowing I used to get bought and sold like a lump of meat. It made you feel powerful.' I roll up Finn's drawings and slide them into my bag. 'It's not Susy who wanted to trap me in my past, it was you. Using what happened to me when I was young to get your revenge on Tommo, and knowing that any time you wanted you could bring me to heel by throwing it in my face.'

The first flicker of comprehension creeps into his eyes. 'You talked to him.'

'He was very forthcoming.'

He comes closer, his expression a mixture of anger and fear. 'Did he contact you?'

'That's not important. What's important is that he told me everything. The whole sordid story of our marriage. How you spent months tracking down the girls on the cards you found in his study.'

'All right! So what? I went looking for someone who could discredit him but then I found you and I… fell in love.'

'Yes, with the fact that I was desperate, naive and powerless. Did you keep the card that had my details on it? Did you lock it away somewhere so you could get it out and gloat over it, knowing you had the ultimate weapon to keep me in line and stop me from ever leaving you?' A flicker in his eyes tells me I'm somewhere near the mark. 'Well, you can stick it on a T-shirt for all I care. Send it to your mother, your friends, everyone at the surgery. I'm not ashamed that I was a victim.'

'Nicci.' He puts out his hands to take hold of me. 'I never judged you for what happened to you. I just wanted to give you what you never had.'

'Don't touch me.' I pull away from him. 'You were licking your wounds after Annabel dumped you and you couldn't believe your luck when you found someone you could not only use to get your revenge on Hugh Rustom-Bennet, but who you could oppress and humiliate the way he had oppressed and humiliated you. So you made your move, and what? Bombarded me with ads for the job at Parkview and reeled me in? I'm such an idiot. I honestly thought you hired me because you saw my potential and, get this – I thought you married me because you loved me.' I try to laugh but the sound sticks in throat. 'God, Donna was right. That was always my weak spot. Wanting to be loved. But the thing I'll never forgive you for is Finn. Pushing him and pushing him to be someone he isn't.'

'That boy needs a firm hand or he'll always be a failure.'

'No, Ian. He'll always be Finn, and that's enough for me.'

The heat seeps from my anger. I feel odd. Light, almost calm. 'I thought you were the most wonderful man in the world – handsome, clever, selfless. But Leon was right. You're manipulative and vain and, worst of all, you're a bully, who's so lacking in self-esteem you can't bear to be challenged by anyone.'

For a moment his body deflates. Everything seems frozen, as if the world has stopped – and then his sneer creeps back. 'If it wasn't for me you'd still be living hand to mouth on a sink estate, wearing cheap, shoddy clothes and eating cheap, shoddy food. Everything I did was for you.'

'Stopping me working? That wasn't for me. That was so I could spend my life shopping, washing, ironing and soothing your ego.' A chill spreads through me as suspicions lurking in the recesses of my brain crystallise into certainties. 'You're the one who sabotaged the appointments, aren't you? That mix-up with Mrs Clarke, swapping the files around, putting broken glass in my tyre so I'd be late.'

'I wanted you to stop working because you were – and clearly still are – stressed, and unstable.'

'And the bits of glass you scattered by the side gate? That wasn't just about undermining me for being scatty – it was an excuse to put in those bloody cameras so you could spy on my every move.'

'It was for your own sake, Nicci. You're falling apart.'

'There's nothing more to say, Ian. I'm leaving.'

He laughs. 'With no money, no car, no friends, no family, no job and no references? Where are you going to go?'

'Susy's.'

'Oh, she's going to keep you, is she? How long's that going to last?'

'Until Finn's inheritance comes through.'

He pauses, uncertain. 'What are you talking about?'

'His father was Ryan Hurley.'

He takes a moment to place the name. 'Sallowfield Court Ryan Hurley?'

'Hugh Rustom-Bennet is the lawyer for Ryan's father's estate and Finn is his only living descendent. As you can imagine, when Mr Rustom-Bennet met me in the flesh he was very keen to make sure that my son gets what's rightfully his. Just as keen as he was to walk out of your mother's life when you sent him our wedding photo. So you *were* right about my past – I can't escape from it, but instead of letting it sabotage the rest of my life, I decided to salvage what I can from the rubble.' I look Ian right in the eye. 'Thanks to Mr Rustom-Bennet, Hurley's trustees are going to buy me a house and give me more than enough to live on while I study for the degree you were so determined to stop me from getting.' I step back towards the door. 'I've packed all our things. They're in the hire car I parked up the road.' His eyes sweep the room. 'Don't worry, you'll barely notice the difference after I'm gone – you made sure that nothing in this house is actually mine.'

'Don't be ridiculous. You can't leave me. I love you.'

I look at him, and it's as if I'm seeing him properly for the very first time. 'I honestly think you believe that – but your feelings for me are as worthless as this ring.' I wiggle my engagement ring off my finger and lay it on the table. 'And, just so you know, you didn't need to pretend. I loved you so much I would have been happy with a ring out of a cracker.' I pick up my bag and walk towards the door.

'You're making a big mistake.' His fist smashes onto the table, making the crockery jump and rattle. 'The biggest mistake of your pathetic little life.'

I lay my house keys on the hall table, along with an envelope of cash – repayment for the money I took from his credit cards. I decided not to pay him back for the Honda – after all, he's the one who said it was my wedding present. I move on down the hall.

'You stupid bitch. You won't manage on your own.'

I close the door behind me.

I sit in the hire car for a moment, watching the twinkling lights of the houses of Juniper Close, and then I turn on the ignition and drive away.

CHAPTER 52

'How do you get a squirrel to like you?' Mr Smartypants raises one heavily painted eyebrow, throws his hands theatrically wide and with as much comic timing as a metronome raps out the punch line. 'Act like a nut!'

The children fall about, chortling with laughter, Finn's giggles loudest of all.

I stand in the doorway, eyes speeding around the room. Lydia is topping up the adults' glasses, Lisa is adding a few more layers of wrapping paper to the pass the parcel, Leon has nearly finished putting out the food and the party bags are named and ready. I may have gone a bit over the top with the decorations but I wanted to make Finn's birthday special. I lean back against the door jamb and close my eyes. So much has happened in the past year – changing towns, starting my university course, moving into a house of my own.

Gordon Hurley's trustees wanted to buy me something much bigger and flashier and they seemed surprised that I chose a little three-bed terrace on the outskirts of town. But I like it. I like the noise, the buzz in the street, the friendly neighbours, the rooms that hadn't been decorated for years that I could splash with bright emulsion, the overgrown garden that I'm slowly reclaiming, the pencil marks up the walls where the last owners measured their children's heights, the feeling of warmth and happiness they left behind.

I open my eyes and Joyce is there.

'I've put the candles on the cake and poured the juice,' she says. 'Anything else you need doing?'

I shake my head and she puts her hand on my arm. 'You've come a long way since your days at Rainbows.'

'I hate to think where I'd be now if it hadn't been for you giving me that job. You caught me before I fell.'

'Well, I'm proud of you.'

'I missed you, you know. All that time when I was with Ian.'

Her lips pucker. 'Do you still hear from him?'

'Not for a while.'

Susy slips in between us, pulling off her coat. 'He gave up trying once he realised he couldn't bully her into coming back. Sorry we're late.' She propels Gaby into the sitting room and catches sight of Mr Smartypants in full flow. 'You cannot be serious! You know his real name's Des Whittle and his day-job's a traffic warden.'

'Finn begged me to book him. He wouldn't have anybody else.'

'Well, keep him away from the alcohol *and* the other mothers, and don't say I didn't warn you.' She waves at Leon, who is adding a tray of dips to the already groaning table, and calls: 'How's college?'

'Not bad. I've got a six-week placement at a hotel.'

'Great! Actually, I was hoping I'd see you. Any chance you could give a talk at Next Steps next week?'

'*Me?*' He gazes at her as if she's gone mad.

'We're running a workshop for new mentors on recognising the signs of exploitation. Your input would be invaluable.'

He drops his gaze and says shyly, 'I'll think about it.'

'Nicci's going to be talking about her own experience of being sexually exploited and pressured into carrying drugs after she left care.'

His eyes swivel to me for a moment, shocked and wide, then swivel away to the kitchen. 'I… I've got to get the pizzas out of the oven.'

'And now I need an assistant,' announces Mr Smartypants. Twenty small hands shoot in the air, twenty necks strain, twenty kneeling bodies sit up and wiggle with excitement.

With the fingers of one hand splayed wide and his wand clasped in the other he sweeps circles across the heads his audience. 'My magic powers are drawing me to the birthday boy. Yes… yes… I can feel it! Here he is!' He flicks the wand and a nicotine-stained index finger at Finn who gazes up at him, fairy lights glinting on the lenses of his new glasses as he pushes them up his nose.

'Come on up here beside me.'

Finn struggles to his feet and steps between the other children, mouth agape with excitement.

'Now, Finn. Are you a scaredy cat?'

Finn shakes his head.

'Are you sure? This trick isn't for the faint-hearted.'

Finn frowns and nods.

'All right, take my wand, here you go.' Finn grips it with both hands like a sabre.

Des whips off his top hat, holds it upside down and covers it with a silk handkerchief. 'Stand back a little. Are you ready?'

'Yes.' Finn's voice is a whisper.

'Now, I'm going to say three magic words. After each of the first two you circle the wand over the hat. The third time you tap it right here on the brim. Wait for it—' Finn's grip tightens. A sudden electric hush. 'Hocus pocus,' Des intones, his voice deep and wobbly.

Finn stirs the wand slowly through the air.

'Shazeema!'

Finn waves the wand again.

Des catches his arm. 'You *sure* you're not a scaredy cat?'

Finn's body twitches. His gaze slides up to Des's face. A steely flash of anger burns cold and hard. Then it's gone, leaving him frozen, staring blankly into nothingness as if a glass shutter has cut him off from the rest of the world. It pierces me to the quick, but it's lost on Des, who checks his watch, lifts the hat a little higher and shouts, 'Shazaam!'

Finn doesn't move.

I call, 'Go on, Finnsy!' and give him a big, upbeat smile. He turns, finds my face and seems to refocus, as if he's seeing me from a long way off, and then he taps the wand against the brim of the hat. A buzzer blasts out an ear-splitting comedy honk as a ball of rainbow streamers shoots from inside the hat and explodes in mid-air, twirling ribbons of purple, pink, blue and yellow onto the guests. Finn throws back his head, whoops with laughter and joins in the rush to catch them.

I turn and push free of the crowded living room. All eyes are trained on the children so no one takes any notice as I make my way down the hall and into the garden. It's a chilly evening, the branches of the little apple tree and the flowering cherry I planted the day we moved in are etched spindly black against the silver twilight. I sit on the wooden bench by the wall and light a cigarette. Laughter and voices from inside my house, music from the flats next door, a group of drinkers emerging noisily from the pub on the corner, the sound of a passing car giving way to another and then another, the lights of a plane drifting overhead. Fragments of life all around me.

Finn's little glitches of fury don't come often but they trouble me when they do. I tell myself it's not Donna's genes or Ian's goading that are responsible for the flash of anger he just showed: it was the entertainer questioning his bravery that snatched him from the safety of our sitting room and flung him back to the horror of that moment in the factory when he faced his demons and threw himself down that chute to save me from Donna. I want to turn back the clock and set him free from the shadow of that day. But I can't. Donna will always be dead, and Finn will always have killed her. I think about her death all the time, trying to work out what I could have done to prevent it, at what moment in our lives I could have stopped it from happening. But it seems to me that that the only thing I could have done differently is to have left Finn on the doorstep of St Johns vicarage and walked away.

I can never wish for that. Not for him. Not for me.

I tell myself that we are safe. That no one will ever find out what really happened to Donna, anymore than they will ever find out what really happened to Jade. But the thought brings almost unbearable sadness. There's no one to mourn either of them, no one to catch sight of the date and remember, with a lump in their throats, that today is the anniversary of one of their deaths and whisper *Isn't it awful?* and *Doesn't time fly?* No one to visit their graves or to remember the way they smiled or frowned or struggled to win out against the hand that life dealt them. No one except me. That's why I planted these trees. The apple for Jade. The cherry for Donna.

I will carry the guilt of their deaths through every moment of the life that I've clawed out of the wreckage of theirs; through the birthdays and Christmases they will never celebrate, and the joys and losses they will never experience. Every time I reach out to another unloved, abandoned teenager, I will do it for them. For Jade and Donna who never had a chance. Two lost, lonely girls who could have been me.

A LETTER FROM SAM

Dear reader,

Thank you for choosing to read *A Good Mother*. I really enjoyed creating the plot and devising the characters and I hope that you enjoy reading it. It's a story about mother-love told from the point of view of Nicci, a young woman who was brought up in care and who was forced to face the adult world without help or support once she left the system. Years later, after she has turned her life around, the tragic events that unfolded during her time as a lost, lonely care leaver return to threaten her life, her marriage and the safety of her son.

I first became interested in care leavers after my husband took a three-year job in Kenya and I volunteered for a local charity that rescues, houses and schools street children. While doing a fantastic job of nurturing the younger children, the charity also strives to provide continued support for those taking their first shaky steps into the adult world. On my return to the UK I was shocked to discover how little support there is for teenage care leavers here and how difficult, lonely and dangerous life can be when there is no one out there who cares.

If you enjoyed the twists and turns of *A Good Mother* you may like my thrillers *Her Perfect Life* and *Gone Before* and I hope that my future novels will also keep you hooked. To keep up to date with all my latest releases, just sign up at the link below

Your email address will never be shared and you can unsubscribe at any time.

www.bookouture.com/sam-hepburn

If you like *A Good Mother* I would be really grateful if you could find a moment to write a review. I would love to know what you think, and sharing your thoughts in a review is a brilliant way to help other readers to discover my books. Thank you!

I always enjoy hearing from my readers – you can get in touch on my Facebook page, through Twitter, Goodreads or my website.

All my best,
Sam

 SamHepburnAuthor

 @Sam_Osman_Books

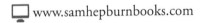 www.samhepburnbooks.com

ACKNOWLEDGEMENTS

Thank you to my lovely editor Lucy Dauman, to my brilliant and ever supportive agent Stephanie Thwaites, and to Noelle Holten and Kim Nash at Bookouture who work so hard to support their authors and their books. A special thank you to the charity I Afrika in Nairobi for giving me the chance to get involved with the wonderful work they do, to my children Charlotte, Murdo and Lily, and, as always, to my ever patient husband, James.

Printed in Great Britain
by Amazon